A THING DONE

Also by Tinney Sue Heath:

Lady of the Seven Suns: A Novel of the Woman Saint Francis Called Brother

A THING DONE

BY

Tinney Sue Heath

A THING DONE

by Tinney Sue Heath

ISBN (paperback): 978-1-7339933-4-0
ISBN (ebook): 978-1-7339933-3-3

BISAC Subject Headings:
    FIC014020 FICTION/Historical/Medieval
    FIC014000 FICTION/Historical/General

Cover design by Jennifer Quinlan of Historical Fiction Book Covers.

This is a work of fiction. Historical names, characters, places, and events are used fictitiously; all others are products of the author's imagination.

To Tim and Joe

And for Connie Lee

CONTENTS

E un ch'avea l'una e l'altra man mozza,
levando i moncherin per l'aura fosca,
sì che 'l sangue facea la faccia sozza,

gridò: "Ricordera'ti anche del Mosca,
che disse, lasso! 'Capo ha cosa fatta,'
che fu mal seme per la gente tosca."
– Dante Alighieri, Inferno 28.103-108

And one who had both one hand and the other cut off,
raising the stumps in the murky air,
so that blood besmirched his face,

Cried, "Remember also Mosca,
who said–alas!–'A thing done has an end to it,'
which was an evil seed for the Tuscan people."
(author's translation)

1. FEAST

It was a fool that began it, but it took a woman to turn it murderous.

Pride and lust, spite, greed, and folly split Florence down the middle in that harsh spring. By late March, when the Feast of the Incarnation gave birth to Christ's year 1216, the damage was done.

Our city by then had rent herself into two warring parties. She split, like a stone splits when the stonecutter drives his wedge into a crack and sunders the rock into jagged pieces, never to be whole again.

Ask any Florentine how the rift began. He'll tell you it started with a banquet, a fight, a man hurt. A marriage offered to make peace. A woman's interference, a betrayal—maybe more than one—and a cry for vengeance. He'll tell you, in wonder, that the great strife began at that banquet with nothing more than a fool's jest.

He might even tell you that the fool played his prank, collected his purse, and danced away, not caring what he had set in motion.

He would be wrong.

All that he's told you will be true until that last. True, but incomplete. There's nothing in his account of blackmail, nothing of secrets, nothing of the bitterness of a rejected woman. Nothing of loyalty bought and sold. And most of all, nothing of violent conflict coldly planned and set in motion for political gain.

A fool began it; that much is true. I should know, for I am that fool, fool by profession and more fool by my actions. But before you judge me, know that the rift, like the crack in the stone, was already there.

*

"I hope his mouth doesn't freeze to that trumpet," Neri muttered, thrusting his hands into his sleeves. The organetto bounced on his chest, hanging from a thick leather strap around his neck. I caught all three balls in my left hand, one at a time as they arrived. I could talk and juggle at the same time, but both activities suffered when I did.

"This job was your idea," I reminded him, and he snorted. Neri had a childlike fascination with the nobility, and he could never have resisted a gathering like this. I could have, and he knew it. I was there only because he wanted me there.

"We need the money," he said. "There's this little problem called rent coming up." True enough, but there were warmer jobs, indoor jobs. Which, I hoped, was what this one was about to become.

2

The youth shivering in the doorway raised his trumpet to his lips, its banner flapping in a gust of wind, and managed to blow a ragged fanfare to summon the diners into the hall. None too soon, either. The watery January sunlight was already past its peak, and Mazzingo's dubbing ceremony had been over for at least two hours, plenty of time for everyone to arrive at the new knight's castle outside Florence for the promised feast.

As far as our proud employer was concerned, it was high time he got the accolade. He'd been strutting around the courtyard showing off his bright new spurs of gold as he accepted the congratulations of the men whose peer he now was. Mazzingo—or messer Mazzingo, to give him his newly-minted knightly title—had spared no expense: as well as a princely feast and a dangerous quantity of excellent wine, he was treating his guests to our talents, and we were some of the best. In his enthusiasm he had invited the knights from both factions, but Oddo's men had grouped themselves at the near end of the courtyard, while the knights of the Buondelmonti and the Donati and their followers pointedly moved to the far end.

Mazzingo needed to get his fellow knights inside and warm and fed before they grew restive. His noble guests in their fur-lined cloaks and heavy gloves were better off than we were, but they were ready to abandon their games of skill in the courtyard and get someplace warm. Few men can throw a knife at a target while wearing gloves; even fewer when bare hands freeze to the hilts.

Our troupe had been trying to provide a bit of background color. I spun my three leather balls in an easy reverse cascade pattern, because that was all I could do with mittens on and I wasn't about to take them off. Rufino turned cartwheels and did handstands, his palms raw and red from the frosty ground.

The musicians had it worse. Playing an organetto and a rebec with icy hands was somewhere between difficult and impossible. Neri managed to pick out tunes on his keyboard with numb fingers, cursing under his breath the whole time, and his bellows wheezed, no happier than we were to be taking in the frozen air. Anselmo sawed doggedly away at his rebec, which had lost any pretense of tuning. All of us were eager to get inside.

The knights fanned out as they climbed the broad staircase, then funneled into the hall, members of the two factions interweaving awkwardly as they approached the door. When at last we in our turn shuffled in out of the cold, I stuffed my juggling props into their leather bag and leaned

3

it against the wall next to the door, for easy retrieval later. This hall had no musicians' gallery, so Neri and Anselmo selected a corner and began tuning the rebec to the organetto, a task likely to occupy them for quite a while as the instruments warmed and shifted pitch. Pipes and strings like a constant temperature, Neri used to say. They grow surly when they're exposed to extremes, which is why musicians like to set up away from the fire.

The windows were shuttered against the cold, yet the big room was bright, with a crackling fire built up in the hearth and torches blazing in brackets at intervals along the walls. Heavy wool draperies of a rich dark green hung in between the torches to shield diners from the damp chill of the walls. Long trestle tables laid with good white cloths formed three sides of a rectangle, separated by gaps to allow the servers and entertainers to move about. Benches were on the outside only, as was the custom, so all the diners faced the open center of the room. Just as well; half of these men didn't trust the other half behind their backs. Low wooden platforms rested under the benches, ready to protect guests' feet from the cold stone floor, but nothing protected them from each other.

Mazzingo's guests shed their cloaks, draping them over the wooden bars along the wall on either side of the door. Some went to warm their hands at the great hearth. Others sat on the long storage chests that lined the hall, tugging off wet boots while their men stood by holding dry footgear. Servants circulated, carrying costly maiolica basins skillfully painted with cross-hatching in brown and watery green and boasting an expensive glaze, and guests gave their hands a perfunctory dunk in the warm, scented water.

Mazzingo took his place under the baldachino; his pet priest mumbled a prayer and withdrew, and the diners fell to. While Neri and Anselmo tried to get their instruments to agree, Rufino and I worked the open center of the hall with our jests and antics. We played the buffoon in front of each table in turn, staying out of the servers' way and making sure we gave equal time to all. We were coarse and crude and vulgar, and they loved us. We took in extra coins aplenty, and drank deeply from the goblets of wine they thrust at us as a reward.

When we heard Neri begin to improvise an istampitta, Rufino and I decided it was time to let our partners take over for a while. By the time we came to a stopping point and retreated from the center to catch our breath, Mazzingo's guests had already gone through an impressive quantity of wine. The hall was growing noisier. My musical colleagues played on, but they might as well have mimed their performance, for by then no one could hear them. We had waited a bit too long to give them their turn. Rufino headed for the kitchen to try to cadge a bite to eat, and I leaned against the wall near the door and watched the feasters.

They had already demolished the starting dainties, the dried figs and the bitter oranges from Sicily that were Mazzingo's proud extravagance, and then the capon pies and bean pottage that made up the first remove. One of Oddo's men banged on the table and cried, "Bring us meat!" Some of the others began stamping their feet rhythmically on their wooden platforms, hard enough that they probably splintered a few of them, and called out their own demands. Gently-born knights and nobles they were, the more venerable among them proud veterans of the fourth Crusade, but right now what they wanted was meat, and they were not asking politely. These were men accustomed to getting what they wanted.

In response, Mazzingo's sweating, livery-clad servants hurried from the kitchen behind the hearth, holding aloft huge trays of carved roast sheep, and the guests raised a raucous cheer. It was not lamb—not in January—but young sheep still, and tender. My mouth watered. Two servers to each row of tables shoveled slices of succulent spiced mutton onto the pewter plates shared by pairs of diners, and then more servers arrived and poured more wine, to an even louder cheer. My stomach growled as the savory aroma of meat filled my nostrils, but I knew those of us working the feast would be lucky if we got the cold leavings later on.

No one's attention was on me in those moments, or so I thought, so I jumped when a beefy hand gripped my shoulder. I turned to face messer Oddo Arrighi dei Fifanti and caught the full force of his foul, winey breath, for we were of a height, though he was considerably broader.

"Fool, I have a little job for you," he said, right in my face. I gulped, and tried to breathe through my mouth. I have a name—it's Corrado—but no one ever uses it.

"My lord?"

"I want you to pick up the plate that's between messer Berto degli Infangati and messer Buondelmonte dei Buondelmonti, and I want you to snatch it away from them." I stared at him. Of all the knights present, no others came from families as stalwartly opposed to Oddo's clan as Buondelmonte, except perhaps the men of the powerful Donati family.

Oddo waited, watching me, as my mind raced to come up with an excuse. Jesters are expected to be outrageous—it is, in fact, what they pay us for—but our survival depends upon developing an instinct for when we risk going too far. My instinct had served me well for years, and

5

I saw danger ahead.

"See them at the back table?" Oddo prompted, pointing. "You know which ones they are?"

I knew. "My lord, they're eating—" I began, but Oddo interrupted.

"You don't have to do anything with the plate, and they can have it back later. I've got some money riding on this, and I intend to win my bet. There's coins in it for you." He held up a bulging canvas purse.

Oddo's eyes glittered with wine and malicious amusement, and he was a man used to being obeyed. Still, it's good to survive long enough to spend one's earnings, and I wanted to avoid anything that linked me in the public eye with either faction. That was a matter of professional good sense, but it could also be a matter of survival if hostilities broke out among the nobles, as had happened so many times before. I'd seen the harm that could do.

"What if they attack me, Lord? They have drunk much of messer Mazzingo's good wine, and they may be angered. I'm only a fool, and I cannot defend myself against knights." I knew I was babbling, but I had a very bad feeling about this assignment.

Oddo grinned. "I'll see you come to no harm, little fool. You have my word on it." He thumped his fist on his massive chest, meaning, I suppose, to suggest his honorable and knightly heart.

"But my lord, what of my employer? I'm hired to entertain for messer Mazzingo, and if this jest doesn't please him, I will have failed in my contract." Maybe that would work.

He looked me up and down appraisingly. "I like you, Fool. You give good service where it's due. I'll speak to Mazzingo and tell him of this private jest. Give me the time it takes to say three Paternosters and then do as I told you." He pressed the purse into my hand and headed back toward the baldachino, where Mazzingo was laughing uproariously at whatever his companion had just said.

Now what? Neri, watching from his corner, signaled for my attention with a dissonant chord, audible now that the knights were busy eating. He raised an inquiring eyebrow, and I shrugged. Nothing either of us could do about it now. Oddo spoke to Mazzingo, who laughed again and nodded his head, and then Oddo turned to me and made a peremptory gesture, plainly telling me to get on with it.

Nothing for it; I'd have to act. I stashed the purse in my sleeve. From the other side of the room Neri watched me intently, alert as always and clearly aware that something unplanned was afoot. He flashed me the three-finger sign for "careful," and I touched my temple in acknowledgement.

I appraised the situation. Mazzingo had carefully mixed the factions at his tables, but the men at each table chose their own cupmates. Messers Buondelmonte and Berto owed each other party loyalty and friendship, and neither one bore any love for Oddo. My scalp itched ferociously, as it always did when I felt threatened. I thought it might be lice looking for a way out, as they say rats will leave a ship before it sinks.

My back was to the door. Oddo stood behind Mazzingo at the white-draped table along the short wall to my right, and the elegant Buondelmonte and his red-nosed companion were seated across from me along the long back wall. The henchmen and squires sat at the table nearest the door, to absorb any drafts while their betters stayed warm, and I stood behind them, shifting my weight from side to side like a cock getting ready to fight. To my left a fire blazed in the great open hearth, shared with the kitchen behind it.

I took a deep breath. Adopting the jester's mincing, scampering walk, I moved into the center space and pranced over to the table where Berto and Buondelmonte were eating and drinking. Both men were richly dressed, but Buondelmonte, a vigorous man in his prime, appeared considerably more at home in his fine garments than did Berto, who kept pushing his sleeves back to keep them from dragging in the food.

The pair grinned up at me from their side of the table, plainly expecting more foolery for their amusement. I grinned back, trying to make it clear that all was in jest, but I was beginning to wish I had said those Paternosters in earnest.

No choice, I reminded myself. I took a deep breath, shot my arm out, and seized the plate even as messer Berto reached for a chunk of meat. I capered away backwards, holding the knights' dinner high over my head. Several men roared with laughter at this, but my eyes were on the two diners I had just robbed, and their faces were like thunderheads. I was sweating.

Buondelmonte glared at me and started to say something, but Berto lurched to his feet and bellowed a curse, fumbling for his knife. I didn't want to turn my back to him, even to run away, so I swallowed hard and dropped to one knee, holding the plate in front of my face, trying to fold up and make myself disappear. Surely someone will stop him, I thought desperately. Oddo, for all his chest-thumping, didn't appear to be coming to my rescue, and I saw nowhere to hide.

It may well have been Mazzingo's potent wine that saved me. Sober, Berto could fling a blade and hit the center of a target many paces distant.

7

Sober, of course, he might not have been so quick to start throwing weaponry around in a crowded feasting hall.

Before Berto managed to get a firm grip on the hilt, Buondelmonte clamped a hand on his companion's hairy wrist and held it firmly. I released the breath I had been holding. Berto snarled something indistinct, and Buondelmonte leaned over and said something in his ear.

By now all were watching, and what was left of the hubbub faded as Mazzingo's guests waited to see what would happen next. Four of the servers were stranded in the center of the room with me, holding their emptied trays aloft, afraid to move, eyes wide and anxious. I scuttled behind one of them while Berto's attention was on Buondelmonte. Crouching now, I threw my left arm around the man's legs, managing— barely—to keep my plate of meat upright in my other hand, the first serious juggling I'd done all day. The poor fellow stood there in terror, balancing his serving tray overhead with both hands, and hissed "Get away!" while he tried ineffectually to kick himself free of me. I held on.

Oddo strode forward to the spot where I had stood when I grabbed the plate.

"What, Berto, do you threaten our little fool? You laughed hard enough at his antics before," he said. He smiled the way a dog bares its teeth.

"Back off, Oddo," Berto growled. "This thieving fool stole my dinner, which is no proper jest. I'll have it back, and I'll have him whipped!"

Oddo threw his head back and laughed. "Look at the grand knight, so hungry that he cannot take a jest!" he said, his voice pitched to carry. "Is there no food at home, Berto, that you must gorge yourself here?"

This bald insult drew a collective gasp from the other guests. Berto's family was much reduced in wealth and prominence in recent years, and that barb would surely sting.

Oddo wasn't done. "If you stand at the kitchen door after the feast, you'll be given a generous handout of scraps to take home and feed your family. But you disgrace your knighthood when you do battle with a pathetic little fool who only acts on orders."

At that, Buondelmonte looked at Oddo sharply. He released Berto's wrist and sat back, never taking his eyes off Oddo.

Berto's face flushed a dark red. His fury must have interfered with speech, for he sputtered and his chest heaved, but nothing coherent emerged.

"Oddo," he finally spat out, "you're the fool here. You lie in your throat!" He banged his cup on the table, sloshing wine, and a stain the color of blood spread across the white cloth.

Oddo chuckled—an ugly sound. "If it's food you want, Berto, I'll give you food." In one economical motion, he reached across the table and picked up a voider, already half full of capon bones, scraps of pie crust, pits and peels and other leavings. He flung it, hard, full in Berto's face.

2. LUCK

The voider clattered to the floor. Berto bellowed in rage, swabbing at his face with both sleeves. This time, at least, he didn't go for his knife. I heard a roar from the other guests, but I didn't see what happened next, because that was the moment when the servant—my reluctant shield—finally managed to free himself from my grip, toppling me over. His tray crashed to the floor and he gave a despairing little squeak as he bolted, darting behind the squires' table and heading for the kitchen as fast as he could move. Most of the greasy meat on my purloined plate slid off onto the floor before I managed to right myself.

The hall erupted into mayhem. I stayed down in a crouch. I caught a glimpse of Berto, still wiping grease and gravy off of his face, and of a furious and spattered Buondelmonte, now on his feet and shouting at Oddo, and then men were up and moving around, and I lost sight of the knights. I thought at first the others intended to part the quarreling knights and put an end to this madness, but my stomach clenched as I realized that they were shoving tables back toward the wall, pushing them out of the way to let the fight go forward.

Buondelmonte's squire flung a handful of almonds at one of Oddo's men. His target ducked, and the almonds hit the floor with a rattle like a shower of hailstones on a tile roof. Another squire, not to be outdone, picked up a saltcellar and hurled its contents at his neighbor, who yelped and jammed his fists into his eyes. A bread trencher sailed overhead, trailing gravy. Pairs of men squared off, distracting their neighbors from the original confrontation. I saw no weapons drawn, but every man in the hall had a sharp eating-knife within easy reach.

Time to leave. I stood up and craned my neck to find my fellow performers. Neri, Anselmo, and Rufino were heading for the door, Neri's arms wrapped protectively around his organetto. Anselmo was lugging my prop bag. I started toward them, but my way was blocked by two muscled young men wrestling while their fellows stood by, cheering on one or the other.

I tried to maneuver around them, but my foot landed on a piece of greasy meat and slid out from under me. I lost my grip on the plate, fell hard on the brick floor, and had to roll to avoid being stepped on. The plate landed upright with a dull clank, and I grabbed it up again before it stopped rocking, for in the confusion I still thought of it as my responsibility.

By the time I got to my feet, my friends were gone, and I had no clear path to the door.

I backed up against a trestle table which had been toppled, its contents dumped unceremoniously onto the floor. That meant I was standing in a puddle of sauce and treading on ruined table linens, but at least no one could come at me from behind. Absurdly, I still clutched the plate, and a few forlorn shreds of meat still clung to it.

A chunk of cheese struck my forehead and fell to the floor. Well, better that than their knives, I thought, twisting to one side to avoid an olive. It bounced off my shoulder and I caught it on my plate, where it rolled around incongruously in the gravy.

I sidled along, the table board at my back, heading for the corner of the room. That took me away from the door—not the direction I wanted to be going, but too many men were brawling between me and the door, and the corner at least was quiet. Once there I couldn't glimpse Oddo or Berto or Buondelmonte, but I did see Mazzingo, still seated under his baldachino, laughing at the uproar. He picked up a slice of meat between thumb and forefinger and sent it spinning through the air, with a flick of the wrist as if he were skipping stones. I could only guess the wine had overcome his careful diplomacy, or perhaps he took care to aim equally at both sides. His table was still upright, but behind it, a torn drapery dangled precariously. Next to Mazzingo, messer Mosca dei Lamberti, a rising star in Oddo's faction, grinned wolfishly as he broke off chunks of bread and lobbed them at his selected targets.

At least what those two were doing was in fun, I thought, albeit drunken and undignified fun. But many of the contests out on the floor were turning vicious. I feared a free-for-all, especially among the squires and younger fighting men. One youngster upended a cup of wine over his neighbor's head, and the drenched lad's howl of rage made me wince.

Apart from it all, across the length of the room from Mazzingo and Mosca, a knight stood alone and motionless. I knew who he was. Every Florentine knew who he was. Messer Schiatta, head of the powerful Uberti family, had been favored with the seat nearest the fire on this bitter day, in spite of the grumblings of older, frailer men. Now he stood next to the hearth like a pillar, tall, lean, watchful, the flickering firelight behind him giving him the look of something unearthly. No flung food came his way, and even the scuffling men managed to give him a wide berth.

The tussle blocking my view of the center lurched to my right, and amidst the flying food and squabbling men I saw Oddo and the pair of gravy-stained knights. Their glowering faces told me the real danger in this hall wasn't the wine-fueled tempers of the young squires, but this tense standoff—Oddo's calculated provocation against Buondelmonte's rising rage. I wasn't surprised to see Schiatta watching too, his calm in marked contrast to all the chaos around him.

Oddo and Buondelmonte were facing each other and speaking, or more likely shouting, but the room was full of such a din that I couldn't hear them. Berto, sitting now, scrubbed at the front of his robe with the edge of the tablecloth. Oddly, he seemed more absorbed with that task than he was interested in Oddo. But Buondelmonte was another story. His color was high, and he stood like a warrior. I couldn't see what he held in his right hand, for too many people were moving around erratically in the space between us.

A man yelped somewhere to my left, distracting me for an instant. When I looked back, to my horror I realized it was no chunk of bread or dried fig in Buondelmonte's hand, but a glittering blade. Metal reflected torchlight, and others too began to notice and drop their own contests, serious or foolish, to watch.

Oddo stood defiantly, his legs firmly planted, his arms folded across his chest. He spoke—I heard his powerful voice, but the noise level still didn't permit me to make out his words—and then he laughed, that same mocking laugh he had directed at Berto moments before.

Buondelmonte moved like a great cat then, supple and fast, and vaulted the table. His knife slashed out and raked Oddo's arm. Oddo's broad face showed disbelief, and then fury. He clutched his left arm with his right hand as bright blood spread like fire along the fabric of his sleeve. He bellowed an obscenity, and everyone heard it, for by now all attention was again on the center of the room, and silence had replaced the uproar.

Buondelmonte stepped back, reddened blade in hand. His expression was uncertain, confused, as if he didn't quite realize what he had done.

If he didn't, others did. Mosca scrambled over his table, dragging the tablecloth onto the floor with a clatter of pewter. In an instant he was at Oddo's right side, his own blade in his hand.

With that, Mazzingo came to his senses. Perhaps he finally remembered he was the host, or realized that having a civil war start at his knighting was not how he wanted to be remembered. Whatever the reason, he sobered up in an instant and stepped firmly between Mosca and Buondelmonte, seizing his authority as lord of the castle to demand their attention. He made a gesture which I read as telling the men to lower their weapons.

After a moment's hesitation, both did. This was the first and probably the last time the new knight would so confront his seniors, and only his lordship in this castle gave him the right. The onlookers exhaled, though they kept their eyes fixed on the two pairs of men, for even those foolish young hotheads who favored war had no wish to see it conducted indoors, with bread chunks and olives and eating-knives, rather than banners and horses and swords and trumpets. Everyone except the principals finally seemed ready to calm down.

There they stood, Oddo clutching his arm, Mosca and Buondelmonte holding their knives down at their sides and glaring at each other, and Mazzingo using the considerable mass of his body to separate the two sides. No one moved, until Schiatta left his place by the fire and walked, slowly and deliberately, over to where the four men were standing. Men made way for him at every step.

He stopped next to Oddo, held up both his arms, and speaking to the whole room said in his sonorous bass voice, "This feast has ended. Return to your homes. We will have no more fighting this day." Not a moment for subtlety, but I heard a hint of emphasis on "this day."

Buondelmonte hesitated a moment, scowling, then wiped his blade on his robe and sheathed it. Mosca sheathed his as well, in a fluid and easy movement.

Buondelmonte headed for the door, his color high and his mouth grim. He strode past Oddo, Mosca, and Schiatta as if they weren't there, motioning to his squires, who scrambled to gather up cloaks and boots and gear and follow their master. Several of the knights chose to leave with them, including Berto and a fierce, sharp-featured man I recognized as one of the Donati. The rest of us stood amid the wreckage of the room and watched them go. I had the feeling Schiatta was making a mental list.

The men who remained in the room grouped themselves into two clusters. One group, the men of the Uberti, the Fifanti, the Amidei, and the Lamberti and their henchmen, moved toward the center of the room, joining the three men who still stood there with Mazzingo.

The other knights began to collect their things and prepare to leave, but they were ostentatiously taking extra time about it, making it clear to the men in the center that they were not leaving with Buondelmonte. Schiatta spoke a quiet word to Mazzingo, and the host turned to his remaining guests, raising his arms to signal his intention to speak.

"My lords, I thank you for your attendance," he said to them, his

13

powerful voice echoing off the far wall. "These unexpected events have interrupted our dinner, but I trust they haven't spoiled our day of games and friendship. I promise you, we'll gather again another day for a finer feast, and that one, we'll finish." He smiled, but only with his mouth. "I bid you good evening."

Now free to go without giving offense, the knights and their men picked up their pace, finished making themselves ready and filed out into the courtyard, thence to wind their way around to the stables and collect their mounts for the ride home.

That left Oddo's faction, and me. My friends were long since gone, and my cloak and the battered old knife that passed for my weapon were still in my props bag, which was probably stuffed in our handcart and on its way home by now. I didn't relish walking the six miles to Florence alone and unarmed in this cold, but I wanted to be back in the city, where I could feel safe again. The Tegrimi castle was not the farthest I'd ever been from Florence, but it was plenty far enough. After nearly being skewered by Berto's knife, I wanted nothing more than to go home to the little house I shared with Neri and tell him what had happened, and let his woman Ghisola fuss over me and bring me wine and comforting food.

Perhaps if I followed close enough behind the mounted guests and if they traveled slowly enough for me to somehow keep up with them, the usual threats to lone travelers would let me pass in peace. I had no wish to deal with wolves, or bandits, or any stranger menaces this night, though had I known what was to follow from these events I might well have chosen the wolves.

I crept cautiously from my corner, heading for the nearest still-standing table to put down my troublemaking plate, hoping no one would stop me and I could head for the door unseen.

No such luck. Oddo noticed me, and he strolled over to me before I reached the table. Absently he reached out with his good hand, plucked the olive from the plate and ate it. "Don't leave, Fool," he said to me with his mouth full. "I have more instructions for you." He spat out the pit. I wanted nothing more than to make for the door, but now I couldn't, so I put the plate down at last, and it sat forgotten on the corner of the table. I waited.

Oddo's left arm was still bleeding. An eager young man, wearing the Fifanti's flamboyant gold with a broad red stripe, begged the knight to allow him to bandage the wound, and Oddo finally agreed. He sat on a bench and stuck out his arm. His man began to work, flushed with pride at being allowed to do such a service for his lord.

While the young man deftly worked the bloodied sleeve off Oddo's arm, Mazzingo approached them. No longer the confident host who had stepped between two armed men to keep the peace, he was pale and hesitant as he stood in front of Oddo, like a boy before his teacher waiting for permission to speak. I wondered if he was regretting his earlier show of evenhandedness. Oddo looked up at him, raised an eyebrow, and waited, still holding his arm out but ignoring his man's ministrations.

Mazzingo took a deep breath and recited, "My comrade in arms and my most honored guest, it grieves me deeply that you have sustained injury while in my home. I am yours to command, should you seek retribution." Oddo nodded his approval and extended his good hand, which Mazzingo gratefully clasped in both of his.

"I thank you, messer Mazzingo. This incident was no fault of yours, and I bear you no ill will. Your support is welcome." Oddo withdrew his hand so he could scratch his nose, and color began to return to Mazzingo's face.

"You'll want a parliament," Schiatta said without preamble. He was standing behind Oddo, his arms folded across his chest.

"Yes." Oddo's expression was grim. "My house. Tonight. All our families."

Mazzingo frowned. "My lord, I—"

"No, of course not, Mazzingo," Oddo said. "You stay and get this mess taken care of. We'll send you word later." He turned back to Schiatta. Mazzingo, dismissed, stood there uncertainly for a moment, then turned and strode off toward his kitchen.

Oddo stood up abruptly, occasioning a small sound of protest from his man. The bloodied sleeve dangled at his side.

"That's good enough, Guido," Oddo told him. "It'll get me home without any more of me leaking out, and Ermellina will want to patch me up herself, once we're there." He inspected Guido's neat rag-bandage job, clearly the result of military training. "Good work, lad." Guido tried to smother a grin, and failed.

"Let's ride," Oddo said, and the men around him started to ready themselves. I tried to make myself inconspicuous, hoping he would forget about me. If he did, I could wait until the knights and their men departed, and then make my own way home.

My stomach rumbled, and I wondered if first I might be able to find a bit of food that hadn't been pulverized during the fracas. I didn't envy the servants who were going to have to clean up after this knightly food-fight, though I supposed they'd get the unserved food still in the

15

kitchen as compensation, which was better than I expected to do. Tables overturned, food and utensils scattered everywhere, fine table linens and wall hangings ripped and fit for nothing better than privy rags—maybe it was as well after all that no women were present, for they would have wept at such destruction. Maybe someone had left a cloak behind in their hurry, and I could snatch it and be on my way.

But it wasn't to be. In all the time I was to know him, Oddo was never to forget about me until just after he had found a way to complicate my life. His small round eyes sought mine and found them, and he said, "And here's another one who did well. Fool, you're coming along to our parliament. I believe you bring me luck. Guido, get him there."

He shrugged on the cloak that Guido held for him, adjusting it around his bandaged arm, his shoulder still bare under the heavy wool garment. He started for the door, turning back just long enough to call out a courteous farewell to Mazzingo. All of the remaining men in the room followed him out, except for the handful that lived in this castle, and Guido grabbed me by the arm and steered me, protesting, after them.

The sky had clouded over and dusk was approaching. Guido and I followed the others swiftly along the narrow walkway atop the wall, moving swiftly through the rapidly fading light. I was shivering, and only partly from the cold. I carefully did not look down, for I am not easy with heights. Anselmo and Rufino took much amusement in watching me try to avoid them whenever I could. Neri, who would joke relentlessly about almost anything else, never joined in. He knew that I've seen what a fall from up high can do to a man. I don't talk about it, but Neri was there.

"You'll ride with me, Fool," Guido said. We were headed for the stables, just inside the main gate to the castle.

If there's one thing I dislike even more than heights, it would be horses. They're fine beasts in their place, noble and useful, but I'm a city lad and I don't need one of the big hulking things to get around. My own two feet do that well enough. So my protests were taking on a more urgent nature as Guido dragged me along, for I realized I was about to find myself perched on top of one of the creatures for the first time, and I didn't like the idea at all.

I had precious little to say about it. Guido and another man hoisted me up onto the damned beast and tossed me an old cloak. Threadbare and grimy and reeking, it was still better than nothing, so I wrapped it tightly around me. Guido mounted adroitly in front of me, and I clutched his middle and clamped my legs tightly against the animal. The stink of horse rose up and engulfed me, which I guess was to be expected.

16

"Hang on, Fool," Guido said over his shoulder. "As soon as we get out of the gate, we're going to move." We started forward at a shambling walk, and I shifted my body around, desperately trying to find a position where I felt securely anchored and likely to stay on the thing, rather than tumbling down among those hard hooves, which is what I feared. The best I could manage was to hang onto Guido even tighter and lean the side of my head against his back. He made a ribald remark which I failed to appreciate, and then we were through the open gate, and he said, "Now!"

I felt those massive muscles bunch beneath me, and then we were off, hurtling over the frozen ground at a pace I had never even imagined, much less experienced. I hung on to Guido for my life while we covered the six miles to Florence, keeping my eyes tightly closed and trying not to whimper.

I knew we would probably pass Neri, Anselmo, and Rufino with our cart somewhere along the road and I wondered if they would recognize me. I doubted it; daylight was fading rapidly, and not much of me showed above the borrowed cloak. And they had no reason to expect me to come thundering past on a horse. In any case, I wasn't going to open my eyes to look for them.

I was too terrified even to wonder what sort of luck brought a man a knife wound, and why he wanted more of it.

3. PARLIAMENT

I might have wished for my first horseback ride to be a gentle experience, conducted at a sedate and dignified walk. Thus are the small sons of knights taught to trust their mounts, or so I've heard. Not so this night, as we flew over those six miles while my heart banged so hard in my chest that I had a hard time drawing breath. The horse's hooves churned the air, and I was never sure they actually touched the ground, though I suppose that's what all the bouncing was about.

I only opened my eyes for the last part, when the animal slowed to a walk as we passed through the city gate. I sat up and tried to pretend I did this every day, but it was probably too late for that. There was laughter, and one man called, "Hey, Guido, your saddlebag's come alive!"

Oddo rode in the lead. The gatekeepers moved smartly out of his way, waving us all through. The slower pace and the relief of being back within the city's walls allowed me to catch my breath and muster something that with luck might pass for dignity, but I was sticky with sweat and my hair and clothes were disheveled from my ordeal. When at last we reached our destination, of the three of us, horse and riders, I was the worst off. The damned horse was comparatively fresh despite having carried us both, and Guido was positively giddy.

We came to a stop outside the Fifanti palace, with its huge blocks of rusticated stone at street level and its hulking wooden jetties overhanging us, cutting off any view of sky from the street. Guido hopped down lightly, giving the horse an affectionate pat on the neck.

"So, Windstorm, the stableboys will give you a good rubdown soon," he murmured, nuzzling the animal's enormous head.

He loped off toward Oddo's palace, but halfway to the front door he remembered me. I must have looked ridiculous, marooned and trembling on top of a heap of panting muscle and bone and sweat, for Guido was chuckling when he came back to rescue me. He hauled me off the thing as ungallantly as he had flung me onto it, and cuffed me jovially on the shoulder.

"Cheers, Windbag. You won't be seeing me again," I muttered to the horse. I contemplated patting it on the neck as Guido had done, but it snorted, and something in its eye, like an egg-white around a baleful brown yolk, warned me off. I backed away, and Guido laughed. He cuffed me again, then ordered me up to the kitchen, where Oddo had gone moments before to explain to his lady wife why he was coming home from a banquet with a gash in his arm and a hole in his sleeve.

Oddo's massive wooden door stood open, and men were coming and going through the portal with much shouting of orders and frenzied activity. I plunged into the confusion and went to find Oddo, climbing two flights of wide wooden stairs and then the narrower steps up to the kitchen.

Oddo sat on a bench in front of the fire. He was in high spirits for a man recently wounded, but his lady wife was having none of it. She said nothing, but her mouth was a thin line and her movements were abrupt and jerky as she worked on Oddo's arm. She had unwrapped Guido's field bandage and was about to improve on it, her strips of linen and pots of salve already laid out next to her on the bench. It made me wonder if Oddo made a habit of this sort of thing. The salve gave off a sharp, astringent herbal smell, not unpleasant.

"So, Fool. Not quite the evening you expected, eh?" said Oddo. He didn't wait for an answer. "You can still earn your coin for tonight. Ouch!" He jumped as his wife applied the salve to his wound.

"Give me some jests and distract me from what this tyrannical woman is doing to my poor arm," he ordered. "But, Fool, see that you keep it clean. My wife is to be treated with all honor." The honorable tyrant said nothing, just kept working, though I thought I saw a dimple appear briefly in one cheek.

I clowned for Oddo while his wife swathed his arm in many more layers of bandage than the scrape required. By the time she finished, I was out of breath and out of jests. Anyone seeing Oddo's swaddled arm would think him lucky it was still attached.

He downed a cup of wine and half of another, then focused his gaze on me. "Fool, you will go down to the door. You will have one of my guards come to me for orders. Not Guido; I want him on door duty. If any more of the consortium have arrived, you will courteously invite them up to the hall to join the others. Move. Quickly." He dismissed me with a wave of his good arm.

I rattled down the stairs as fast as their unfamiliarity and steepness allowed. At the foot of the first flight was a hall with other rooms running along three sides of it. No torches or fire burned there, and everything was in shadow. I hurried down the next flight, past the larger hall, where the men who had arrived with us were dragging out benches and making themselves comfortable around a large brazier. A lad and two young women scurried around pouring wine for them, and two men were lighting torches with a candle and stuffing them into brackets. I

19

went down the last flight toward the entrance, where a single lit torch illuminated a group of men.

Guido was one of two guards on duty at the door. Messer Mosca and several other members of the Lamberti family had arrived and waited in the entry. The Conti Gangalandi were there, standing in a group apart. They wore their distinctively old-fashioned clothing: outer sleeves only to the elbow, showing the coarse undertunics beneath, and riding slits up the sides of their robes, instead of front and back.

I told Guido and the other guard of Oddo's summons and then greeted the waiting guests with as much dignity as I could muster, considering I was still wearing my fool's weeds and that foul cloak. I recited Oddo's message to them, and they started up the stairs, Mosca taking the lead. Close behind them came the Amidei, who arrived while I was speaking, with their patriarch Lambertuccio, Oddo's brother-in-law, at their head. Guido's fellow guard brought up the rear.

This was my chance, I thought, and I turned to the door. It was barred. I looked at Guido, puzzled.

"Nobody leaves. Master's orders," he said, leaning on his staff and watching me.

"I never heard him give any such order." I was indignant, and I wanted out of this mess before things got even worse.

"Aye, he did," Guido said, grinning. "He said 'parliament', and those are the rules. The family comes in, and nobody else except if they're with the master. And nobody goes out until he says."

The other guard hailed us from the top of the stairs. "Up to the hall, Fool. Now!" he ordered, making a peremptory gesture with his staff. No escape yet. Reluctantly I started up the stairs.

A sudden pounding on the door made me stop. Guido lifted the bar and eased the door open a crack. An imperious, high-pitched voice demanded entrance.

Guido spoke to this new visitor with deference, but he didn't open the door wide enough to admit anyone. Whoever was seeking entry must be someone short, I thought, for Guido's chin was almost down on his chest as he spoke. The guard who had summoned me upstairs started down the stairs toward us, holding his staff horizontally, as if to block passage to the hall in case the visitor managed to gain entry.

Which she did. The person shrilly berating Guido was a stocky little woman draped in a tawny mantle, and she pushed her way in, over his protests. Her face was hidden by her hood, but her voice was harsh and demanding. Judging from Guido's cautious, respectful demeanor, she

20

was a lady, though you wouldn't have concluded that from the language she was using.

"My orders are no women upstairs, my lady, even family," he said, as if apologizing, all the while trying to position himself between the woman and the staircase. I supposed the serving maids didn't count—they usually didn't, with these people.

The lady did her best to get around Guido, repeatedly ordering him to get out of her way, and they continued this odd dance for a few moments while she called him some richly imaginative names. The poor fellow kept trying to block her while at the same time being obsequiously polite. I could probably have found material here for a jester routine, but I was glad I wasn't the one trying to deal with her. I watched from my position on the stairs.

Finally Oddo must have heard the ruckus she was making, because he came to the top of the stairs and bellowed at us. "We're in parliament, Guido. Tell her to go home. Give her an escort if she hasn't got one. And Fool, get on up here." He went back to his guests, and the upstairs guard followed him. Obediently, I started to climb again.

Guido and the woman stopped their maneuvering. She hissed in frustration, then decided to take it out on me. "You. On the stairs. Stop right there. Who the hell are you, that you were watching us like that? Come here."

I stopped halfway up, turned, and glanced at Guido. He gave a small nod and I came slowly back down, presenting myself before the lady with a bow. This was not good. I needed to get back up there. Soon.

She looked up at Guido and said, "Go upstairs and tell my uncle I do not require an escort. My men are waiting outside." He opened his mouth to say something, then closed it again. He caught my eye and gestured with his chin toward the barred door. So now I was Oddo's temporary guard, I supposed. Guido gave the woman a little bow and went up the stairs.

My turn. She looked me up and down, bold as a man, and I lowered my eyes from her plain, doughy face. She was young and her mantle was costly, but she had no grace or beauty to her. She was scowling, and her face was red and blotchy, yet she had a look of sharp intelligence about her. Ghisola had that same alertness, only without malevolence.

"You're going upstairs to the parliament," she said. It was a statement, not a question.

"Yes, my lady."

She stuck her hand inside her mantle and pulled out a folded scrap of

21

vellum. It looked like it had been cut from a page in a book, and I saw a scribe's faint parallel guide lines sketched on the outside, as on a last page whose text did not extend all the way to the end. She thrust it out to me.

"Here. Take this to Mosca dei Lamberti. Do you know who he is?" I nodded.

"Give it to him before the meeting, and don't let anyone see you do it. Tell no one. Do it now." Arrogant bitch, I thought, but I was in no position to argue. Mutely I took the scrap from her stubby fingers, bowed, and turned back to the stairs. As I started to climb, Guido hurried back down; as he passed me, we heard the door close with a solid "clunk", and the lady was gone. Guido made a comical gesture of wiping sweat from his brow as he rebarred the door. Safe now, I thought, and I grinned at him. I was tempted to tell him about the note and ask who she was, but something in the way she had looked at me stopped me. Instead, I went on up the stairs.

When I reached the great hall Oddo was still greeting his friends and kinsmen, going over the day's events for the benefit of those who had not been at the knighting. His description was beginning to sound a bit more heroic than I recalled the actual brawl being, but I suppose these things grow in the telling. He carried that scratched and much-bandaged arm as if it gave him great pain, and his guests exclaimed over it as if the injury were nothing less than an assassination attempt. I took advantage of the general commotion to sidle up to Mosca, who was making steady headway on a large goblet of wine, and proffer the note.

I looked around to be sure we were not being observed. "A lady sent you this, my lord," I said quietly.

"A lady, hmm?" he said, smiling. Mosca's teeth were startlingly white, in contrast to his swarthy face. He snatched the note from my hand. "Let's see it, then." He unfolded the scrap of vellum and read it, and his smile vanished.

The blood drained from his face, and he crumpled the scrap in his fist. He scrunched his eyes shut, and his tall body swayed a little. I thought he might be about to faint. Alarmed, I scanned the room for a stool or a bench to steer him towards, but none were unoccupied. I grasped his elbow and tried to direct him nearer the brazier, but he would not move. He let his wine cup tilt crazily in his hand, and wine splashed out onto the floor. Fortunately, everyone else was otherwise occupied, and no one noticed.

At last he opened his eyes again, but his face was ashen.

"You didn't tell me it was that lady," he said, so softly I barely heard him.

"I don't know who she was," I said, confused. I hadn't expected this reaction, and I was afraid others would begin to notice. I was pretty sure that would not be a good thing.

He uncrumpled the note and read it again.

"Damn her," he muttered, but he pocketed the note and gulped what was left of his wine.

"My lord, are you well? I fear I've brought you bad news," I said, still uneasy. What was this about? What I was witnessing made no sense to me.

He shook his head in lieu of answering. "There's nothing for it, then," he murmured, mostly to himself. "It will be as it must be. Maybe this will satisfy her." His voice sounded brittle and weary. "So much better if she didn't know." I still had no idea what he was talking about.

Oddo clapped his hands loudly then, twice, to call his parliament to order. All of us turned to face him, and the room fell silent.

I stood at Mosca's side, near the back of the room, where we could see and hear everything. Torches, hastily stuffed into wall brackets and lit, burned fitfully, giving forth a garish light and chasing erratic shadows across the men's faces. The room might have been a warrior's den from a century ago. Behind Oddo, shields and weapons hung on evil-looking hooks, and a fresco of a hectic battle scene full of improbably ferocious horses ran the length of the wall at his back. Perhaps the artist had felt the way I did about the beasts. I took the measure of the painting: middling quality work, no more. My father's freehand work had been finer. Oddo had probably been overcharged.

Oddo explained his purpose: the insult and injury done him by Buondelmonte must be resolved honorably. He called on all present to witness that he was doing the right and proper thing by bringing the question to his kindred and friends and requesting their advice on the matter. For that, he got a murmur of approval.

"Was there injury or insult done by our side?" I didn't recognize the speaker.

"None to match an injury that drew blood," Oddo replied. Apparently deliberate provocation didn't count with these men.

Ideas started to fly. One young hothead suggested inflicting a wound on Buondelmonte in turn, but others favored demanding a public apology and the kiss of peace. A cut to the arm did not justify a full vendetta, yet drawing blood was a serious insult, not to be ignored. Most importantly,

Buondelmonte must be seen to bow to the consortium's wishes. Honor demanded no less.

An older man suggested taking the matter to city officials and demanding a fine. It sounded reasonable to me, but another man jeered at him and told him that was a coward's way. The first speaker bristled. I braced myself for a repeat of the afternoon's ridiculous brawl, but Oddo silenced both men with an impatient gesture.

Mosca muttered something I didn't catch. His robe bore the stains of the food-fight he had recently been part of and the wine he had just spilled, but he smoothed the fine fabric with his hands as if it was fresh from storage, marred only by a crease or two. He squared his shoulders and left my side, making his way through the men to the front of the room. Thinking he had regained his presence of mind, I was relieved.

At a nod from Oddo, he turned to face the assembled men.

"The object is to achieve a peaceful resolution, is it not?" I heard general agreement, though not without some grumbling.

"Peace, but with our honor intact and Buondelmonte chastened?" Louder assent.

"What, then, about proposing a marriage between the families? To make peace, but on our terms?" That seemed to catch some of the men by surprise, but others voiced their approval.

"That's good," said Lambertuccio. "Who's marrying who, though?" He ran a hand through his gray hair. "On his side, it has to be Buondelmonte himself, or close kin to him, else honor won't be served."

"Buondelmonte, then. He's recently a widower," Mosca replied. That was quick, and a little glib, I thought.

"True. That would do it, then," Oddo said. "Who have we got?"

"My sister lost her husband. She's taken the right of tornata, so she's back with me and she's mine to give," said one of the Fifanti whose name I did not know. "Do you want her?"

"Not for this, though she's a fine woman," Mosca said. "For a peace pact, we need to offer a virgin."

Then his face lit up as if he had just had an inspiration. I didn't trust that look; I thought it false and exaggerated.

"Lambertuccio, how about your girl?" he said.

"Selvaggia?" Lambertuccio stroked his grizzled chin, considering. "Possibly. She's niece to you, Oddo, so it might work, and I do need to place the girl. He's rash and foolish, but at least his family is an old one, and noble."

Niece. The girl in the mantle had said, "Tell my uncle..." Could it

24

be? Oddo might have scores of nieces for all I knew. But I wondered.

"Indeed it might work, Brother-in-law," Oddo said. "We would show Florence that Buondelmonte takes his orders from us. And as you say, it places the girl—as I recall, that problem has been preying on your mind of late."

"That it has. I've no wish to hand that braggart a generous dowry, though."

"All the better," said Oddo. "He'll accept whatever we offer. Maybe as much as you'd give a convent to take her, no more. That will make it doubly clear to everyone that we are the ones making the decisions here. And he's rich enough to take care of her, and he'd be too afraid of us to treat her with anything less than honor."

"And he dares not refuse us," Mosca added quickly. "He knows he's in the wrong, and if he did refuse us, it would mean war. His own people wouldn't back him if he tried to sacrifice them for his boorish behavior." Smoothly said, but I wondered if Mosca spoke truth.

The scheme solved a sticky situation neatly. It tied Buondelmonte to Oddo's sister's child, ending friction between the families on Oddo's terms. Such peacemaking marriages were common, if not often successful for the individuals involved.

Oddo beckoned to a little man who had been waiting over to one side.

"Ser Opizzo, you will draft this contract for us," he declared, and the notary bowed his head. "Are you ready to prepare the document?"

The man fished a large flat pouch from under his cloak. He took a wax tablet and a stylus from the leather pouch and looked up at Oddo, awaiting instructions. Oddo and Lambertuccio led him to the bench closest to the fire, and there the three men sat. The little notary crouched low over his tablet, scratching away, while Oddo and Lambertuccio dictated to him.

Oddo's guests milled around drinking wine and discussing the day's events. I managed to acquire a cup of wine, for by then I needed it. The wine was good, the room warm and well-lit, and I was beginning to think I could learn to be comfortable in such luxurious surroundings, were it not for the company I'd have to keep. Until Mosca took his opportunity to speak to me.

"Fool, does anyone else know about that note?" He spoke in a low voice. I shook my head. "Good. See that no one learns of it, for if anyone does, I'll know who to blame. And you don't want me blaming you, Fool—is that clear?" He looked into my eyes, a hard stare. I gulped, and

25

felt my scalp itch again.

"It's clear."

Satisfied, Mosca wandered off to talk to other knights.

The little man finished his chickenscratching, and the three men stood. "My friends," Oddo called. Again everyone turned to him. He put his good arm around the notary, who clutched his wax tablet to his chest and blinked at the roomful of men. "Ser Opizzo has drawn up the contract, and within the hour he will have transferred it to parchment. I propose that we go as a delegation, first thing tomorrow, to Buondelmonte and take our notary with us, so we can contract the betrothal immediately. Are we agreed?" Heads nodded.

"Excellent. My friends, I thank you for your wisdom and your advice. All who wish to come along tomorrow are welcome. Let us meet here, dressed and equipped as the great families we are, and proceed from here to Buondelmonte. Let us plan to meet, say, an hour after the city gates are opened. Thus, any men who stable their horses across the river will have time to fetch them. What say you?"

Oddo's guests shouted out good-natured cheers, and Mosca's voice rang out over the others: "Until tomorrow, friends and kinsmen!"

The guests began to leave then, placing their emptied wine cups on the sideboard and filing down the stairs. I made to do likewise, when for the second time that day I felt a heavy hand on my shoulder.

"I want you with us, Fool," Oddo said. "But don't dress up—I want you in your motley. There'll be more money in it for you, don't worry. Be here in the morning, without fail. And do not, understand me, do not talk about this to anyone." He punched my arm for emphasis, and I winced. Oddo was a powerful man.

If he wanted me in fool's garb, it could only be as an insult to Buondelmonte. I would have preferred not to play that role, but it was impossible to argue with Oddo, so I had to agree. Only then was I at last permitted to descend that wide staircase and go out into the night.

By then most of the guests had left for their homes. Clouds obscured the moon and the stars, leaving the streets treacherously dark. The knights were guided by their torchbearers, but I made my way alone through the inky streets. As exhausted as I was, I tried to marshal my thoughts as I walked, for soon I would face Neri's questions, and I had just been ordered to keep silent, both about the next day's plans and about my own reluctant role in shaping them.

4. BUONDELMONTE

Late as it was, Neri and Ghisola were up and waiting for me. Ours was a frugal household—not that we had much choice—so no candle was burning, and in the gloom I could barely see them. After the blazing torches at the banquet and the Fifanti palace, the contrast was stark. The fire was down to embers, and our drafty house was not much warmer than outside. Even so, I dropped the grimy cloak on the floor before I went any farther.

Even in the meager light I noticed Ghisola's gap-toothed smile, one of giddy relief. I felt a twinge of guilt for worrying her. Still, after all that had happened, it was pleasant to know that someone cared about my safety and my well-being. Someone besides me, I mean. To be fair, Neri was relieved, too, though he didn't intend to show it, but I knew him too well to be fooled.

"We left you your supper." She pointed to the pot squatting on its low tripod over the coals. "Or did your brawling employers stop throwing things long enough to give you a meal?" Neri said nothing, but sat watching me, his arms folded.

"Not unless you count flinging food at me." I dished up the fragrant stew. Ghisola was a skillful cook, one of those women who could take a bit of salt meat, last year's onions, and a handful of garden greens and turn it into a meal as savory as you'd find in the noblest kitchen in Florence. We had eaten well in the two years since she moved in with Neri. And I was famished.

Neri stretched his long legs out on the bench. "So what happened?"

I sat on a stool with my stew and a hunk of bread and wolfed down several bites before replying. It did not disappoint. He waited, drumming his fingers on the bench. The room was too dark for me to see his expression, but I knew Neri's impatient frown—I had seen it often enough. His curiosity was boundless; he always had to know everything that was going on. No harm in that, except he also liked for everyone to know that he knew.

"Fight," I finally told him, still chewing on my bread. "Buondelmonte cut Oddo's arm, Mazzingo stopped Mosca from killing Buondelmonte, and Schiatta told everybody to go home." Brief but accurate.

I heard Ghisola's sharp intake of breath, and Neri whistled. "He drew blood?" he said.

"Yes. Not serious, but it was enough." A blood-insult would have to be answered.

"Did you walk home alone?" He poked at the embers and the fire flared a little, finally giving enough light to see by.

I took another bite to give myself time to think before answering, and studied my housemates. Neri was still wearing the red tunic he liked to perform in. It had been much mended and its color was faded, but he wore it with a sort of pleased-with-himself swagger, for it had once been fine. Ghisola's straw-colored hair was working its way out of its thick braid. She was a tidy woman, but her curly hair had a will of its own, and it did not fancy being confined. Both of them were watching me intently, waiting to hear more.

I was so tired I was tempted to tell them everything without trying to sort it out first. If I did, maybe Neri would let me go to bed, which is where I fervently wished to be. But Oddo had ordered me not to tell anybody about what I had witnessed or about the next day's excursion. If I told Neri, and he went to the tavern after I went to bed, as he often did, he might drink overmuch and brag about what he knew. And if Buondelmonte got wind of the morning's visit, he might just arrange not to be at home for it. I didn't want Oddo tracing that problem back to me, so I thought it safest to dodge the question. I could tell them about it later, once this was all settled. Maybe even about the note.

"I was with some others." Naturally they had worried; even a group of well-armed men would think twice about walking that road after dark.

"We realized when we got home that your knife was still in your props bag. Were the others armed?" I nodded. This wasn't so difficult—so far I hadn't even needed to lie.

"Whose cloak were you wearing?" He pointed to the grimy garment I had dropped on the floor when I came in.

"Somebody's servant loaned it to me." My own cloak had been returned to its place on the rod beside the door. "I'll have to take it to the Fifanti palace tomorrow." Good. There was my excuse for going out in the morning.

Ghisola wrinkled her nose. "Don't know why anybody would want it back."

"Ghisi, you didn't even see it. It was too dark when I came in, and now it's in a puddle on the floor, over there." I waved in the direction of the door.

"Smelled it, though. Smells like horse. You do, too." Damn. She would have to notice that. I glanced at Neri to see if he had heard, but he was busy scraping live coals into a heap, ready to cover for the night, and he didn't say anything.

Best not to answer, I thought. I put my empty bowl on the shelf and stretched. "I'm going to bed. I need to sleep."

Neri looked up. "You aren't going to tell us all about the fight?" he said, sounding like a little boy deprived of a bedtime story.

"Tomorrow. Nothing much to tell, anyway."

"Tomorrow, then. You do look tired." He hesitated, then said, "Sorry we left without you, but we had to get the instruments out of there. We waited for you outside for a while, but you didn't come, so we went on." He must have expected me to be angry, but in their place I would have done the same.

"I couldn't get out the door—too much fighting. I just kept low and stayed out of it." I went to the door and picked up the discarded cloak, so Ghisola wouldn't be tempted to explore it further.

"Best thing to do," Neri agreed. "I was worried about you at first, but by the time we got out they weren't paying attention to you any more, so we figured you were probably all right." He grinned. "That was quite the feast. Good thing we got paid in advance."

We bade each other good night and went to our sleeping corners, he and Ghisola to whatever rest or pleasures they chose, and me to lie awake worrying about the next day's doings. When I pulled back the patched curtain that separated my sleep space from the rest of the house I saw my bag of juggling props, neatly put away on its shelf.

*

I was watery-eyed and dragging when I left for Oddo's palace early the next morning. I wrapped myself in the threadbare cloak before I emerged from my sleeping corner so that Neri and Ghisola wouldn't see that I still wore my motley, but they were still abed—though not, I think, asleep—so I changed it for my own cloak before I went out, wadding up the disreputable one and tucking it under my arm. It was even fouler by daylight and smelled no better. On my way I dropped it in front of the legless beggar who sat daily in the porch of Santo Stefano. When I turned the corner I saw him holding it out at arm's length and sniffing at it gingerly.

The narrow street in front of the palace was crowded with men and horses. Oddo's hunting dogs were milling around, confused—such a gathering usually meant a hunt, but the men were not dressed for hunting, and the dogs didn't know what to make of it. I managed to avoid all the beasts, especially old Windy, and find Oddo to let him know I was there.

"Good morrow, Fool." He looked me up and down, and a slow smile spread across his face. "Good. You'll make my point, right enough." I was fairly sure that wasn't a compliment; I tried to run my fingers through my hair, but some bits of Mazzingo's feast had created an impassable tangle.

"Don't suppose you want a horse this morning, eh?" I flinched, and he laughed at his own joke. He pointed to a cluster of young men standing nearby. "Go there," he said, and turned away to talk to somebody else. I went.

One of the lads told me we were to follow on foot behind the horses, once Oddo got his entourage organized. It looked like all of the men who had attended the parliament were present, plus quite a few more. Mazzingo was there, too, but he wasn't looking happy. All were dressed to impress, in a carnival of bright colors. Oddo, his arm still spectacularly bandaged, inspected the riders for visible weaponry and armor, though he didn't bother inspecting his foot soldiers. I didn't doubt that plenty of not-so-obvious weaponry was coming with us on the persons of those knights and squires, most of whom, by the look of them, had enjoyed a more restful night than I had and were eager for this morning's adventure. I wasn't, but before I could spend much time worrying about it, Oddo lined everybody up and we were off.

The day was crisp, overcast, with diffuse light. In the occasional intervals between bits of overhanging architecture we glimpsed a colorless sky. Oddo and the other mounted men rode with practiced ease, moving along as briskly as the narrow streets allowed. Those of us on foot had to push ourselves to keep up. Guido was riding just behind Oddo, a proud grin on his face. I jogged alongside a younger man, one who had greeted me with a friendly word when I joined the group. The young ones always like us fools. This one introduced himself as Pierino. He wore Oddo's colors, garish red and gold.

"So who is this girl they're offering?" I asked him. "Is Buondelmonte a lucky man?" I was puffing with exertion, for the pace was quick, and speech came hard.

"Oh, that's Selvaggia," Pierino said, striding easily along at my side. Not for the first time, I wished God had granted me such long legs. He could have held back some of the nose, in compensation. "She's messer Lambertuccio's daughter. It's a good enough match for Buondelmonte, though his family's been here forever. She's got money, lots of kinsmen, allied with the old families. Better than he deserves. Only, the girl herself

. . ." He shook his head.

"Never say I told you this," he said, lowering his voice, "but she's none too fair, and she's one as will have her way no matter what. Her two big sisters are proper Amidei ladies who married well, and their husbands have no complaints. But this one—well, there haven't been a lot of offers. We were all thinking she was for the convent. If you bring in enough money there, they'll take you, even if you're bad-tempered and short and stout with a face like a turnip."

We quick-stepped along, dodging the horses' leavings. Dogs barked, pigs scurried out of our way, and children flattened themselves against buildings and stared at us.

Short, face like a turnip—as I suspected, it must be the girl in the mantle. She wanted this marriage, then. I'd love to know what kind of hold she had on Mosca for him to turn so pale at her message and do her bidding, for I had no doubt it was her note that had spurred him to speak at Oddo's parliament.

"But then this business came along," Pierino waved a hand to indicate the mounted knights ahead of us, "and the lords saw a chance to fix things without a vendetta and still show the world that Buondelmonte dances to their tune. It will be a huge relief to her parents, too. I hear it's been hell living with her since her last sister married." I could well imagine.

The morning was well advanced and the streets teemed with people, people who had little choice but to crowd up against the rough stone buildings and make themselves small as our party thundered by. A shoemaker and his apprentice hurried to haul their worktable off its trestles and lean it against their shop wall, out of our way.

We rounded the last corner onto Buondelmonte's street. The Buondelmonti palace and tower were a street or two north of the river and near the marketplace. Too near, according to his enemies. Most of that space was in the hands of Oddo's people. The Buondelmonti presence was a pricking thorn to them, and especially to the Amidei. That family's tower crowded close to the city side of the bridge, overlooking all the traffic across the Arno and the shops that lined both sides of the bridge. No better vantage point existed in Florence. From that tower they could spit cherry stones at the ancient statue of Mars guarding the end of the crowded bridge.

The riders drew up in front of the Buondelmonti palace, and those of us on foot bunched up behind them. Oddo ordered Guido to announce our presence, and Guido dismounted and strode up to the palace door.

31

He banged on it with his fist, at the same time crying out, "Open! Messer Oddo dei Fifanti awaits."

Slowly the heavy studded door opened, but only a crack. A servant peeked out from behind it and stammered out a question, which I couldn't hear from the back of the party. Oddo was in fine form this morning. He gave the traditional speech about coming in peace, having business to transact with the master, and so on, and the servant bobbed his head respectfully and withdrew, pulling the door shut. The mounted men joked among themselves as we waited for Buondelmonte to appear.

Above us, the Buondelmonti palace boasted a wooden gallery that overhung the street, jutting out like the lower lip of a sulking child. We heard a noise up there, and looked up to see Buondelmonte standing at the railing, gazing down at us. His brother Gherardo was at his side.

Clever, I thought, watching Oddo's expression darken. They claim the advantage of height. Both men were dressed with care and elegance, as if they had been expecting this visit. I supposed that meant I could have told Neri about it after all. Too late now.

Oddo tilted his head back to look up at Buondelmonte, raised his elaborately bandaged arm in a gesture of greeting, and waited. Buondelmonte took a step forward to the edge of the gallery, which was plastered and brightly painted in his family's distinctive blue and white. He inclined his head, a minimal movement, and then spoke to all of us in a resonant voice.

"Be welcome, my lords, to my house, and that of my brother Gherardo." Gherardo, in his turn, inclined his head. Buondelmonte greeted each of the mounted men in the front rank by name and title, mentioning any relationships between his family and theirs when such existed—only a few, and none forged recently. He went on to pray them to honor him by entering and taking a cup of wine, adding platitudes about the day being brisk and his home warm and welcoming. Merely a formula, but the courtesies must be observed. And while they were being observed at tedious length, all of us in Oddo's party strained our necks staring up at the Buondelmonti brothers on their balcony.

As Buondelmonte made his stiff little speech of welcome, I took the opportunity to study him. He was a proud man and well formed, his long nose a little red from the sun or from yesterday's drink. He stood erect and tall, and he wore a surcoat of brilliant blue which must have cost more than I have spent on clothing in my lifetime. His brother Gherardo, at his right side, was the younger of the two. Gherardo wore a surcoat of the same cut as Buondelmonte's, but his garment was gleaming white, the two of them side by side comprising a heraldic statement. Both men appeared unarmed, but something in the way they held themselves told me that like our own men, they were not unprotected. I caught a glimpse of movement behind the lowest window of the lofty tower attached to the palace. A group the size of ours need not fear ambush, but we were being watched.

Buondelmonte invited us all inside, and Oddo accepted. Buondelmonte's eyes swept the group as Oddo spoke, and they lingered for a moment on me, in my rumpled and food-stained jester's motley. A flicker of annoyance crossed his face, but then it was gone. The servant opened the great door wide and held it for us, and the knights dismounted and followed Oddo inside, talking and joking. Those of us who had arrived on foot followed, except for a few appointed by Guido to hold the horses. I would almost have preferred that assignment, even though they were horses, but I wasn't among those chosen. I trooped inside with the others, acutely aware that my very presence was an affront to our hosts. When I crossed the threshold, Buondelmonte and Gherardo were just descending the stairs to meet their guests face to face.

We found ourselves crowded into the ground-floor entry and storage area of the Buondelmonti palace. A few storerooms lined the back wall, curtained off with wool drapes of a blue so dark it looked black. A staircase led up to the living area. A few benches stood against the walls, bare of cushions or carpets, and wine barrels were lined up along one side.

Buondelmonte's home was less warm and welcoming than his speech had suggested, and no invitation came for us to climb up those stairs to the hall and the hearth. No braziers smoldered on this level to take the chill out of the air, and I suspected that was deliberate. Of course, he could always claim he didn't know we were coming. Perhaps he and his brother always wore their fine blue and white garments at home in the morning.

Buondelmonte's servants were there, at least. They ladled wine into cups, adding water to make a morning drink, and passed the cups around to all of us. It was pewter and brass for the knights, wood and ceramic for the rest of us. Did they own so many cups, I wondered, or had they borrowed from friends and kin? And yet we saw no members of the Buondelmonti consortium present other than the two brothers.

Oddo, Lambertuccio, Mosca, and the Buondelmonti brothers consulted briefly, then entered a small room over to one side of the main door and pulled the curtain closed, leaving the rest of us to drink our wine and take our ease.

So we waited, and drank the wine, which was not as fine as the wine Mazzingo had served. Not their best, I suspected, but then, why should it be? We talked among ourselves and kept half an eye on the curtain that separated the five men from the rest of us, until Oddo stepped out and beckoned to ser Opizzo, who obediently approached and was ushered into the little room, clutching his leather folder.

Not many minutes passed before the curtain opened and all six men emerged to make their expected announcement. We toasted Buondelmonte's upcoming nuptials with good-natured cheers, and a few bawdy comments and jests began to make the rounds among the men. Both of the Buondelmonti brothers stood stiffly and their smiles were forced, in contrast to Oddo's jocularity and Lambertuccio's good cheer. Mosca was subdued, but he downed his wine with a good enough will.

After much handclasping, back slapping, and many fine words of brotherhood and friendship, and even the kiss of peace—and remembering Oddo's foul breath, I didn't envy Buondelmonte that—Mosca at last called for our delegation to depart. Most still wore their cloaks, but those who had shed them now put them back on. With one last embrace between Oddo and Buondelmonte, and then between Lambertuccio and his future son-in-law, we began to file out the door. Oddo stood with Buondelmonte and Gherardo next to the door and watched the men go. Knights went first, as is proper, and then the rest of us started to leave, but before I reached the door, Oddo grabbed my arm.

"Fool," he said, deliberately loud enough for the Buondelmonti brothers to hear, "I owe you a purse. Meet me at the Amidei palace tomorrow, and you'll have it. Be there." At his side, Buondelmonte didn't bother to hide a scowl. Oddo turned away to give Guido an order and I headed for the door, more eager than ever to get away.

I would have made it if there hadn't been a clump of men bunched in the doorway, but once again I felt a hard hand on my shoulder. Not Oddo this time, but Buondelmonte. What was it with these pompous blowhards, I wondered, that they couldn't keep their hands off me?

"Fool, you stay," Buondelmonte muttered in my ear. "Now it's my turn to employ you." I turned to Oddo for help, but he was still talking to Guido. Buondelmonte jerked his thumb toward the curtained room where the men had met, and I went, for I saw no choice. Oddo had already forgotten me.

I ducked behind the curtain. Recently disturbed dust made me sneeze. The space was small and plain, but at least the knights' negotiations had not taken place in a storeroom, for the room contained nothing but a bench, two stools, a small brazier with live coals, and a little table covered with a small carpet. On the table, good wax candles burning on two of the candleholder's three prickets shed adequate light. A few wax tablets and other writing supplies were piled on one corner, and five wine cups, recently emptied, ranged around the candleholder. I guessed ser Opizzo didn't get to drink while he worked.

I stood there wondering what I was about to get myself into now, listening to Oddo's smugly hearty farewells and Buondelmonte's neutral reply, and finally the heavy door eased back into place with a sound like a giant's sigh. I waited.

A large, rough hand grasped the curtain and pulled it aside. Buondelmonte stood there glaring at me.

"Well, little Fool, it's a fine uproar you and your idiotic jest have caused. You've gotten me either a wife or a war, and I'm not sure I'm liking either one. What do you have to say for yourself?"

"My lord, I regret any difficulties—"

"You regret! A fat lot of good that does anyone. If you hadn't snatched that plate of meat, this city would be at peace today, without all this accursed posturing. Are you proud of yourself?"

"Messer, I was only doing what I was ordered to do." I thought that perhaps sticking a knife into Oddo might also have contributed to the troubles, but it seemed wisest not to say so.

"And you'll follow orders again, only from now on, I give them. Is that clear?"

I hesitated. The last thing I needed was to be in the employ of both Oddo and Buondelmonte, those two enemies supposedly turned friends. If I worked for either one of them, half the city wouldn't employ me. If I worked for both, that meant the whole city. Buondelmonte took a small pouch from his sleeve. Unlike the utilitarian canvas pouch Oddo had handed me yesterday, this one was silk, in the Buondelmonti blue and white. He tossed it to me, and I caught it and looked inside.

5. GUALDRADA

Up until that moment I had done nothing more than my job. Had I refused Buondelmonte's purse, handed it back to him and walked away, it would have gone hard with me, for he would probably have decided to teach me obedience. But I would likely have survived, and I could have avoided taking part in what was to follow.

But when I looked into the purse, I saw coins of a sort and number I had seldom seen, let alone held in my hand. How can I describe what such money means to a fool who lives from hand to mouth? Who sweats the sour sweat of fear whenever the rent comes due? I've stolen food; I've slept on the bare dirt floor of a room I hadn't paid for; I've spent a penny for a dead man's clothes and never asked what he died of. I couldn't refuse those coins, even though they came from a nobleman.

So I slipped the elegant purse into the pocket inside my sleeve where Oddo's canvas pouch still rested, and I listened while Buondelmonte gave me my orders.

"You'll be delivering a message for me, Fool," he said. "You'll be taking it to monna Gualdrada of the Donati. Do you know where she lives?"

The Donati had two compounds, one central, the other at the city's eastern wall, near San Pier Maggiore. The lady's name sounded familiar, but I couldn't place it. "Monna" told me she was married, but I didn't know who her husband was. "I don't know which is her home, my lord."

"The smaller of the palaces near Santa Margherita. It's the one with the leatherworker's shop at street level." I knew the building. "You take her the message, wait for her reply, and bring it straight back here. Got that?" I nodded.

"When you return, if I need anything else from you I'll tell you."

This confused me. Nothing in merely bearing a message merited that princely purse, so I knew that bearing the message couldn't be the whole of it.

And indeed it was not.

"And Fool, you are never to speak of this errand, nor of any other you carry out for me, to a living soul. If you do, you not only forfeit the purse, you forfeit your miserable, pathetic life. I trust this is clear." His words chilled me and set my scalp to itching, but it was too late: the purse was in my sleeve, and I had received my first orders. I was employed.

I waited in silence while Buondelmonte picked up a wax tablet and a stylus from the pile of scribal supplies on the table. He warmed the tablet between his huge hands, and then sat at the little table and scratched a few lines into the wax. He read it over, nodded to himself, and slipped the tablet into a leather envelope.

He held a stick of wax over the brazier, then let it drip onto the flap of the envelope. He stamped the seal with his ring as the sweetish smell of hot beeswax filled the little room. He handed the envelope to me and watched while I stored it well out of sight.

"Go quickly, and come back as soon as you have her answer." He walked me to the door, opened it, and gave me a little shove on my way. Thus I finally found myself on the other side of that massive door, but without anything like the sense of freedom I had hoped to find there. Nothing for it; I had an errand to do.

*

I set off for the Donati compound. The most direct route would have taken me past the Fifanti houses, which I didn't want, so I took the winding, muddy back streets around San Michele in Orto and avoided the streets where I might have encountered Oddo's kin and friends.

The Donati enclave in front of me consisted of a tower, two imposing stone palaces, and a courtyard that could be fully blockaded in case of attack, as well as several houses owned by the family and rented out. This ancient and noble family, for all its quarrelsome history, practiced the virtue of hospitality by providing a commodious stone bench for weary passersby. Two old men were sitting there, talking and sharing a cup of something. They might have been there all morning, and perhaps intended to pass the afternoon there, as well.

The larger palace presented a forbidding front, with no windows lower than the first floor of living space, up a flight of outdoor stone stairs. The smaller, however, had its ground floor converted to shop space, a stone counter running the length of the building, about waist-high. On it, the leatherworker displayed his wares to the street while he worked just inside, keeping a sharp eye on his merchandise. He was no shoemaker, but rather one who dealt in luxury leather items, such as belts, purses, saddlebags, and intricate leather fastenings and tooled cases. He closed up the shop at night with a wooden awning that could be lowered and latched for security, and which met the counter to form a wall across the front of the palace. His daily presence was itself a kind of security for the Donati living above, since anyone headed for the great staircase up to the family's living quarters had to go through the shop and past the leatherworker.

I knew the man slightly, though I couldn't remember his name. He was a friendly, garrulous fellow, a little stiff and awkward in his movements. He had once done a commission for me—my set of leather juggling balls and the pouch I kept them in, an extravagance that used up most of my fee for performing at a wedding feast. With the coins jingling in the two purses up my sleeve, I could do more business with him soon, if I chose, without even sacrificing the rent this time. Maybe a new jester's cap in yellow and green, to match my motley.

I thought at first he was talking to someone, perhaps lecturing an apprentice somewhere out of sight, for his voice droned on with few pauses and little change of pitch. But as I made out his words, I realized he was attempting to sing a lauda in praise of the Blessed Virgin. What he lacked in ability he made up in enthusiasm and fervor, and he didn't notice me until I stood directly in front of him.

He broke off his tuneless song and greeted me with a broad smile. "Fool! I bid you welcome. Have you come for more balls, or other playthings of your trade?"

"No, not this time. I bear a message for monna Gualdrada. Can you let me come up?" I wasn't supposed to tell anyone of my errand, but there was no other way to get in.

He shook his head. "I can't just send you up. There's only women in the house—the Donati widow and her girls and the servants. And their cousin, and she's a widow too. I'll call Elisa for you and she'll take you up if the mistress says it's all right. You may have to wait while she gets one of the mistress's brothers-in-law from next door." He got up awkwardly, leaning on his work table for support.

"Who's Elisa?"

"She's monna Gualdrada's maidservant. You could just give her the message, and she'll take it up to the mistress for you."

"Can't. I promised the man who paid me that I'd wait for a reply."

"All right, then, I'll get Elisa. Have a seat, if you want." The leather-worker hobbled over to the staircase and tugged on a rope that ran the length of the wall up the steps, held up by hooks placed in the wall at every second step. I thought I heard a bell sound, upstairs. He waited at the foot of the stairs, humming in a monotone, and I sat on the stool he had vacated. The shop had a pleasant smell of good leather—not the stench of the tanning process, but a smell I associated with men dressed for the hunt, before they come back reeking of blood and sweat.

Soon I heard quick footsteps, and a fair and shapely young woman came running lightly down the stairs. She was simply dressed, but her dove-gray gown suited her well. She and the leatherworker exchanged a few words and she glanced over at me, then shyly lowered her eyes. She spoke to him, too quietly for me to hear, and then turned and went back up the stairs as effortlessly as she had come down them.

The leatherworker stumbled a little as he made his unsteady way back to where I was waiting, and I jumped up to give him his stool, wondering if I should offer an arm to help him sit. He winced as he settled himself back down.

"Can't be standing too long, you see. Got a touch of the gout."

More than a touch, I thought. His health had deteriorated since I saw him last. "An awful thing, the gout. God grant that it leave you in peace. What did the maid say?"

"She's checking with the mistress. Won't be long." And it wasn't, for the lovely young woman was soon back. She came over to me and greeted me in a soft voice, keeping her eyes lowered. I was charmed. Most of the women I knew weren't so modest.

"My mistress asks you to please come up to the kitchen," she said, almost in a whisper, her eyes at my chest level. "She'll meet with you there." She started up the stairs, then turned and beckoned me to follow. To do so was pure pleasure. This house full of women was already a refreshing change from the swaggering warriors and their strutting hangers-on with whom I had been keeping unwilling company the past couple of days. As we climbed, I heard the leatherworker break into song again. At least, I think he was singing.

We climbed one flight, my eyes on the maidservant's swaying backside, and came to the great hall. It was a large room, empty except for a few trestle tables and benches stacked along the walls, adorned with a painted border about halfway to the ceiling, a repeated pattern of flowers and foliage. With the windows shuttered I couldn't see much, but I thought the frescoes were probably quality freehand work. Large hooks had been mounted high up on the walls, for attaching hangings.

The staircase continued upwards, and so did we. The rope alongside us continued as well. We reached the next level, which consisted of a smaller hall, or at least a hall that had given up some of its space to chambers created by the addition of wooden partitions at the far end. Women had been working with cloth in there, near a window—a clothing assembly project, with pieces of white linen spread out on two low trestle tables. This small hall was brighter than the bigger one. Its windows were covered with oiled cloth, and the shutters, which could be closed in sections and set at different angles, were arranged to direct maximum light to the work tables. The rope ended here, attached to a small brass bell. We crossed that hall, maneuvering between the tables, and climbed the narrow wooden staircase up to the kitchen.

The kitchen was pleasantly warm, though a little dark, and not too smoky. A skinny old woman with papery skin sat at a bench next to the fire, idly poking at it with a stick. She looked up when we arrived and studied me. I stared right back at her. Eventually she nodded.

"Elisa, get him a cup of hot wine," she said, her voice more vigorous than her fragile appearance suggested. Too old and too plainly dressed to be Gualdrada. The widowed cousin, perhaps?

Elisa took a ladle from its peg and dipped it into a pot suspended from a tripod over live coals. She filled a wooden cup and handed it to me, her eyes downcast all the while. I took it and thanked her, and she murmured something and disappeared behind a curtain.

I looked around. The kitchen was tidy and well organized. A thick block of wood on a cutting table held several large knives at an angle. Spoons, graters, strainers, and other kitchen tools hung from pegs in a neat row along the wall, and clean white towels hung from hooks under a shelf, out of reach of mice or other vermin. A stout broom leaned in a corner. Maiolica jars, decorated in brown and bluish green, lined a high shelf, and a large brass basin sat ready on a three-legged stool, a few dishes in it waiting to be washed.

The old woman turned to me abruptly. "What do you want with monna Gualdrada?" she said. Her voice rasped with kitchen smoke and age.

"I bring her a message from a friend, Grandmother," I said courteously, having concluded that she held a place of importance in this household. She wrinkled her nose.

"A friend, is it? Well, that may be a matter of opinion. You don't belong in a house with two marriageable girls and no men present. I'm not so sure you belong in a Donati house at all."

I decided to leave that one alone. I took a seat, unasked, at the far end of the bench and held my cup of steaming wine, still too hot to drink. Already I was too warm, but I didn't want to shed my mantle and expose my tawdry jester's costume here.

For the first time I noticed the gray cat. It was curled up on a towel in front of the fire, asleep and snoring a little, with an occasional shuddery outbreath. Now that I thought about it, I caught a faint odor of cat in the room, but not enough to be unpleasant. The worst of it probably escaped with the smoke and the cooking odors, through the louvred opening in the roof.

Footsteps and a rustling of cloth signaled someone's approach from the chambers that lay beyond the kitchen. I stood up as monna Gualdrada swept into the room.

The Donati widow was a handsome woman, with an impressive bosom and a face that must once have been beautiful. Mature but by no means old, she wore a simple blue gonnella. The unadorned garment was entirely appropriate for wearing at home, but it was made of good cloth and fitted her well, laced close to her body down to the hips, then flaring out in graceful folds to the floor. An expensive hint of rose and lavender surrounded her, subtle but effective. She wore her hair uncovered, in a thick red-brown plait down her back.

This informality served to remind me of my place. Had I been Buondelmonte himself, or Oddo—not that Oddo would ever have entered a Donati house—she would have greeted me with her hair covered, and with a cioppa or a guarnacca over her gonnella. And one, at least, of her male relatives would have been with her. The old woman had been right about that. Was this why Buondelmonte hired me? Because I was so insignificant I could get in and deliver his message without arousing anyone's attention? It seemed likely.

I made an elaborate bow, sweeping my arm in a semicircle which pushed my cloak back and exposed the garish yellow and green of my fool's outfit. I felt ridiculous.

Then she smiled at me, and with that she was no longer merely handsome, but lovely. She had wide blue eyes and full lips, and her smile made her at once young and desirable, and womanly and mysterious. Was Buondelmonte dallying with this woman? Was that why the secrecy, why the unlikely choice of me for a messenger? I knew now that she had marriageable daughters, so she had to be at least his age and probably more. Yet it was possible. Was I perhaps carrying the news of his forced betrothal to one who would be distressed to hear it?

"Monna Gualdrada, I bring you greetings and a message from messer Buondelmonte," I said, holding out the leather envelope.

She took it from me, still smiling. "Please, my friend, be seated and enjoy your wine, while I read your message," she said in a rich and musical voice. I sat. I was pretty sure no member of the nobility had ever called me "friend" before.

"I take it you will wait for a reply?" I nodded, and she moved closer to the fire's light. With her fingernail she broke the seal on the envelope and withdrew the tablet.

41

It disappointed me that she could read. I would like to have read it for her, for I was curious about the contents. I could have read it, fool though I am, even if Buondelmonte had written it in Latin. My mother, God rest her soul, wanted me to make my career in the church, and she saw to it that I got the necessary education. Not that I used it much, these days, but you don't forget these things.

I pretended to gaze absently at the window as the lady read, but I watched her from the corner of my eye. She frowned; then I heard her suck in her breath and let it out again in a long hiss. The old woman watched her steadily, but said nothing. Gualdrada read the message over again, walked over to the hearth and held the tablet over the fire until the wax started to drip, erasing Buondelmonte's words. Then she began to pace the length of the hearth and back. On her third circuit, when she neared where I sat on the bench feigning inattention, she cleared her throat softly.

I looked up. The dazzling smile was gone. "My answer to our mutual friend is brief, and I prefer not to commit it to writing. Can you remember it and convey it to messer Buondelmonte?"

"Yes, my lady." I waited.

"Tell him, then, that I understand his situation, and that I wish to see him. Tell him to come to me, right away, and together we will find a way to resolve this. Bid him come, for his honor depends upon it."

If this was dalliance, surely her honor was more at stake than his, I thought, suppressing a smile. "I have it, my lady," I said.

"Say it back to me." I did. She rehearsed me a couple of times until she was satisfied.

"Go now, friend, and take this with my thanks." She pulled a coin out of the small purse hanging from her belt and offered it to me. It was generous payment, but I couldn't take it.

"Messer Buondelmonte has already paid me, my lady, though I thank you."

"Good service merits fair payment," she said, still holding out the coin.

"I'm sorry, my lady, but I cannot." I was already being paid by one person too many.

She smiled her assent and put the coin away. She slipped the wax tablet, erased and now cooled, back into the envelope and handed it to me.

"Elisa," she called over her shoulder, and the girl emerged from the pantry. "Take our friend to the door and see him out. He is in haste, but

42

offer him sweetmeats to take with him if he wishes." And with that and a brief smile for me, monna Gualdrada withdrew into the chamber from which she had emerged. The old woman, still not saying a word, got up and hobbled after her, without so much as a glance at me.

6. DISHONOR

I refused the sweetmeats and followed Elisa down both flights of stairs, where she left me. The leatherworker bade me a cheery farewell. He was singing again as I left, and I retraced my steps to the palace of the Buondelmonti.

By now the bells had already rung for Sext. The day turned warmer and brighter, and my mood brightened with it, for I believed that soon I would recite the lady's message to Buondelmonte and be free to go at last, my bright new coins jingling merrily in their pouch. That reminded me, I still had payment to pick up from Oddo, too. This little adventure was not without risk, but it did pay well.

Buondelmonte's man remembered me from the morning's delegation. He didn't look happy to see me, but he had orders to admit me and send me up to the hall, so up I went. I heard two men speaking in the hall, and I recognized both voices: Buondelmonte and his brother Gherardo, and they were arguing. I didn't want to walk in during a private conversation, so I took the stairs slowly, and while I climbed, I listened.

Buondelmonte said something about the Donati that I didn't catch, and then Gherardo answered testily, "Brother, you're too headstrong. Your foolish act at the feast was bad enough, and now you're making this decision without consulting the family. You can't expect us to back you in anything so dangerous."

Dangerous. Deliver the message and get out, I told myself. Don't linger to see where this is going. You don't need to know.

I coughed deliberately, and trod more heavily on the stairs to make enough noise for them to hear me coming, for I wanted no surprises. I reached the hall and bowed to the brothers. They were seated on two cushioned stools with a small glowing brazier on the floor between them; the long hall was otherwise empty, and gloomy. Three of the windows were shuttered, but a fourth admitted weak light through the oiled cloth stretched across the opening.

"Well?" said Buondelmonte, holding out his hand.

"She wanted me to speak it to you, my lord."

"Do so, then."

I recited monna Gualdrada's brief message. The two brothers looked long at one another. Buondelmonte's face was flushed, and a little smile played around his lips. Gherardo's face, in contrast, reminded me of one of the snarling demons in the Last Judgment painted on the wall of my parish church.

"May I go now, messer Buondelmonte?" I asked. A good time to leave, before a fight erupted between these two.

Buondelmonte ignored me. His eyes did not leave Gherardo. I sidled toward the stairs.

"Well, Brother?" he said.

Gherardo spat on the floor. "I won't try to stop you, Buondelmonte, but you endanger all of us if you set this folly in motion." He glared at his brother. "I stood with you this morning. Don't ask more of me than I can give."

"I've made no decision yet, Gherardo. But I'll go, and she and I will talk, and we'll see what, if anything, may be done."

Gherardo frowned, but he said no more. Buondelmonte turned to me. I had almost reached the stairs, but not quite.

"Not so fast, little fool," he said. "If my brother won't come with me, then you will. You have work yet to do to earn those coins." He looked jaunty, like a boy about to set off on an escapade. From the way he was grinning at me, no one would believe that an hour ago he had threatened my life. Gherardo made a noise of disgust, got up, and stamped out of the hall.

"Do you ride?" Buondelmonte asked me.

"Not well, milord," I said. Neri would have hooted at that, I thought.

"Very well, we'll walk," he said, and I privately gave thanks.

I was becoming a familiar fixture in those narrow streets around the oratory of San Michele and its little garden. This time, however, I was accompanying a well-known knight, and it was a different experience. Several men greeted Buondelmonte or spoke a few words to him, but a few turned their heads away. Some offered their support, or at least a pithy comment about Oddo. Buondelmonte was gracious to all, but he simply said that a resolution was in progress and he couldn't stay to talk about it just now. We moved farther away from Buondelmonte's neighborhood, past the parish church of Santa Maria sopra Porta and beyond, and there fewer people approached us, though from the stares that followed us, I guessed that the whole city knew what was going on.

And what exactly was it that was going on? Why were we heading off on foot to that house of women, and why was Gherardo so troubled? Now that Buondelmonte was not being stopped by acquaintances every few steps, I ventured to speak to him myself, for he seemed in a friendly enough mood.

"Monna Gualdrada of the Donati is a fine and gracious woman," I said. A safe beginning—even her worst enemy couldn't have argued with my words, and clearly Buondelmonte was no enemy to her house.

He favored me with a wide smile. "Wait till you see her daughter," he said, and the big man's eyes were sparkling. He started to walk even faster.

Her daughter. So that was what this was about. But he had just contracted with Selvaggia, and the lady's message had said—oh, God's teeth, but this was going to be trouble.

"Her name's Isabella, and she's the fairest woman in Florence, without a doubt. If you think the mother is fine, the girl will astound you."

"She must be fair indeed," I murmured, lengthening my stride to keep up with him.

"She's not yet formally promised to me," Buondelmonte said, "but we had an understanding. That's what this meeting is about. We need to figure out some way I can get out of this new contract and have Isabella instead."

Worse and worse. If he broke that contract—I didn't want to think about what it would mean. Now I understood why my silence had been such an important part of our deal. If any word of this got out, it meant war. If he broke the contract, it meant war. For all I knew, if he married Selvaggia there might be war anyway. And if there was war, and Oddo learned that I was working for Buondelmonte, then I would be the first casualty. And even if I was insignificant enough to somehow survive, conflict among the great families endangered and disrupted the lives of all of us, great and small. My life, and Neri's, and Ghisola's, and the lives of all of our friends and neighbors.

Still, I had seen Selvaggia: I couldn't blame him, even if this Isabella was not the miracle of womanhood he described.

At the Donati palace the leatherworker was surprised to see me back, and in such company. He greeted the knight with formal courtesy.

"Messer Buondelmonte, welcome. The belt you ordered will be ready soon. Would you like to see the tooling I have done thus far? I have been working on it this very day, and I think the design will please you—"

Buondelmonte put up a hand to interrupt him. "No, my friend, not today. I come on urgent business with monna Gualdrada. Will you call Elisa for us, and I'll view your fine craftsmanship another day?"

"Of course, my lord. Do you wish me to fetch monna Gualdrada's brothers-in-law too?"

"No, that won't be necessary, Lippo." Lippo—that was the name I had forgotten. Lippo the lauda-singing leatherworker. "This is business monna Gualdrada can transact alone. In fact, I prefer that you not mention this visit to anyone." Buondelmonte held out a pair of coins. His eyes met Lippo's, and Lippo took the coins and nodded his assent. He limped off to get Elisa, and we stepped inside the shop. I was the one in jester's weeds, but I noticed it was Buondelmonte who was careful to stay in the shadows.

Again Elisa came down the stairs lightly and spoke shyly, but this time she addressed her words to Buondelmonte. Again she led us up the stairs, Lippo droning contentedly in the background. This time Buondelmonte came between my gaze and that tantalizing backside, and his presence did nothing to improve my view. Again we walked across the cluttered smaller hall and climbed the narrower staircase that led to the kitchen. Women must transact all their business in kitchens, I mused.

The old woman sat at the fire as before, and monna Gualdrada stood in front of the hearth waiting for us. Her hair was covered with a gauzy white veil, and she had donned a handsome guarnacca of darker blue over her gonnella, making the womanly lines of her body only a little less obvious. But still no male of the family was present.

Gualdrada gave Buondelmonte that dazzling smile and welcomed him, offering him a cup of wine. He accepted with a broad smile of his own, and Elisa ladled hot wine from the pot into a costly maiolica cup with a geometric pattern, well made. She handed it to him and then, unasked, she filled another cup of the same fine manufacture and gave it to me. I was moving up in the world. For me, this was not necessarily desirable.

Gualdrada sat on the bench and patted the place next to her, inviting Buondelmonte to sit, and he did. Forgotten again, I continued to stand, to sip my wine, and to listen. The gray cat, which had eyed us curiously when we arrived, settled back into sleep. The old woman frowned at me, and then she went back to watching Gualdrada and Buondelmonte.

The two of them exchanged a few pleasantries, but soon they got down to the real business at hand. Buondelmonte gave her his version of recent events, and as he spoke his boyish eagerness drained away. He grew ever more downcast, as if hearing his own voice tallying the forces opposing him was enough to make him realize, finally, the seriousness of his situation.

"Gualdrada, I know this ruins everything, but don't you see, I had no choice. A knight must protect his honor." He shivered, despite the fire's warmth, and tugged at his sleeves to pull them down over his hands. He didn't meet her eyes.

"Men have strange notions about honor, my lord," she said tartly. "Would that you had answered words with words, and left your blade sheathed."

Buondelmonte recoiled as if she had slapped him. "He offered much more than words. What would you have had me do, Lady? You were wife to a bold knight. Would he have stood there and quaked like a base coward while a boor attacked him with a vessel full of garbage?"

"Forese would never have gotten himself into such a ridiculous situation," she snapped. "Or any situation where the Uberti and their kind could give him orders." Her mouth twisted into an ugly grimace when she spat out that name. "My husband was no coward, as you well know, but he was also not a rash, hotheaded fool."

Her harsh words startled me. I braced myself for rage in response, but to my surprise, Buondelmonte hung his head and said nothing.

"Do you, then, withdraw your suit?" Gualdrada pressed him. "Do you no longer wish to wed my daughter?"

The woman was relentless. What could he possibly say to that? Buondelmonte's face was a mask of pain.

"Gualdrada, you know well what I want, but I have all of them arrayed against me. They will have this marriage, and they leave me no choice. The contract is signed, the dates are set. They've left nothing undone. What is there for us to do?" His voice was anguished.

Gualdrada stood up abruptly. She looked down at him, her blue eyes cold and her slender hands curling into fists.

"Messer Buondelmonte dei Buondelmonti, I thought better of you than that. Will you be a dishonored knight, dancing to the tune of the Amidei and the Fifanti? Are you a Buondelmonti, or do you take your orders from the Uberti and do the bidding of the Lamberti? They want you to tie yourself to a girl so much less noble, less fair, less desirable than my daughter that all will know you do it only because you have no choice. They're insulting you, and never doubt it, they will laugh at you. Is that what you want? Are you nothing more than Oddo's puppet? If that's all there is to messer Buondelmonte, you don't deserve my Isabella."

Buondelmonte flushed. "Gualdrada, try to understand. Of course I want Isabella. She's infinitely more fair and more noble. She is everything any man could want, and I would give all I own to have her. But to go back on the contract now would mean war. It could destroy both of our families, and that includes Isabella. And you." His shoulders slumped.

A brief silence followed, broken by Gualdrada. "So, you'll marry that ugly daughter of an Uberti lackey, and make your heirs with her. And what blood will they carry then? Can they be true Buondelmonti if their mother is beneath you, and you only took her out of fear?"

They'll be true Buondelmonti if their mother was beneath the right man at their getting, I thought, but nobody asked for my opinion.

"I do not fear them," Buondelmonte said, his voice rising. "Gualdrada, you don't understand the implications of this. It isn't as easy as you think. I'm in an impossible position."

She raised one perfect eyebrow. "I'm sure, my lord, that you would indeed find it less difficult to meekly do as they tell you. But if instead you follow your own noble heart, people will rightly call you brave, and know you for a true knight. You can do this thing, Buondelmonte. You can defy them."

"And if you and I made a contract? Will your brothers-in-law support it?"

Gualdrada hesitated, but only for a moment. The old woman watched her, unblinking.

"If we make the contract, they'll support it," she finally said. "Better not to speak of it before it's done." The old woman closed her eyes and sighed loudly. Gualdrada ignored her.

"If I do this thing, I drag my own family into a nightmare." He was wavering.

"Would you see her again, my lord?" Gualdrada's voice was suddenly soft and persuasive. Like the sirens, I thought. "Would you see what you propose to give up?"

He sucked his breath in sharply, then spread his arms in a gesture of defeat. He lowered his head.

"Yes," he said in a whisper. "I would see her."

"Then I'll show you both my daughters, as is proper," she said, and she walked over to the door to the bedchambers and called, "Girls, come now."

Two young women emerged from the bedchamber. The first was small and slender, an exquisite child-woman with pale hair and delicate features. I gawked. The girl was a rosebud, a fruit just coming into its sweetness, a crescent moon in a starry sky. I had seldom seen her equal.

But the older girl, the girl who followed behind—ah, she was a rose in bloom, a ripe summer fruit, the full moon at its zenith. She was Elena of Troy, she was the fair Isotta, she was the goddess Venere herself. Her hair was a richer gold than her sister's, her eyes the same intense blue as her mother's. Buondelmonte had not exaggerated. This woman could stop the tide, could hold back the Arno in flood. I didn't breathe; I only looked.

Both girls wore fine garments in colors chosen to show them off to greatest advantage: flowing silver-blue for the younger, and a soft, clinging rose gonnella for the one who must be Buondelmonte's intended.

"Isabella," Buondelmonte breathed. He rose to his feet and stared at her worshipfully.

And then that vision of loveliness gazed upon her knight, her long eyelashes fluttered, her luscious lips parted, and she emitted a high-pitched little giggle.

It broke the spell for me, that silly sound, but Buondelmonte was only more enchanted, a fond and foolish smile on his face. Oh, yes. This was serious.

"Do you want her, Buondelmonte?" Gualdrada asked softly.

"Yes. Yes, I want her," he murmured, never taking his eyes from the girl.

"Then be the knight she deserves." Her voice was warm honey.

Buondelmonte whirled to face her. "Yes! I will have her! We'll make the contract now, before I leave this house. Damn the Amidei and the Fifanti and the rest—messer Buondelmonte of the Buondelmonti makes his own decisions. I am no coward."

You may be no coward, I thought, but you are an idiot. And as for making your own decisions, well, monna Gualdrada looks pretty pleased with herself just now.

Gualdrada knew how to follow through, using all the tricks employed by persuasive women throughout time. She smiled that remarkable smile and added a little lash-fluttering of her own, her eyes wide with admiration.

"All of Florence will praise your courage, my lord, and rejoice at your decision. Never will it be said that messer Buondelmonte dei Buondel-monti lets lesser men tell him what to do. I'm proud to give my dearest, my loveliest daughter to such a knight, as bold as Lancialotto. What a couple you will make!"

Buondelmonte beamed, first at Gualdrada and then at Isabella, who giggled again. Her sister rolled her eyes. I quite liked the sister.

"Girls," said Gualdrada, clapping her hands together, "go and make yourselves ready. I'll have ser Rinaldo brought, and we can make the contract and have the ring ceremony this very day." The girls curtsied. Buondelmonte and I watched them go.

Buondelmonte bit his lower lip. "Gualdrada," he said, still looking in the direction the girls had gone, "can we do both in one day? It isn't usual."

"No, my lord—my son! Not usual, but there are compelling reasons for it," she said. "If we only make the contract, my brothers-in-law might challenge it, for they, too, are the girls' guardians. They might even say that a woman can't act alone. But if the ring has been given, there can be no turning back. She'll be yours. Is that not what you want?"

"Yes—you're right. I regret, for Isabella's sake, that we must proceed in such haste, without proper pageantry, but I'll make it up to her later. Later, at the nozze, when I lead her to my house. That I swear to you, and to her. I don't even have gifts for your household today, but I promise you they'll follow, as soon as the time is right."

"Elisa!" Gualdrada called. Once again the young woman emerged from the pantry, wiping her hands on her apron. "Fetch ser Rinaldo," Gualdrada said, and Elisa was off. She didn't even get a purse every time she did this, poor girl.

Gualdrada turned back to Buondelmonte. "It would be folly to let anyone know of this until the day you lead my daughter. What will you say to the Amidei, and to Oddo?"

"Nothing. I'll say nothing to them at all. They expect me to be at Santa Maria sopra Porta in three weeks, to take that girl to wife. I must lead Isabella before that day."

Gualdrada's eyes glittered dangerously. "But, my son, I can't possibly have her trousseau ready any sooner than that. We have so much to do, and we're beginning so abruptly. As soon as you slip a ring on her finger, she's yours. Surely you can give us time to make a proper trousseau, to clothe her adequately, to plan the feast, to get the traditional gifts for your household and for you to choose such little keepsakes as you will for ours. You must not lead her until all these things are done. A gently-bred girl can't be expected to marry like a foundling dowered by charity."

"But we can't do it after the three weeks have passed, because by then they will have enforced their contract. I can't marry both girls." Pity, I thought. Things would be so much easier, though possibly not for Buondelmonte.

"Not before, and not after. Then perhaps a more precise timing is best."

"What are you suggesting?"

"Lead her on the same day you are expected at Santa Maria sopra Porta." By all the saints, she wanted him to humiliate them.

"Leave them standing at the church?" Buondelmonte was aghast. "But that insults them!" Now it was my turn to roll my eyes. Buondelmonte's grasp of the obvious was underwhelming.

"Of course it does. It pays them back for insulting you by trying to force you to take a wife you don't want. They've treated you like a naughty child, not like the bold knight you are. And besides, even if you were to announce it to them first, it's no less insulting. Refusing the girl is refusing the girl, whenever you do it."

Buondelmonte's brow furrowed, as well it might. "Well, it's true that it will be an insult no matter when I do it, and it's also true that I'd have to be a complete dolt to announce it to them before it's done. But, Gualdrada, the cost is too high, for all of us. They'd be publicly shamed. We'd leave them no choice—they'd have to act."

"It's what my husband would have done. He wouldn't have been afraid. And if the city charges you a fine for breaking that forced contract, I'll pay it for you."

"That wasn't the cost I was thinking of, though your offer is generous. They won't take this lightly. They may well want blood, not money."

"What they want and what they get are two different things," Gualdrada said with a dismissive wave of her hand. "They'll bluster for a while, but they won't take action, not of that sort. Not over refusing a girl nobody else wants either. You and Isabella can stay on your land in Montebuoni for a while until things settle down. And I know Bishop Giovanni well—he and my husband were great friends—and if they make threats, I can persuade him to make a peace between you."

Buondelmonte shook his head. "I'm less certain of that than you are, Gualdrada. What you propose is the sort of insult that can't be ignored." He picked up his wine cup, only to find it empty. He stared into it as if wondering where his wine might have gotten to.

"Indeed it can't. Think of it, Buondelmonte. Florentines will tell this story for generations. Centuries from now, everyone will know that you were the proud knight who turned the tables on those who would have bullied you. They'll sing your praises in ballads and in stories. Young boys in their games of make-believe will vie to be the one to play messer Buondelmonte, and their weaker fellows will have to play the men of the Fifanti and Lamberti and Amidei." I noticed she did not mention the Uberti. Perhaps that would have strained credibility.

The image made him stand a little straighter. "I would not have it said that a Buondelmonti feared them," he said.

"And yet it will be said, unless you lead my daughter on the very day they await you."

Buondelmonte stroked his stubbly chin, thinking it over. Don't do it, I thought. You'll doom us all. There will be hell to pay.

The old woman clutched her poker like a weapon, never taking her eyes from Buondelmonte. I realized I was sweating, and not just because the room was warm. No one breathed, until at last Buondelmonte spoke.

"Yes. I'll do it. And on the day."

7. RING-GIVING

Before any of us could react to this, Elisa appeared with ser Rinaldo, another ink-stained man who might have been ser Opizzo's taller brother. To get him here so soon, this house full of women and surprises must have had their notary stashed nearby and ready.

"Let's go to the hall below us to draw up the agreement," Gualdrada said. "The light is better, and we can use one of the tables."

Gualdrada, Buondelmonte, and the notary went down the stairs, Elisa vanished into the pantry and I was left once more in the company of the old woman.

She was scowling. Evidently she wasn't particularly impressed with my most recent employer, or else some other aspect of these machinations didn't appeal to her. Either way, it showed good sense. This house of women, however fair and gracious, was a dangerous place.

Without thinking, I turned to my disgruntled companion and asked the first question that came into my mind: "So—were you once gorgeous, too?" She stared at me for a moment, then burst out laughing.

She must have needed the relief, for she laughed until she wheezed, and had to wipe a stream of tears from her eyes with a kitchen towel. Finally she said, "No, Fool, I was not. I was nurse to monna Gualdrada, and if you had seen her when she was a girl, you wouldn't be so impressed with those young ones. There never was a girl to equal my Drada."

Not the cousin, then, but still a part of the family. Perhaps I could make an ally here, for whatever that might be worth.

"I believe it. Even now she's extraordinarily fair," I said.

"Aye, she is," the old woman said, nodding vigorously. "The young ones won't age so well, you mark me. I know they're fair now, but they haven't half of Drada's sense, and a woman needs to be intelligent if she's going to age well."

That was a new concept for me, but it might bear thinking about, another time.

"The young ones lack a grown woman's sense, then?"

"Isabella, yes. Nothing but air in that pretty head. Fiammetta's more like her mother, but she's young yet."

Fiammetta. A lovely name, and it suited the child. The old woman poked at the fire, lapsing into a moody silence. We sat watching the flames and listening to the wind whistling through the window for a while, and then I turned to her again.

"Grandmother," I said, "is this marriage wise? Will there not be danger?"

"Danger? Oh, aye, there's plenty of that. And no, it isn't wise. Drada is clever, but she's so set on this that she can't see what she risks. I've talked to her until I can talk no more, and she will not hear me. Nothing will do but Isabella weds Buondelmonte, and Drada's blind to the cost."

I was afraid of that, but I still didn't understand. Even if Gualdrada refused to recognize the danger she was courting, others in the family must see it. I would have expected her to modify her plans rather than defy the powerful family she had married into.

"Surely Isabella could marry any knight Gualdrada chose for her," I said. "Why must it be Buondelmonte?"

"The Donati have long been allied with the Buondelmonti." She watched me, clearly waiting to see if I accepted this as sufficient reason.

"The Donati have many friends who are noble and wealthy and powerful," I persisted. "Messer Buondelmonte isn't the only knight in need of a wife. Why him?"

She snorted. "You're a nosy one, aren't you? Fools aren't entitled to know family business." She turned her back on me.

I shrugged, and waited. Considering how much she had already told me, I was pretty sure the old woman would eventually fill the silence, but when she finally spoke, I was startled by the roughness of her voice.

"Her sister." She still did not face me.

"Isabella's sister?" I said, confused. What could pretty Fiammetta have to do with Gualdrada's determination?

"Drada's. Her sister was married off to an Uberti. To make peace."

Now that I thought about it, I did vaguely remember some flap about a marriage-for-peace between those families a few years ago. I didn't recall how it had worked out, though. I waited to see if anything more was forthcoming, but it wasn't, so I tried again.

"I gather it failed to do so."

She slammed her fist down on the bench. "Do you see any peace?" she demanded. "Of course it failed. Drada loved her sister and she hates the Uberti. She would die—or more likely kill—before she'd let that family tell her what to eat to break her fast in the morning, let alone who her precious airheaded daughter can or cannot marry. And the chance to shame the Uberti or their allies is a thing she would never pass up. She couldn't pass it up and still be Drada."

That explained a lot. I started to ask the old woman what had happened to Gualdrada's sister, but something in her face warned me off.

Instead, I said, "What about the bishop?"

"Drada thinks he'll do her bidding for the sake of her late husband, but he won't. Her husband lies in his grave, and Drada's only a woman, with no power of her own. The bishop will do as he pleases, you mark me."

That did seem likely. I couldn't imagine the proud and mighty Bishop Giovanni da Velletri being swayed by a woman, even one as persuasive as Gualdrada.

"What do you think will happen, then?" I asked.

Nothing good, it appeared. I thought it a mark of how strange this business had become that I was now discussing politics with an old woman, but she had plenty to say. I learned I had been right in thinking Gualdrada's late husband's kinsmen would not welcome this contract, but that they would grudgingly support it once it was made. She told me, too, that Buondelmonte offended his own family by the headstrong and solitary nature of his actions, first at the banquet, next in making a pact with Oddo, and now in contracting with Gualdrada for Isabella. No knight was free to act alone in these matters. Family must be consulted, and except for Gherardo's presence at the meeting with Oddo, Buondelmonte had failed in that duty.

If Buondelmonte had sought counsel instead of merely borrowing cups, maybe he wouldn't now be reversing himself and plunging the city into an uproar, for despite Gualdrada's confidence, I didn't believe the outcome would be anything less. Before I could express my own fears, though, we were rejoined by Gualdrada, Buondelmonte, and ser Rinaldo, who held up a sheet of vellum covered in small, neat writing.

Buondelmonte grinned at me. "It's done," he said, pointing to the vellum the notary held up for us to admire. "We have our contract, we're in agreement on dowry and dates, and now we have only to give the ring. Fool, you'll stand with me, and Isabella's sister will stand with her."

Oh, Mother of God, could I possibly get any more deeply involved in this mess?

Gualdrada went into the bedchamber to finish readying her daughters. The old lady glowered at Buondelmonte.

Oblivious, he favored her with a gracious smile. "Grandmother, I know it's right for me to remember you with a gift on this occasion, but I've had no opportunity to get anything yet. What would you have me bring you?"

"Nothing."

"No, don't be shy. Would you like a coif, or slippers, or a purse? I know you serve this household well, and I'll see you have the best."

"I want my girls to be safe. You of all people can't give me that, unless you do it by going away and leaving us alone." She gave the fire a particularly vicious jab with her poker, and a log flared up.

Buondelmonte opened his mouth to argue, but his eyes fell on the notary and he said nothing. Admirable restraint, I thought. Too bad he didn't practice it more often.

Ser Rinaldo sat on the bench, heavily. He nodded at the old woman and then to me. "Good day, Grandmother. Good day, Fool."

She grunted, and I greeted him cordially. This situation was no more his fault than it was mine, after all. Buondelmonte found a stool, pulled it up to the fire, and sat, staring moodily into the glowing embers and the little low flames that tickled the wood.

I wanted to know the contents of that document. I was anxious to know whether the contract set the date, but I couldn't ask the notary with Buondelmonte sitting there, and anyway I doubt he would have told me. Professional ethics and all.

We sat in silence, each lost in his own thoughts. I stared at the small kitchen window, not quite able to make out, through the oiled cloth stretched across it, whether I was seeing snowflakes swirling in the air, or just a trick of light and shadow. In this warm room we wouldn't know it if the temperature outside had dropped enough for snow. If it had, we'd have a chilly walk home.

My stomach growled, and I remembered I had missed dinner. The old woman must have heard my rumblings, for she got up and shuffled over to a table next to the wall. She unwrapped a chunk of bread and uncovered a cheese, then busied about cutting both and arranging them on a wooden platter, along with dried figs from a heavy terracotta jar.

She brought them to the bench and set them down between the notary and me, saying nothing. I grabbed a piece of bread and a good-sized hunk of cheese and began to eat. Ser Rinaldo helped himself to a fig.

Buondelmonte sighed, a bit theatrically, I thought. "It's a mean wedding feast for my bride," he said mournfully. "She should have every delicacy Florence can provide, and all we have is a plate of bread and cheese."

The old woman sniffed. "It's food. Eat it if you're hungry," she said.

"I need no delicacies," said a high-pitched voice, girlish and breathy. We all looked up. Isabella stood across the kitchen from us in a splendid scarlet gown, with much gold thread embroidery and a complex design stitched in pearls across her bodice. As she walked toward us, hips swaying, we became aware that she was surrounded by a cloud of scent—flowers and spices and oranges, at once more innocent and more alluring than her mother's artful blend of rose and lavender. That astonishing waterfall of golden hair tumbled down her back, loose and gleaming. She was magnificent.

Her mother and sister followed behind her, also in more elaborate and elegant clothing than before, and the sight of the three of them was overwhelming. Several paces behind them was a fourth woman I had not seen before, young, black-haired, and far advanced in pregnancy. Her head was shyly bowed.

Buondelmonte stood up, dazed. He walked forward slowly. Reaching Isabella, he took her slender hands in his, and the two of them gazed into one another's eyes while the rest of us watched. Ser Rinaldo's jaw had dropped at the sight of the women, and he was only now remembering to close his mouth, which still contained half a fig. I had seen it all before, except for the fancier clothes; I kept chewing.

Gualdrada went to the pregnant woman and took her hand, drawing her forward. This one, too, was fair, though Gualdrada and her daughters outshone her and her distended belly made her awkward. "Messer Buondelmonte, this is Isabella's cousin monna Bianca, widow of the late messer Antonio dei Galigai. Isabella would have her beloved kinswoman present at her ring ceremony." Buondelmonte barely managed to turn away from Isabella long enough to murmur a courteous greeting. The young woman stood silent, looking down at her feet—or rather at her belly, which blocked her view of her feet.

Buondelmonte turned back to Gualdrada. "What ring will I use?" he asked her, as if he had just realized that he might need one for a ring-giving ceremony. Not the quickest horse in the palio, the good messer Buondelmonte.

Gualdrada looked at his hands. "I can lend you one, or you can just use one of the rings you wear. Unless, of course, you'd rather not give them away."

"No, no, I'll happily give her every ring I own, not just these, but they're big enough to be bracelets for her, she has such tiny hands," he said, gently lifting one of Isabella's hands to demonstrate. He wore two large and elaborate gold rings, one on each hand. On one, two prongs secured a polished dark blue stone, and the other was intricately carved with his personal crest. This was the ring he had used to seal his message to Gualdrada. I was amused to see all of the women, even the old lady and the pregnant cousin, appraising Buondelmonte's rings.

"Well, then, use either," said Gualdrada briskly. "We need to begin the ceremony now, before anyone discovers you are here. I wish we could do it in the great hall, but it's too public. If Lippo has any customers, they would hear everything. And there isn't enough room in the little hall, so it will have to be here. Married in a kitchen is still married, after all." She pointed to a spot on the floor. "You, Isabella, stand here, and Fiammetta and Bianca behind you. Buondelmonte, you be here." She pointed again. "Ser Rinaldo, here. And Fool, you stand behind Buondelmonte and be prepared to give him a good clap on the shoulder just as he gives Isabella the ring."

So now I was to wallop a knight who two hours ago threatened my life. This was proving to be a strange day indeed.

Buondelmonte turned to me. "Make sure the blow you give is solid, Fool. It's for luck." I knew this. I did it for Neri, when he married Duccia. Not that it had helped much; she'd been living back with her family the past two years. Though that part was lucky for Neri, luckier by far than the marriage had been.

We took our places. The old woman shuffled to Gualdrada's side, behind the notary. Ser Rinaldo began to read aloud rapidly from the document he had prepared, detailing the dowry (more money than I'd ever see, but middling for the knightly class), the promised trousseau (elaborate), the finery with which Buondelmonte swore to bedeck his young bride (outrageous), and, finally, the date of the nozze—the eleventh of February, the same date Buondelmonte was to appear at Santa Maria sopra Porta and take Selvaggia to wife. The old lady met my eyes and grimaced. We were in agreement, but we could do nothing.

Ser Rinaldo was in mid-sentence when the gray cat leaped straight up, uncoiling in the air, talons out. A mouse on the hearthstone gave a tiny shriek as the cat pounced on it, rending it with teeth and claws. It was over in an instant. Ser Rinaldo stopped reading and gaped. I was rattled, Fiammetta looked away, and Bianca crossed herself, but Buondelmonte and Isabella just went on gazing into each other's eyes. Gualdrada smiled and murmured, "Good puss," and the old woman merely stared, first at the cat and its mangled prey, and then back to Buondelmonte and Isabella. Finally she fixed her eyes on Gualdrada and kept them there.

Ser Rinaldo composed himself and got on with it, talking about uniting the families and so on, obtaining the consent of each party (consent, indeed—Buondelmonte could hardly keep from picking the girl up and carrying her off to the bedchamber), and finally, the call for the ring. Buondelmonte took Isabella's hand while she lowered her eyes modestly, and he drew the carved ring with the crest from his right forefinger. He slid it over her slender finger, where it dangled absurdly, and I drew back my arm and gave him a whack that made him stagger a little. May it bring us all luck, I thought. We're going to need it.

Isabella looked up at him solemnly with those huge blue eyes, and impulsively he drew the other ring from his other hand and placed it on her finger, too, where it slid down and hit the first ring with a solid clank. Her face brightened at this, and she favored him with a smile. The two enormous rings were ridiculous on her hand, but they represented a fair chunk of wealth. Gualdrada and Fiammetta beamed at the couple and clapped their hands, and even silent Bianca smiled a little. The notary and I offered our congratulations, and the old woman grunted and returned to her bench.

Buondelmonte continued to hold Isabella's hands and gaze into her eyes. Isabella's eyes kept darting to the rings, but she did keep that enchanting smile going. And she had managed so far not to giggle.

Gualdrada broke the spell, placing her hand gently on his arm. "Buondelmonte, you must go," she said, her tone insistent. "It's done, and it would not be well for you to be found here now. Go, my new son-in-law, and I'll send a messenger for you soon."

Buondelmonte glanced meaningfully toward the chambers within. "You don't think this would be even more secure if . . . ?"

Gualdrada shook her head, though she was smiling. "It is secure. You ask too much of my girl for a single day. She woke an unpromised virgin, and she'll go to bed a wife."

"But a wife in name only—"

"It's enough, for now. Go. Girls, go change your garments." All three young women went, Isabella tugging her beringed hand free and dazzling her new husband with another smile.

Buondelmonte watched them go, his shoulders drooping. "I could have at least kissed her," he said, a note of complaint in his voice.

"You wouldn't have stopped." Gualdrada was businesslike. "I know you want her before the nozze, and I'll arrange it if I can, but secrecy and safety must come first. I'll see that no information leaks from here, and you must do the same." She looked over at me and then back to Buondelmonte. "I assume you can control your friends and your family."

"Of course. All will be as we've planned." Buondelmonte picked up the cloak he had draped across the bench. Mine was still fastened around my neck, though I had pushed it back behind my shoulders because of the warmth of the room. Gualdrada was clearly in a hurry to see the backs of us, so we each grabbed a handful of bread and cheese—I guess Buondelmonte hadn't eaten either—and with a few more words between mother-in-law and son-in-law, we were off.

We went out through Lippo's shop and hit the street, walking against the cold wind. Buondelmonte turned to me with sheer triumph on his face and said, "Well? Was I right? What did you think?" No furrowed brow now; none of the anxiety and foreboding he had shown earlier. You infatuated fool, I thought. What have you done?

What I said aloud was, "Oh, she's fair indeed, my lord. You did not overpraise her. But I would happily take the sister."

He roared with laughter and slapped my back. "You? In your dreams, Fool," he said amiably. I'd settle for that, yes.

The snow had stopped. Only a light dusting remained on the street, but the day was noticeably colder than before. We walked along side by side, more like companions than master and servant, or jester and employer, or whatever we were. Despite my fears, I allowed myself to feel a sort of camaraderie between us because of our shared experiences that extraordinary day.

Buondelmonte put an abrupt end to that when he said to me, his mouth still full of cheese, "Fool, we need to have an understanding. You've seen and heard more this day than you should have, but it couldn't be helped. Remember, when I gave you those coins a big part of what you were being paid for was your silence."

"Of course, my lord."

He swallowed the cheese. "Good, because if I ever have the slightest reason to believe that you have spoken of these events, I will have you killed. Maybe I'll even do it myself. Either way, it will be done slowly, painfully, and very, very thoroughly. Do we understand each other?"

So much for shared experiences. "Yes, my lord."

"Good. Now we go our separate ways. If I have need of you again, and I hope I won't, I'll send for you." And he was off, around a corner. I headed home, hoping no one would be there to ask me how my day had been.

8. PAYMENT

My steps dragged as I got closer to home. I believed Buondelmonte; I could not afford to tell Neri what had happened. Telling him would endanger both of us. But Neri and I kept no secrets from each other, or at least we hadn't until I failed to tell him about Oddo's parliament. Our fathers had worked together. I couldn't remember a time before I knew Neri. We'd both been apprenticed to his father, after mine died and I had to end my schooling. There was a period in my life when I probably wouldn't have survived had it not been for Neri. We shared everything except our women, and it made me a little queasy to think of trying to keep all of this from him, especially since I knew he'd do everything in his power to get it out of me.

The wreath was hanging over the door at Simone's house, which meant his ground-floor tavern was open for business. I realized I could use a cup of hot wine and an excuse to delay going home, so I tapped on the door.

Simone opened up. "Come in, come in. Don't leave the door open—it's cold out there." I stepped inside and waited for my eyes to adjust to the dim light and the smoke. Most people's braziers burned cleaner than their hearths, but Simone's was smokier. I don't know where he bought his charcoal, but I'll bet it was cheap.

Simone wiped his raw red hands on his apron and went to get me some wine. His establishment was simple: a trestle table, a few stools, the smoking brazier, a wine barrel in the corner, and a shelf with a few cups. So few that he was constantly having to wash them, dunking them in a basin of cold, murky water, which is why his hands always looked like a laundress's.

He had three other customers already—not capacity, but getting close. Our neighbors Bicci and Tommasso were there, playing at dice, and standing behind Bicci, watching the game, was Neri.

Should have gone on home, I guess.

I exchanged greetings with all three men, and pulled a stool up to the table and sat. Neri sat down across from me, leaving Bicci and Tommasso to their game at the other end of the table. They were hunched over and playing intently, even though the stakes appeared to be raisins.

"So where've you been?"

"Took the cloak back."

"And that took all day?"

"No, one of the knights hired me for the day." I was thinking fast, trying to come up with something he'd believe.

He took a slow, deliberate drink of his wine.

"So now you're the star performer, is that it?"

We were on dangerous ground. Neri was proud of being the leader of our little troupe of four, and he didn't take kindly to potential customers negotiating with any of the rest of us. I'd been planning to say that I entertained for some rich twit's dinner, but seeing Neri's irritation I changed my story to something a little closer to the truth.

"He hired me to deliver a message, and to wait for a reply and bring it back to him."

Neri's frown smoothed out. My being an errand-boy didn't intrude on his territory, I guess.

"Quite an errand, to take up all those hours."

"Had to wait a long time." I took a drink from the cup Simone had set in front of me. It was warm, harsh, strong, and comforting.

"So you didn't perform?" he said, too casually.

I shook my head.

"Who hired you?"

"Just—one of the knights. I can't say who. I had to take an oath." He wouldn't like that, but at least he couldn't argue with an oath.

"Well, I hope he paid you enough to make it worthwhile." I shrugged and took another drink.

He studied me for a while. I sipped my wine and stared past him, at the wall.

"You look out of sorts. They're really not that bad, you know. Your 'people with surnames,' as you call them."

"Yes, they are," I said. This was non-negotiable.

"They hire us and pay us," he insisted. "We can't get by without them."

"All right, I have to work for them. That doesn't mean I have to like it." That sounded childish, even to me. But Neri knew why I felt the way I did about the nobility. Why was he being so persistent?

"Let it go, Neri," I said.

"No. Not this time. You need to face this. You have good reason to hate one family, I'll grant you that, but they've been exiled for years. There's nobody with that surname left in Florence. Not all of the nobles are like them."

They're all close enough, I thought, but I didn't want to argue with him, so I didn't say it aloud. Neri had more reason than I did to like the nobles, or at least less reason to hate them. To me, the whole concept of a family name was pretentious and ridiculous. I'm Corrado di Ugo di Benvenuto. What more does it take to identify a man than his name and his father's, plus his grandfather's if there's any confusion left?

As for having to work for them, that was true enough. I'd have been happier if we could have worked for others like ourselves, but there was no money in that. People like us can't afford people like us.

Neri was watching me impatiently. "So what's up?" he said. "Something's bothering you. What happened today?"

I sighed. I didn't need to be interrogated just now; I needed peace and quiet and sleep. And some more wine. I waved at Simone, who came and took my empty cup.

"Neri, I had a difficult day yesterday. If you recall, I almost got skewered by a knight for following another knight's orders. Today hasn't been so great either, or maybe you think it's a privilege to run around doing errands for some surnamed idiot. Can we please just give it a rest?" He glared at me, and I glared back. We were like brothers, in pretty much every way.

Simone brought back my cup, filled. Not as hot this time, but I didn't care.

Neri pushed his stool back from the table and got up. He grabbed his cloak from the peg and told the room in general, "I'm going home. Goodnight, all," and he stamped out the door.

Bicci, Tommasso, and Simone all looked at me, but I probably didn't appear very approachable. I didn't meet their eyes, and I kept drinking steadily. They tried a couple of times to get me to describe the previous day's knightly food-fight, but when I responded with monosyllables they finally gave up and left me to my wine.

I drank until I judged Neri would have gone to bed, then, unsteadily I made my way home and fell into bed without undressing.

*

When I woke the next morning it was fully light, and Neri and Ghisola were bustling around near the hearth, talking. I pushed the curtain aside and emerged, still wearing my bedraggled motley, hoping Neri had slept his way into a better mood.

He looked up, his expression somewhere between exasperation and amusement. "You're a disgrace," he said, amiably enough, though I thought I still heard an edge to his voice. "Your hair is sticking straight up, and you look like you've been wearing those clothes for a month."

Had it been a month? I shook my head, to clear it. No, only two days, though it felt like more.

"Too much wine," Ghisola said, not unsympathetically. "Here, drink some water. You'll feel better." She dipped a wooden bowl in the water barrel and handed it to me. I took it and drank. The draught made a small start at washing away the sour, stale taste in my mouth, and I did feel a little better for it, though my head was still aching fiercely.

"Go wash up and change your clothes," Ghisola said. "It will help, you'll see." She peered at me. "I have to deliver a batch of wool this morning, and I can stop at the apothecary for you if you're ill."

I must have looked pretty bad. "No, thanks, Ghisi, I'm all right," I told her.

Ghisola spun wool for her meager living. It wasn't much, but it helped with the household expenses, and as she liked to point out, the lanolin kept her hands soft and youthful. I had from time to time considered suggesting that she try sleeping in the woolsack, but she probably wouldn't have taken it well. Ghisola was all right, though. Not as small and gentle and modest as I like my women to be, but a good soul, and a good friend. And a huge improvement over the pretty, shrewish Duccia, Neri's estranged wife.

Changing clothes sounded like a fine idea, when I thought about it. Most of the frightening things I had been involved in of late had to do with those jester's colors. Maybe if I shed them, I could also shed the sense of dread I was carrying around.

I took a basin of water back to my sleeping corner and managed to improve my state of cleanliness considerably. When I stripped off my food-spattered motley, the two purses, canvas and silk, fell to the floor with a clank. I scooped them up and started to stuff them into my prop bag, but then thought better of it and decided to carry them with me. I didn't fear theft, but I did fear Neri's curiosity. He aimed to find out what was going on, and I didn't trust him not to come searching for clues once I was out of the house. I hung my jester's weeds to air, then put on a reasonably clean shirt and my sturdy brown tunic and tucked the purses away in my sleeve. Now I looked much soberer than I felt.

I waited in my bed corner until I heard Neri and Ghisola leave. Then I shuffled out and sat in front of the hearth, but the fire was down to embers, and the room was cold. I opened the door a crack and got hit with a blast of frigid air, so I slammed the door shut. A good day to stay at home and recover, but I didn't have that luxury. I had to go to the Amidei house to pick up my payment from Oddo.

The idea of seeing Oddo again made me groan. Still, I'm a working man, and it goes against the grain to do a job without pay, especially a job that had proved as risky and touchy as what I had done for Oddo. I might as well get the coin owed me.

I pulled on a second pair of hose for warmth, laced up my high shoes, grabbed my cloak, and headed out into the cold, bound for the Amidei house. It wasn't far from the Buondelmonti palace, but I wouldn't be passing by there again. Ever, if I could help it. Oddo scared me, but Buondelmonte, all impulse and unpredictability, scared me more.

The day was blustery, though the wind was at my back, and I pulled my hood down over my face for protection from the stinging cold. That was lucky, for as I neared the Amidei palace, who should I see coming toward me, walking into the fierce wind with a fiercer scowl on his face, but Buondelmonte himself. Two of his retainers scrambled to keep up with him, for he was moving double-time, his head down. He didn't notice me, and I thanked the saints for my hood and my change of clothes. If he came from the Amidei palace, he must be keeping up the pretense that the wedding they demanded was going to take place. For a hopeful moment I wondered if perhaps he had changed his mind, but no—the ring was given. Too late for that.

We passed each other, close enough to brush shoulders, and within a few heartbeats I stood at the Amidei door and pounded on it with my fist. I didn't wait long before one of the servants opened the door, though it felt long in that wind. I gave the man Oddo's name and my own and gratefully stepped inside while he went upstairs to tell Oddo I had come.

This entryway was plainer than those of the Buondelmonti palace and Oddo's home. It was utilitarian, with storage containers neatly arrayed around the walls. Here were no benches or curtained-off rooms. The layout was similar, though, in that a stairway in the back led up to the living quarters. A wooden bar along one wall was draped with three or four oiled cloaks. Several pairs of winter boots stood ready underneath. I guessed that a stout door on the back wall led to a courtyard, perhaps with brick ovens or a private well.

In the time it took me to observe this much, the servant was back. "Go on up," he said, jerking his thumb toward the stairs. "Messer Oddo is with messer Lambertuccio in the hall, and you're to join them there."

I thanked him and climbed the stairs, which were narrower than those in all the other palaces I had visited recently. This building was considerably older, and its tower had the reputation of being one of the most ancient, as well as the most formidable, in Florence. Ideally located for military purposes, it looked directly down onto the river and the only bridge that crossed it. The palace was three stories high, unlike the more ostentatious four levels of Oddo's palace and of the Donati's, but it was long, presenting a narrow face to the street and extending a fair distance back, and the adjacent tower soared into the sky, higher than any mortal man should ever try to go.

I reached the hall and found the two knights there, wrapped in their mantles. The windows in this hall gave plenty of light, but they were wide open to the cold and the wind. The Amidei were a hardy lot.

Oddo and Lambertuccio were talking, the rapid, overlapping speech of two men who know each other well. Oddo gesticulated with his bandaged arm as if he had forgotten his injury completely.

"Did you see the look on his face when I told him to be sure to obey the law and limit the number of men he brings with him?" Oddo grinned with relish at the memory, and Lambertuccio laughed. No wonder Buondelmonte looked like he was ready to kill someone, I thought. That law was one of the most selectively-enforced on the city's books, and obeying it would have put him at a clear disadvantage. I didn't expect Oddo to observe any limits on the allies and henchmen he would bring to the wedding. The non-wedding, I thought, as I reminded myself that Buondelmonte would not show up at all, with or without an entourage.

"He wanted to demand that we do the same, but he didn't have the courage," said Lambertuccio.

"In this situation, we make the law," Oddo said. "He's in no position to demand anything."

As I entered the room, shaking my hood back from my head, I saw that the men were not alone after all. A woman sat on one of the pair of stone seats that flanked a window, using the light to work on her embroidery. I thought it unusual for a woman to be privy to the men's discussion, so I looked at her curiously, for she was concentrating on her needlework and I could watch her, at least until the men acknowledged me. She was young and plump, and she wore a handsome dark green guarnacca over her gonnella, the looser outer garment concealing bulges the fitted gown underneath would have revealed. The guarnacca was probably for warmth, for she also wore a shawl against the cold, and fingerless gloves.

Oddo finally saw me, and he cut off Lambertuccio's reply with a sharp gesture. I bowed to both of them, then, just to be safe, I bowed to the woman. That was when she looked up at me, and I recognized the dough-faced girl in the mantle, the shrew who used me to convey her orders to

Mosca. Selvaggia, daughter of Lambertuccio, niece of Oddo—the willing bride who was about to be mortally insulted by her bridegroom and didn't yet know it. I watched her recognize me, but she said nothing, and went back to her stitching.

I wished fervently then that I was somewhere else. Just about anywhere else would have done, for knowing what I knew, I didn't want to be around these people. No amount of payment was enough to be in this position, yet here I was.

Well, best to get it over with.

"Well met, Fool," said Oddo, reaching into his pouch. "I owe you more coin, and I'm pleased to give it to you. What did you think of our little adventure yesterday?" He chuckled. "Pity you didn't arrive earlier. Buondelmonte was just here, to meet his bride." He indicated Selvaggia, who didn't look up. "Did you enjoy our little visit?"

I inclined my head. "I am happy to have served you, my lord, and honored to be in such company." A diplomatic answer, utterly untrue on both counts, and one that satisfied him. He placed several coins on the bench beside him, and beckoned me to come forward and take them. Then he turned back to Lambertuccio and picked up their conversation where they had left off.

They started discussing the upcoming wedding feast, and I suppressed a shudder as I approached the bench to take the coins. These amounted to a fraction of what Buondelmonte had paid me, but they added up to a fair enough sum for merely accompanying the men on their visit to the Buondelmonti palace.

I reached into my sleeve to pull out Oddo's canvas purse so I could add the new coins to it. I was watching Selvaggia from the corner of my eye, and, distracted, I pulled out the blue and white Buondelmonte pouch by mistake. Horrified, I stuffed it back in my sleeve and looked at Oddo to see if he had noticed, but he and Lambertuccio were still deep in a conversation that involved wafers and table linens. I felt a wash of relief, which halted abruptly when I saw Selvaggia staring straight at me with those alarming opaque eyes. She had seen.

I pulled out the right purse this time and added Oddo's coins to it, my hand shaking so that I dropped one and had to pick it up off the floor. I stammered my thanks, was ignored, and headed for the stairs. My scalp itched ferociously. To my relief, no one tried to stop me, and I was able to get away and out, into the now-welcome icy wind.

All the way home I argued with myself. It meant nothing, I said. Yet she did see it. Yes, but she may not have recognized it. Oh, come now, is there anyone in Florence who doesn't know the Buondelmonti colors? But she wouldn't necessarily suspect anything. For all she knows, he employed me once in the distant past.

I couldn't shake the sinking realization that once she had been left standing at the church door, she would put the pieces together and realize what I had done. Or, if not exactly what I had done, at least that I had been in the employ of someone who by then would be her worst enemy in the world. She's only a girl, I told myself. How could she harm me? What could she do?

Well, to start with, she could tell Oddo.

9. UNEASY

The eleventh of February was the day of Buondelmonte's marriages. That is to say, the day set for him to give a ring to Selvaggia, and also the day for him to lead his fair Isabella to her new home. Since both of these things were supposed to be done in the public eye, complete with witnesses and all the appropriate festivities, I couldn't shake off a feeling of impending disaster. If Oddo had called a parliament over a scratch to his arm, what was he going to do over a serious public insult to him and to his family?

If word reached Oddo of what Buondelmonte had done, it might well mean war, sooner rather than later. And if word reached Oddo that I had been there and taken part, my life wouldn't be worth a clipped penny. For that matter, if word did reach Oddo, Buondelmonte would assume it was my doing, and then it was just a matter of which one of them got to me first. It might even be the one thing they could manage to agree on.

So I waited, counting the days and keeping my own counsel. On the Saturday when, by my calculations, we had five more days to live through before hell was loosed, I was sleeping in after a late job the night before when a loud knock on the door jolted me awake.

Neri answered it, and I heard a familiar voice asking for the fool. It took me a moment to place it, but by the time Neri yanked my curtain open, I was pulling on my stockings and getting ready to come out and talk to Guido.

What on God's own earth was Guido doing here? And how did he even know how to find me? Had Oddo found out about Buondelmonte and sent Guido to get me? If he had, would Neri and I be able to drive him off, or would he be armed, or would there be other men with him, waiting outside? I didn't want Ghisola involved in anything ugly.

Only one way to find out what he wanted. I emerged from my alcove to find Guido in polite conversation with Ghisola, who was working some magic with a few dried herbs and some eggs and cheese and a fry pan.

He looked over at me and grinned. A good start, I thought, relieved. That looks friendly enough. But what was Guido doing standing there next to my hearth? What did Oddo want now?

"Well met, Fool," he said. "I was telling your—the lady of your house that I've come to offer you a job."

"A job?" I said stupidly. Surely he wasn't going to make me appear at the wedding in motley as another insult to Buondelmonte. Neri, next to me, watched us both intently. Go carefully here, I told myself. This could be trouble on more than one front.

"Messer Oddo has decided to give you and your companions the honor of performing at his niece's wedding." Guido's grin widened, and he waited for my response. I suppose he thought I would be grateful and eager, maybe overwhelmed by this great privilege, and would stammer out my profound gratitude, which he would graciously accept on Oddo's behalf.

What I said was, "No."

Guido and Neri both started. With Guido it was simple surprise, but with Neri, unless I was mistaken, it was a combination of irritation that Guido was trying to negotiate with me instead of with him, and sheer amazement that I would peremptorily turn down such a plum of a job. I really did know him too well.

Guido tried again. "I don't think you understand, Fool. Messer Oddo gives you this honor." Oh, I understood fully—for Guido, that would be all he'd need to know. It was for me, too, but not in the way he expected.

"No. We can't do it. We have other plans. Tell him thanks for thinking of us."

Guido and Neri both started to talk at once. An acrid smell from the hearth told me that Ghisola's attention was on us and not on her frittata.

"You can't refuse, Fool. This is what the big man wants. He'll pay you handsomely. Just cancel your other job."

At the same time Neri was saying, "I am the leader of this troupe of entertainers, my good man, and if you want to hire us, you speak to me."

My head was spinning. Oddo didn't suspect me, he wanted to hire us, Neri was becoming indignant, and the last thing in the world I wanted to do was to be present at the wedding that wasn't going to happen.

Unexpectedly, it was Ghisi who broke the impasse. She handed Guido a cup of wine and said pleasantly, "My lord, Corrado is not the one who books jobs for the troupe. Neri does that. Perhaps you would be good enough to speak to him?"

Guido, who probably wasn't used to being called "my lord," looked confused. He took the wine from her and looked from Neri to me and back again, unsure what to do next.

People saying no to Oddo would not normally be a part of his experience, I thought sourly. With Ghisi's words I knew I had already lost this one. Neri was not going to turn down this job, no matter how I felt about it. And I had no way to let him know just what a bad idea it was, especially with Guido present. My secrecy had caught up with me.

Neri took charge. "There are four of us, then. Two musicians and two who juggle and tumble and all that sort of thing. We all sing, and we can put on short skits. What does your master offer, and what does he want us to do?"

I stopped listening while they negotiated. Ghisola gave me a troubled glance. I glared at her, and she lowered her eyes and went back to her cooking.

It wasn't her fault, not really. She didn't know what my reasons were, and she probably thought I was refusing because I disliked the nobility, or maybe because I'd had a bad time at the Mazzinghi knighting thanks to Oddo. It made sense that she would try to placate Neri, and she knew we always needed money. I couldn't blame her, but I did wish she had kept silent.

Neri and Guido finished working out the details. Guido took Neri's oath that we'd be there, and he in his turn swore to a generous payment.

"Wear good clothes," he told us. "No motley for this occasion." Neri nodded. I wasn't sure I owned anything that these people would consider good clothing, but I knew Ghisola would turn me out looking respectable somehow. She always did.

As soon as the door closed behind Guido, Neri turned on me furiously. "How could you refuse a job like that?" he demanded. "It isn't up to you to refuse, anyway. And where else do you think we're going to see that kind of money? What's the matter with you, man?"

"All right. Have it your way." Not that I had any real choice left. "We'll do the job and you'll get your money. Happy now?"

"No. I still want to know what you were thinking. What could have made you say that? You had no right. You almost ruined everything. This is the biggest opportunity we've ever had." He glowered at me.

I couldn't explain. I couldn't even come up with a believable lie. Defeated, I shrugged and said, "I don't like Oddo. He almost got me killed once, and I don't trust him. But you're right, the money's good. So we'll do the job, and that's the end of it." With that I turned my back on him and stomped back into my alcove. If I could have figured out how to slam a curtain behind me, I would have.

I knew Neri would go out soon. He'd need to let Anselmo and Rufino know about the job and set up a rehearsal schedule. So I waited, wanting to give us both a chance to cool down.

If I hadn't given him that concession, he would have followed me into my tiny, disorderly space and kept the argument going. I'd removed his excuse, but I knew he would still be angry.

72

I also knew it wouldn't last. Neri had always been quick to anger, but as soon as something more interesting distracted him, he let it go. I figured I would defuse whatever remained by offering some ideas for skits that I had been working on lately, and maybe coming up with a flashy new juggling routine, since this cursed job meant so much to him. I couldn't tell him that his precious job wasn't going to happen, so I would have to play along. And anyway, we'd be able to use the material another time. With that in mind, I was scrabbling around in my props bag when I heard the door close and then Ghisola's hesitant voice on the other side of my curtain.

"Rado?"

"What do you want, Ghisola?" I didn't mean to be so curt, but I guess I was still annoyed.

"Can we talk about it?"

I pulled the curtain open and gestured at the bench. We both sat down.

"I'm sorry if I said the wrong thing. I can see why you don't want to work for messer Oddo, but wouldn't it be dangerous to tell him no, if he's that kind of man?"

She had a point. It was hard to imagine Oddo taking no for an answer.

"Maybe. Yes. Yes, I suppose it would be. Maybe I spoke too quickly. But I wish you and Neri would talk to me before you decide what the troupe should do."

"Well, we couldn't exactly do that, could we, with that man standing there?" She tilted her head to one side and watched me.

I gave in, as I always did with Ghisi. "No, you couldn't. Just as I couldn't tell you any more about why I don't want to do this job."

"There's more?

"There's a lot more. But I can't talk about it, and I don't want Neri to get obsessed with finding out, so just don't say anything, all right?"

"All right. Anyway, all I know is that there's something I don't know, and I'm used to that. But you will do the job?"

"Yes." Well, no, actually. And neither would the others. But we would be there, ready to go, just as if the wedding was really going to happen.

"And you will try to keep Neri happy?"

"Ghisi, I've spent most of my life trying to keep Neri happy. I'm not going to stop now."

"He's worth it."

She had me there. "Yes, he is."

"He'll settle down, you'll see. He's probably already told Anselmo all about it. By the time they get to Rufino and tell him, Neri will be so busy thinking about the job that he will have forgotten he was angry."

*

He hadn't exactly forgotten, that much was plain, but he did seem to want to make peace. He even told me, in front of the others, that he understood why I didn't trust Oddo, and he didn't blame me.

"You won't be at any risk during this job," he assured me. "We'll keep him away from you." Neri could have no idea how naive that sounded, but I refrained from laughing and instead thanked him gravely. Neri, in his turn, lavished praise on all of my ideas for skits and sets—he was not always so easily impressed—and so the two of us were reconciled.

Ghisola, though, knew us both well enough to see that our exaggerated politeness with each other masked considerable discomfort, but she said nothing. She was to be in charge of props, instruments, and clothing, and that kept her busy. Neri drew the line at letting her perform, though her voice was fine and melded well with his, but he saw no harm in letting her help out. Or, as she put it, "do all the work." In fact, some of our best routines betrayed Ghisola's signature wit and facility with words.

We decided among the five of us which acts to work up, including our new ideas. Rufino and I spent hours practicing a new juggling routine, while Neri divided his time between working out music with Anselmo and practicing langue d'oc love songs on his own. He had a musician's ear for languages, and he could have passed for a real troubadour. Anselmo ached to bring his pipe and tabor, for all eyes would be on him as he played both at once. He was good: the fingers of one hand danced around the holes in his tabor pipe while the other hand drew forth elaborate rhythms from a simple drum. But the vielle was a more appropriate instrument for a wedding, so that's what he concentrated on. Neri would play his organetto, of course, but also bring a small harp to accompany his songs.

Rufino got it into his head that he would be able to train our neighbor Bicci's dog to dance on its hind legs and jump through a hoop. Masetto, so named after Bicci's previous landlord (and it was not a compliment to either), was neither a sleek hunting hound nor a lady's fluffy lapdog. He was more of a flea-infested afterthought. He looked as if his ears, his tail, what was left of his scruffy fur, and his rheumy eyes had come from four entirely different creatures, adding up to a sort of ungainly chimera. He was smart enough, as Rufino kept insisting, but he didn't take direction well, and that's putting it kindly. His one passion in life was chasing rats.

74

If Rufino could have constructed an act around that, it probably would have worked. Still, my ever-optimistic colleague was determined, so we shrugged and left him to it, though I did insist he also spend some time rehearsing the new juggling act with me.

While we worked up our acts, Ghisola somehow managed to supply us all with decent clothing. This involved some borrowing, some buying from secondhand dealers, some mending, and a certain amount of improvisation, but she did it. Not everything we wore would stand up to close scrutiny, but it would all look fine from where the audience stood.

There was never any doubt about what Ghisola herself would wear— her best gown, the blue of chicory flowers. If I hadn't watched her work on that garment, I wouldn't believe it was the same one she had brought home in triumph the previous year from the secondhand shop. Faded, ripped, and bedraggled, it had looked a hopeless case to me, but over a period of a month she transformed it. First she bartered some of her almond cakes for the privilege of dunking it in the dyer's vat, to freshen the color. Next she mended the rips and snags so cleverly that they were invisible, and let it out where she needed more room and replaced the frayed side lacings with good silk cord. Then, with infinite patience, she added intricate embroidery to the sleeves, the neckline, and the full circumference of the hem. And now she wore it with pride. It would never compete with the fine clothes of the people with surnames, but she looked good in it, and she knew it.

We all had a lot to accomplish in a few days, but we were professionals, and it came together well. I threw myself into the preparations because I did not want to leave myself time to think about what I knew.

That never works. I worried constantly. I couldn't forget that we were in a frenzy of preparation for a wedding that wasn't going to happen, and that we were going to find ourselves right in the middle of a volatile situation. I wanted to warn the others of what they might be getting into, but I couldn't speak of what I knew was coming. There should be no immediate violence, I reasoned with myself. Oddo will have his parliament first. Maybe he'll even pay his entertainers anyway, in a spirit of knightly largesse.

My sense of dread grew. My dreams were all of hands now—huge hands drawing weapons, hands holding out purses, hands ring-stamping seals on letters, tiny hands with two giant rings dangling, a deeply disturbing dream of a raging man with two hands cut off, dripping blood. And always, two familiar hands grasping a full plate of meat and snatching it away.

75

The tenth of February arrived, and Anselmo and Rufino joined us at our house for the final rehearsal. I noted a few rough spots, but overall we weren't bad. Oddo should be pleased, I told them, and they grinned.

Rufino and Anselmo left for their homes, promising to come for us in the morning. That night Ghisola was so excited she chattered on for what felt like hours about the people with surnames. She babbled about who among them was who, and their alliances and towers and arrogance and crimes, and about their women and their fine clothes and jewels and servants and horses. Neri good-naturedly let her prattle, but it got on my nerves. I went to bed early, but I slept fitfully.

The eleventh of February dawned.

10. INSULT

Three mellifluous langue d'oc love songs, one spectacular round of juggling, a few uneasy moments of Rufino wobbling around on my stilts, and still no Buondelmonte. Oh, and there was also the unfortunate episode with Bicci's dog and the rat, but the less said about that the better. We thought it likely that the flea-ridden Masetto would come back home eventually, and Bicci, who was part of our audience, didn't seem worried.

Oddo did, however, though he was doing his best not to let it show to the crowd of onlookers. We were gathered under cloudy skies outside Santa Maria sopra Porta, where we were supposed to welcome the bridegroom and his party, but so far the wedding was a one-sided affair.

And I was the only one there who knew it was going to remain so.

In contrast to Oddo's instructions to Buondelmonte to limit the size of his entourage, the Amidei, the Lamberti, the Fifanti, and the Uberti were there in force, dressed as befitted their rank. The women, in their jewels and fine gowns and gauzy veils, clustered near the church, but the men kept themselves where they could see if someone was coming.

We four performers had set up opposite the women, on the other side of the piazza. Ghisola, behind us, was muttering under her breath as she struggled to replace a broken string on Anselmo's vielle while he tapped a tambourine in time to Neri's organetto. Rufino and I tossed my leather balls back and forth, nothing tricky this time, just a little background color. It left me able to watch Oddo and Lambertuccio and Mosca. They were in a tight circle, talking animatedly, looking up frequently to see if anyone had spotted Buondelmonte yet.

Among the ladies was Selvaggia, dressed in a magnificent scarlet gown with the gold sleeves of her undertunic showing. She looked short and squat compared to the other young women, but her hair, dark and glossy and abundant, was bound up in an intricate pattern of gold netting and pearls, and I had to admit that it, at least, was lovely. With her were her mother and several other older women, and also ladies of around her own age or not much more, some wearing a married woman's coif, others with the uncovered plaits or flowing hair of virgins. The other young women talked and giggled together, but I noticed that Selvaggia stood a little apart.

One of the coiffed ones was a rare beauty, wearing an artfully fitted gown of a tawny gold, the color people call pelo di lione. Not even Selvaggia's dress and hair could have diverted attention from that shape and that face.

When we first arrived and were setting up, Neri had eyed her appreciatively.

"Buondelmonte probably wishes he was marrying that one," he said.

"She's wearing a wimple, you dolt," I said. "She's married. She's not available."

"That doesn't mean a man can't look, and wish, does it?"

"It ought to mean that," Ghisola said tartly.

Neri had grinned archly and launched into his first song, while Ghisola wrinkled her nose at him. They were joking. I think.

Meanwhile, it was hard to miss a certain growing agitation among the men. Buondelmonte should have presented himself long before this point, and I sensed that these men feared a public humiliation. And with reason. I could only hope the big lout would have the sense not to ride past these men with Isabella in tow, for I had no wish to witness a bloodbath.

"Who's the one who looks like an old lion?" Rufino asked, not missing a ball.

"Lambertuccio. And the one who looks like a hawk is Mosca," I said, returning yellow for red as blue spun overhead. Mosca had keen eyes and a hooked nose in a lean, angular face.

"Oddo's more of a bull," Anselmo chimed in, tapping on his tambourine.

Neri, still playing his organetto, said out of the side of his mouth, "Don't talk. You'll drop something."

"No, we won't," I told him. "And don't talk out of the side of your mouth. It looks ridiculous." The balls kept dancing through the air, the tambourine kept jingling, and Neri kept pressing his little mushroom-shaped keys while we spoke. Ghisi just shook her head. She knew when we were showing off for each other.

Neri finished his istampitta with a flourish, and set his organetto down gently on the ground so that he could take up the little harp he owned jointly with Anselmo. Ghisola had passed Anselmo's restrung vielle back to him, so he took over the background music while Neri quietly checked his tuning.

I juggled with Rufino and kept an eye on Oddo. This whole situation made me uneasy, but all I could do was to continue to pretend I was as ignorant of what was going on as everyone else was. I still feared they would make a connection between Buondelmonte and me, but I thought an innocent demeanor would be my best defense, allowing me to claim convincingly that I knew nothing of his plans.

I saw Oddo send one of his men off toward the bridge. They must be expecting Buondelmonte to come from his family's lands outside Florence. Where was he, I wondered? Maybe he would quietly sneak Isabella back to his house, and this day would end in disappointment and puzzlement but not—yet—in open hostility. Maybe.

Among the women, Selvaggia's mother, madonna Lauretta, dabbed at her eyes, and Oddo's lady put a sympathetic arm around her shoulders. Not only the gathered nobles were restive, but it was becoming clear to the onlookers that some sort of problem was holding up the show. Oddo, Lambertuccio, and Mosca, now joined by Schiatta, huddled together, talking quickly.

Oddo's man returned, a little out of breath, and reported. Oddo scowled. What had he just learned? If it had been the whole tale, that Buondelmonte and Isabella's bridal procession had been spotted, I would have expected more of an explosion, so I guessed that the only news was that there was as yet no sign of the bridegroom. Whatever had been reported, Oddo looked at Schiatta, who gave a decisive nod. Oddo stepped forward, clapping his hands for attention.

Unfortunately that was the moment when Neri launched into his next love song, and Oddo turned to him and glowered, making a "cut!" gesture, slashing his finger across his throat. Neri's hands dropped from the instrument and his mouth snapped shut. His face reddened, and I liked Oddo even less than I had a moment before, if that was possible.

"Messer Buondelmonte has been delayed," Oddo announced to the wedding guests, loud enough for everyone to hear. "Let us return to his bride's home and await him there." With that, the family members began to form a straggly column and move toward the street.

Selvaggia walked up to Oddo and said something to him. At first I thought he was going to shoo her away, but then he said something back. Then she gestured in our direction—in fact, she pointed right at me. He nodded, and she turned to join the women headed back to the Amidei palace.

We sat watching them go, uncertain what to do next.

"What was she pointing at us for?" Anselmo asked. I was afraid I knew, but before I could suggest a hasty retreat, Oddo strode over to us.

"Fool. There's been a change of plans, so you and your friends can go. I'll let you know if we have need of your skills later. Here's your payment." He handed me another canvas bag bulging with coins. Smoothly I passed it to Neri without even looking at it, as if that had been Oddo's intention all along, and Neri's face reddened again. Oddo handed me what I thought at first was a coin.

"You I do need again. Come to me at the Amidei palace in two hours. Bring this token—you'll need it to get in. Be there."

He turned and followed his family back to the street. The five of us looked at each other.

"What did he give you?" asked Rufino. I looked down at the disc in my hand. It was lead, crudely stamped with Oddo's name on one side. I held it out for the others to see, but none of them could read, so I had to tell them what it said.

No one had much to say as we packed up. Neri counted the coins in the pouch and reported that we had received the agreed-upon amount plus a little, and there was a general sigh of relief.

We all went back to our house, dodging the people on the street who wanted to ask us about what had just happened. We put the props and instruments away and plopped down in front of the hearth, and Ghisola poured wine for all of us.

"Well, I guess that's that," I said.

"It isn't going to be the end of it, though," said Neri, and Anselmo and Rufino nodded. "After all, this is no small thing. The greatest families in Florence have been insulted, and they aren't going to stand still for it. Especially your friend Oddo." There was an edge to his voice for that last remark. I wished Oddo had not handed the purse to me, and had not summoned me in front of Neri. For that matter, I wished Oddo had not summoned me at all.

"Insulted by one of the other greatest families in Florence," Anselmo added. Two, I silently amended, thinking of the Donati's role in all this, which my colleagues didn't know about yet.

"Is there anything to eat?" Rufino asked Ghisola, putting down his empty cup. She shook her head.

I felt ravenous.

"I need food before I try to deal with Oddo," I said. "Selmo, Fino, if you'll go out and get us dumplings or something, I'll pay." That met with an enthusiastic response, so I handed over a few coins from my share of the contents of the canvas bag, which Neri had distributed as soon as we arrived.

They headed out with a couple of our towels to see what they could find to make up for a missed dinner. Ghisola called instructions after them for where to find the best street vendors at this time of day.

They didn't know yet about Isabella, but did Oddo, I wondered? If he did, I didn't look forward to answering his summons, not that I had any real choice.

Neri and I settled onto the bench, and Ghisola built up the fire a little. Neri looked at me with what was becoming his signature mix of concern and irritation.

"So what does Oddo want with you now?

I shrugged. "How would I know? All he said was to come to him later. I assume he'll tell me when I get there."

"No doubt. If he wants to hire us again, though, remember he talks to me, not to you." That didn't deserve an answer, so I didn't give it one. Our performing jobs were the smallest of my worries.

Neri put his feet up on the bench and leaned back against the wall. Ghisola sat down next to him and cleared her throat, and he grinned. "Before I forget, Ghisola wants to tell you something she thinks she saw," he said.

"I did see it," she snapped. "Men don't ever notice anything."

"We were a bit busy, love," Neri said, putting his arm around her waist and squeezing. "You didn't have to be putting on a show for them, so you could just have yourself a good look, couldn't you? Now tell what you saw, then, there's a good girl."

"Well, I don't know what it means, exactly," she said, nestling against Neri, "but at one point I saw one of the women trying to get the attention of the man you said is like a hawk. That's Mosca, isn't it?" I nodded.

"I think it was one of the Uberti ladies. The young pretty one in the tawny gown. She passed by Mosca and spoke to him, but he moved right away from her and wouldn't even look at her. I thought she was surprised and kind of upset, like she had expected a different reaction. And all the while, that bride was staring at them with a little smile on her face. Of course, that was at the beginning, before she knew she was going to be jilted, so she could still smile then. What do you think that was all about?"

"I have no idea. Did anyone else see it?" Could this be the hold Selvaggia had on Mosca? Surely he had better sense. Whoever's wife she was, she wasn't his; Mosca was unmarried.

"I don't think so. Everybody else was watching you perform, or watching the men out in front. I was behind you, where I could see all the women, and I just happened to be looking at them."

"And why was that, my dear?" said Neri, with mock innocence.

"Because I like their dresses, that's why." Ghisola blushed, but she went on doggedly. "I'm never in all my life going to own clothes like those, so at least I can get me a look, when the opportunity is there. There's no cost to looking, is there?"

"No, looking is free," I said, amused. "That's the whole point. They want you to look." Although they probably didn't want people looking on while Buondelmonte made idiots of them, I thought. Had he led Isabella yet? And did they know?

I didn't have to wait long to find out. Anselmo and Rufino burst in, out of breath, and their words tumbled out in an incomprehensible blur of voices until Neri managed to get them to slow down and take turns. I was pretty sure I knew what was coming, but at least the towels were full of something that smelled like food, so we had that much good news.

"It's Buondelmonte. He's gotten himself married to somebody else, and his wedding procession just went by." Anselmo was almost sputtering with excitement. I could see it in my mind—Buondelmonte and the incomparable Isabella, elegantly dressed and riding their well-groomed horses, heading from the Donati palace to that of the Buondelmonti.

"God's balls!" said Neri. "Are you sure? Did you see them?"

"Yes, we saw them," said Rufino. "We were in the back of the crowd, but we saw them go by. So did half of Florence."

"Who was the woman?"

"Don't know. She was a looker, though—even better than the one in the gold dress at the wedding."

They described the procession—the men armed and armored, in defiance of law and custom; Buondelmonte's glowering brother Gherardo at his side; other family members and friends escorting bride and groom and the ostentatiously displayed trousseau: lengths of rich cloth and other household treasures mounded up in several huge baskets, and servants bearing iron-banded coffers that presumably held jewels. Far from traveling quietly as one might have expected, they went forth with shawm players, tumblers, and singers. Worse and worse, I thought. Buondelmonte, you arrogant bastard, were you so eager to show off your bride that you had to rub it in their faces?

"Who did they hire?" Neri asked, his professional curiosity aroused.

"Nobody local," said Anselmo. "They must've been from Montebuone or someplace." I didn't think so. Buondelmonte's family seat was too tiny a hamlet to produce a troupe of performers. More likely they were from Prato, or Lucca, or even Siena. But it did make sense that Buondelmonte wouldn't have taken the chance of hiring Florentines, when secrecy was so vital to him.

"Were they any good?"

"Nah. They were pretty awful," Anselmo told him, and Neri grinned.

"Well, at least Oddo got the best show. Do the Amidei and their kin know yet?" Good man. Neri was beginning to get the hang of figuring out what was important in these matters.

"Don't know," said Rufino. "If they don't yet, they soon will. They were back at home when the procession went by, but they're bound to hear about it. It was a bold thing for Buondelmonte to do, to stand up the Amidei girl on the very same day he took another girl to wife."

Ghisola's eyes were round. "Oh, that poor girl," she whispered, but it occurred to me that her words might apply equally to either one. The secret wife or the jilted bride, the pretty giggler or the clever schemer, he endangered one even as he insulted the other.

Rufino and Anselmo could tell us little more than they already had, so we unwrapped the towels. One was filled with cheese dumplings, the other with little fried meat pastries. They were not yet cold and we ate with gusto, discussing the day's events with our mouths full.

At last we could prolong the meal no further, and I got up with a sigh to pull my outdoor shoes on and go see what Oddo wanted of me this time. I felt a prickling of fear that Selvaggia knew my role in what had happened, for when she spoke to Oddo it must have been of me. She had pointed right at me, after all. But how could she know? She had seen enough to associate me with Buondelmonte, true, but she wouldn't have known the magnitude of the outrage at that point, for they didn't know then about Isabella.

Of course, she would know by the time I got there.

11. MESSAGE

I found myself walking briskly as I came closer to the bridge, even though I wasn't eager to see Oddo, nor to enter the ancient palace of the Amidei. The day was crisp and fine, and my legs wanted the exercise. Besides, whatever Oddo wanted, I wanted to get it over with.

If Oddo already believed I had betrayed him, I suspected he would have given me no token and no summons—just sent his thugs to destroy me, unless of course he'd prefer to do it himself. I hoped the summons meant he didn't know, although Selvaggia's gesture in my direction worried me. I would have to proceed very carefully.

I presented myself and my medallion to the man at the door of the Amidei house. He took the token from me, looked carefully at both sides, and dropped it in an open casket on the floor where it clanked against others. He let me in and told me to wait in the entryway while he fetched an escort.

"I can just go up," I told him, starting toward the stairs. "That's what I did last time."

He grabbed my arm and held it firmly. "Times are different now," he said. "Your token shows messer Oddo's name, but his arms aren't on the reverse side. That means you come in, but you don't come in alone. You wait."

That didn't sound promising. I waited in the bare storage space while the guard ducked behind the rod with oiled cloaks hanging on it and rapped on a door I hadn't noticed before. It wasn't the latrine; that was on the other side, and unmistakable to anyone with a nose. Another man wearing Oddo's colors opened to the guard's knock. I had seen him a couple of hours ago, at Santa Maria sopra Porta. The two men spoke briefly, and the new one came over to me, bobbed his head in acknowledgement, and gestured toward the stairs.

I was relieved. Nothing threatening so far, no rough handling or threats or bluster. If Oddo had it in for me, these men didn't know it. I climbed the stairs to the hall, the man in Oddo's livery right behind me.

The windows in the great hall were still open to the air, though this day was milder than the day I had first stood here and the chill was less. This time the hall was richly hung with fur-trimmed drapes, and the floor was strewn with lavender and other sweet herbs. Tall candlestands, each with several prickets holding unlighted candles, were set up in all four corners. I realized with a pang that these were the decorations for the wedding that would never happen.

Lambertuccio sat on the bench, exactly where he had been the last time I was here. His shoulders were hunched and his mouth a thin straight line. Oddo paced furiously back and forth, still wearing his wedding finery. The hard leather soles of his outdoor boots slapped the herringbone brick floor. He stopped, and both of them looked at me as I paused on the top step.

"Have you heard?" Oddo demanded, scowling.

"Heard what, my lord?" I asked innocently, entering the room. Oddo waved my escort back down the stairs.

He had to be asking if I knew about Isabella. They must have heard by now, if everyone on the street already knew. Could I get away with pretending I didn't?

"Has messer Buondelmonte—" I began, but Oddo cut me off.

"Don't speak that name!" he roared. "Never speak that bastard's name in my presence again!" He spat on the floor.

I bowed in apology. "My lord, I'm sorry for this trouble and for this unwarranted insult to your family." I turned to Lambertuccio. "And especially to your daughter, my lord."

Both men seemed to expect more, so I blundered on. "Is it possible that illness or injury or another cause outside his control kept him away?" I could try to appear ignorant of the full magnitude of Buondelmonte's act of betrayal. And no matter what happened, I was not going to admit to knowing about Buondelmonte's marriage ahead of time. That would be suicide.

Unexpectedly, it was Lambertuccio who answered. "No. We've learned that he was seen leading another bride to his palace." Not a young man, Lambertuccio had aged ten years in the two hours since I saw him last.

"A Donati bride!" Oddo was red-faced and hoarse. "On the day he was to swear to my niece, he led a Donati woman to his home, with full pageantry and display. They came within a stone's throw of this palace. They'll be feasting even now!" He turned on his heel and began his furious pacing again.

Lambertuccio gave me a searching look. "Do you see what this means, Fool? He planned this. He gave a ring to the Donati woman after he signed our contract. It couldn't have been done before, or he'd have used it as an excuse not to sign. And he led her on the very day he was to wed my daughter." Selvaggia's father looked old and tired, but there was something else there, smoldering under the surface. The old lion was a man to be reckoned with, no less than the bull and the hawk. I didn't know what to say to him, so I remained silent.

This was not good—they knew all. Of course they were enraged: Buondelmonte's act was an enormous, unprecedented insult to the family and to all its allies. But at least they were telling me about it as if they thought it news to me. That made me feel safer.

I felt an unexpected pang of sympathy for the girl. What must this be like for Selvaggia, shamed in front of the entire city? The Buondelmonte enclave is neighbor to that of the Amidei. Many in the street who saw Selvaggia waiting in vain for her bridegroom also would have seen that same man, now another's husband, joyfully leading the incomparable Isabella to his family home. And Selvaggia had wanted this marriage, wanted it enough make Mosca cause it to happen. Or almost happen.

Oddo had paced his way to the far end of the room, so I took a chance and asked Lambertuccio, "My lord, is there a way I can serve you? I am unsure why I have been called to your house."

By the time I got that much out, Oddo had stalked back to where Lambertuccio sat, and he answered me.

"You can talk to the girl, that's what. For some reason she wants to see you, though what she wants with a fool at a time like this, I have no idea."

Lambertuccio had. "My daughter says she wants to talk to you because you were there for that meeting with Buon—with that base knight. First she wanted to find out if you knew why he didn't show up, and now she wants to know whether you've heard anything about this Donati slut, and whether anyone on the street knew this was coming, and what people are saying now."

"My lords, I've heard nothing."

"Best you haven't," said Oddo, "or the first thing you should have done was to come to me. We've already told her you're just a fool and you won't know anything, but she's still determined to see you, so now you go and tell her yourself. And remember, Fool, the girl's upset, so be careful."

"She's afraid for what may become of her now," Lambertuccio said. "She feels as any woman would feel, so insulted." He sounded painfully tired.

"The fool doesn't need to hear family business, Brother-in-law. Just pass her along to the next suitor on your list," said Oddo impatiently. Lambertuccio opened his mouth to speak, and then closed it again.

Oddo turned back to me. "You'll meet with her upstairs in the kitchen, Fool." Of course. Women. Kitchens. Where else? I bowed to both men and started toward the stairs.

"Fool!" I stopped and turned to face Oddo.

"I want her pacified, not more upset. There's enough trouble around here without a woman's hysterical screeching. So remember, calm her down. That's your job. Do it, and you get your coins. Go."

He pointed up to the kitchen, and I went. Behind me I heard Lambertuccio say plaintively to Oddo, "Her mother is the one who's hysterical, Oddo. The girl's ready to kill someone, and she doesn't much care who."

Better and better. I arrived at the kitchen level and took a deep breath.

The rejected bride sat stiffly erect, still as a statue, the day's bright light silhouetting her in the window. A servingwoman worked quietly at the hearth, tending to a pot of onion-scented liquid bubbling away on a tripod over the coals. Selvaggia was no longer wearing her elaborate wedding costume. Her simple gonnella of dark red did nothing to disguise her ungainly shape, and the sides strained a little.

She fixed me with a basilisk-like stare and my stomach sank. This one knew. She had seen what she had seen, and she was bright enough to put it together and to understand. To my annoyance I realized I was trembling. Not even Oddo had made me tremble.

"You knew."

"Lady?" I couldn't meet those hard eyes.

"You knew what he was going to do to me. You have his purse. You're in his pay." Her voice rasped.

"Lady, I had no choice—"

"You could have warned us and spared me that shame. You did not, Fool. You betrayed my uncle, and you insulted me."

"Lady—"

"Did you?" Her voice rose to a shriek. The servant jumped, stared at us, and then quickly looked away. "Did you warn me?"

I took a step back. There being nothing I could say to that, I held my tongue. She, too, was silent for a while, turning her head to look out the window. She had a prominent nose, seen against the backdrop of sky and river.

Just as I began to hope that she had spoken her piece and was now done with me, she spoke again, and this time her voice was calm and well-modulated. Even more than the shriek, that made my scalp itch.

"And what do you think my lord uncle will do if he learns of your betrayal, Fool?" she asked, sounding merely curious.

I shuddered. That was precisely what I had been trying not to think about.

Selvaggia then described to me, in exquisite detail, how Oddo had dealt with a retainer who displeased him. I listened, though all Florence already knew that gruesome story. I will not relate it here, except to say that a simple execution would have been more merciful.

She reached the end of her tale, a tale I thought she told with unseemly relish given its nature, and smiled at me. "I take it you don't wish to undergo a similar experience?" she asked.

I shook my head. No, I fervently wished to avoid that or any other consequences of Oddo's displeasure. She had me exactly where she wanted me, and I could only wait to see where that was.

"Then in exchange for my silence on this matter, may I assume that I have your cooperation?"

I had to swallow before I could answer. "You do, Lady," I said.

She studied me. "I am no false Buondelmonte, Fool. I am of the Amidei and my word means something. I say now that if you do as I tell you, I'll keep your secret forever. If you don't, I will unleash the full fury of the combined families on your lice-ridden head. Do you understand me?"

It was clear enough. "I do, Lady. What would you have me do?"

She laid out her plan. Oddo intended to call a council of the allied families within the next few days. The assembly would be bigger than the one hastily convened after the Mazzingo knighting, for the affront was much more serious. The families, then, would decide what manner of vengeance to exact.

"You will hear those, Fool, who want him publicly humiliated, and those who want him to forfeit money and power as a result of what he has done. Others will want him insulted and permanently marked by a wound." She looked up at me, waiting.

I won't hear them, I thought. Not this time. What I said was, "Do you not want some of those things too, my lady? You were grievously ill treated."

"I want him dead."

Dead. I had expected no less, but it gave me a shock to hear it stated so matter-of-factly, and by a girl. No Isabella-like giggles here.

"I understand your wishes, my lady, but I cannot help you in this," I said. Murder was no part of a fool's job—surely not even Selvaggia expected me to kill.

"You will do exactly as you did before," she said. Her face and voice were serene. "You'll deliver my message to Mosca, because I can't get it to him any other way without arousing suspicion. I daresay he will

88

be expecting it, this time." She reached into her sleeve and withdrew a scrap of lined vellum like the last one, folded twice, and held it out to me. This woman was hard on books.

"Get it to him before the council. Hand it to him only, no one else, and don't let anyone else see you do it."

"Lady, I don't know when the council will be, or where," I said. I put my hands behind my back to avoid taking the note from her and took a step backward.

"Find out," she snapped, shaking the piece of vellum at me impatiently. Reluctantly I took it and slipped it into my own sleeve. I bowed to her, and started to go.

"Fool," she said. I turned.

"It will be in Santa Maria sopra Porta, where I was to have been married," she said softly. Cold venom in her voice, but a hint of something else as well. "Vengeance will be sworn at the place where he committed his offense. And now you have only to find out when."

I bowed again, and this time she let me go. In my eagerness to get away I all but ran down the stairs, but the presence of several men who had joined Lambertuccio and Oddo in the hall made me slow down and take a look.

The men were standing in a knot, and in the midst of them was the towering, unmistakable figure of messer Schiatta degli Uberti. As I passed, I saw him register my presence. At Oddo's parliament after the knighting, he had said little, only listening. If he was taking an active part now, it indicated how serious things had become. Remembering the cold and calculating way he had looked at Buondelmonte during the fight that began it all, I shuddered. I didn't think Buondelmonte's chances were good.

I slipped through the room and down the stone stairs unnoticed by the others, and once more I was relieved to leave that place. The day was as bright as before, but it seemed colder and more forbidding as I made my way through the winding streets toward the home of Mosca dei Lamberti.

12. SEEKING MOSCA

The small bell for None had not yet rung when I reached the market-place, one of the busiest parts of this teeming city, even when, as now, it was not market day. Just off the piazza the Lamberti palace loomed over the street with an even more forbidding face than the grim Amidei tower, its mammoth blocks of rusticated stone uninterrupted by windows at the street level. No welcoming bench waited outside. In this cramped part of town, where buildings crowded in on each other and upper stories jettied out over the narrow streets and blotted out the sun for those below, no room remained for such amenities.

The palace's street level was not a shopfront, only an expanse of dark gray stone blocks with a sturdy door in the middle. A painted stone shield with the Lamberti golden balls in relief on a blue field overlooked the entrance. A bird, perhaps allied with Buondelmonte's faction, had left its contribution on the top ball, streaking it with white.

I knocked on the great door and waited. Nothing. I knocked a second time, harder, but still no one came, and I wondered if anyone listened behind that formidable stone facade. I took two steps back, the better to see the windows on the second floor, and bumped into a woman with a market basket. She scowled at me and cursed me for a clumsy fool, and I shrugged, for she was at least half right.

Not knowing what else to do, I left the Lamberti palace behind and wandered into the street. I knew many of the shop owners and not a few of their customers, so I asked around to see if anyone knew when the council would be, or if it had even been decided yet. No one I approached knew, though they all knew it would be happening. The red-cheeked girl selling her dried fruits would have been happy to keep me talking with her, and another time I would have been glad to oblige, but not this day. I told her I had to meet someone, and moved on before she could argue. Just as well—given the nature of our last encounter, I should have remembered her name, and I didn't.

I hovered around a knot of women gathered outside the little church of Santa Maria in Campidoglio and listened to their gossip until one of them noticed me and told me to be off, flapping her hands at me as if shooing a chicken. All I learned from it was that people throughout the city were abuzz with what Buondelmonte had done. And popular opinion had already fingered Gualdrada as the author of the outrage. Women were quick to blame one of their own.

The bell chimed None and still I lacked the information I needed. I walked back to Mosca's house and banged on the door again, in case anyone had returned. No one had, or at least no one chose to answer my knocking.

There was nothing for it but to try again first thing in the morning. It would be market day, which should make it easier to find the information I sought. Remembering Selvaggia's matter-of-fact voice as she threatened to tell Oddo of my betrayal, I knew I couldn't afford to be late. More lives than the lovesick Buondelmonte's were at stake, and I had a particular interest in preserving my own.

I took one more quick turn around the neighborhood, stopping anyone I knew to ask if they had seen Mosca. No one had, so I got no help there. Tired and frustrated, I headed home. On the way I found a food vendor and bought her remaining scraps of cold meat pie for a bargain price, for despite the dumplings and pastries we had eaten earlier, I was hungry again. I ate as I walked. The fat had congealed, and the tough crust stuck to the roof of my mouth.

At home I found Neri and Ghisola sitting at the hearth, waiting to learn what had happened to me. Anselmo and Rufino had long since gone, no doubt to spend their earnings in a tavern, but Ghisola must have persuaded Neri to stay home with her to hear my tale. I collapsed onto the bench and waited for the inevitable questions.

"So what did Oddo want?" Neri said, without preliminaries. He sat with his right leg crossed over the left, jiggling his foot.

How much should I tell them? I had to come up with something they would believe, but I was too tired to think of anything, so I settled for a partial version of the truth.

"He wanted me to talk to the girl. The bride."

"The bride!" Ghisola said.

Neri whistled. "Why on God's holy earth did he want you to do that?"

"He said she wanted to see me because I was along for the meeting with Buondelmonte."

"You were there?" said Neri, incredulous.

At the same time Ghisola said, "You saw her? What was she like?"

It was easier to answer her than him, so I said, "She was angry. She's been insulted, and she wanted to know what people are saying in the streets."

"But why ask you?" said Neri. "And why didn't you tell us you were at that meeting?" One look at his face told me this wasn't going well.

Ghisola said, "Was she still wearing her wedding dress?"

91

Neri first, this time. "She asked me because everybody else who went to that meeting was linked with her family. I think she figured people would speak more freely around me than they would to her people," I improvised. This might be believable, though it didn't explain why I hadn't told him before about my presence at Buondelmonte's home that day, at a meeting that had already attained the status of legend even before these latest doings.

"But—" Ghisola said, and Neri raised a hand, silencing her.

"I want to know exactly what's going on here," he said, slowly and deliberately, his foot bobbing furiously up and down. He studied my face as if the truth was written there, if he could only read it. I hoped he couldn't. "You went with Oddo to meet with Buondelmonte and didn't tell us about it, and now you're a guest in his palace and talking to the jilted bride. At the knighting you were just a performer like the rest of us until you grabbed Buondelmonte's dinner and started an uproar. What are you up to?"

I sighed. "Neri, none of this was my idea. I had no choice about the plate. I think Oddo would have killed me on the spot if I'd refused to do his stupid little joke. And I couldn't get away afterwards, because he grabbed me and dragged me back to his house. On a horse, no less."

The thought of that made Neri chuckle in spite of himself, but then he remembered our earlier talk and his amusement vanished. "You let me think you walked back alone," he said, his eyes narrowing. "Here I was feeling sorry for you."

"I wish I had walked back," I told him. "That ride was a nightmare, and feeling sorry for me was exactly what any decent person should have done."

"Nevertheless, we'd do better with a little more honesty here," he said, and hearing the irritation in his voice, I didn't want to press my luck.

"All right, then. Next I had to juggle for him while he got his arm bandaged. And I had to sit in on his council, and then he got the bright idea of bringing me along to Buondelmonte's the next day in my motley, as a walking insult. He ordered me not to tell anybody, so that's why I didn't tell you. After that, they started using me as a message carrier. I hoped they would all forget about me, but obviously they didn't. They hired us for the wedding, it didn't happen, Oddo gave me the token, and I went to his house. Oddo had me talk to the girl, and that's the whole story. He paid me a few coins for the messages, and that's what I've been using to pay for household costs."

Both of them stared at me with their mouths open. All at once I realized just how exhausted, scared, and helpless I felt, and I slumped, cradling my head in my arms on the small table by the fire.

My dejection must have awakened Ghisola's sympathy, because she got up and poured a cup of wine and brought it to me unwatered. "That isn't all of it, is it?" she asked, her voice uncharacteristically gentle. "You're still involved in this, aren't you?"

I took a deep swig. It was neither as sweet nor as smooth as the wine served in the great houses, but its familiar sharpness was reassuring. Plus, it was better than Simone's.

"Yes," I said. I couldn't tell them about my association with Buondelmonte, but it felt good not to be hiding everything any more. "I still have a message to bear. I'm hoping that will be the last of it, but I need some information I haven't been able to get, and I'm worried I won't be able to get it in time. Those people scare me."

"Well, at least they weren't dealing with you instead of me because they had some cockeyed idea that you run our troupe," Neri said, leaning back. "They just knew you because they were already hiring you for errands." He passed me a little dish of olives. "Is the message from Oddo?"

I took an olive and ate it while I thought about what to say. I placed the pit in the cracked dish Ghisola kept on the table. The olive was salty and good, and I realized I was still hungry, so I took a handful. Neri waited, drumming his fingers, not bothering to disguise his impatience.

Now I had to lie again, or at least mislead. If I told them everything, they would be in danger along with me, and I wasn't sure Neri was capable of keeping the story to himself.

"Not Oddo. Somebody a lot less important." Maybe that would put Neri in a better mood. "I wish I could tell you who, but I'm sworn not to reveal who gave me this message. I have to get it to the man it's intended for before Oddo's consortium meets to figure out what to do about Buondelmonte." That such a meeting was in the offing could not come as a surprise to anyone in Florence. That the message came from a woman was not something Neri needed to know.

"The meeting might be tomorrow, or the next day or the day after that, but I haven't been able to find out yet, or to get the message delivered. I'll have to go out first thing in the morning and try again." All three of us looked up at the window in the side wall. Day was waning, but it wasn't yet dark out, and our fire still gave adequate light indoors. Neri's rule was no candle or lamp lit until we could no longer make out colors, and then only tallow, and only if we had need of light in the late hours. I had rented this house before Neri left his wife and moved in with me, but these days he was the one who made the rules. I didn't mind; his rules were as good as any.

"Can't you just go back to the Fifanti palace and ask?" Neri said.

"I don't want to go near that place again. They'll just grab me for some other harebrained errand. It won't be hard to find out when the meeting is going to be, but I have to do it soon so I can get the message delivered on time. First of all I have to know what day, in case it's tomorrow."

"I can find that out for you," Ghisola said. Neri and I both looked at her, surprised.

"You?" he said, chuckling. "Do you have friends in the Fifanti household, then? Or maybe the Uberti?"

"Never you mind where I have friends," she said, flushing a little as she got up from the bench. "I'll have that information for you by morning. See if I don't."

"Where are you going?" Neri asked. "Off to sip a cup of wine with your old friend messer Schiatta, I suppose?"

"Out. I'll be back," she said, and she pulled her cloak down from the rod and was gone before he could order her to stay.

Neri shrugged. "I don't know what she thinks she's doing, but I can go to the market with you tomorrow morning, and between us, we'll find out somehow," he said.

"Thanks, Neri. I can't afford to mess this one up. It wouldn't go well for me if I did." I was grateful for his help, though it still felt strange not to be telling him everything.

"I know you can't tell me who sent the message, but can you tell me who it's for?"

I considered that. I saw no harm in it, and maybe Neri could help. And knowing more would give him satisfaction, Neri being who he was.

"Mosca dei Lamberti."

He gave the three-note whistle that meant he was impressed. "When you start playing with the big boys, you don't mess around, do you?" he said. "Well, we'll go out early and head for the market. We can probably find out just by listening to what people are saying, but if we have to ask around, we can do that, too."

The shadows were growing deeper. In a spirit of generosity Neri lit a candle and put it on the table, thinking, perhaps, to lighten my heavy mood by dispelling the gloom. It guttered and smoked, but it did add a bit of cheer. He asked me many questions about the families, their councils, their palaces. I answered him as well as I could, trying to satisfy his curiosity without telling any more than I had to about my own involvement.

After we had been talking for a while and I had begun to relax, Ghisola returned. She slipped inside and fastened the bolt, then turned and grinned at us, displaying the little gap between her front teeth.

"Here's how you find out whether it's tomorrow or not: go to the corner, look up toward my sister's house, then look at the balcony on the house across from hers. There'll be a laundry line out. Look for a red swaddling cloth. If it's the thing closest to the window, the council is tomorrow. If it's the second thing from the window, it's the next day. If it's the third, it'll be the day after that."

Neri beamed at her. "Well, that beats everything." He got up and went over to her. "How did you do it?" He put his arm around her sturdy shoulders and squeezed, and she smiled up at him.

"My sister's sister-in-law has a cousin whose brother's widow is in service to the Uberti. We just sent a message 'round to the widow, and she'll pass the word through the laundry system."

"Clever girl," said Neri approvingly, and he kissed the top of her head.

I shook my head. All of this plotting and scheming and secrecy on the part of Florence's knights, and meanwhile the women were passing information through their laundry lines. "Ghisola, thanks," I said, meaning it, and she smiled.

Then a thought struck me. "But what happens if it's raining? They won't put laundry out in the rain."

"If it rains, the cousin will send a water boy with the message, but you'll have to pay him."

"Fair enough." I could afford that. I would pay dearly for this information. I would pay more dearly if I failed to obtain it, but thanks to good friends, maybe that wasn't going to happen.

The three of us sat and drank for a while longer while the fire died down. Neri took the long pole and maneuvered the shutters closed on the high window, to keep out the night air. He and Ghisola talked of our information quest as if it was a grand adventure, and I tried not to ruin it for them, but my own feelings were darker. If I could have left them to deal with it, I would have, but I saw no way to extricate myself. I drained my cup and stood up, ready to head for my bed corner and leave my friends some privacy, for it began to look like they would want it. Ghisola flung the contents of the dish of olive pits onto the coals, and the sweet, oily smoke immediately perfumed the house. She cuddled up again next to Neri, and they bade me good night.

It took me a while to fall asleep, with the uninhibited noises Ghisola and Neri were making behind their curtain, but I wished them joy of it and waited patiently for silence and sleep. Tomorrow would be soon enough to find Mosca.

*

All too soon I woke abruptly, to the first hint of predawn light coming through the cracks in the shutter. My housemates were still snoring in their alcove, so I grabbed my cloak and stepped out into the street. The corner, the house across from Ghisola's sister's house, the balcony—and no laundry line. It's too early, I told myself. Laundry lines don't appear till there is sunlight to expose them to. Still I was disappointed, and I returned to the house full of dark premonitions for the day to come. I bustled around the hearth, trying to make enough noise to rouse Neri without seeming to do so on purpose.

When he finally emerged from behind his curtain, yawning and stretching, he looked rested. Must be nice, I thought sourly.

"Laundry out yet?" he asked me.

"Not yet."

"We can go check the line again, and whether it's there or not, we'll head up to the market next and see what we can find out for you. Once you know the day, you'll still need to know the time of it. Missing him by minutes is as bad as missing him by hours." That was true, though I had barely thought that far ahead.

He took the pole and poked the shutter open, and thin light and cold air trickled in. It was day.

We put on our cloaks and went outside. This time the balcony had a line stretched between it and the next window over, with space to hang several garments. Nothing on it yet, though. I swore, and we were just about to give up and head for the market when a young woman appeared on the balcony with a basket balanced on her hip. We stood still and watched her as she shielded her eyes from the sun with her hand, peering off to the east. She must have found whatever she was looking for, because then she began to arrange her laundry: a shirt went up, then a child's tunic, three towels, a chemise, a few rags, all with gaps in between. At last she produced a bright red swaddling cloth and pegged it second in line, beyond the shirt. Then she disappeared inside.

"Not today," we said together. We had a day to work on getting the note to Mosca, and I already felt better.

I was eager to get to the market and find out the rest of what I needed to know, but Neri insisted we go tell Ghisola.

"She's earned it," he said. I couldn't argue with that. "Besides, I want some sturdier shoes." He was still wearing his leather-soled hose. It was colder than the day before; another layer of clothing would not be amiss, so I agreed to a quick stop at the house.

Ghisola was up and pulling on her own cloak when we got back.

"I was just coming to find you," she said. "Did it work? Did you find out?"

Neri told her what we had seen and what we still needed to do, while I grabbed my extra tunic with the warm lining. She nodded in smug satisfaction.

"Usually does work," she said. "You mentioned a chemise. Was it right side up, or upside down?"

I thought back. "Upside down," I told her. "Was that a message too?"

Ghisola cackled. "Yes, but not for you." Neri, who was lacing up his outdoor shoes, looked up curiously and opened his mouth to speak, but I steered him toward the door. We needed to get going.

Ghisola reached for her cloak again. "I need a few things," she said. "Maybe I should come with you."

"Come another time, love. We're spies today. Besides, it's cold," said Neri, patting her backside in a proprietary sort of way. She stood on tiptoe to give him a quick kiss, and left her cloak on the rod.

"Take the basket, then, and get me a sausage and some lentils, if Ceci is there—his are good." Ghisola had laid in her usual prudent supply of dried beans and lentils before the winter, but Neri had upset a cup of water into the lentil barrel, and the result had been mold and spoilage. She had patiently picked over the survivors and rescued all she could, but now we had run out. "And see if you can get me a bundle of kitchen rags. Mind that they're clean, if you do." She took the basket off its peg and handed it to him. "I'll get the bread at the bakeshop." She settled in for a quiet day of spinning in front of the hearth, and finally we were off.

13. MARKET

Neri and I split up to see what we could overhear. Between us we probably knew most of the people in the market piazza, so I thought our chances of finding what we needed were good.

The marketplace is vast. Covered permanent stalls ring its perimeter, and many temporary selling stations crowd the middle—everything from flimsy tables with makeshift cloth awnings to sturdy collapsible wooden structures. The market traffic is heaviest in the early morning, so we were there at the perfect time.

Even in the winter Florence's market is raucous and bustling, from the time the city's gates open for the day until its activities finally cease many hours later. It's an endlessly entertaining, ever-changing stew of sights and sounds and smells. Everything you could possibly need, most of what you might want, and some things you could well fear are there somewhere. Ordinary shopping, clandestine gambling, whores soliciting business, singers, pipe-and-tabor players, puppeteers, preachers, poets, trained animals—all there. Once the weather turned warm and the fruit and vegetable sellers returned, it would be even more packed with people, for the city's population grew with every year, until I wondered how we all managed to fit within her walls.

I strolled through a steady stream of news and gossip. Not surprisingly, much of it had to do with the Oddo-Buondelmonte affair, and it was easy enough to find out what I needed to know: the meeting would be the following day, confirming what the laundry had told us; the location, the parish church of Santa Maria sopra Porta, as I knew from Selvaggia; and the key piece of information now fell into place, which was that the council was to be held at the hour of Sext.

Now all I had to do was get my message to Mosca, and I had more than a day to accomplish that. I scanned the crowd for Neri and saw him walking toward me munching a crisp chickpea fritter. He offered me one from the napkin-wrapped package in his basket and I took it and ate it while he told me what he had learned about the meeting time. He wasn't surprised to find I already knew it.

"Everybody's talking about it," he said, popping another fritter into his mouth. "There'll be a crowd at the church tomorrow just to watch who goes in."

I looked in the basket. He'd found the sausage Ghisola asked for, and when I poked the muslin bag, the lentils inside made a swishing sound.

But we still needed kitchen rags.

The ragsellers were all in one area of the market, not scattered around like most of the other vendors. Two of their number had adjacent permanent stalls, and the others set up nearby for companionship and competition. Each hawked his own wares and insulted the others', but by and large they were a good-natured bunch and they enjoyed each other's company, even if their camaraderie mostly amounted to trading coarse insults.

We didn't know which seller Ghisola preferred, so Neri just called out to the lot of them, "Who's got clean kitchen rags, eh?"

Naturally, they all did. One of them was a young woman, bold and friendly, and it didn't take much to persuade Neri to look at her wares. The others responded by calling her a slut and worse. Their words were harsh, but the tone was not. After a little banter back and forth and some haggling ("For that coin, you'd be lucky to get women's rags and rags for the privy, let alone good clean kitchen rags." "Clean, you say? Let's have a sniff, then. Look greasy to me.") we came away with Ghisola's rags, neatly bundled.

"Now," I said, helping myself to another fritter, "all we have to do is get this message to Mosca, between now and Sext tomorrow."

"That's all, is it?" said Neri. "I thought you couldn't get anybody to answer there all day yesterday."

"That was yesterday. Let's go try again."

Neri shook his head. "When I think about the choice between standing around some high mucketymuck's palace door trying to get his attention, or getting this sausage back to Ghisola in time for it to be in our dinner, I think my duty is clear." He offered another fritter, holding up his index finger to indicate "one." I took it—it was still warm, though just barely—and Neri was off, with a grin and a wave.

My mood darkened immediately. It had been a relief to have his company for a part of this venture, and I wanted him with me for the next, more difficult part. But he had his own day to plan, and little reason to think that accompanying an errand boy would do much to ingratiate him with the people with surnames. I could only be grateful for his help and Ghisola's so far, and grateful that I no longer had to keep everything a secret, even if the full extent of the danger wasn't something I was free to share with them.

Leaving the disorderly corner where the raucous ragsellers held forth, I made my way through the crowd toward an area of the market where more upscale vendors set up their stalls, thinking that the sort of people who might know Mosca's whereabouts were more likely to congregate there. I passed a table with skillfully-carved wooden kitchen implements—Ghisola would have been tempted—and another displaying luxury leather goods, though none so fine as Lippo's work, in my opinion.

My goal was a sprawling semi-permanent stall displaying fine mercers' goods. All I had to do was follow the fiddle music, for this merchant often hired entertainers to draw customers to his stall. He had hired me a few times, but once after an hour had passed in which I collected more coins than he did, he dismissed me as too much of a distraction.

His goods attracted shoppers with fat purses. Finely-stitched linen coifs and veils so delicate they were transparent, brilliantly-colored woven belts, silk purses and sturdy aprons, lacings in every color, embroidery threads and needles, patterned cushions, enamelled studs and fastenings, children's linens, and the costly gloves and stockings he sold for a healthy commission from their makers, all competing for attention, artfully arranged on lengths of fine wool in rich greens and blues, or hanging from rods attached to the wooden frame of his stall, under a generous awning of the same vivid colors of sky and meadow. His display extended the length of two long trestle tables.

Unusually, only one small group of customers stood in front of the stall, five men and a woman. Otherwise the marketgoers held back, though not so far back that they couldn't watch that little knot of shoppers. The fiddler kept playing his repetitious saltarello, but instead of crowding the stall as usual, the other marketgoers left the six customers a wide berth. The crowd was restless, murmuring and glancing nervously around, and one woman crossed herself as she stared wide-eyed at the backs of the six.

I approached from the side, curious about who might spark such interest among the marketgoers. The shoppers' backs were to me and I did not recognize them, though I saw that one of the men was richly dressed. His cloak was a fine dark blue, and a costly fur-lined hood trailed down his back.

Something about him was familiar to me. As I was trying to figure out why, he turned my way, and even as I registered whose face was grinning at me, his all-too-familiar voice said, "Fool."

Buondelmonte.

"My lord," I managed to say, inclining my head, and the others turned toward me too. The woman was Elisa, in her dove gray gown and a dark mantle with a hood. Her eyes were wide and frightened, darting around the crowd as if she feared an attack any moment. Sensible girl. What in hell were they doing in a public place? Were any of Oddo's people in this crowd? If they were, would they act? Thank God and all the saints that Oddo had not yet held his meeting, at least. Surely, surely nothing would happen in the market. I felt myself start to sweat.

Two of the men I recognized as a couple of Buondelmonte's young retainers. One of them carried a basket, and both had formidable knives, just shy of swords, tucked in their belts. They, too, scanned the crowd, and the one without the basket kept his hand hovering near the hilt of his knife.

The other two I also recognized, as anyone in Florence would have, but I had never thought to associate them with Buondelmonte: Dino and Vanni, a pair of thugs, two brothers from Pistoia who lived by hiring themselves out as protectors of those who believed themselves endangered. They were good at what they did. They had a reputation for dirty fighting, for they had worked as strong-arm men and enforcers for wealthy merchants back in Pistoia, and they left because even that lawless city would no longer tolerate their tactics. Vanni bore a livid scar across his left cheek, and Dino lacked most of his front teeth. They were always together, always armed, and they had few friends. Both were physically powerful men, not noted for intellect or wit. And right now they were watching me suspiciously, reminding me of nothing so much as a pair of vicious, hungry guard dogs.

"Come here, Fool, and look at what I've bought," said Buondelmonte, motioning me closer. He was the only one in the area who seemed perfectly relaxed, except possibly for the merchant, who must have figured that whatever happened would eventually attract business. I came closer and nodded to Elisa, who gave me a wan, anxious smile.

Buondelmonte reached over to the basket the young man was holding and plucked a white cloth off the top. He rummaged around and pulled out an elegant pewter cup. "See, this is for Lippo. I'm buying the wedding gifts for my lady's household, and I thought this would please him."

"I'm sure it will, my lord," I murmured. All of my instincts told me to scan the crowd for danger, but four men plus Elisa were already doing that, so I resigned myself to having a conversation with Buondelmonte and leaving security to the professionals—and to the poor scared girl who so plainly didn't want to be there.

As he showed me trinkets and as I dutifully admired them, I wondered if a knight with Buondelmonte's considerable training in war could really be so unconcerned for his safety, or if this was all for show. I watched his face as he talked, and I realized that even as he spoke with casual

101

nonchalance, he was moving his eyes systematically back and forth over the crowd, every now and then shifting to face in a slightly different direction. He had a knife at his belt too, one with an ornate hilt, but the blade was made for business. It wasn't the weapon that had fatefully scratched Oddo, but a longer, more no-nonsense version. And what finally convinced me that he wasn't as unconcerned as I had first thought was a glimpse of an iron gorget at his throat, all but hidden by his fur-lined mantle. Now that I looked more closely, I saw a telltale bulkiness under his garment. He was armored. Nothing as obvious as chain mail, or as useful, but at least a padded perpunto under his clothing.

That made me feel a little better, but I still didn't want to be here, with half of Florence watching me talk with Buondelmonte even as I carried in my sleeve the note that could spell his doom. I started to excuse myself, but he would have none of it.

"We're looking for a gift for the old woman now," he told me. "Elisa thinks she might accept an apron, and I'm thinking we ought to find a nice one here. Elisa!" he said, and the girl started. "See if you can find an apron she'll like. The very best one he's got, and then let me know how much you need." He turned back to me as she obediently flicked through the snowy white aprons hanging on a rod, gently feeling each hem between thumb and forefinger while the merchant fed her a steady stream of sales talk. It had never occurred to me that anyone would buy an apron, for such simple garments were usually made at home. But I guess wealthy people will buy anything.

Buondelmonte's shopping had not been limited to the marketplace. He showed me a string of pearls and a silver-and-gilt girdle with semi-precious stones, gifts for Fiammetta and Isabella, extravagances which could only have been purchased in a jeweler's shop. As he showed off his prizes, Vanni and Dino and the two retainers kept up their surveillance of the crowd.

"Messer Buondelmonte, the young lady has made her choice," said the merchant, his voice oozing with obsequiousness. "The finest linen, bleached in the sun for many weeks." He held up a roomy apron with an ingenious five-pocket design. Two pockets opened on the sides, so the wearer could slide either hand in, and the middle three opened at the top, the central one wider and deeper than the others. Buondelmonte nodded and handed over a handful of small coins.

"What more can I show you, my lord?" the merchant asked. Buondelmonte put a finger to his lips, caught my eye, and pointed to Elisa, who was studying a handsome tablet-woven belt, luxuriously long and with a lozenge design in blue and purple extending the entire length. She reached out and touched it tentatively, then quickly withdrew her hand and turned away. It was fine work, but it must have been costly.

"Now go to that stall over there and pick up a bag of honeyed almonds, if you'd be so kind, Elisa. My lady is fond of them," he said, handing her a coin, and Elisa smiled a silent farewell to me and did as he bade her. The rigidity in her shoulders relaxed as she moved away from him.

"We'll take that belt too," he said, pointing to the one Elisa had admired, "and wrap it." The merchant smiled, deftly coiled it and wrapped it in a square of muslin, and handed it over to the knight, murmuring an outrageous price.

Buondelmonte winked at me. "I've been trying to figure out what she wanted all morning, but she kept insisting she didn't need anything," he said, handing the wrapped belt to the man holding the basket. "It will look well on her gray gown."

I didn't think I could bear much more of this. That scrap of vellum was all but scorching me from its hiding place, and right now I did not want to see Buondelmonte as a human being. The merchant was doing his level best to persuade the spendthrift nobleman to throw in a pair of gloves and a couple of coifs, and as far as I know he succeeded, because I took advantage of the distraction to speak a quick farewell and make my escape. I felt Dino's and Vanni's eyes on my back as I hurried away.

I shook my head to clear it, wishing I could erase that entire encounter, for it was time to try Mosca's again. I skirted the edge of the market and dodged a street preacher and his growing audience, and again I found myself looking up at Mosca's forbidding front door. I approached it and knocked. Still no reply. I pounded again, waited in vain, and then I backed up, this time colliding with a boy struggling along under a heavy sack of grain. I peered up at the windows high above the street, and I was sure I saw motion behind one of them. It could have been a person—wondering, perhaps, who was banging on the door. I might have suggested an easy way to find out.

This was beginning to drive me mad. I had to get that note to Mosca, and I would dearly love to do it soon and be done with it. Then they could have their murderous council and do what damage they chose, and I would not be involved in it.

Except, of course, I would be. If I didn't deliver this note, a chance remained for Buondelmonte to escape with his life. True, someone else might hold out for a fatal outcome even if Mosca never learned Selvaggia's wishes, but it seemed less likely. Cooler heads would surely prevail. I was no expert in these matters, but even I could think of many sound reasons for not launching a lethal vendetta. Most of the chatter in the marketplace held that we would see some sort of revenge, but no killing. "It was only a wound to the arm and a bit of a flap about a couple of women," I heard one man point out to another.

But if I didn't get the note to Mosca, Selvaggia would tell Oddo I worked for Buondelmonte and knew of the jilting beforehand, and that would be it for my "miserable, pathetic life," as Buondelmonte had called it. Especially if Oddo somehow got wind of my conversation with Buondelmonte in the marketplace, and God knows enough people had witnessed it. And while I didn't want to see the big handsome idiot dead even if he deserved to be, even more than that I didn't want to be dead myself. No help for it: now, more than ever, that note had to get to Mosca.

I looked at that door again, as if staring at it hard enough would release its bolt and cause it to swing open on its mighty hinges so I could stroll inside. It didn't.

Again I thought I saw movement behind one of the windows above. All right, then, I'd get their attention another way. I scooped a handful of small stones up from the street, drew my arm back, and took careful aim. But before I could fling my missiles through Mosca's window, a sharp tug on my elbow from behind made me drop the stones with a clatter and nearly toppled me over.

"I wouldn't do that, if I were you," said the man who had grabbed me, as I spun around to confront him. "Not a good idea at all." His tone was mild, but at a head taller than me, he could afford to be mild.

"Yes, you would, if you were me." I spat. "There's no other way to get anybody to answer."

I knew this man, though I couldn't remember from where. He had probably been with Mosca on our trip to see Buondelmonte, or perhaps I had seen him at the Fifanti home. He was the Lamberti's man, I did remember that much. He'd been wearing blue and gold livery, before. He recognized me, too, and his mouth quirked in a lopsided smile.

"Looking for the master, were you?" he said.

"Yes. Got a message for him."

He stuck his hand out. "Give it."

"Can't. My instructions are to hand it to him directly." Selvaggia had been adamant on that point, understandably.

He shrugged. "Not going to happen, friend. Not today. You know where he'll be tomorrow?"

104

"Yes." So did everyone in Florence.

"You can give it to him then, but he won't be back in town before that."

"Why didn't they answer the front door?" I asked irritably.

"Orders. When the master's away, nobody gets in, so what's the point of answering?" The logic of that eluded me, but it was clear that I couldn't accomplish any more until the next day, so I bade him farewell and set off for home, trying not to think about Mosca and to dwell instead on something pleasant, like the sausage, instead.

I didn't get far, though, before I saw something that made me stop short. Ahead of me was Neri, his back to me, talking to a woman. He should have been home by now, I thought. With Neri between us I couldn't see who the woman was, but her bright orangey-rose skirt wasn't anything Ghisola owned. Something made me duck into a recessed doorway and stay back, watching.

On the surface there was nothing particularly odd about it. Neri knew people all over town, and before Ghisola came into his life he had had his share of women. He'd even been known to seek out a friendly whore sometimes, when he was otherwise unattached, and he still greeted all these women cordially when he saw them, and they him.

Something in his posture, though, put me on alert. It didn't seem likely he was negotiating with a whore now, but not many respectable women would wear a color like that, and whoever she was, she was standing very close.

And then Neri shifted his weight and I glimpsed her angry face. Not a whore, but Duccia, Neri's estranged wife. Or perhaps she had started to charge for what she used to give away for free, and the term applied after all.

This was not a friendly exchange. Neri held one arm stiffly at his side, his fist clenching and unclenching, the other arm still carrying the market basket, and Duccia appeared to be talking furiously. She wasn't shouting, or I would have heard her from my doorway, but she glared at him and her mouth moved busily.

At one point she reached out and grabbed the arm holding the market basket. He shook her off, turned his back on her, and walked away with long strides. She scurried after him, grabbed him again, and he shoved her away. Then I did hear her, shrilly calling him names most women wouldn't have uttered. He kept going, and eventually she stopped dogging his steps, raised her fist in the fig at his retreating back, and flounced off around a corner.

I emerged from the doorway and started walking again, slowly, thinking about what I had seen. It was disturbing. Duccia had been a disruptive influence in Neri's life from the moment he met her, and he should never have married her. He had been infatuated, though, and wouldn't listen to me. Seeing her with him made me uneasy, and I wondered if he would say anything about the encounter when I got home.

I found Ghisola cooking and Neri sitting on the bench looking sullen. He was taciturn, returning my greeting with a monosyllable. Ghisi caught my eye and shrugged a little.

We spent a quiet evening engaged in our separate activities, which in Neri's case involved drinking several cups of wine. I had hoped one or both of them would be coming with me the next morning to Santa Maria sopra Porta, but it didn't seem like the time to ask, so it looked like I was going to be on my own.

14. A THING DONE

It was well before Sext the next day when I arrived at the tiny piazza in front of Santa Maria sopra Porta, a few paces north of the bridge. I should have been in plenty of time to catch up with Mosca before the council, but already the square was suspiciously full of people. Some of the onlookers made an effort to look as if they had good reason to be there, but most unabashedly settled in to watch. Unsmiling men stood at both of the open doors of the ancient church, and several knights were already in the piazza, talking quietly. I didn't think anyone had gone inside yet, but I couldn't be sure.

Lambertuccio was there. His fur-lined cloak sported the bold red and gold stripes of the Amidei, so obviously related to the single red stripe on gold that identified the Fifanti. This was the Amidei parish church and that family was its principal patron, so Lambertuccio's people would be, in effect, the hosts of this meeting.

I recognized the four men at the doors as Schiatta degli Uberti's men. My pulse sped up as I realized the Uberti intended to play a major part in whatever was to come. When that large and mighty family consortium became involved, the seriousness of the matter rose to a new level.

The Uberti were universally feared and respected; their attempt to claim lordship over Florence a generation ago had come within a hair of succeeding, and even their allies weren't altogether sure whether or when they might try it again. Some said Florence could do a lot worse, especially now that Schiatta headed the family, but those who favored keeping the city a consular commune—or who would like to rule it themselves—thought Schiatta nothing less than a demon from Hell.

I heard a commotion, and the crowd parted to make way for a half-dozen men on horseback. Oddo rode in their lead, and several other men of the Fifanti lineage, elaborately dressed and grim-faced, followed close behind him. The people in their path drew back respectfully. The Amidei men came forward to greet the newcomers, and Oddo dismounted. He embraced Lambertuccio briefly, a greeting between kinsmen.

Next to arrive were the Conti Gangalandi, also mounted but coming from the south. They must have come from their property in the countryside, across the bridge. As usual, they stayed bunched tightly together, their austere garments reminiscent of an earlier, more primitive time. Oddo and Lambertuccio together made a show of welcoming them.

But where was Mosca? Many men had already gathered, although

I hadn't yet seen the Uberti or the Lamberti, and the time set for the meeting was approaching. I began to fear that Mosca was inside already, though none of the men whose arrivals we had witnessed had yet entered.

The church was old and small, and I wondered how it could hold so many men. Most of them had arrived on foot, for their homes were not far away. The Conti Gangalandi and Oddo's people left their horses in care of their men. A few finally began to enter the church, though Oddo and Lambertuccio remained outside to greet new arrivals. By now I was fighting down panic. Had I missed Mosca?

At last I saw a party of mounted men in the Lamberti blue and gold approaching. I squinted to see whether Mosca was with them, but I couldn't find him. A heavyset man I recognized as one of Mosca's kinsmen was leading the Lamberti contingent. They arrived, dismounted, and were welcomed as the others had been, but Mosca was not among them. My panic rose, and my breathing was quick and shallow.

Schiatta and his men arrived, on foot. People fell back to let the tall, stern-faced man pass, and he strode through the piazza without a glance to either side. He had an air of power and purpose that managed to subdue the crowd's festival mood without a word or a gesture. Oddo and Lambertuccio welcomed him, and he clasped hands with both of them.

My own attention, however, kept returning to the Lamberti. Where was Mosca? He had to be here, and I had to get him my message. Little time remained. The rest of the Lamberti and most of the others entered the church, leaving Oddo, Lambertuccio, and Schiatta huddled in intense conversation outside.

I looked to the north, from whence the rest of the Lamberti had come. Surely this council wouldn't begin without Mosca, and surely he wouldn't have arrived before his family and hidden himself away inside while the others strutted in the piazza.

From the west the bells chimed for Sext. Oddo and the others looked up and to the north. After a few more words among themselves, they turned to enter the church, Schiatta first speaking to his men guarding the door that faced the square.

I felt sick as I watched the men draw the door closed behind the leaders. Mosca had not come. My stomach knotted and my head began to ache again, and my scalp itched.

If he avoided the meeting, could she blame me? Yes, because I was supposed to have given him her message ahead of time. Never mind that it had not been possible to do so; she'd blame me.

Through my distress I heard an excited murmur from the crowd, and

I saw a lone rider trotting briskly into the square, coming from the south. It was Mosca at last, and from the look of him, he had galloped into the city and taken the bridge at a canter before slowing down for the narrow street that followed. I'd like to have seen the chaos such a ride must have caused. His dark hair was plastered to his head, his robe askew, and his sleek black mount's sides heaved, glistening with sweat.

Mosca dismounted like a dancer, motioned for one of the horseholders to take his reins, and loped toward the church. By then I was on my way, holding the message out and calling to him.

"My lord!"

Several of the henchmen moved to stop me, but Mosca heard me and turned. I halted in front of a protective line of very large armed men and brandished the note over my head.

He scowled, but motioned me forward. "Let him through."

Too late, it occurred to me that his absence and last-minute arrival might have been an attempt to avoid receiving another message from Selvaggia. If so, he would not appreciate my waving it in the air in front of this crowd.

The line of men melted away, and I walked toward him, all eyes on me. All right, waving that note around had not exactly been subtle. But in a matter of seconds I would hand it off to him and be free to go, safe again, having done what was required of me. And I would never have to talk to these people again.

"Hurry up," Mosca barked. By that time, the guards had opened the doors again and were ushering him through. I caught up with him, thinking to hand him the message and back away, but instead, to my dismay, he grabbed my sleeve to pull me inside with him.

I squawked an incoherent protest and dug in my heels, but to no avail. He pulled and I skidded along behind him, my shoes scraping on the stone pavement, my gorge rising in my throat. I looked back at the crowd, and to my surprise I saw Neri and Ghisola, newly arrived in the piazza, staring back at me. Their mouths were open in comically identical round O's as they watched me disappear into the church.

The door shut firmly behind me, and I swallowed hard. It took a few seconds for my eyes to adjust, after the bright daylight outside, but I could tell that the church was full of men, smelling of horses and wool and too many male bodies close together.

Mosca still had me by the arm, and he dragged me over to a pool of light under one of the high windows. He plucked Selvaggia's note from my hand unceremoniously and opened it, still gripping my left sleeve.

The heavy bolt on the door fell into place with a thud. Too late—I would be attending this council, as unwillingly as I had attended the last one. More unwillingly, in truth.

Oddo, Lambertuccio, and Schiatta stood in front of the altar, still conferring among themselves. Light from the main window over the altar fell on them, like torchlight illuminating the actors in a mystery play.

Next to me, Mosca made a sound of disgust and grimaced. "Vicious bitch!" he muttered under his breath. The man on his other side glanced at him curiously. Mosca made the note disappear into his sleeve and turned his back on the onlooker, who shrugged and turned away.

"You know what she wants, don't you, Fool?" Mosca said. His mouth was a thin line, his eyes hard.

I nodded. "She wants him dead. She told me." We kept our voices low, and our conversation was only one of many as men waited for the meeting to commence. We made certain we were not overheard.

"Dead, and it's up to me to make sure it happens. It's not good enough to let the families decide, like in any normal conflict. No, it has to be her way."

For the first time, I was beginning to sympathize with Neri's raging curiosity, for I was burning to ask Mosca why he had to obey the girl. But I was afraid. She had a hold on him, and maybe I didn't want to know the nature of it. After all, she had a hold on me, too, and I wasn't about to share that with Mosca. Let him think I was just in it for the pay.

"When will it happen?" I asked. Maybe even if Mosca persuaded the men to call a vendetta they would take no immediate action. That could give Buondelmonte and Gualdrada time to sort things out later, somehow.

"Who knows? We can't do it during Lent, or Easter week, because the bishop would have our heads. We'd be exiled, at a bare minimum, and more likely excommunicated. No, it'll have to wait that long, at least. She can't expect otherwise."

"Why can't it be done before Lent?" I bit my tongue. True, that would avoid the penitential season, with all its emphasis on peacemaking, but I didn't want to encourage them.

"Buondelmonte's not in town any more. He and his people went to their villa yesterday. He won't be back before Holy Week, and we can't get to him out there."

I had a thought, at once reassuring and disturbing. "These men may not even agree to kill him," I ventured.

"They'll agree," Mosca said grimly. He scowled as Oddo stepped forward to speak. "We'll worry about the timing once this part is done. Right now, I need to concentrate." He turned his attention to the men in front of the altar.

Oddo spread his arms wide, his eyes sweeping the crowd. He pitched his voice to carry to the back wall of the church.

"You all know why we are here. You know what insult has been done to all of us by this arrogant and stupid knight."

Not a bad description, I thought.

"He has shamed us all, and honor leaves us no choice but to respond. Today we—you, my family, my friends, my allies—will decide how to cleanse this shame and right this wrong. We will be avenged and our honor restored, this I promise you."

"Honor!" someone shouted, and an old man thumped his walking stick vigorously on the floor as others called out their support and encouragement.

Oddo waited for the men to be quiet, then went on to sketch what had happened. He used few words, but they were words chosen to stir passions—words of honor besmirched, of broken promises, of peace denied, insult given. The mood of the crowd was restless, indignant, with simmering anger barely below the surface.

Then the venerable Lambertuccio rose to speak, his luxuriant gray hair catching the light like a corona around his haggard face. I was not prepared for his fiery eloquence, and I think I was not the only one taken by surprise.

"My noble daughter, left standing at the church! Rejected, as if she were not good enough for him. It could have been any of your daughters, my friends," with a sweeping gesture that took in all the men standing in the church. "Think how you would feel, if your own kin was treated so. And so it has been, for all of you are kin to us, by blood, by marriage, or by solemn alliance. This insult done my daughter shames us all." He looked at the Amidei group in the front of the crowd, which included his son and two sons-in-law, as well as the usual assortment of brothers, cousins, uncles, and others allied by marriage.

An ominous rumbling began among his listeners.

"Are we to be treated so by this arrogant Buondelmonte? Will we stand for this? Not only has he broken his promise, shamed us in the eyes of all of Florence, and violated the peace he agreed to, but he has wed a woman of the Donati, a family with no love for any man here." A louder rumble greeted these words.

"My daughter, my flesh and blood, dragged into this man's foul schemes." Lambertuccio lowered his leonine head to his chest, and his powerful voice broke as he said softly, "I would she had been spared this."

This show of pathos inflamed the crowd, and here and there a man called out for vengeance. Next to me, Mosca raised an eyebrow and sniffed. I don't think he saw Selvaggia as a victim, exactly.

Lambertuccio raised his eyes and lifted his arms dramatically. "My kinsmen, my friends—I say to you, there must indeed be vengeance," he thundered, to shouts and raised fists. "We must erase this shame!"

Oddo watched him with an expression of mild bemusement, as if he hadn't expected such rhetorical heights, but he added nothing.

Then Schiatta stepped forward. By then, nothing less would have quieted the agitated crowd, but Schiatta's presence claimed instant silence.

"Good my lords," he began in a voice fully an octave lower than that of any other man in the room, "all of us know that Buondelmonte must pay. We meet today only to decide the price, and in what coin." Mosca shifted at my side.

"It is for the offended families to decide," Schiatta went on. "Whatever you choose, I tell you now you have the full support of the Uberti." This elicited cheers, and among them, to my alarm, I heard the war cries of some of the families.

Oddo stepped forward and stood next to Schiatta. "What say you?" he asked the men in the church.

"Fine him!"

"Banish him!"

"Beat him soundly, for the base knave he is."

"Wound him in the face! Scar him and shame him!"

"Blood for blood!"

"Kill him!"

That last came from a young hothead in the Amidei group. Several men began to argue, all speaking at once. Mosca watched them intently.

"Are we prepared for a full vendetta?" said an older man among the Conti Gangalandi, his voice carrying over the rest. "We are at peace now, albeit a shaky peace. Is it for this reason that we will break that peace?"

Lambertuccio glared at the speaker. "Is my daughter's honor not reason enough? Is not all of our honor reason enough?" The crowd was once again paying close attention.

The Gangalandi count held up both hands in a placating gesture. "Yes, my friend, of course it is, but the safety of all of our families may depend on what we decide here. If we cause a death, inevitably some among us will die in our turn. A vendetta cannot be stopped when people decide they've had enough. It rolls along under its own power, destroying as it goes. It is no small thing to call for a death, if an answering insult could suffice."

By now all the men were talking among themselves, debating what was being said. The thrum of voices was getting steadily louder.

Mosca left my side and moved swiftly to the front, nodded to the three men standing before the altar, and turned to face the crowd. He held up his hands for silence, and got it. This was it, I thought. Buondelmonte's death warrant.

"Buondelmonte's family does not support him in his action," Mosca declared in his silken voice. "They are angered that he acted without counsel, and rightly so." His audience reacted with murmurs of surprise, for it was unusual for families to fail to offer support in such matters.

"If we wound him, they will have to oppose us," he went on, his words carrying effortlessly. "If we hound him from the city, they cannot let him go unsupported. If we exact a financial penalty, as kin they must back him." His eyes scanned the crowd, giving little signs of acknowledgment here and there.

"But if he dies, will they seek other deaths to avenge him, after he has acted alone? It is too much. I say they will not." That voice, like soothing oil.

Shouting erupted among the younger men. Mosca was swaying the crowd. Oddo and Lambertuccio exchanged a glance, but Schiatta, his face impassive, looked steadily out at the men. He folded his arms across his chest and stood like a rock, his legs a little apart, his eyes searching the faces before him.

"Let him die!"

"He deserves death!"

"Death for his insult!"

Excited voices vied with one another to be heard, but Mosca's floated above them all, his diction crisp and clear:

"A thing done has an end." Oil can ignite, as well as soothe.

The crowd roared. Their shouting soon coalesced into a rhythmic chant: "End it! End it! End it!"

The chanting went on and on. Mosca, Oddo, Lambertuccio, and Schiatta conferred briefly among themselves, and finally Oddo raised his hands for silence. It required first Lambertuccio, then Mosca, and finally Schiatta himself to repeat the gesture before the din subsided.

Oddo spoke. "My friends, you have decided," he declared. "It is the will of this council that Buondelmonte shall die." He raised his hands again to forestall more shouting. "It will be done. How and where it will be done we do not yet know, but we will send word to all of you. And now messer Schiatta will speak." Oddo stepped aside and Schiatta came forward, his spare frame straight as a rod, taller even than Mosca.

"My lords, you have given your judgment," said that bottomless voice. "This deed must be done, and it must be done with honor. I claim the right to enact this vengeance for messer Oddo, who sustained the first injury. I claim it also for messer Lambertuccio, whose daughter suffered intolerable insult. And I claim it for myself. Will any among you gainsay us?" I noticed he gave no reason for including himself, but it didn't matter to the crowd. For these men, having the Uberti with them was tantamount to having God's own endorsement.

Pandemonium erupted. The men cheered, the Amidei, Fifanti, and Uberti groups each trying to outshout the others. Even some of the Conti Gangalandi were caught up in the general enthusiasm, but not the old man who had spoken earlier, whose mouth was clamped grimly shut.

The meeting devolved into a strategy session. Oddo told the men again that once a plan was in place, the families would be notified. In response to questions, he said he thought it unlikely that anything would happen before Easter, as too little time remained before Lent. The Florentines wouldn't look with favor upon vengeance enacted during the holy season, no matter how justified, and in any case Buondelmonte had taken his bride to his country estate, putting them out of reach for the time being.

At long last the meeting started to break up. One of Oddo's men rapped on the church door, and the guards outside hauled the heavy doors open. The attendees filed out, but Mosca stayed behind, talking earnestly with Oddo and Lambertuccio. I slipped through the door just after the Conti Gangalandi and looked around to see if Neri and Ghisola were still there, but the sun's position told me that at least two hours had passed, and the crowd was smaller than it had been. Neri and Ghisola were not part of it, so I trudged on home, my steps heavy and my head full of all I had just witnessed.

15. CARNIVAL

I wondered whether Neri and Ghisola would have learned the out-come of Oddo's council by the time I got home. I wondered, too, how they would feel if they guessed the nature of my message from the outcome of the council. I did not think it would sit well with them.

Before long everyone in Florence would know, for vendettas were never meant to be secret. Part of their sinister effectiveness was their public nature. Honor was not served unless everyone knew what was to come, and why. Thus the intended victim either went about his business as a marked man, protecting himself as best he could, or he shamed himself and his family by running away. Or he tried to broker a peace, if his family had the right friends. Most did not.

Years might pass before a vendetta was fulfilled, which made for serious disruptions in the lives of entire families. That was part of the power of a vendetta. But if Mosca had anything to say about it, this was one vendetta that would be enacted without delay.

The gossip had arrived before me, and so had our neighbors. Bicci's dog waited outside—Ghisola wouldn't let him in—so our next door neigh-bor must be within. I found him sitting with Simone the tavernkeeper at our hearth, both of them leaning forward, one man's words tumbling out over the other's as they recounted their news between swallows of wine. Their free hands waved erratically in the air, trying to illustrate the rush of words. Neri and Ghisola listened, their faces expressionless, both of them uncharacteristically silent. I shut the door behind me and took off my cloak, tossing it over the rod next to the door, and joined them on the bench.

"They'll get him, you'll see," Simone said. He turned to me. "The knight, Buondelmonte, I mean. Do you know about it?" Simone loved to be the one to convey news. I nodded, and a flicker of disappointment crossed his face. Oh, yes. I knew.

"Well, they can't, can they, as long as he hides out of town," said Bicci.

"Oh, it's hiding, is it?" said Simone with a sneer. "So if that lot had you marked for a nasty death, you'd just saunter through the streets minding your own business and hoping for the best."

Bicci laughed. "In the first place, that lot wouldn't call a vendetta against the likes of me. They'd squash me like a bug. But Buondelmonte's a knight, for the love of Christ. He's supposed to be able to take care of himself. And he's got family, too. It's not like he's all alone in this."

Was he? Mosca had said he was, but on sober reflection, I agreed with Bicci. The wedding procession had included not only the reluctant Gherardo but several more Buondelmonti men as well, and Gualdrada's brothers-in-law and other men of the Donati. They may not have approved of Buondelmonte's action, but they were there, as family should be. Would they support him in this disastrous marriage, yet not back him in the vendetta that resulted?

"He won't stay away forever. He's got business in town, and his house is here, and his new wife's people are here. Sooner or later he'll relax and come back, and they'll get him, sure enough." Simone banged his fist on the bench for emphasis.

How had word reached this part of town even before I did? I hadn't been the first one out of the church, but I was still surprised at how fast the news had traveled. Probably the women's laundry lines were telling the tale by now. I'd have to ask Ghisola later which garments added up to a death sentence.

"What do you think, then?" Simone asked me. "Deserves it, doesn't he?"

I didn't want to get into this. "Don't know. I don't pay attention to the knights' affairs," I said, and Neri snorted. Bicci raised an eyebrow at that, though Simone seemed oblivious.

I didn't know what Neri's problem was, but I had little patience for it. A man was going to die—a man I had walked with, who was vigorous, headstrong, in love, and robustly alive. I had watched the men at that meeting and heard their council, and I no longer saw any hope for Buondelmonte. Simone was right. They'd get him, sooner or later. Even if Neri hated that thought as much as I did, he knew my part in all of it was unwilling, so why this contemptuous, angry attitude? But I had no intention of confronting him while others were present.

"I'm going to bed," I said, standing up.

Neri, too, stood. "Not yet. We need to talk," he said coldly, and shot a look at Bicci and Simone. This time, even Simone caught on. Taking their cue, they handed their cups back to Ghisola, made their farewells, and left.

"Ghisola, go to bed," said Neri as the door closed behind them, and without a word she went, pulling the curtain shut behind her. He motioned for me to sit on the bench with him, and after a moment's hesitation I sat, but on the stool, a few feet away. He folded his arms across his chest and glared at me.

"We know what happened," he said. Well, that was obvious. "We

116

know what they decided, and we know what Mosca said."

A thing done has an end. I couldn't shake the feeling that this thing, once done, had no end any of us would live to see.

"It was because of the note to Mosca, wasn't it?" he said. He was looking at me as if I were something unclean. "This happened because of what you did."

That was more than I could accept. Not everything that happened in this turbulent city was my fault. "The note wasn't the only reason it went the way it did. Plenty of people wanted it this way. They could have reached the same decision if there had never been a note," I told him, not bothering to keep the irritation out of my voice.

"But there was a note, and you gave it to him, and Mosca is the one who pushed it the way it went. And you got Ghisola and me involved too, trying to find him for you."

"And if I hadn't given it to him, someone else would have. You and Ghisola haven't done anything wrong—you didn't know what the message said. You weren't there, you don't know how it happened, and you've got no right to pass judgment on me. This isn't your business, Neri. It's between me and my confessor." By this time I was so angry my voice was shaking. I needed his friendship now, not this blind condemnation.

"Have you confessed, then?"

"I just got home from the council. When would I have had a chance to make confession?"

"And do you fear it?"

I put my head in my hands, defeated. He knew me too well. "Yes," I muttered through my fingers. "I never meant to be involved in any of this, and I hate it that I am. I would give anything I have to make this vendetta go away."

He looked at me steadily. "Would you give the church that purse full of Oddo's coins you've been spending?"

If you only knew, I thought. Most of those coins are from Buondelmonte. You would think me a monster indeed, if you knew that.

"I need that money to pay for my share of household expenses."

"This house does not run on blood money."

"How will I pay my way, then?" Money was always tight with us.

"You could try working," he said, stretching out one hand as if offering up an idea. "It's less than two weeks until Lent, and we've got some jobs."

"Have we?" It had been days since I thought about work.

"Yes, as you'd know if you weren't so busy being a spy and a lackey to a lot of murdering knights." His voice was hard.

"Well, they ought to leave me alone now. It's done. And believe me, I never had any other choice. Do you think I like being part of all of this, even a small unimportant part?" All of the tension and dread of the past few days was starting to wear on me. I slumped down. Let him think what he would; I was too disheartened to argue any more.

Neri stroked his chin. "I believe you, that you didn't want to be involved," he said slowly, "and I can well imagine that they didn't leave you much choice. But profiting from it is another matter."

Many people tended to underestimate Neri's astuteness; that was a mistake. With that observation he had gone right to the core of the matter.

"So will you give Oddo's coins to the church, and live on what you earn with the rest of us?"

I hesitated, then said, "Yes. I swear I will give Oddo's coins to the church." He nodded, satisfied, and his face softened into a smile.

"Then we'd better do all the jobs we can between now and Lent, because you've lost time already, working for those knights."

I stood and stretched, and Neri put his arm around my shoulder and squeezed. "I've feared for your soul, my friend," he said, almost tenderly. "I'll pray for you. For all of us."

We embraced briefly and awkwardly, then retired to our sleeping alcoves, he to join Ghisola and I to think bitterly on how little sacrifice it was to donate the few coins of Oddo's that remained, when I had no intention of giving up Buondelmonte's.

*

During the next eleven days we worked every chance we got. Neri pushed us, uncharacteristically preoccupied with earning every possible coin. When we weren't working a contracted job, we were doing routines in the street, entertaining passersby. With Lent fast approaching, Florentines were quick to indulge their love of pleasure while they could, and we did well.

Anselmo and Rufino were glad to have me back with them, but Neri was quieter than usual, and he kept a certain distance. At home I often felt him watching me. Something else was bothering him, too, something to do with money. Instead of his usual it'll-all-work-out attitude toward finances, he was keeping careful track of every cent we earned.

I gave Oddo's coins to the church, as I had promised. I even gave a little of the money from Buondelmonte to the blind beggar who sat at the church door, but it didn't make me feel any better. Neri never asked me if I had donated Oddo's money, but I think he must have known. I did not make my confession. We were performing every day, and I would have ample opportunity during Lent. I hid the rest of Buondelmonte's coins well. I didn't think Neri was spying on me, but I was no longer sure of anything.

We heard snippets of news from time to time about the activities of the great families—Gherardo's fortifications of the family complex; an occasional sighting of Buondelmonte and Isabella in town, Vanni and Dino always close by; various comings and goings and meetings involving Oddo and Mosca and Schiatta.

One of these last, relayed to us by Simone, troubled me particularly, though on the surface it was more innocent than many of the others: Oddo had been seen coming out of the bishop's palace, laughing and joking with the men who were with him.

It might have meant nothing, yet still I wondered what those two had to say to each other, the warrior and the churchman. But Bishop Giovanni was a wealthy landowner, like Oddo; a shrewd businessman, like Oddo; ruthless and intelligent, like Oddo. He was a politically adroit man who walked the line between pope and emperor with as much skill as Rufino walked a tightrope. The two of them could easily have had a business deal to transact. They moved in the same exalted social circles and they might have simply been friends. But I remembered Gualdrada's confident words to Buondelmonte, of how she could call on Bishop Giovanni if the situation became dangerous, and I was convinced she was deceiving herself.

*

Our last big bash, our Carnival show, was by tradition in our own neighborhood. The weather was fair that Tuesday, and that was all our neighbors needed to justify a big, extravagant party. The butcher contributed all the meat he had left after people had finished shopping for their pre-Lenten feasts, and Ghisola and the other women roasted some of it on spits over a bonfire laid in front of the well. Smaller pieces of meat were grilling on two big braziers, which had been provided by the man who owned the cookshop next to the tavern.

A trestle table held every kind of food, donated by each household according to what they had left and what needed to be used up before the lean days. Frittatas, grated hard cheese, sliced sausages, and ravioli stuffed with forcemeat and herbs tempted us to indulge. Tomasso the barber, whose luxurious mane of dark hair was at odds with his profession, had provided a tray piled high with honey almond cakes and wafers, and he looked suitably proud of himself. However careful people had been in measuring out their food stores to last the winter, now was the time to enjoy whatever remained, or at least those things that must not be eaten in Lent. Our household had little to give except our performing talents and Ghisola's cooking skills, but we gave unstintingly of those.

An area was roped off for the youths to wrestle and to mock-duel with clownish wooden swords, with a couple of the older men refereeing. Younger children had the run of the square, and the women who weren't involved in cooking the meat kept an eye on the littlest ones. One of those women was Ghisola's sister Lapa, which made good sense considering she was mother to a significant number of those children. Her husband, who was older, was probably relieved to be one of the referees, freed for the moment of any responsibility for his own brood.

Bicci had set up a little stage by flinging a much-mended tablecloth over two stools, and he delighted the younger children with tricks of sleight-of-hand, accompanied by a steady stream of distracting chatter. Bicci was a skilled woodcarver, responsible for the sly grotesques gracing misericords in several of Florence's churches, but we knew him best for his devastatingly accurate impersonations of prominent Florentines. He drew forth gales of laughter from the older children by performing his chatter in the voice of a pompous local schoolteacher.

Bicci and his smiling wife Tedora were both sandy-haired and freckled, more like brother and sister than husband and wife. Tedora stood along-side to hand Bicci his props, but after the first hour or so, she pulled up a stool and did her job sitting, every now and then arching her back and rubbing it a little, for she was well along in her first pregnancy. Carrying a baby would wreak havoc on a tumbler's body, I thought, watching her. That distended belly would completely wreck his center of balance. Good thing the task of bearing is left to women.

I had little space for juggling, but managed a brief performance, to loud applause. I earned that applause, too, because juggling in such close quarters takes more skill than many realize. I limited my props to colored balls, for I hadn't enough space for the clubs.

At one point I gave in to the children's pleas and got up on my stilts, but with so many people crowded into a small space I couldn't find enough room to walk. Also, a group of boys was playing an impromptu game of bocce, weaving in and out of the crowd. Last June's San Giovanni celebrations had taught me painfully that rolling bocce balls and stilts are a bad combination, so I hopped down again. The children complained, but Bicci distracted them by causing an egg to disappear.

I took the stilts back to the house and put them away. When I came back, I gave Bicci a well-deserved break by settling in to tell a few stories, and he went off to the food table.

Several tales later, as I was beginning to want a respite myself, Tedora appeared at my side with a slab of trencher bread piled high with meat tidbits, which she handed to me. I stood down, and Bicci pulled his pair of battered marionettes from a sack, to excited applause. He enchanted the children with a puppet rendition of the fable I had just told them, along with a spot-on imitation of my narrative style. I watched, munching contentedly.

All of this activity barely left any room for dancing, but people found the space somehow. Anselmo played for the dancers, scraping away at his rebec while a boy kept time by banging on an upended bucket. Neri had left his organetto at home, afraid it would be damaged in the crush, and it seemed he had left his melancholy mood behind as well, for once. His fine strong voice led the singing, everything from ballads to raucous marching songs, as the spirit moved him. Later in the festivities, as the wine barrel grew steadily emptier, the spirit moved him more toward bawdy songs and parodies, and others joined in haphazardly. Ghisola's throaty alto lent a pleasing richness, and she knew all the lyrics—not surprisingly, for she had probably invented many of them. Her sister was a match for her. Lapa and Ghisola had been singing together since they were small, and I found it pleasant to hear them, and to watch the two of them together, so alike, Ghisola's coloring fairer than Lapa's but both of them with the same irrepressible gap-toothed smile.

We knew that elsewhere in the city more dangerous celebrations were going on—adolescent boys throwing stones in risky mock-battles, young men jousting recklessly, everyone drinking to excess. With any luck, I thought, Oddo's faction and Buondelmonte's would have enough sense to keep their parties separate. Even with the hot-headed knight out of town, things could turn violent in the blink of an eye, given the rancor Buondelmonte's betrayal had set in motion. Inevitably at Carnival, even in calmer times, somewhere in the city wine-sodden men swaggered and strutted and provoked each other. Later, we would hear of injuries, likely even deaths. But in our neighborhood we had thus far succeeded in keeping things under control.

It was a fine party, and a fine way to say goodbye to the fat times and to worldly pleasures for the forty penitential days of the Lenten fast. The night was far gone when Neri, Ghisola and I doused the bonfire and stumbled drunkenly home, sated and happy and still singing, to fall into our beds and sleep at last.

And then it was Lent.

16. LENT

That lean and sober season arrived as if to mock us, just as spring made her first tentative appearance. The breezes were a little warmer, the sunlight a little brighter, the occasional showers less bone-chilling. Too early for blossoms but not for buds, and the orchards that clustered just inside the city walls were full of promise. It wouldn't be long now until women set their herb pots out on roofs and balconies to catch the sun.

With each passing day we woke to birdsong livelier and more varied than the morning before. We walked with a sprightlier step, even as we put away our colorful garments and began the long haul of eating salt cod until we were all heartily sick of it.

Spring had its somber side, too. Processions of barefoot penitents moved slowly through the streets, mournfully chanting their psalms and praying. They struck themselves rhythmically with rods as they walked. Always they looked straight ahead or else down at the ground, with a sorrowful demeanor. Always, churchmen were watching them.

About three weeks into Lent, Neri and I stood outside our house watching one such procession pass. We were at loose ends, our performances in abeyance for the penitential season.

I was worried about him. For all his preoccupation with money, sometimes when it was his turn to supply the house he returned with strong wine rather than foodstuffs, and I had to make up the difference. He took his wine unwatered even in the morning, and he was often in his cups by Sext. He showed no sign of wanting to talk to me, and I didn't press him.

Neri stared at the passing procession moodily. I wondered if something was wrong between him and Ghisola, but I heard them talking long into the night as I tried to sleep, and he drank less when she was home.

As we watched the last of the sackcloth-clad penitents disappear around the corner, I decided to see if I could find out what was troubling him. I was trying to figure out how to begin when he spoke first.

"Let's go to the church," he said.

That caught me by surprise. Neri was usually a moderately pious man, but lately he had been going to Mass only on Sundays, and as far as I knew he hadn't been near the church the rest of the time.

"Why?" I asked. "There's no service."

"I want to see San Cristoforo," he said.

That surprised me even more. Our parish church, like many others, had a large image of the saint on one wall for the benefit of parishioners. The worn fresco was big enough to be seen from a considerable distance, because on a day you gaze upon San Cristoforo with his sacred burden, you will not meet a bad death. That is not to say you won't die on that day, but you won't die unshriven.

I didn't know why this appealed to Neri, but for myself it wasn't a bad idea. I was not free of the shadow of the threat posed by Selvaggia and Oddo, and for that matter, Buondelmonte, and if the saint could provide a measure of safety, I would gladly seek him out, though I'd prefer safety for my body as well as for my soul. In fact, if I could have steered Buondelmonte toward such an image, I would have. I told Neri I'd come with him, and we walked the short distance to the church together and went in the men's door. A stink of stale urine lingered in the porch, but inside, a faint, sweet memory of incense replaced it.

When my eyes grew accustomed to the gloom I saw we were alone, except for a couple of women kneeling on the Gospel side. The clumsily painted Last Judgment on one wall flickered in the light of the few candles that burned in front of the altar. Funny, I thought, how candlelight can make a mosaic appear to come alive, but a bad painting just looks deader than ever.

I knelt near the back and faced the altar, but Neri knelt facing San Cristoforo, who was depicted as a huge, comically ugly man up to his knees in a wavy blue river, carrying the haloed Christ child across on his shoulders. Neri gazed at the image intently while he prayed, as if he was trying to store up the sight against some future need. I tried to pray, though my mind was unsettled, until a noise distracted me and I looked up.

Father Pietro was standing behind the altar, peering at us through the gloom of the church. He was notoriously nearsighted, as well as being a relative newcomer to the parish, and he was probably trying to recognize us—not that I, at least, was a very familiar sight to him, but Neri should have been. I scrambled to my feet, made my obeisance to the altar, and ducked out the side door.

To my surprise, Neri was right behind me.

"I think he saw me," he muttered.

"He probably couldn't tell who you were, from up there," I said, wondering why it mattered.

"I hope not." Neri started walking, not toward home, but toward the communal well that served our neighborhood. I fell in step with him.

When we reached the little square, we walked around to the far side of the well and sat on the circle of three stone steps that surrounded it.

It was a good place to soak up the sunlight. A few women were coming and going with their buckets, but they trudged up the steps on the other side and didn't come close enough to hear us, as long as we spoke quietly. Neri smelled of wine, and his eyes were bloodshot. I wondered what tales the women would carry, seeing us there.

After sitting for a few minutes in silence, I grew impatient. "Neri, what's up?" I said, trying to sound interested but not too curious. "What are you so worried about?"

"Remember the procession we just saw?" His eyes were red-veined.

"Of course I remember," I said, puzzled.

"I'm afraid you're going to be seeing me in one of those, and Ghisola too."

That made no sense, I thought. They were hardly such great sinners as all that. Their liaison was adulterous, since Neri's estranged wife still lived, but so many couples lived thus that not even the church had the manpower or the will to punish them all.

Unless someone filed a complaint.

"Is it Duccia?" I asked. I felt a prickle of anxiety as a memory of that pretty, bitter face surfaced in my mind.

He nodded. "She's been pestering me, wanting money she says I owe her. She's been making threats."

The thought of that scheming little bitch aiming her poison at my friends made my gorge rise. Neri had been well rid of her; neither of us had thought to see her again once they parted.

"And do you owe her anything?" I asked. Surely he had not been so foolish.

"I gave her most of her dowry back. All I had left, anyway. And she's a cheating whore who didn't deserve to see any of it."

He did owe her money. This was not good. I had urged him at the time to take her to court, so she could claim nothing from him later, but he refused. At least I began to understand why he was so concerned lately with making money.

"If she comes forward and says anything, she knows we'll tell the world what she did. Maybe you wouldn't, but Anselmo and I wouldn't hesitate to tell it. She's not going to risk that." I spoke with more confidence than I felt. Quite a lot of the world already knew, and it hadn't slowed her down much.

He shrugged. "Well, so far she hasn't done anything but nag and threaten, so I think she does know what she'd be risking. But what worries me most is that she might accuse Ghisola. I don't want Ghisi involved. It's dangerous for her, and I can't expose her to that."

He was right, of course. It would be disastrous for both of them. Punishment for adultery was barbaric, ruining people's lives and sometimes their bodies, and always harshest for women. I felt sick at the thought.

"But if the church acted, and forced you to become a public penitent, you'd have to swear to give Ghisola up, wouldn't you?" I asked.

His face crumpled. "I can't give up Ghisola. And I can't put her at risk, and I can't promise to repent if I'm not going to. So what can I do? I know I'm sinning and I can't repent, so I can't confess it. And that's not even the only sin I'm worried about. I can't even confess that I helped you deliver that note, because that would get you involved, and whoever gave you the note, too. All I can do is look at San Cristoforo every day in case... in case something happens." We both crossed ourselves hurriedly. I hated it that his generous gesture of helping me with the message was partly the cause of his pain. Such talk made my scalp itch, and he wasn't through yet.

"And if anything does happen, I need you to swear that you'll take care of Ghisola."

I did not consider myself superstitious, and I know people say all manner of things when they're upset, but I couldn't shake the feeling that he was tempting a malicious fate.

"Neri, don't talk so. Nothing will happen—all of this will work out. You'll see."

"Swear it, though."

"Of course. I swear it." Maybe my oath would content him and we could drop this disturbing conversation.

"Swear by something."

"I swear by the saints, and—and by my mother's soul, if anything happens to you I will take care of Ghisola. Now will you let it rest?"

He put a hand up as if to say yes, enough, and we lapsed into silence, sitting dejectedly, watching the women come and go with their buckets.

Despite my anxiety, I felt a little impatient. I still thought it unlikely that Duccia would dare to file a formal complaint, though she could certainly work a lot of mischief just by gossiping. And at least he wasn't struggling with guilt on the scale of mine, for he had not knowingly involved himself in an impending murder. But a look at Neri's face made me repent my lack of generosity, for pain was pain, and my friend was clearly hurting.

"Let's go home," I said, standing.

Neri stood too, and stretched. "I don't want Ghisola to know about Duccia," he warned me, and I promised to say nothing. We headed home, and it seemed to me that the tension between us had diminished a little. For that, at least, I was glad.

After we supped that night, the three of us sat in front of the fire together, talking. Neri was not drunk, but all of us had our fair share of wine. His share loosened his tongue to the extent that he talked to us about his spiritual concerns, though he tried to couch it in general terms as merely a theological debate—if a man and a woman sin, but do no harm, how great is the fault? Whose sin is greater? Is it possible to confess if one cannot repent?

Ghisola, not taken in for a moment, placed her hand over his. "You're good, Neri, to think these things. Many men would do what they pleased, never caring if they sinned or not. And I'm grateful for your care for me."

"Do you fear for your soul?" he asked her, his face troubled.

She thought for a long moment. "No, I don't," she finally replied. "I am as God made me—a woman with many weaknesses, but one who means no harm to anyone. I would wed you, if I could. I'm faithful to you. I know I violate God's holy law by what we do, yet at the same time I feel as if we'll be forgiven. I pray to Our Lady, and always I come away filled with peace."

He embraced her, smiling at last, and I stole away to my bed, leaving them together. Knowing, finally, the reason for his concerns about money, and knowing how afraid he was, I was awed to think that he had urged me to get rid of my ill-gotten coins—coins he knew I would have lent or given him in an instant, had he only asked, coins that could have solved at least one of the problems eating away at him. And now, having let him think those coins surrendered in an act of penitence, I couldn't even offer. And even if coins were to solve his immediate practical problem, I was beginning to realize Neri's guilt was real, and it ran deep, and that I bore responsibility for at least a part of it.

17. FLOWERING SUNDAY

Lent dragged on, and it wasn't only salt fish that wearied me. I chafed at not being able to work. I missed eating meat and cheese and eggs, I missed music, and I missed Florence's colorful street performers, whose numbers often included our own little troupe. Unless you counted penitential processions and lugubrious street preachers as entertainment, and I generally didn't, little of interest was going on anywhere. I was bored, idle and restless. I had too much time to think, and too many things I didn't want to think about.

Even now all was not well with Neri. Sometimes he acted like his old self, but at other times his anger flared without warning, and both Ghisola and I soon learned to avoid provoking him. He paid daily visits to San Cristoforo. He still drank enough to worry me, and he and Ghisola quarreled, which was a new thing. He fretted about money, yet he spent it on wine. If he talked to Duccia again, he didn't choose to tell me.

And so we went along, the three of us all aware of a tension just beneath the surface of our daily lives. Ghisola was subdued and quieter than usual, Neri quick to find fault and tell us both how we should be doing things, and I found myself more and more often avoiding arguments by absenting myself and taking long walks around the city.

When Flowering Sunday dawned I awoke feeling hopeful. I had convinced myself that the mood would lift and things return to normal after Lent, especially if Buondelmonte managed to stay out of trouble, which probably meant staying out of town. Only another week to get through. The day was warm, the sky a brilliant blue, and I looked forward to the great procession. I had missed it only once since I was old enough to take part. I was ill that year, and my mother brought me my blessed branch to keep for the year to come. I wept to miss the wonder of it.

On this day, all Florence takes part in the solemn ritual that enacts Christ's entry into Jerusalem. All of us assemble in the space between the cathedral of Santa Reparata and the Baptistery and form a long column of worshipers, moving reverently, with slow steps, to the church of San Lorenzo north of the old city walls. There we celebrate Terce; there the bishop blesses the palm fronds and olive branches and strews the great cross with flowers. Churchmen chant their ancient antiphons as the procession forms anew and returns with measured pace to Santa Reparata. There we laymen receive our blessed branches and hear mass.

I was eager for the music, and for the color and the beauty and theatre, but I wanted to go with Neri, and he was still abed. Ghisola had left earlier to join the women's part of the procession. I waited, impatient, not wanting to leave without Neri and wondering whether I should risk waking him. I didn't know how he would react, so I abandoned that idea.

Finally I could wait no longer. The bells told me that even now I had to hurry to catch up with the tail end of the procession, so I set off alone at a fast walk. I calculated that the worshipers would already have left the cathedral square, and I was going to have to take a more direct route and move smartly to join them before they reached San Lorenzo. I wound my way through the empty streets and caught up with the procession just as it snaked through the old city gate.

When we got to San Lorenzo we couldn't squeeze everyone in, so those of us in the rear crowded as close to the open doors as we could. I was only a few steps from the doorway, and peering past the men in front of me I saw a huge pile of branches to one side of the altar. I stared at the heap in awe. With that many olive branches piled up, would we have an olive harvest this year? But then, I had that same thought every year, and always the olives and their oil appeared anyway.

I couldn't see much from where I was, nor could I hear the sermon, but the chanting, coming first from the churchmen on the east side and then answered by others on the west, was enough to call forth tears for its spine-tingling majesty. At least we little people at the end of the line could have that much.

When the procession formed again for the return to Santa Reparata, officious clergy shooed us latecomers away from the door and kept the processional order as it had been, with the addition of many young clerics bearing giant baskets piled high with the blessed greenery, and allowed us to fall in line only after everyone else had filed out. It was fair enough, I suppose, but the arrogant way they did it took away much of the day's joy for me. All of the wealthy men, the church patrons and nobles, were assured of their favored places in the procession, but were the rest of us not also part of God's congregation?

As the procession moved on, I knelt, prayed, and sang when I was supposed to, but no longer did I worship. Back at Santa Reparata I was again crowded out of the church, unable to hear or see anything. The cathedral was huge, but men were standing shoulder to shoulder, back to belly, wedged together. I wasn't even sure I'd get my blessed branch, but the clerics did at least make sure that everyone got something, even us latecomers. The blooms I received were the stragglers among the other branches and flowers, as I was a straggler among the other worshipers.

Yet another thing to thank Neri for, I thought sourly, though to be fair, he had not asked me to wait for him. I clutched a spray of wilting purple flowers that had been suffocated under a pile of olive branches, though its scent was still sweet.

And as I thought of Neri, I spotted him, farther back in the crowd than I was. His hair was uncombed, but his eyes were alert and he mouthed the words along with the cantor. I motioned for him to join me, but he shook his head and stayed where he was. Not that moving would have been easy in that crush of people.

After mass I managed to keep him in sight and catch up with him as he was leaving, and I fell in step beside him. He accepted my presence without comment. He held a browning, drooping lily, perhaps a little more disreputable than my own limp purple sprig. We didn't see Ghisola among the women, but she had probably been near the front.

We took our time on the way home. We chatted with Bicci and walked down to the river with him, and on our way back we tossed a stick for his mangy dog, the errant Masetto, near the neighborhood well. Neri's mood seemed to lighten with these idle pastimes, and he even smiled once or twice. The tightness in his hunched shoulders began to relax, and he stood a little taller.

When we finally arrived at our house, Ghisola was there before us. Her olive branch lay on the bench, and she was at the hearth stirring a soup that smelled garlicky and good. Neri kissed the top of her head in greeting.

"So how'd you rate an olive branch?" he asked her. "We just got these rotting flowers." He set his lily down next to the branch.

"I got there in time," she said tartly, but she didn't look at us. I thought she would be relieved to see us together and not arguing, but something was bothering her.

Neri saw it, too. "What is it, Ghisi?" he asked.

"Nothing. I just overheard some silly talk after the procession, and I guess I let it bother me. It's nothing," she said, staring into the pot.

"Tell us," ordered Neri, now serious, his good humor dissipated like steam off a pudding.

She took a deep breath and obeyed. "I heard a priest talking to two of his acolytes, and he told them that everyone who had anything to do with the vendetta against Buondelmonte will be damned. Everybody. Even the knights' servants. Their wives. Anybody who even talked to one of them about it. He says it's an abomination in the sight of God, and God will strike everyone who had anything to do with it." Her voice shook, and I thought she was near to tears. My own first reaction was to laugh, but I controlled that urge when I saw Neri's face turn a deep, angry red.

So there we were, one of us ready to weep, one furious, and me ready to laugh. All at once I felt disgusted with myself. How did I know it wasn't true, after all?

Neri slammed his fist down on the bench, making both the olive branch and the lily jump. The olive branch landed back on the bench, a little askew, but the lily tumbled to the dirt floor.

"Damned!" he bellowed. He whirled to face me. "I should have known better than to try to help the likes of you. Now I'll be damned along with you, and Ghisi will too!" With that, she made a little strangled noise and started to cry, and that made me angry. He could have left her out of this, even if he had to vent his anger on "the likes of me."

"Calm down, Neri," I said testily. "What would a priest know about it? He's probably allied with Buondelmonte and the Donati. And why would the people against Buondelmonte be damned and not Buondelmonte himself? He's the one who stabbed Oddo and then insulted their family."

"This is your fault," he snarled, pointing an accusing finger at me. "If you hadn't meddled in matters that don't concern you, this entire city would be safer today."

I supposed that was true, but I was in no mood to hear it from Neri.

"What's that to you?" I snapped.

"I'll be damned, thanks to you. Cursed for all eternity, my soul in hell because you had to interfere with your betters. I had enough sins on my conscience without this."

The idea of that lot being my betters would have been laughable if I hadn't been so infuriated.

"Your soul is your own responsibility. I've nothing to do with it. What kind of senseless gibberish are you talking, man?" I had had about enough. "Helping a friend is no sin. You didn't know murder was at stake. As for the rest of your sins, don't go blaming me. All that's between you and God."

Ghisola stared at me in alarm, her finger to her lips in warning, but I was not to be deterred.

"And speaking of hell, what do you think you've been making of all of our lives lately? What is wrong with you?" I would have gone on, but Neri's enraged roar startled me into silence.

His face was contorted into a mask of anger and misery. He looked like one of the damned in the Last Judgment painted on the cathedral wall, so hopeless and frightened that I almost took pity on him despite

131

my own flaring anger. But then he heaved himself up from the bench and took a threatening step toward me, and instinctively I raised an arm to protect myself.

"That's enough," said Ghisola quickly, and she stepped between us. Neri glared first at her, then at me, and he turned on his heel and stomped out the door, slamming it behind him.

Ghisola sank down on the bench, sobbing. I didn't know what to say, so I just picked up Neri's lily from the floor and set it down again on the bench next to her olive branch, along with my spray of rapidly-browning flowers. For all the good it was doing us, our blessed greenery might as well have gone into Ghisola's soup, though I doubted my flowers would have improved it any.

Ghisola's crying grew quieter, though it did not stop. Every now and then she gave the soup a stir, even as tears trickled down her face. Finally she said, "He was wrong to blame you."

I shrugged. Maybe it was all my fault. I didn't know any more. Nothing was making any sense, and that was as good an explanation as any.

"He can't help it," she said, snuffling. "Everything's been wrong for him lately, and he's upset. And he's worried. I am, too."

I wanted to comfort her, but she was Neri's woman, and if he walked back in and saw us, any closeness between us could look wrong to him. Things were already bad enough without that. Finally I put my hand gingerly on her shoulder, for that seemed innocent enough. "I know, Ghisi. I'm worried about him too."

She pulled a kerchief from her belt and blew her nose. Her eyes were red and puffy.

"Is it Duccia?" I asked, forgetting I wasn't supposed to mention her.

She shook her head. "Not this time. Sometimes it's her." I wasn't surprised to find that Ghisola knew about that situation. She was an astute people-watcher, and she was perfectly capable of letting Neri think he had fooled her when he had not.

The two of us ate our soup in gloomy silence. It was savory, but we needed more than that to cheer us—we needed nothing less than Neri being his old self again. And if that miracle had occurred, I think we would have been the happiest two people in Florence. Especially if the Buondelmonte vendetta would somehow just go away.

Neri didn't come home that night. When he did make an appearance the next day, no one said anything. On the surface it was as if nothing had happened. That afternoon Ghisola made an excuse to go visit Lapa for a day or two, leaving Neri and me hanging around our tiny house in stony silence, avoiding each other.

*

The long-anticipated end of Lent was approaching, but I needed a change of pace now. And, to be honest, I wanted to spend some of that Buondelmonte money I had gone through so much to earn. My thoughts strayed back to Lippo the leatherworker and my earlier idea of ordering a jester's cap from him. It lifted my mood to think of performing again soon, and a fine leather hat dyed yellow and green would be a worthy addition to my professional tools.

I could afford it, even after surviving the Lenten weeks without employment, for I had been even more frugal than usual in my effort to keep Neri from learning how many coins I still had, even after I donated Oddo's payment to the church. Someone might as well benefit from them. Besides, thus equipped I'd be in a better position to help Neri earn the money he needed to pay off Duccia, or so I reasoned. Was I lying to myself? I still don't know.

My decision made, I waited indoors through two days of steady rain, ducking out only as far as the bakeshop for bread and a fragrant leek pie, until the Wednesday before Easter dawned overcast and drizzly. This was the last day businesses were open before the Easter vigil, so I set off for the Donati palace, wrapped in an old oiled cloak.

With every step, as my shoes squelched through the mud, more of those things I didn't want to think about came back to me. I considered going to a different leatherworker, but I liked Lippo's work, and he was an honest man. I needn't pay any attention to the Donati palace itself, or to its residents, I told myself. My business was only with the shop on the ground floor. I don't know why I listen when I tell myself things like that, but listen I did.

Lippo was his usual cheerful self. My arrival interrupted his singing, and the boy cutting leather in the back of the shop gave me a grateful smile. Lippo ushered me in behind the counter and out of the drizzle, and when he learned I was there to see him and not the women upstairs, he bade me sit on a stool next to a small brazier, and he pulled up another stool next to it for himself. We talked of the design for my hat, as well as of materials and cost, and he sketched a picture on a scrap of rough paper. I liked it. He fetched a collection of color scraps, and we began rummaging through them, looking for the right colors. He had a nice piece of leather in an acceptable yellow on hand, but we decided he needed to order the green we wanted, as he had nothing bright enough. The dyer would be doing a batch of green fairly soon, he thought. We even talked of making a matching domino mask out of the scraps, weaving strips of the two colors diagonally to make a pattern of alternating green and yellow diamonds.

We agreed on payment, and Lippo leaned back and stretched his arms. "So, I suppose you know all about the Donati girl's marriage and all the trouble? You were there, weren't you, with messer Buondelmonte that day? I didn't learn of it till later."

I did know. More than he had any idea, in fact. "It was the talk of the city. How are monna Gualdrada and the lady Fiammetta doing?"

"Monna Gualdrada is frightened for her daughter, and her brothers-in-law haven't been kind. They blame her, and they do it so openly that even I have overheard them. I always act as if I've heard nothing, of course."

"And Fiammetta?" How had this affected that lovely woman-child?

He smiled. "Oh, she's worried, too, but mostly she's all excited about her cousin's baby. I never saw a woman so addled over a little one. She'll be a fine mother herself one day, that one."

"Is Bianca's babe given to the light, then?"

"Oh, yes, born only a week after the lady Isabella rode off with her knight. Another female for the house."

"I trust the mother is well?"

"Well, and happy and relieved to be safely delivered. She was just churched a day or two ago, so now she's off with Fiammetta taking the baby to one of the baptism scrutinies. The babe'll be part of the communal baptism."

So would hundreds of other children born around Lent or a little before. Unless a babe's precarious health required immediate baptism, parents waited until Holy Saturday. The magnificent spectacle which transformed hundreds of infants into both citizens and Christians at once was one of Florence's most solemn and memorable rites.

"Fiammetta's one of the godmothers? Then I expect monna Gualdrada must be the other," I said.

"No, Fiammetta's one godmother, and Isabella is the other. Monna Isabella, I mean. I can't get used to calling her that—she was just a little girl, only a short while ago." He smiled, and his eyes crinkled. "And her new husband's the godfather. They've been staying out of town, on account of the troubles, but they had to come back in for the scrutinies. Now that the lady Bianca is churched, she can go with the babe, so this time Fiammetta and Bianca took the little one by themselves, with messer Cione for an escort."

That explained those sightings of the well-guarded couple in these last few weeks. Godparents! How could they have taken the risk? They would have to be in the midst of that crush of people on Holy Saturday—had been in crowds with each scrutiny they attended. What was Buondelmonte thinking? Had the Donati women managed to persuade him to take this risk, all for family pride and honor? I had thought him safe enough until Easter was past, and he must have believed it, too. But what if we were wrong?

I was pondering the recklessness of this, surprising even with all I knew of Buondelmonte's impetuous nature, when a woman spoke to me from outside the shop.

"Hello, friend Fool," said Fiammetta's light voice.

18. BABY MARGHERITA

I looked up to see Fiammetta and Bianca in front of the counter, cloaked and hooded against the fine drizzle. Bianca held a squirming bundle that was making little mewling sounds. A tall man, well dressed and well armed, stood behind them. He was massive and powerful, and I had last seen him hurrying out of Mazzingo's castle in the company of Buondelmonte. He hadn't been happy then, and he didn't look happy now.

I stood up hastily and made a little bow. "My ladies."

Fiammetta smiled. Lippo lifted the gate for her, and she and Bianca and the baby stepped in out of the wet.

"This is my lord uncle, messer Cione," said Fiammetta to me, gesturing toward the tall man, who remained outside the shop. "Uncle, this is the gentle fool who witnessed my sister's ring-giving. He's been a friend to us and to messer Buondelmonte." The tall man looked at me, expressionless, and said nothing. Surely, I thought, this man recognized me from Mazzingo's ill-fated knighting. And if he did, would he believe that the fool who caused Buondelmonte to be spattered with gravy was now a friend to his household? I bowed to him also, and watched a rivulet of rainwater trickle down a crease in his face.

"Niece, kinswoman, I've seen you safely home," he said to the women. His voice was low pitched and strong. Neri would have liked him as a duet partner. "I shall leave you here. Send for me when you have need of an escort again." Fiammetta thanked him, adding a graceful curtsy which made even that impassive face soften with the hint of a smile. He pulled his hood tighter against the rain, which was picking up, and squished through the mud toward the imposing palace next door, where a servant was already holding the door for him.

Fiammetta greeted Lippo affectionately while Bianca cooed to the baby. Then she turned back to me. "Friend Fool, will you not come up and see Mother? She will welcome you, I know, and you can see Bianca's little one where it's warm and we can unwrap her from all these blankets."

"My lady, you are kind, but it would not be proper," I began. "I—"

She interrupted, a finger to her lips. "My uncle Manno is there to assure propriety. Please, friend Fool, my mother is despondent over my sister's problems, and it will cheer her to see you."

It troubled me that these women considered me their friend, when since I saw them last I had proved myself the contrary by my attendance at Oddo's council and by carrying Selvaggia's message to Mosca. Clearly to them I was only the fool who had once accompanied Buondelmonte. I was as enchanted as ever with Fiammetta, but I felt a strong pang of guilt at her gracious welcome. Nevertheless, when I looked down at that lovely heart-shaped face I couldn't say no to her, so, reluctantly, I followed the women up the stairs. We all left wet footprints behind us.

By the time we got to the hall, the babe was wide awake and squalling in earnest. Bianca took her complaining daughter up the stairs, whether to the smaller hall or all the way up to the kitchen I didn't know, and the babe was soon quiet.

Another man, shorter and less imposing than messer Cione, sat on the bench in front of the huge brazier. I knew who he was, but he at least hadn't attended Mazzingo's knighting, and therefore had not watched me steal his soon-to-be nephew's dinner. He smiled at Fiammetta and looked at me curiously.

Fiammetta introduced me to Manno, uncle to her and to Isabella, brother to messer Cione and to monna Gualdrada's late husband messer Forese. He greeted me pleasantly enough, not as an equal, but as a great man might speak to a lowly neighbor or a potential client. Courtesy mixed with condescension, for although the younger brother lacked Cione's knightly title, he was still a Donati. The hall was dim, the shutters partially closed against the rain, and it was hard to see details, but I thought he bore a little resemblance to messer Cione in his strong facial features. I couldn't find any trace of Isabella's or Fiammetta's extraordinary beauty in the Donati men I had met so far, but the fair Gualdrada was enough to account for that.

Manno indicated we should sit on the bench, and asked Fiammetta to see about bringing wine. Smiling, she assented, and started up to the kitchen, her wet cloak over her arm. "I'll tell Mother you're here," she said to me over her shoulder.

Manno chatted inconsequentially, suggesting various occasions where he might have seen me perform. None of them matched jobs I had done, but we agreed that if I was familiar to him, he might have seen me juggling in the street. Neither of us mentioned my unfortunate performance at the knighting, though I had no doubt he knew of it. I didn't know what else to talk about, and apparently neither did he, for he soon fell silent. I wanted to put my feet up, the better to dry my shoes and hose, but it would have been too much of a liberty. I shivered, still wrapped in my cloak. We both sat in the dim hall, lost in our own thoughts, until footsteps on the stairs caused us to look up.

Fiammetta was coming down carrying two cups, with a level of care suggesting they were full. How women managed to do that in their long skirts I could not guess, but they all seemed to have the knack. Just behind Fiammetta came Gualdrada, both of them illuminated from behind by the light from an open window in the hall above.

I stared at Gualdrada. She might have aged twenty years since I last saw her. She had lost a great deal of weight, and her face was drawn and gaunt. The change was far more drastic than the slight slimming plump women like Ghisola welcomed as a compensation for the trials of Lent. She looked as if she hadn't slept or eaten for weeks, but she was still impeccably dressed and groomed, a fine white linen veil covered her luxurious hair, and her posture was erect.

Manno sat stony-faced, not looking at Gualdrada. I stood respectfully, and she rewarded me with the ghost of the dazzling smile I remembered. Fiammetta handed cups of wine first to her uncle and then to me.

"Please, be seated," Gualdrada said, her voice not more than a whisper. "Be welcome to our hall."

I mumbled something meant to be polite and sat back down obediently. She pulled up a stool and sat on it.

"I'll go see if Bianca has finished feeding little Margherita yet," Fiammetta said. "Our guest will want to see her—she's such a beautiful baby." She smiled at us and went up the stairs.

Manno turned to Gualdrada. "That babe should be sent out to wet-nurse. It's not proper for a woman of one of our houses to feed her own." His ease and friendliness had disappeared, and his tone was cool, critical.

Gualdrada shook her head. "The girl fears her late husband's family will claim the child if she lets it go away from here."

"Hmph. Best thing for everybody if they did," he said grumpily. I concentrated on the far wall, pretending not to hear.

"They won't. They would have, perhaps, if the babe had been a boy, but they aren't going to want another girl to dower, and no father to pay," Gualdrada said. "And they won't challenge the Donati."

"That babe is no Donati," Manno said, scowling. "It belongs to its father's people, and they're the ones who should raise it. The girl should have stayed where she was, if she wanted to keep the child."

Gualdrada bristled. "Not the way they were treating her. Would you have a Donati woman living like a servant?" Manno shrugged, and she glared at him.

"They won't come for Margherita," she said firmly. "I've told Bianca this, but she's fearful, and these are not easy times." Gualdrada sounded as tired as she looked, but she faced Manno stubbornly.

"And why might that be, Gualdrada? Could it be that these are not easy times because you chose to make a marriage alliance behind our backs, and set in motion a nightmare that may yet be the end of all of us?" He was talking to her as if I was not there. I wished I wasn't.

Gualdrada pulled herself up a little straighter. "What's done is done," she said. "As for the babe, that's not yours to decide. Bianca is in my house, and Forese left me the use of this house for my lifetime. If she wants to stay here with her child, then stay she shall. As for my daughter, she's well married, and it's not her fault or mine if murdering fools insist on making trouble." Manno raised a skeptical eyebrow.

"Why do you look so, Brother?" Gualdrada said, a hint of challenge in her voice. "Do you not think messer Buondelmonte a fine enough husband for Isabella?"

"I think him a vain, hotheaded fool," Manno snapped.

What a coincidence. So did I.

Gualdrada went on as if he hadn't spoken.

"Widows don't seek their lot, but Christian women of good birth can raise their children alone if they must, as I have done. Yes, Isabella's marriage would have been for her father to decide, but he left me as her guardian, and so I've done my duty. Had it been left to you and your brothers, both of my girls would have languished unmarried while you tended to your own."

"Sister-in-law, you speak too hastily. Cione and I are your co-guardians. You sidestepped our role, and you've taken upon yourself the responsibility for all that has happened and all that will happen." Manno's voice was harsh. "You are no more a Donati than that babe. Your husband's dead. You're of your father's house again, and you had no right to make a contract for Forese's daughter."

Gualdrada went even paler, if that were possible. And no wonder, I thought, surprised once again by the ways of the great families. Forese's daughter was also hers, after all, and Gualdrada had lived in that house as part of the family for perhaps eighteen years.

She didn't speak, but neither did she look away. She gazed at him with the calm dignity of a woman who no longer has much to lose, and I shivered.

To my relief, the two younger women came tripping down the stairs, bringing an end to the standoff between Gualdrada and her brother-in-law. Fiammetta carried the baby—a pink-faced little thing with a shock of dark hair, her limbs tightly swaddled in bright red cloth. Around her neck was a piece of coral, for protection, hanging from a silk cord.

Fiammetta brought her over to show me. "This is little Margherita," she said proudly, gently stroking the scrunched-up little face. "Isn't she beautiful?"

In fact she looked like every other baby and she smelt a bit like new cheese, but that probably wasn't the right answer. "She will be fair enough to take her place in this household of beautiful women," I said, hoping I was being sufficiently courtly, yet not too familiar. Fiammetta's smile told me I had hit the right balance. She and Bianca sat on the bench opposite ours and occupied themselves with playing with the baby, who cooed and gurgled contentedly.

Gualdrada turned to me. "I'm glad to see you, my friend, but I've been unwell. I must go now and rest, but I would ask you before you leave us to come up to the kitchen and see monna Ortolana. She'll be pleased to see you again."

That must be the old woman. "With great pleasure, my lady. I am sorry you are unwell, and may God give you a good recovery." I stood as she did, and with another of those ghostly smiles she took her leave, climbing the stairs slowly.

"Friend Fool, let's go upstairs and see Auntie Ortolana," said Fiammetta. I liked it when she called me that, even while it made me feel guilty. "I think Margherita is ready for her nap, too."

Bianca smiled at her cousin, silent as ever. Fiammetta held the drowsing babe, who had a thin trickle of milk dribbling down her chin.

"Uncle, we'll be in the kitchen only for a few moments," Fiammetta said to him. "Can you stay a little?" Obviously the rules had tightened when it came to male visitors.

"I'll wait, but not long, Niece. I'm expected at home soon."

Fiammetta promised we would be brief, and the two young women climbed the wide stairs and then the sturdy steps up to the kitchen, little Margherita cradled tenderly in her kinswoman's arms. I followed them, noting as we passed that the small hall was once again crowded with sewing paraphernalia, only this time it was baby-sized pieces of linen shirting.

The kitchen was warm, and it felt good after the chilly hall. It was exactly as I remembered it, except for an elaborately carved wooden cradle next to the longer bench. Over that bench, Fiammetta's fine but sodden cloak was still steaming a little in the heat from the fire. It would carry the scent of wood smoke, once it was dry.

140

The old woman sat at the hearth, her poker in hand. She looked at me without any sign of surprise. She wore her old apron; a new white one with five pockets hung on a hook. Gualdrada was nowhere to be seen.

Bianca took the baby back from Fiammetta, who handed her over reluctantly, and gently placed her in the cradle and began to rock her, head to toe. I have heard that in France they rock their infants from side to side, but in Florence we stick to the old way. It must work well enough, for the child was soon sleeping soundly.

The old woman studied me. "You're back," she finally said.

"Yes. Good morrow, Grandmother."

"Did Mother go to her appointment?" Fiammetta asked her, speaking softly. I didn't know whether the cause of her lowered voice was the sleeping babe or her uncle downstairs, or both.

"She did. I went with her to the bishop's palace, and he saw her, as he had agreed. Manno thought we went to church to pray."

"That was good of you, Auntie. I know it must have tired you. Were you waiting where you could hear them?"

"Aye. Your mother told him I was deaf, so he let me stay." So Gualdrada had lied to the bishop. That was a measure of the extremity of the situation.

"Did she tell him of messer Oddo's threats, and the danger to the Easter peace?"

"She did, and he assured her he will have no violation of the holy season, on pain of excommunication. He's going to call Oddo in and swear him to that."

Fiammetta smiled, and the gloomy kitchen was lighter for it. "I'm glad of it. I thought it unlikely that they would be in danger during Lent, or for the baptism, but I'm grateful for his reassurance, nevertheless. And did Mother mention making a permanent peace?"

"She did, but he wouldn't hear her out. He said the men themselves would have to make that request before he could act."

Fiammetta's smile faded. "I was afraid of that. Is she very disappointed?" The old woman nodded.

"Aye. Drada kept after him, and he finally told her to get Buondelmonte to come in and speak for himself." She pronounced the knight's name as if she spat out a piece of rotten apple.

Fiammetta sighed. "Well, maybe he will, after we get through Easter week," she said, but she didn't sound very hopeful. "And at least we know they're safe for the time being."

141

As far as I knew, Oddo had already figured out that violating the Easter peace would not be wise, but the bishop's involvement was news, indeed. Remembering Simone's news of Oddo's earlier visit to the bishop, I found it hard to believe that Oddo had much to fear. But at the same time I believed that the formidable churchman would enforce the Easter peace, and that any lack of respect to his churches or his rituals could cost the perpetrator this man's valuable friendship. Too bad I was less certain of his concern for the peace in other times and other places.

The old woman—I still couldn't get used to thinking of her as monna Ortolana—turned to me. "Manno and Cione don't need to hear any of that, Fool," she said. "Nor Lippo, either. Monna Gualdrada's business is her own, and the men don't need to be meddling in everything she does. Do you understand?"

"Yes, Grandmother. I hear only what is said directly to me."

She grinned at that, showing a shortage of teeth. "I don't believe that for a minute, but I think you get my meaning."

Manno called up the stairs. "Niece, I must go now. Bring your friend downstairs." The old woman wrinkled her nose and poked at the fire, and both the young women turned toward the baby, who stirred but didn't wake. Fiammetta and I stood, and she smoothed the front of her gown, which had acquired a few suspicious wet spots while she held the baby.

She took both my hands in hers. "Friend Fool," she said, looking up at me with those clear blue eyes, "thank you for your visit, and for your discretion, and for your friendship. One day I'll be married, and it would delight me to have you and your friends perform for my wedding."

"Do you wish to be married, then, my lady?" What an idiotic thing to say. Where did I come up with that?

"I want to have babes of my own," she said softly, beaming down at little Margherita. "I can hardly wait."

I didn't know what to say to that, so I merely squeezed her hands and wished her God's blessing. She wished me a blessed Holy Week, said farewell, and turned back to the baby. The old woman and I exchanged a glance, and I was on my way downstairs.

Manno had his cloak on. As soon as he saw me, he headed for the stone stairs down to the leatherworker's shop, clearly expecting me to follow, and I did. I heard Lippo's tuneless voice happily praising the Virgin as we descended.

When we reached the street level, Manno turned to me and said coldly, "You have been a guest in a Donati home. This requires your complete discretion, do you understand me?"

"You have it, my lord," I said. He acknowledged this with a grunt and left, walking toward the same palace messer Cione had entered earlier. This time, no one was holding the door open.

My thoughts were roiling as Lippo showed me a few refinements on his design for my hat, all of which I agreed to without really seeing them. I made my farewells, arranged a date to come back for the hat, and without further delay set off, away from that remarkable household of women.

I hated it that Fiammetta thought me such a sound friend, when I had been anything but a friend to them. Even the old woman trusted my discretion. I resolved to give them that, at least, even if I had been an uncertain friend in the past. And I felt some small relief at knowing that the bishop himself demanded of Oddo that he keep the peace, at least during Easter week. That meant that Buondelmonte and Isabella were safe coming into town for the baptism on Saturday, even if they then stayed to celebrate Easter, which I assumed they would. I knew that Gherardo had taken steps to further fortify the town house, including setting up moveable barricades that could seal off the Buondelmonti enclave efficiently and thoroughly, if necessary.

Still, something was nagging at the back of my mind. I couldn't figure out exactly what it was, so I tried to let it go. The thoughts that came instead were of Gualdrada's distress, Manno's anger, and a steady sense of danger that soaked into me as thoroughly as the day's dismal rain.

19. BAPTISM

I hated waking to silence on Friday morning, and again on Holy Saturday. To wake without bells was like waking in another world—like waking in Hell itself, for surely anywhere else we would hear bells.

We Florentines are city people, born to the voices of the great bells. We wake to the bells, we pray and work, dine and go to mass, end our workday and close our city's gates to bells, and when our time is come we die to the bells and are buried to them. Bells peal in celebration, in warning, in lamentation. They ring to inform, to proclaim, to summon, to alarm, to call to prayer. We hear their voices bouncing off stone walls, echoing across the river, following us down narrow, twisting streets.

No wonder, then, that on the fearful mornings of Good Friday and Holy Saturday we wake disoriented, for on those dark days the bells are silenced. It is right that in this small way we share in Our Lord's passion, but still I find it hard.

On the second day to break in that unnatural silence, morning dawned bright and clear, the light strong, the air fresh with anticipation. I was up and out before Ghisola and Neri emerged, for I wanted to witness Buondelmonte and his party arriving at Santa Reparata for the final anointing before that afternoon's solemn baptism ritual.

A crowd was already gathering in the square outside Santa Reparata. This morning it was mostly parents and godparents with their little catechumens, but they filled the narrow area between the cemetery and the Baptistery, and some of them sought shade among the tombstones while they waited.

Though it was still early, most of them were dressed for the baptism, wearing snowy white garments and garlands of flowers. The men were freshly shaved, their Lenten beards already a memory. Noblewomen wore gowns of dazzling white, but even the poorest of the parents and godparents had managed to find something white to wear, even if they had to rent or borrow their garments.

With so many lively infants the crowd was far from quiet, and as more people arrived the noise level rose. Here and there, mothers or wet nurses fed their babes, huddled in their own clusters of well-wishers and godparents to hide them from strangers, and godmothers fed their young charges goat's milk through pierced cowhorns. I was glad most had chosen to ignore the rule that a catechumen must be fasting, for the screaming and crying and squalling and yelling was shrill enough without adding the spur of hunger to it.

And here came my party. Buondelmonte and Isabella, in gleaming white, rode white horses, the gilded spurs and pommel of his knighthood glittering in the sun. Fiammetta and Bianca sat astride a gray. Their voluminous white skirts spread gracefully over the animal's blanketed flanks and sides, and the sinister Pistoian bodyguards rode close behind them. Bianca, behind Fiammetta, cradled a bundle that had to be little Margherita. Fiammetta guided their mount expertly through the crowd. She stayed close to Isabella, who also rode with an easy grace. Buondelmonte's face was serious and alert, but the women were smiling. They greeted other women, admired babies, and took their joy in the morning.

I stayed concealed behind others in the crowd. I wanted to watch over Buondelmonte and the women, but I was not eager to be seen. I wasn't even sure why I was here, exactly. If something was going to happen today I would be unable to stop it, but here I was anyhow, if only to bear witness.

A churchman came out onto the steps and rattled his wooden clapper to announce the anointing of the infants. The clattering wooden bars sounded like skeletons dancing, a macabre image I tried in vain to banish. As a substitute for bells, it did not satisfy.

Family groups began to file inside. Buondelmonte and the women dismounted, leaving Vanni and Dino with the horses, and joined the others making their way toward the open cathedral door.

Was that wise? I wondered, then shook off the thought. Nothing would happen in the cathedral; the bishop would never permit it. Nothing would happen on this day.

Family after family filed in, their infants crying lustily, laughing, or just yelling for the pure noise of it. None of them slept, not with so much commotion all around them.

Once all the baptizing families were inside the church, few people remained outside. A handful of servants awaited their masters and mistresses, boys held horses' reins, and Dino and Vanni sat in their saddles like great hulking lumps.

Since the catechumens and their families would be tied up in the ritual for some time, I decided not to wait. Seeing all those clean-shaven men reminded me that my own scruffy Lenten beard and a few inches of unruly hair needed to go. Then I could go into Easter Week looking like a good Christian, even if I was not so sure I was one in fact. I headed back to my own neighborhood to find Tomasso, who by now would have moved his barber shop out into the street and should be well started on his busiest day of the year.

I found him, as I had expected, with a line of customers waiting their turns. Among them was Neri, grumpy and red-eyed. I suspected he was there at Ghisola's prodding.

I spoke to the last man in line and asked him to hold me a place, and then I went up to where Neri was waiting, leaning against the wall of a house. I touched his arm, and he turned listlessly in my direction.

"You were out early," he said.

"I watched the people coming to get their babes anointed."

"I thought other people didn't go to the cathedral until the real service, later. Or maybe you're a godfather for one of your knightly friends, so you had to be there. Is that it?" His tone was teasing, but it had something not altogether friendly in it.

I shook my head. "I think they choose their godparents elsewhere." I was a godfather, once, a long time ago. My brother's boy. His mother didn't survive his birth, the babe didn't live long, and my brother, too, was no longer among us. Of that baptismal party three years ago, only I was left, for both the other godfather and the godmother had gone to their rest in the intervening years. They were victims, like my brother, of a summer fever that had raged through the city.

Neri was silent, and turned away from me to gaze vacantly off down the street. I didn't try to talk to him any more; it only made things worse.

Handsome Tomasso loved an audience. He was in his element, his razor flashing in the sun, picking up speed as he went along. He was skillful, but I didn't want him to be striving for his top speed while he attacked my stubborn beard. He was working fast and talking faster—no customer of Tomasso's ever escaped without a barrage of words. A brazier next to him kept a pot of water simmering, ready to moisten his supply of clean white towels.

Neri's turn came, and I watched while Tomasso made short work of his wiry reddish-brown whiskers. When Tomasso tried to make his usual lively conversation, Neri responded only with grunts, though admittedly that might be the safest approach when an overexcited barber with a half dozen sharp blades laid out in front of him is scraping one's throat.

When Neri was shaved, he got up, paid, and walked away without a glance at me. Tomasso looked at the wet towel he had just used, wrinkled his nose, and tossed it aside. He took a fresh one from the pile at his feet and beckoned to the next customer.

I took my own turn when it came, bantering back and forth with Tomasso and enjoying first the feel of warm rosemary-scented water on my face, and then my smooth chin and shorter hair. He asked me if I knew what was wrong with Neri, and I assured him I had no idea. Or too many ideas, more like. He shrugged, and I paid him and moved out of the way so that the next shaggy customer could be served.

It was still early for dinner, so I walked around and thought about things for a while. I kept telling myself Buondelmonte and the others were safe, at least until the end of Easter week, by which time he and Isabella could be safely out of town and stay there as long as it took for things to calm down—although that might well be the rest of their lives, unless Oddo's faction got itself exiled, or the bishop intervened to force a peace, and even those unlikely solutions might be only temporary.

Something was worrying me, something I was trying to remember, and it continued to elude me. It had to do with Easter week, but I couldn't call it into my mind. Perhaps it would come to me later, I thought.

I went back to the house for a little while, but there wasn't much to eat there, and Neri and Ghisola were not home. The tavern was closed for the holy days, so I had to make do with yesterday's bread dunked in salted oil. By the time I ate and then took a cup of wine with Bicci, it was nearing time to go back for the afternoon's ritual, starting with the baptisms and then the day's other rites.

I changed clothes. This was the season to put away dark clothing, so I dressed in my light blue robe, which had lain folded in my chest since last autumn and had deep creases that refused to relax. I should have hung it out a day or two before. Looking now almost like a proper Florentine should on Holy Saturday, I headed back to the cathedral.

The square was already packed with people. I didn't see Buondel-monte and his ladies, though I knew they had to be there somewhere. The crowd was so dense I couldn't see anything but the people immediately around me. Nobles found themselves squashed up against merchants and woolworkers, despite their best efforts to hold themselves apart and protect their fine apparel. I envied the towering height of Schiatta degli Uberti, or even Mosca—either of them could have seen over the heads of the crowd to find anyone they were looking for.

I was so preoccupied with trying to reassure myself that Fiammetta and the others were safe that it never occurred to me to take part in the service myself. Many a year I had joined in, carrying my unlit candle in procession, chanting the responses, watching and listening in awe as the bishop baptized the first male child and the first female, to be known from that moment forward as Giovanni and Maria, for our city's patron and for the Queen of Heaven. And waiting, eagerly, for that blessed moment when the bells began to peal at last, after the long, awful silence, and the world came right again.

It was not right yet. I scanned the crowd again, searching for familiar faces. I found many—I have lived in Florence all my life, and few of her citizens are completely strange to me—but not those I sought.

One sought me, though, or at least found me, whether he sought me or not. I felt a tap on my shoulder and turned to find Pierino, the talkative young man who had walked with me that morning in January when Oddo's group made its way to the Buondelmonti palace, the one who had regaled me with information about Selvaggia and her family.

"Hey, Fool, it's good to see you again. How are you?" he said, grinning at me. I liked the lad; I couldn't help grinning back.

"Pierino. Good to see you, too. Are you here in service to messer Oddo, or are you on your own?"

"Oh, I'm working," he said. "I'm here with Captain Guido and a couple of others. We're supposed to be getting some information. Can't talk about it, though. It's a secret." He said this with considerable self-importance, and then looked at me expectantly. He wants me to ask, I thought. Well, why not? I'd play along.

"Oh, come on, Pierino, you can tell me. Remember, you told me all about Selvaggia while we were on the way to the Buondelmonti palace," I said, wheedling.

His face took on a sly, conspiratorial expression, and he pointedly looked to both sides. Plenty of people were close enough to hear us, but nobody was paying any attention, and that was enough for my eager young friend.

"Well, you're pretty much one of us," he said in a whisper, "so I guess I can tell you. We're to confirm that Buondelmonte is here acting as godfather for some Donati brat."

"Is he?" I said, as if surprised. "Why do you need to know about that?"

"You know about the decision, right? You were there."

"Yes. But surely they can't enact it now?"

"No, not on this holy day, or tomorrow, or in fact any time during Easter Week. My master and his kinsmen are good Christian men."

That wasn't the first description that occurred to me, but never mind. I felt relieved to hear him confirm that the attempt would not happen this week.

"Why do you need to know about Buondelmonte, then?"

Before he could answer me, the archpriest stepped out into the square, and an anticipatory murmur swept through the crowd. Some then knelt, others stood, but all stopped their conversations and were silent, waiting. Even the squalling infants quieted, although not completely. His Holiness himself couldn't have silenced a horde of babies.

The nervous lad whose job it was to carry the firebowl held it out carefully before him, while the priest worked clumsily with a flint to rekindle the Easter fire within it. It took him several tries, but at last he succeeded in striking a spark that caught the kindling in the bowl, and the new fire blazed up.

Pierino and I stood shoulder to shoulder, watching. I wanted to hear the answer to my question, but now was not the time for speaking.

The archpriest turned to face the great door of the cathedral and raised his arms, his back to the crowd, and in a loud voice that echoed off the stone wall in front of him he chanted "Lumen Christi" three times. He took the firebowl from the boy and carried it, slowly and with dignity, into the great church. The crowd formed itself into a sinuous, snaking line and followed him in.

I took advantage of the activity to ask Pierino again, "Why do you need to know that, if nothing can be done this week?"

"Because," he said, still whispering, "if he's a godparent today, he'll have to come back a week from tomorrow, on Easter Octave, for the chrism ceremony. We'll know where to find him, and the Octave will be after the end of Easter Week."

That was it. That was the thing that had been tugging at the back of my mind. Godparents must accompany their charge back to the church on that day to have the chrism cloth removed, washed, and returned to the child's parents, and I had forgotten. My brother's child hadn't lived out the week, so my own godparent experience didn't include that ceremony. My stomach clenched.

"Doesn't that still count as Easter Week?" I asked. "I mean, it's the final part of the baptism, and they have to be here."

Pierino grinned again, this time more wolfish than cheerful. "Well, that's exactly it, isn't it? They have to be here. And messer Oddo says it's more'n a week past Easter, so it doesn't count, or at least it's close enough."

"But what's the hurry? Vendettas can go on for years."

"This one won't. Messer Mosca's convinced our master that it's better to do it soon and have it over with, so people won't be laughing at us. He's real persuasive, that one. Not that it took much, with the big man already furious."

Easter Octave. Surely Buondelmonte had thought this through, I told myself. Surely he would find a way to avoid it, perhaps leaving this final responsibility to Fiammetta and Bianca.

No. Not Buondelmonte. He would come back, publicly and ostentatiously showing off his magnificent young bride, his knightly spurs, his high-stepping white horse, and his luxurious clothes. I had no doubt of that. But at least now he had Vanni and Dino with him. Scowling lowlifes they might be, but they amounted to good, solid protection.

And yet, would two men—even those two—be protection enough? Buondelmonte would be better off by far if he knew when to expect Oddo's attack, so someone needed to tell him. And that someone was going to have to be me.

That thought scared me. It had to be me because I was probably the only one outside of Oddo's circle who knew, but by that same token, it wouldn't take much for Oddo to figure out how Buondelmonte learned of his plans, if he quizzed his men. And he would.

Perhaps if I didn't approach Buondelmonte directly, but got a message to the Donati women, or even to Lippo, it would be harder to trace. But I had been seen talking to Buondelmonte in the marketplace; I didn't think using a go-between would be enough to keep me safe.

I had said nothing in response, and Pierino looked at me, puzzled. Over to my right I noticed Guido loping toward us. Most of the crowd that had lately filled the square had by now entered the cathedral, and only a handful of us remained outside.

Guido reached us, unsmiling. "Fool," he said, acknowledging me, and turned to Pierino. "I trust you've kept silence?"

Pierino's eyes opened wider. "Yes, I—I only spoke to the fool, and he's one of us," he said, but he sounded unsure of himself.

Guido spat. "You're the fool here, Pierino. He's not one of us. Did messer Oddo say he was?"

Pierino was close to tears. Younger than I thought, even. "But he was with us before, so it won't do any harm—"

"That's not for you to judge. My orders are, if anybody finds out, I bring 'em back to the master, and he tells us what to do about it. And even if he says this one is all right, he's not going to be happy about you flapping your mouth." Pierino shut that mouth tight, trying to regain control. I wasn't any too happy about knowing, myself. Now I had the burden of warning Buondelmonte, and that was going to be even riskier if I had to see Oddo first.

We heard a rustling sound from the church. The worshippers began to file out of the cathedral, led by churchmen, all of them still carrying unlit tapers. The clerics began to march solemnly toward the Baptistery, singing the litany of the saints.

The churchmen in the lead began to circle that ancient octagonal building so beloved of the Florentines, and as they walked, they continued to sing. The worshippers added their voices, and I realized that both Guido and Pierino were singing softly as we watched. It was a moving sight, the white-robed parents and godparents and the other worshippers in their light garments on this brilliant afternoon, and I heard my own voice joining in, even while my mind roiled.

Take me to Oddo? What happens then? And how could I get my information to Buondelmonte without risking my own neck, when Oddo had just been reminded that I knew his plans?

I heard Guido whisper, "Look! There they are." Buondelmonte, Isabella, Fiammetta, and Bianca had come out of the church, all in their gleaming white, and Fiammetta held the infant Margherita tenderly. All were singing the litany. I imagined I could hear Fiammetta's sweet, pure voice above all the rest.

"We've got what we want, then," Guido said decisively. "We need to take this one back to the big man, and you, boy, had better hope our news puts him in a good mood." Pierino swallowed hard, but didn't say anything.

Guido put a hand firmly on my arm. "I'm sorry about this, Fool, but you can blame the stupid boy. Messer Oddo needs his plans kept secret for a while longer, and he says that if anyone finds out, he wants to see that person before they talk to anyone else. So that's where we're going now. Don't worry, I'll tell him it wasn't your fault."

"But he asked me," Pierino wailed, and Guido gave me an appraising look. He tightened his grip on my arm. I did not like the way this was going.

"Well, then, time to go report," said Guido, and off we went.

Leaving the pageantry and solemnity behind, the three of us walked swiftly toward the Fifanti enclave. Guido didn't loosen his grip on me, and he didn't speak to me again until we were inside Oddo's palace. He sent Pierino off to the barracks, and pulled me along with him toward the stairs.

151

20. EASTER

We started up the great staircase in Oddo's palace, and Guido spoke to me quietly as we climbed. "Fool, I don't know what you're playing at, but you want to be very careful, or you'll find yourself in a lot of trouble. Messer Oddo is determined to have everything go smoothly, and having people find out the when and where of it was not in his plans."

"Pierino did tell me the when, but I don't know anything about the where," I said, keeping my voice low. At least I hadn't completely lost Guido's good will, or he wouldn't be issuing warnings.

"All the same, we can't take chances. When we go into the hall, let me go first and give him our report, and then we'll call you. Just stand there and wait. Don't do anything, and don't even think about trying to leave. Vito is on guard downstairs, and you won't be going anywhere." I had noted Vito when we came in. He could have been Dino and Vanni's big brother, and I was not about to challenge him. I nodded. As for me being in trouble, Guido didn't know the half of it yet, I thought sourly. I would just have to trust to Buondelmonte for protection, once I gave him my warning.

Oddo sat alone in front of the window, watching us. Guido marched over to him and saluted. He reminded me of a boy playing soldier, lacking only a wooden sword and a makeshift helm to complete the illusion.

He spoke to Oddo, and the big man's face lit up. He and Guido exchanged a grin, and then Oddo's attention fell on me.

"You." He motioned me to join them. I did, giving him a bow that was correct and nothing more.

"Guido, what's this one doing back here?"

"He knows when, my lord. Pierino found him and spouted off."

Oddo scowled. "We could have done without that. What was the stupid boy thinking?"

"He remembered the fool from the trip to Buondelmonte's, I think, and he thought it was all right."

"It is not all right. Fool, you'll have to stay here now until after Easter Octave. It's unfortunate, but there's no alternative. You can blame the boy for that. We'll see that you're compensated, but for this week, you are either with me or with Guido every moment, understand? You don't even hit the latrine alone."

I did understand, and I didn't like it. How could I warn Buondelmonte if I couldn't get out of here? "My lord, this is not an easy thing for me to do—"

"It's plenty easy. You'll sleep in the barracks with my men, and when I want you, you'll entertain for the Easter games. You'll be well paid and well fed. If anybody asks, we hired you for the week. It may turn out to be a good thing, having a fool in residence—distract everybody and keep morale high. Guido, make a space for him and keep an eye on him. You did well to figure out what happened and bring him here." Guido beamed. He lived for Oddo's approval, as far as I could tell.

"And do something about that idiot boy. Feo's boy, isn't it?"

"Yes, my lord. Do what? Do you want to keep him?"

Oddo made a face. "I suppose so. Feo served my father; he's under my protection. But teach the boy a lesson, and make sure he learns to keep his mouth shut." His eyes met Guido's, and Guido nodded. I felt a pang of guilt for getting Pierino into a bad situation, or at least for helping him get himself into one.

Oddo turned his attention back to me. "Is there anyone you need us to notify?" he asked. "Anyone you live with?"

"I have a job coming up, so if I must stay here, I'd be grateful if you would let me go home first and tell Neri, so he can get someone to take my place." No such job existed, but I didn't want Ghisola and Neri to worry. And that way I could get one of them to take the news to the Donati palace, even if I couldn't do it myself. Neri, I thought. Ghisi would be more reliable, but I didn't want to risk her safety, even to save Buondelmonte.

Oddo shook his head. "You stay. I'll have him told." He turned to Guido. "Corrado's house. Tell the musician or the woman he's spending the week in our hire." He snapped his fingers. "Do it," he ordered, and Guido was off.

And there went my chance to warn Buondelmonte. All I could do now was pray that Dino and Vanni were protection enough, even without my information.

Oddo once again appeared to forget all about me, and he sat for a while staring out the window while I stood nearby. Finally he sighed heavily and got up. As he did, we heard the first of the cathedral bells begin to peal. The other bells of the cathedral joined in, and then the bells from other churches, near and far, added their voices, one, then another, then too many to distinguish, until all were speaking joyfully together. The long silence was over. Oddo and I looked at each other and crossed ourselves.

I joined him at the window, and we watched the sky grow black with starlings. They boiled out of the church towers, shrieking in alarm, startled from their rest when the great bells began to wake and speak again. They swooped in great agitated spirals, fleeing the sounds they had forgotten in two long days of silence. Knight and fool together, we looked out at our city and drank in the sound of the bells.

When the pealing at last wound down, Oddo shook his head and swept his hair back with his hands. The gesture apparently signaled a return to business, for he bellowed for Vito, who sprinted up the stairs and saluted, out of breath. Oddo turned me over to him "until Guido gets back," and told him to take me down to the barracks and introduce me around as the fool who would be entertaining during Easter Games. He was not, Oddo emphasized, to let me leave the palace for any reason.

The barracks was a plain long room, with ten straw pallets laid out in two neat rows, a simple wooden storage chest at the head of each one. Many more men than that were in Oddo's service, but they didn't all live in his palace. This barracks was for the single men, those without family nearby, and they lived in this palace as part of Oddo's family—family in the larger sense, encompassing servants and other dependents and employees as well as relatives.

Vito consulted with the oldest of Oddo's rough soldiers and then assigned me a pallet and a blanket, neither of which was much dirtier or more verminous or smelled any worse than the one I slept on at home. I stretched out and waited for Guido's return.

No entertainment was permitted on that sober day, even though the bells had pealed again to herald the beginning of the great Easter vigil. All would continue fasting, quiet and reflective, until the Easter services—those most holy rites of the Christian year—were over. Only then would the citizens at long last untangle themselves from the privations of Lent and begin to celebrate, giving voice to their joy in Our Lord's resurrection, the coming of spring, and the end of the long fast all at once.

I was sure that not all of Oddo's soldiers would march off to the cathedral for the Easter service. Oddo didn't strike me as a man who would ease his security, regardless of the day. Vito, who was affable enough despite his forbidding appearance, confirmed that at least half of the men in the barracks were to remain on the premises.

Being confined here was in one way a relief to me, because I still had not made my confession, and thus I didn't know what to do about taking communion. Maybe, I thought, it was best to miss it altogether. With luck, I would live to see more Easters.

I couldn't avoid it, though. Oddo had a care for his men's spiritual health, and he had arranged for his parish priest, one Father Salvestro, to come to the palace after Saturday Vespers and confess all those who needed it, and then to return late on Easter to give communion to all those who remained on duty, unable to attend the cathedral services. Oddo's patronage of the parish church bought him certain privileges.

When Oddo came down to the barracks to ask which men still needed to make their confession, I spoke up, hopeful for a moment that he might let me return to my parish, where I could have contrived somehow to send a message to Buondelmonte. I should have known better. Instead, Oddo ordered me to come upstairs with his men and meet with his priest.

"But, my lord, the church says I must confess to my own parish priest." This was a new ruling, not yet in place in all parishes, but worth a try.

Oddo was in no mood for theological arguments. "This week, you're living here, so he is your parish priest," he said with finality. So be it. I shrugged. If these men could confess, so could I, for we were all contributors to the same massive, as yet uncommitted sin.

Four of us obediently followed Oddo up to his hall, where Father Salvestro waited, tapping his foot with impatience. Not an easy day, this, for a priest to be away from his church, but Oddo was not to be denied.

The soldiers went first, and because no attempt was made to make these confessions private, I was able to listen closely to the formula they used. It was a quick and all-encompassing list of sins by category, and the good father obviously didn't want to wait around for specifics. That suited me well. I couldn't have used the confessional to give the alarm, anyway—not to Oddo's tame priest. I took my turn at the end, kneeling and confessing to all the categories of sin I might have committed, and received the same rote absolution as the others. I didn't feel cleansed, but at least I had done nothing to call attention to myself. And in this place I had nothing to hide except my ties to Buondelmonte. All else, my complicity in this vendetta and my service to Oddo, I shared with the others.

After promising Oddo that he would return with the host late on Easter, Father Salvestro hurried away, and the soldiers and I marched back down to the barracks. Guido was back. He told me he had delivered the message to the blonde woman with the gap between her front teeth. Neri had not been at the house.

Pierino was there, but he turned away rather than look at me. He had a livid bruise on his left cheek, and his eye was swollen shut. He moved stiffly. I had the feeling the other young ones resented my role in Pierino's punishment, but the three older men took it in stride and made me welcome. The off-duty soldiers and I spent the rest of the day variously in prayer or dozing on our pallets or in quiet conversation, and so my first day as Oddo's reluctant guest came to an end.

*

Easter dawned with a great peal of bells, a sound I welcomed with all my heart. Easter dinner would be after the services, later than usual, so I trooped up to the kitchen with the other men to break our fast, and on the way I got my first glimpse of the Fifanti women, emerging from their chambers behind the hall and ready to go to church.

These dignified and devout ladies passed silently through the hall and waited for the last of the soldiers to reach the top of the stairs so they could proceed down. Oddo joined them, taking his wife's arm. She smiled at him affectionately, and he patted her hand. Her face was softer, gentler now than it had been the night she bandaged his arm, and they looked comfortable together. It was a side of Oddo I hadn't seen before.

With master and mistress and much of the household off for a long day at church, those of us who remained took our ease, lounging around the kitchen with our feet up on the benches. Guido was part of Oddo's escort, as was the damaged Pierino, so I was left without anyone in particular to talk with. But the men were friendly enough—even the younger ones who had been sullen at first over Pierino's ill luck had by now accepted me, so that quiet afternoon spent together in the barracks hadn't been a waste. In fact, they made it clear that they were eager for some entertainment from me.

The cook was a middle-aged woman who looked strong enough to take us all on. She was aided in the preparation of the Easter feast by a plain, timid young girl with her hair tied up in a towel, doing her best to follow the cook's orders while pretending the rest of us weren't there. A couple of the men couldn't resist pestering her and trying to get her attention, but she worked doggedly on, holding back tears, and ignored them.

The cook grumbled at having to work around us, but she obviously enjoyed the soldiers' friendly banter. She even brought out a few additional things for us to eat along with our sops in wine, including almonds and a small bowl of fresh ricotta streaked with honey, which we stuck our fingers into with gusto. It felt strange to be eating something made from milk this early on Easter, but then, the whole feast would be over before Father Salvestro showed up to give us communion, so we would have to reverse the order of things for today. The kitchen was filled with sweet and spicy scents, but it was going to smell even better once the herbed chunks of lamb were roasting. It had been a long time since any of us smelled or tasted meat, and a longer time since our meat was fresh and not salt.

"There'll be another feast tomorrow," one fellow told me, "but not for us. Monday's the women's day, so messer Oddo's daughters and their families and the Amidei will be here. This year, some of the Uberti women are coming, so there's even more than usual."

The cook looked up from crumbling dried rosemary in a mortar. "And the Uberti are sending their cook, too," she said, sounding aggrieved. "I can make that feast perfectly well on my own, and now I'm going to have that incompetent woman in my kitchen, and she'll probably try to run things."

"Well, the Uberti tried to run all of Florence once, not all that long ago, so I guess their cook is likely to try to run your kitchen, sure enough," the soldier said.

"They didn't take over the city, though, did they? And she's not going to take over my kitchen," the cook said grimly, grinding hard enough to pulverize the rosemary.

"I think they'd like to try it again, though," another soldier said.

"But it would be good for our master and good for us if they did, wouldn't it?" said the first. "Then we could squash Buondelmonte without having to go through any formal vendetta. We'd drive him clean out of the city, and we wouldn't have to ambush him and do him in."

"Don't talk about such things on a holy day," said the cook sharply. The soldier mumbled an apology. I was relieved, for that situation was not something I wanted to be thinking about, since I couldn't find a way to do anything to prevent it.

The conversation meandered. Soon they were asking me for jests and entertainment.

"Do you juggle, Fool?" asked one, proffering a pair of kitchen knives. I juggle your master and his worst enemy, I thought, automatically checking the knives for balance.

"A little. Not with sharp things. That takes a specialist." So did juggling knights, come to think of it. I was no specialist at that, either, though I was learning fast. The cook scowled and retrieved her cutlery.

"Do you tumble?" That I did, and I demonstrated with a series of forward and backward somersaults, which occasioned a stream of cursing from the cook while I brushed off the debris I had picked up from the floor.

157

"There's not enough room for that in this kitchen," she said, glaring at me. "You want to perform, give us a song, or a joke, or a story. Don't be throwing yourself around while we're trying to make your dinner."

Obediently, I started to run through my repertoire. I wished Neri was there to lead the singing, but I did my best, and I managed to get them all lustily warbling a paean to spring. When I ran out of verses I improvised new ones, and the men bellowed the refrain back at me. After a while I found myself reaching for ever more ridiculous ideas and rhymes. The men loved it, and even the cook snickered at my more far-fetched efforts, while her shy girl proved to have a lovely soprano voice.

We were thus engaged in singing questionable spring ditties when we heard the lord and lady of the house return with their retinue. By this time the cook had the lamb pieces sizzling on a spit and our mouths were watering enough to interfere with our singing, so we brought the concert to a close and trooped back down the stairs to report to Oddo.

The first of our group reached the great hall from above just as Oddo and his group of women reached it from below. The soldiers saluted, Oddo returned the gesture, and Oddo's lady nodded to us and went on to her chambers off the upper hall, followed by the other women. Oddo tossed his mantle to Guido, who hung it on a rod, handling it as if it was something precious.

"A joyous Easter to you, men," Oddo said jovially. "I heard your voices raised in song as we came in. A hymn to our Redeemer, I don't doubt?" He grinned.

"Oh, yes, my lord," said the soldier in the lead with wide-eyed mock innocence, and we all laughed. Oddo assigned Guido and Vito to take a turn watching the door, dismissed the rest of us, and we went back to barracks, where those who had attended the service described it, in all its grandeur and magnificence, to those of us who had missed it.

It was amazing to me how much everyone's mood had lifted with the return of the bells, and with the celebration of the Resurrection finally underway. Even so, I had a hollow feeling in my gut, born of the knowledge that I had not yet taken communion and that my confession had been less than complete, and also that I had information Buondelmonte needed and no way to get it to him. Still, I could do nothing about any of it now. At least I had received absolution from a priest who, I hoped, knew what he was doing for the good of my soul, for by now I needed all the help I could get.

Remembering Neri's outburst and his firm conviction that he was damned, I wondered if he had taken communion. I was still worried about him, and I wished Guido had seen him as well as Ghisola when he delivered Oddo's message. But Ghisola had sent me no message in return, so I could only assume that all was well.

The rest of Easter passed pleasantly enough. Since only the immediate family was present, the soldiers and I ate with them in the great hall. Everything was delicious, but the meat was what we had been waiting for. We polished off every scrap of the succulent lamb, leaving only bare bones to be taken downstairs and tossed to the dogs tethered in the courtyard behind the palace. Eggs, cheese, and a delicate ricotta pie also re-entered our lives with this meal, and we received them all enthusiastically. Ghisola would have wanted to know what spices were in that pie, I was sure, but I couldn't have told her. Something subtle and expensive, probably. The soldiers took turns at the front door, taking short shifts so no one had to miss much of the feast.

Replete at the end of the meal, we sat back with cups of fine wine. The men called for me to entertain, but I was so full I couldn't even consider it. I told them I would perform when one of them came forward to tumble with me, but I got no volunteers, only groans as people patted their bellies and loosened their belts.

We were still groaning happily when Father Salvestro showed up. Oddo led the priest and all those of us who had missed the service into the chamber that served as the family's private chapel. It was a small room with wood panels for walls and no windows, and the flickering candles barely illuminated a few religious paintings. A little altar was covered with a fine embroidered cloth, and a painted wood crucifix hung on the wall behind it. The harried priest set up what he needed, then proceeded to run through the ritual quickly and without inflection. He gave us communion, albeit in a rather perfunctory way, beginning with the cook and her helper, and then the men, with me last. I felt little as we knelt and went through the motions, though I tried to pray with my whole mind and keep my fears and doubts at bay. There was nothing much to it; we all politely thanked the exhausted priest as he packed up his supplies and made ready to go, first making a stop in the women's chambers to administer the host to a bedridden servant.

That night, as I stretched out on my pallet with Oddo's men all around me, I took what comfort I could in my full belly. I didn't want to be there in Oddo's palace. I wanted to be home, with Neri and Ghisola. I had made it through Easter in this strange place, but that most holy of days ended for me with no sense of peace or joy, only a feeling of dread for what was coming.

21. WOMEN'S GAMES

I was curious about what Easter Monday would be like in Oddo's militaristic household. In my neighborhood it meant a lot of horseplay and clowning around, the women bossing their men about, beating on them with sticks (usually, but not always, in jest), and playing silly and insulting jokes on the poor males, who had to put up with it or be reviled as spoilers of everyone's fun.

Since the men got to do all of those things on all the other days of the year, it wasn't too much of a sacrifice. Last year Ghisola had come into her own as the leader of the women, and she came up with truly diabolical games. Watching Neri's reaction had been one of the highlights.

Somehow, though, I couldn't quite picture Oddo's demure wife leading her ladies in such antics. I asked Guido what they did to celebrate the day.

"Not too much. It's pretty mild compared to some households. Monna Ermellina invites the other women over, and they hire somebody to entertain them—you're probably it, this year—and they make a day of it. The men generally stay out of their way."

"No bossing the men around?"

"Well, you might hear the occasional request for the men to bring wine or fetch cushions or some such, but mostly it's all pretty genteel."

"Who comes?" I asked.

"One of their daughters—the other one is running a livelier show in her own home, as I hear it—and the two daughters-in-law, and the lady of the Amidei and any of her girls who are at home. I guess that means our jilted little harridan, this year. Should make for a wonderful party, don't you think?" Guido chuckled. "I hear she's been a demon ever since she got left at the church."

"Better not let messer Oddo hear you laugh about that," I said, holding up a finger in admonition. Guido's smile evaporated.

"You're not going to say anything to him, are you?"

"Of course not. Is that all? I heard something about Uberti women, too."

"Messer Schiatta's been spending a lot of time with the big man and messer Lambertuccio lately. They'll probably all be here, and that means Schiatta's wife and his other women, I guess."

Sure enough, I was to be the entertainment. Oddo would save a few coins by using his tame jester rather than hiring the musicians his lady wife probably preferred. He came to the kitchen to talk to me as we were breaking our fast, and with him was monna Ermellina, a plump, pleasant lady who questioned me about what she might need to provide so I could entertain, and about what sorts of things I could do. I liked her much better when she wasn't fretting about her man.

Her tastes ran toward music, as I had suspected, and we agreed on my playing the flute for the ladies' dancing and perhaps giving them a song or two. But music was not my main skill. I offered a bit of tumbling and juggling, and she told me there should be ample room in the hall as long as we left the trestle tables unassembled until just before dinner. In any case, we'd have to put them away again promptly afterwards to allow for the dancing.

I was to take my place somewhere out of the way in the hall and play on the flute they provided, quietly and in the background, until I was summoned to entertain. Monna Ermellina asked me to be thinking of things I might do that fit the theme of the day, and she smiled at me encouragingly.

"I'm sure that whatever you do will please us all," she said. "My husband tells me you're both talented and clever." I bowed and thanked her, as graciously as I could. She was a gentle lady, and I would do my best to make her little gathering a pleasant one.

She took me down one flight from the kitchen to show me the upper hall, where the party was to be held. It was completely different from Oddo's large hall, with his shields and weapons and battle frescoes. This room was all softness and color—embroidered cushions on the benches, elaborate stencils of birds and flowers on the walls, costly hangings, and woven reed mats on a floor composed of alternating square tiles of blue and red. I suppose it was all very fashionable, but to me it felt fussy and overdone. My father had been scornful about such decor. He always said a fine name was no guarantee of fine taste. That floor made me feel like a pawn on a giant's gaming board, which was perhaps a little too close to the truth for comfort.

Nothing would begin for at least another hour and a half, for Monna Ermellina and her guests had to attend the solemn Easter Monday services and rites before their party could start, so I took the time to practice. One of monna Ermellina's ladies brought me the flute, as well as a set of juggling balls. I tried out the balls: they were not weighted as well as mine, but they would do. I didn't have my motley, but the tunic I wore was cut generously enough to allow me to do my tumbling routine. This should work, I thought.

161

The flute was nicely in tune, its muted voice perfect for background playing. I would have to push it a bit for the dancing, and perhaps round up someone to bang on something, if none of the ladies brought a tabor along. Even if they did, and a tabor pipe with it, I couldn't handle pipe and tabor simultaneously—that was Anselmo's specialty—and so I would have to stick to the flute and let someone else provide the rhythm.

After satisfying myself that I was ready, limbered up, and familiar with the space and with my tools, I took my place in one corner of the hall and waited. Monna Ermellina returned from church and popped her head in to make sure I was where I was supposed to be and tell me it wouldn't be long.

Two servants had finished readying the hall while I was rehearsing. They draped the benches in the hall with costly carpets in intricate Eastern designs, and they sprinkled the floor lightly with fragrant herbs, which meant I would look like a haystack after my first somersault. The shutters were fully open to let in the bright daylight, for the day was mild. Small tables covered with embroidered white towels held dishes of sweetmeats. I leaned against the wall and noodled a tune on the pleasing little flute.

We heard a rapping on the door downstairs, and Oddo and his lady hurried down to greet the first of their guests. I heard a mixture of voices, high and low, as the nobles greeted one another. It sounded like several people had arrived at once.

I continued to play as they came up the stairs. I was, of course, only part of the party decorations, so no one would be introduced to me, but I amused myself while warbling on the flute by seeing who I could recognize.

Some of them were easy. Oddo and Ermellina's daughter was a younger and slimmer version of her mother, with a round face and a rosy complexion. She had two small children with her, a boy and a girl. I wondered if I was going to have to amuse the children as well, but once the children's grandparents had greeted them affectionately and spoken with them, the daughter's servingwoman ushered the little ones into a back room. From the noises that emerged, I guessed there must be plenty of toys there, and room to play.

Two other women about the same age must have been the daughters-in-law. I had seen them all, standing together at the wedding-that-wasn't. Whatever man or men had accompanied those ladies had not come upstairs with them, but Lambertuccio was there, and with him his thin, haggard-looking wife monna Lauretta and their remaining unmarried daughter, the redoubtable Selvaggia. With them also was a child, a skinny, serious girl of about ten. A granddaughter, I assumed. She remained with the women rather than joining the younger children, and monna Ermellina made a special point of seating the girl next to her, with the child's grandmother on her other side. She had brought a drop spindle, and she took it out and began to spin as she sat with her legs dangling, listening to the women chatter.

Lambertuccio and Oddo stood apart, talking quietly, while Lauretta greeted the Fifanti women. She looked older than Ermellina, and I had an impression of nervous blinks, fluttering hands, and anxious little glances. Disquieting dark circles shadowed her eyes, and her skin was sallow.

None of the other women so much as turned in my direction as I sat there playing quietly. Selvaggia, however, stalked in at her mother's side and looked right at me. She noted my presence but didn't acknowledge it. She was wearing the dark green dress she had worn when I saw her sewing in her father's frigid hall, in contrast to the other women in their light-colored spring gowns.

No sooner had I sorted out who was who in this first group than the door downstairs opened to another, louder tap, and we heard more voices, high and low. Very low. It was, unmistakably, Schiatta degli Uberti who spoke to the guard, and Oddo and Ermellina went down once more to greet their new guests.

They returned with Schiatta and a half dozen women, as well as three more small children who were hustled off into the noisy back room to join their fellows. One woman I assumed was Schiatta's wife, based on her age and on the simple dignity and luxurious fabric of her gown, though the extravagant courtesy Oddo extended to her would have sufficed to identify her. With her were five younger women who I supposed to be daughters or daughters-in-law, clothed like a rainbow, or a garden in bloom. They might also have been at the almost-wedding; I wasn't sure.

One in particular, though, I recognized. She was striking, with a shapely body and ripe lips. Her eyelashes were extraordinarily long, her dark eyes large and almond-shaped, and she wore a distinctive and flattering gown of greens and blues, with borders and sleeves contrasting with skirt and bodice and giving the effect of a sensual water nymph. When I saw her last, she was in pelo di lione, turning heads outside Santa Maria sopra Porta.

What interested me about that one even more than her enticing beauty was her reaction when she saw Selvaggia. Her cheeks first lost color and then flushed, and she immediately turned away, seeking a place as far from the younger girl as she possibly could. Selvaggia, as usual, missed nothing, and I thought I saw a little smirk.

Eventually everyone had greeted everyone else, and the ladies distributed themselves along the three benches prepared for their comfort. Selvaggia sat a little apart at one end.

Meanwhile Oddo, Lambertuccio, and Schiatta stood together, talking among themselves. I watched them while I played. If Oddo was a bull and Lambertuccio a lion and Mosca a hawk, then what was Schiatta? Something cold, I thought. Something scaly.

Ermellina stood up and clapped her hands for attention, and all the women politely turned to face her. The men fell silent.

"Gentle ladies, this is the day our menfolk do our bidding," she said to smiles and scattered applause. "I would begin by commanding my lord husband to bring us wine." More applause as the ladies turned to Oddo, waiting for his response

Oddo bowed deeply to his wife, his eyes twinkling. "My lady, I obey," he said, with a flourish, and started up the stairs to a tinkle of laughter from the ladies. Lambertuccio made to follow him, but Oddo signalled him to wait, and Lambertuccio turned back to Schiatta.

I played on. By now I was repeating tunes, but no one seemed to notice either the repetition or the fact that I was playing at all. The women were cheerful and talkative, except for Selvaggia and her mother. The nymph in green and blue talked animatedly with two other young women, but she never looked in Selvaggia's direction.

Soon Oddo returned, ostentatiously holding up a large pitcher filled with wine. Guido followed him with a tray full of glasses and cups, and another man came behind him with a pitcher of water for mixing. The three made a great show of pouring and watering the wine and distributing the cups, beginning with Schiatta's wife and working down by age until Oddo finished by presenting Lambertuccio's little granddaughter a cup of well-watered wine, along with an exaggerated bow and a flourish. The child giggled a little as she took it, thanking him prettily.

This glimpse of Oddo as a family man was disconcerting. Before this week I had only seen his blustery aggressive side, and I had thought it the only one he had. I should have known better; few men are so simple. But now, his duty discharged, with grave courtesy he asked permission to take the other men to his study. His wife granted it, theatrically and to laughter, and all three men bowed and made their way back into the warren of private chambers off the hall. From the burst of noise that followed, I surmised Oddo had made a brief visit to the children's playroom on his way to his study. I wondered how much these women knew of the matters their men would be discussing. More than they wanted to admit, I suspected.

Still I played the flute. All of the women chattered, except for the little girl, who listened wide-eyed, and Selvaggia, who sat in stony silence, and monna Lauretta, who looked tired and strained. I was beginning to run out of tunes I hadn't already played multiple times when at last Ermellina summoned me to her. I scrambled up and presented myself.

"Will you give us a show to please us, Fool?" she asked courteously. Apparently male underlings were exempt from being summarily ordered about on this day. "On this day of the ladies, we want to be amused. Will you show us your skill?"

In answer, I risked a backwards somersault. Not the best move to warm up with, but I had stretched well before the ladies arrived, and I felt limber enough. Ermellina, delighted, applauded me, and a couple of the others joined in. By now most of them were looking at me, rather than at their needlework or at one another, so I took advantage of the moment to run through my tumbling routine.

I extemporized a narrative in which I was playing the part of a domineering husband who has had the tables turned on him by a clever wife, in honor of the theme of the day. They liked it, and a couple of the younger women added their own comments and suggestions, some of them almost worthy of Ghisola. It was obvious that had the older ladies not been present, the tone of the day would have been much rowdier.

I did my signature cartwheel into a handstand to finish, and was rewarded with applause and cheers. Ermellina looked pleased, and rather proud of herself.

"Fool, we would next like to see you juggle," she said, but as I stood before her, panting and mopping my brow with my sleeves, she laughed and relented. "After you've had a rest, of course." So I passed the time until dinner alternating between juggling and playing the little flute quietly in the background, which was not quite resting and not quite performing, and in between, plucking bits of lavender and rosemary out of my clothes.

When the servants set up the trestle tables and brought out the tablecloths to cover them, I went up to the kitchen to get my own dinner. That gave me a good long break, while servants took the capons and salads and pottage down to the guests. From the mix of voices I heard below, the men must have rejoined their women for the meal. Most of what I heard was right there in the kitchen—Oddo's cook squabbling with the Uberti's cook, a woman as wide as she was tall who had no intention of backing down. She answered the Amidei cook's scolding with grunted monosyllables. How those two ever managed to send out a decent meal without killing each other, I'll never know.

I was lounging on a stool, my eyes closed, enjoying a plate of figs and nuts and letting the cooks entertain me when the bickering voices went silent, and I heard a familiar flat voice say, "Fool."

Selvaggia. "My lady?" I said, getting to my feet, still holding the wooden plate in one hand.

"I would speak with you," she said.

"Here?"

"Here." The cooks and the shy helper were across the room, busy with a stack of dirty dishes, scraping plates and salvaging leftovers and scraps. They carefully avoided looking at us. If we stayed where we were and spoke quietly, we would not be heard.

She sat unceremoniously on the stool I had just vacated. I set my plate down on a shelf and remained standing.

"You did as I told you, Fool, and I have kept your secret," she said.

"I thank you, my lady."

"Yet I find you among us again. Why?"

This could be tricky.

"Because I learned by accident of messer Oddo's plans."

"You helped make those plans."

"Not the what of them, but the when and where."

"You learned by accident," she repeated, emphasizing the last word.

"One of Oddo's men told me. I didn't ask." That was not quite true, but it was close enough. And poor eager Pierino would have told me whether I asked or not.

"Hmph. So then my uncle had you brought here, to make sure you don't betray us, yes?"

"Yes."

"He did well. So here you are, and perhaps after you have given your talents to this house for a day or two more, I'll send for you to lighten the mood at the Amidei palace. We need it. My lady mother is distraught, while I grow impatient."

I inclined my head. "My lady, I am here to serve."

She let out a short bark of a laugh. "You're here, Fool, because you have no choice. I don't know what you would be doing right now to undermine our revenge if you weren't a prisoner here, but I will tell you that I don't trust you, and I'm very glad my clever uncle has enough sense not to trust you either."

166

I was on dangerous ground here and I knew it, but I couldn't help seething at her arrogance. I never asked for any of this—these people forced me into it. If they don't like my way of doing things, I thought, they can go find someone else to play their vicious games.

"My lady, I feel no regret at not being trusted by people who plan murder, and especially a woman who wants to kill." I didn't believe I had just said that.

Selvaggia only looked amused. "So the little fool has a spark to him after all," she said. "All right, then, Fool, I'll tell you what. I've seen you watching all of us. I know you've been talking to my uncle's men, and I don't believe for a moment you were given that piece of information out of the blue sky. I know how curious you are. So right here, right now, I am going to satisfy your curiosity. What is it you want to know? Do you wish to know who will strike him, or with what weapon? Do you long to learn how we've assured ourselves that he'll be unprotected?"

I stared down at her. To hell with it. "No, my lady. I have only two things I want to learn from you."

She waited calmly.

"First, I want to know if you intend to destroy anyone else."

"Besides my promised husband?"

"Yes."

"Not specifically. It wouldn't be a good idea to get in our way, but we've no need to make a target of anyone else."

Not Isabella, then. Not Fiammetta, or Gualdrada. I felt the weight on my heart lift, ever so slightly.

"And what's the other thing, Fool?" she said.

"I want to know what hold you have over Mosca dei Lamberti."

Selvaggia laughed out loud. The cooks and the helper managed not to look at us.

"I know something about him he doesn't want known."

"What?"

"He has something he shouldn't have."

"What does he have?"

"A woman."

"It does a man no dishonor to have a woman."

"This woman is different. He has done a thing that would enrage his friends and delight his enemies. Be assured, he can't afford to have me tell what I know."

"Why did you think Mosca could persuade them?"

"He's honey-tongued. How do you think he got the woman? She knows better."

I thought about this, remembering Ghisola's observations about him at the near-wedding. "Is the woman here?"

Selvaggia didn't answer, but a little smile played about her lips.

And I was sure. "The sea nymph."

She laughed. "Sea slut, more like. Yes."

God's blood. Mosca was putting horns on one of Schiatta degli Uberti's sons. As if to confirm it, Selvaggia placed a thumb in each ear and waggled her index fingers suggestively in the air. The man had to be howling mad, and no wonder he was at the mercy of this ruthless young woman. I could think of nothing more to say.

Selvaggia stood up. "Come downstairs, Fool. The ladies want you again, and I said I'd come and get you." She started for the stairs, then turned to face me again. "I'll send for you before the week is out. You've been a part of every scene in this drama as it unfolds, and it would be a pity for you to miss the final act." Then she was gone down the stairs, her footfalls heavy, like a soldier's.

Numbly, I followed. It was time to play for the dancing, even while I, like Mosca, danced to Selvaggia's tune.

22. THE AMIDEI

Selvaggia kept her word. On Wednesday she sent for me, asking her uncle to let me relocate to the Amidei house for the remainder of my captivity. It made no difference to Oddo—he had seen all of my tricks by then, and his mind was on other business.

Monna Ermellina, however, was genuinely sorry to see me go. Her party had been a social success, and she had called on me for more music and foolery several times since. I was sure Ermellina knew what was going on but was determined not to talk about it or think about it if she didn't have to, and with me cavorting around making silly jokes and singing songs, she didn't have to.

But Selvaggia had spoken, and no one wanted to argue with her. Besides, she emphasized to her uncle that her mother was fearful and upset, and a distraction would be just what she needed. Monna Lauretta was said to be Oddo's favorite sister, and he was not likely to deny her.

"So, Fool, we lose your company, but if you can ease my sister's anxiety it will be for the good," he told me as we waited for Guido to hand off door duty so he could escort me to the Amidei palace. "This has been hard on her, and she dreads the finish of it. You keep her as happy as you can, ease her through it, and I'll make it worth your while."

I had nothing to say in reply. I didn't want to go to the Amidei house, where I feared I would be even more in the midst of things than under Oddo's roof, but Oddo had brushed aside my objections and overruled his lady wife's pleas to let me stay.

"Don't pull such a long face, Fool," he said, punching me in the arm. I don't know if he meant it to, but it hurt. "Just do whatever my niece tells you to, and you'll get through it all right." He chuckled. "It's what everyone in that house does. By God, she should have been born a male. She would have run the family, and the city too, someday." I didn't doubt it.

Guido arrived, eager as always to do Oddo's bidding, and the two of us left the Fifanti home without delay. I think Oddo had already forgotten about me by the time the front door closed.

"I don't know why I have to do this," I grumbled to Guido as we walked. "All I know is what day it's going to happen. I still don't know where, or what hour. What harm can I do? I don't understand why I can't just swear to keep silence and go home."

Guido shook his head. "Doesn't work that way, friend. You know too much if you know enough to wreck our plans, and you do. I'm sorry you have to go, because we've enjoyed all your tricks and antics, but now it's the Amidei's turn to watch you give them a show."

I sighed. I needed a break from this constant entertaining, but at least I could start fresh with my usual repertoire, and I wouldn't have to strain to create new material. I wondered sourly what it took to amuse Selvaggia. Maybe I could beat some puppies to death with my juggling clubs, if I had them, or slit the throats of a few small children with a dagger. Which I also didn't have.

We were nearing the bridge. It was another bright day, midafternoon, and I longed to stay out in the sunshine. If I were free, I thought, I could walk over to the Donati palace and leave my information with Lippo. If I were really free, even of that burden, perhaps I'd stroll across the bridge. The butcher shops that lined it would be doing a brisk business now that Lent was over, selling live animals and meat and the other useful bits of their livestock, things like horn, bone, down and feathers, sinew, and tallow. Already we could hear the bleating and squawking and grunting of caged creatures soon to be dinner. The bridge was colorful, but also noisy and malodorous. At least the flies weren't as thick as they would be later, when summer's heat was fully upon us.

We would not be crossing the bridge today. There before us, at the near end of it, stood the ancient statue of Mars. We Florentines boasted of our Roman past, and the antiquity of the battered old equestrian statue was a source of considerable pride. The thing was barely recognizable, having been struck by lightning so many times and buffeted by the rains and winds for so long. It had even been trapped at the bottom of the Arno for several years after a flood carried it off, before they dredged it up and put it back in place.

Countless people had touched it or bumped it or brushed against it over the years, but with a little imagination it was still just possible to see the visage of the mighty God of War in the worn stone that remained. For more generations than any of us could remember, Florence's citizens had garlanded that statue in good times and pelted it with mud and worse in bad. And the Amidei tower had looked down on it for almost as long.

That tower was just ahead of us, and attached to it by a covered wooden walkway, one floor above the ground, was the family's palace. We were admitted by a bored servant who probably also would have preferred to be out enjoying the sunshine. Guido, obedient soldier that he was, escorted me up to Lambertuccio's hall and delivered me into the care of the old lion himself, giving me an affectionate clap on the shoulder as he left me there. Wistfully, I watched him go. I hadn't chosen to be in Oddo's house, but I felt far easier there than I expected to here.

I was in the hall again—only one hall in this palace, but it ran the full length of the venerable building. The room was warmer than it had been the last time I was here, but plain, stripped of those sad wedding ornaments. The walls were frescoed in repeating geometric patterns, lozenges, squares, and diamonds, but the once bright colors had faded with age. Next to both windowseats the paintings were nearly eradicated from years of being leaned on and rubbed against. Likely these paintings had been executed by the generation of painters before the one that included my father and Neri's.

Lambertuccio looked less dejected than he had the last time I saw him, but still I suspected the last thing he wanted to see was a jester. Nevertheless, he duly welcomed me to his house, and he called over a gangly youth who had been standing at the window when Guido and I came up the stairs.

"This is my son, Amadio," he said. The boy, who was simply if richly dressed and whose hair was tonsured, greeted me soberly. I remembered him from the meeting at Santa Maria sopra Porta, though he had not said anything on that occasion. His face still bore the telltale spots and blotches of youth.

"God's blessing on you, young man," he said, and I suppressed a smile, for I was sure I had at least a decade on him. Taking his religious calling a bit too seriously, I suspected. I greeted him respectfully, addressing him as "Father."

"No, not yet," he said, clearly pleased at my mistake. "I've only taken minor orders thus far, though I do hope to earn my place in the priesthood one day. Meanwhile, I study and pray." His eyes rolled upwards in what I would come to recognize as his pious expression, and he steepled his hands, placing his fingertips together.

"Amadio will be in charge of you while you're a guest here," Lambertuccio said. "He's back from his studies to help out the family until this business is done, so talk to him if you need anything. He's to find you a place to sleep and to stay with you whenever the ladies aren't asking for your services." He turned to his son. "I'll be in my study if you have need of me." He left us there in the hall, going out through a side door.

It took me a moment to figure out where the door might lead, since I knew the living chambers in this palace were on the upper level along with the kitchen, but then I realized it must connect with the adjacent tower, that ancient and impregnable pillar of stone. The tower had no entrance on the ground floor, either from the street or from inside the palace. Any of his men who lived on the premises would likely be quartered there.

In days past, when bloody street fighting had been even more common, the tower had stood completely separate from the house. The only access was via ladders that could be pulled up inside. The Amidei had knocked a door through that thick palace wall in recent years and built the wooden walkway, which looked like a long, rickety room suspended in the air and led to a corresponding door on the tower side, where the wall was thicker still.

Amadio gestured to me to sit down. "Have you dined?" he asked.

"Yes, I thank you. Could I trouble you to show me where I'll be sleeping, and where the latrine is?" A household with this much wealth should possess such a convenience.

Amadio was a puppylike young man, eager to be helpful. He showed me the necessary closet, curtained off and located near the door to the tower. At first I thought the curtain was a hanging, the fabric lying flat against the wall, for the latrine jutted outward, built as an addition to avoid using up living space in the hall. The little closet was buttressed by sturdy beams wedged at an angle between the palace wall and the closet's floor, which was made of wood planks rather than brick, in order to keep the structure light. One didn't want to have the privy collapsing underfoot, after all. The ground floor latrine I had noted below must have emptied directly into the cesspit, but this one was served by a drainpipe that doubtless led down to the same destination. A quick look inside the structure assured me that this was the uppermost such facility in the palace; thus, the chambers upstairs must be served by closestools and chamber pots. This was a well-run house. The odor was kept to a minimum, at least on this level. The servants must have hauled water up often to flush the pipe, or, more likely, hauled the kitchen waste water down.

I was to sleep on a bench in the hall, not a bed in a chamber. Not surprising—I was somewhere between a prisoner and hired help, hardly a guest in this palace, in spite of Lambertuccio's courteous words. Amadio showed me the long chest that held blankets, which doubled as a bench along one wall. I would be comfortable enough, though I couldn't seek my rest until all in the house were finished with the hall, and I would wake in the morning as soon as anyone else stirred.

It would do. The weather was so perfect in these spring days that I decided to claim a sleeping place under a window. No need to draw the shutters tonight, and I could look out at the bridge, the river, and the statue of Mars and watch the city until it got too dark to see.

Amadio asked me earnestly if I needed anything at all, anything to make my stay more comfortable. I thought about asking him if I might return to my house and pick up some clean clothes. That might give me a chance to speak to Ghisola, and to Neri, if he was there, depending on how well guarded I was. But I had just taken my blue tunic out of winter storage a few days ago, and Ghisola had made sure I put it away clean. Lambertuccio would never have agreed to let me go anyway, so I gave up on that idea. Instead I asked if I might wash a little, and Amadio took me up to the kitchen. He told the cook to pour me a basin, and told me I could wash where it was warm.

The Amidei kitchen was smaller and more cramped than the other noble kitchens I had been in recently, for much of the upper level was partitioned into chambers, but it did have a washing area curtained off on one side. The sour-faced cook dutifully ladled water into a basin, adding a panful of heated water to take the chill off, and she handed it to me along with a sturdy towel. I ducked behind the curtain, where a large wooden bathing tub lined in coarse white cloth stood ready, and performed my ablutions. I didn't have enough water to fill the tub, and using it would have been presumptuous anyway, so I dipped one end of the towel in the water and daubed myself until I felt cleaner. Then I finished by dunking my head in the basin and washing my hair, though with my recent barbering, it barely needed it. Still, no sense in wasting an opportunity. By then I heard low voices in the kitchen, beyond the curtain.

When I emerged, Amadio was on his knees praying aloud. Also kneeling were the cook and monna Lauretta. When Amadio heard me, he opened his eyes, and he brought things to the "amen" promptly and stood up. He helped the women to their feet, first his mother, then the cook.

"Feeling better?" he asked me.

"Yes, thank you," I said, handing the basin and towel back to the cook, who took them silently. I bowed respectfully to Amadio's mother. Monna Lauretta looked even more nervous and distressed than she had on Monday at monna Ermellina's party Then she had at least been elegantly dressed and tidy, but now she was carelessly attired and on the verge of being unkempt, with sprigs of graying hair sticking out from under her veil.

Her ingrained graciousness caused her to remember to say, "You are welcome here, young man." That again. Her voice was reedy and tired. "I know my daughter and my brother have brought you to me to raise my spirits, but I must tell you that nothing except more godly behavior on the part of my family will do that, so don't think to try to entertain me, however generous the thought."

"My lady, I don't wish to intrude," I said. "I'm here to serve you in any way I can."

"How kind. What you can do for me, then, is to keep the children of this house happy and distracted."

I was alarmed. "My lady, will there be children present—"

"No. They'll be with their cousins in the Uberti palace. But keep them busy and out from under my feet until then, for I will be in prayer."

"My lady, I will do my best." She gave me a wisp of a smile, which reminded me of Gualdrada when I saw her last. Those two suffering women—their families bitter enemies, their pain so alike. Fear for those they loved, for their families' future, perhaps fear for their city itself, if either had that much imagination. And yet Gualdrada had set so much in motion, and this woman had spawned Selvaggia.

She left us, disappearing behind another curtain toward the private chambers. Amadio made sure I felt warm enough to leave the fire despite my wet hair, and asked the cook to bring us a light supper downstairs. We descended into the hall.

The room was warm enough, although any sense of comfort was countered by the presence of Selvaggia, who was sitting at her window seat waiting for us.

23. TELLING TALES

Alarming as her presence was, Selvaggia didn't have much to say, at least not to me. I think she was only there to make sure everything was going according to her plan. Amadio stiffened in her presence, answering her cautiously when she asked where I was to sleep, what their mother had said to me, and what I would be doing during my time there. His brief answers satisfied her.

"Fool, I'll bring the children to you once you've supped," she said to me. "Tell them stories this evening. Nothing frightening—just give them pleasant dreams. You can show them your tricks and sing them your songs tomorrow."

She watched while Amadio and I ate from the tray the cook brought down for us. Our meal was bread and oil, a little dish of olives, and some smoked fish, and I remembered it was Wednesday and a day of fasting. I had dined on a more elaborate fish dish at Oddo's earlier, so it was enough. Dried apples and sticky honeyed almonds finished our meal, and then Selvaggia stood up. "I'll get the children," she said, and went upstairs, leaving the tray on the bench.

Amadio smiled apologetically. "My sister sometimes forgets she's a woman, I think," he said. "She can be abrupt at times, but you must remember she has suffered much of late."

"And do you believe it's God's will that your family take a fatal revenge for her suffering?" I was curious about what this young priestling thought. Still chafing over my lack of freedom, I saw no reason to watch my words.

He seemed surprised that I asked. "It's my father's will, and he's head of the family," he said. "God wills that all of us obey our fathers." And yours obeys Selvaggia, I thought.

"So you take time off from training to become one of God's priests, so you can take part in a killing?"

He had the grace to look uncomfortable, but all he said was, "I do my father's will."

I relented. This poor youngster was not the person to be tormenting with my questions. In a way he was right: he had little choice in what he did. No point in making things worse for him, so we lapsed into silence, waiting.

Across from me I noticed for the first time a stenciled painting of stylized birds and geometrics surrounded by a pattern of vines, in vivid reds and blues and greens, on the ceiling above the stairs going down to

175

the great door. The design was still bright, too high and too far from any source of smoke to have been eroded or obscured like the other paintings in the hall. It could only have been painted from a scaffold, I thought, and I felt the familiar tightness at the back of my throat. I looked away.

Children's voices, high-pitched and excited, floated down the other stairs, the ones going up to the kitchen and the chambers. The voices were followed by the children themselves, six in all, though the youngsters thundered rather than floated. Amadio, obviously a favorite, greeted them affectionately and introduced me to them. They told me their names all in a rush, but the only ones I caught were that of Lucia, the oldest girl, and of Manente, a tall and energetic boy whose features reminded me strongly of Schiatta. Lucia I had seen before. She was Lambertuccio's granddaughter, the grave, wide-eyed child who had spun her thread and listened so avidly to her elders at Ermellina's party. She was delighted to see me again, shyly complimenting me on my performance that night. Selvaggia was nowhere to be seen.

The children rushed to the long chest and flung it open, tossing out blankets and small cushions in what must have been a familiar exercise. Dried herbs flew everywhere. The children wrapped themselves in the blankets and nestled among the cushions on the floor, settling in and looking at me expectantly. Amadio practically bounced as he sat on the bench, as excited as the children.

I gave them several stories, starting with familiar tales and moving on to others I thought they would be less likely to know. They listened to me with wide-eyed fascination. As Selvaggia had instructed, I steered away from any frightening, violent, or alarming stories. It lessened my pool of possibilities considerably, but not so much that I ran out of material. This was one of the things I did best, so I forgot my cares for a while and threw myself into entertaining the young ones.

At one point Lambertuccio emerged from the door he had gone through earlier, but the children were so spellbound that they didn't pay any attention as he crossed the hall. He stopped to watch the children for a moment, his head tilted a bit to one side and a little smile on his craggy face, and then he went on up the stairs.

Daylight faded, and Amadio went upstairs and came back down holding a candlestick with a lighted taper. He used it to light four more in a candelabra in the corner, and then he brought those lights and his original candle over to where we were sitting and set them on the floor near me, where their flickering light allowed the children to see me while I wove my tales.

Eventually the servingwoman the children called Tana came to the top of the stairs and listened from there for a little while. Firelight from the kitchen behind her revealed her to be young and apple-cheeked, and her main duty appeared to be monitoring the children. After I finished the story, she called down, "Bedtime, children." My audience groaned loudly, even Amadio, for he had been listening as eagerly as anyone. The servant put her hands on her hips and frowned at the children with mock sternness, but she couldn't sustain it, and she broke into a smile in spite of herself.

The children got up obediently, still grumbling a little, and left their cushions and blankets in a pile. Lucia herded the younger ones ahead of her up the stairs, looking back over her shoulder to wish us a good night.

It would soon be dark. Amadio extinguished the candles and returned the candelabra to its corner, leaving just the original light burning. Only he and I were left in the hall, and I wandered over to the window. The horizon, with its silhouettes of towers, churches, and houses, was a luminous dark blue. The stone Mars looked different, and on closer inspection I realized an owl sat perched atop that ancient head, though I could only see it in outline against the darkening sky. I heard a low voice behind me. Amadio was on his knees, praying again. Thinking it might be the courteous thing to do, I knelt too, and softly spoke my own prayers. He seemed unaware of me, and he didn't try to lead me in my devotions as he had led his mother and the cook, earlier.

After a time I got up, having felt a certain constraint in what I said to God lately. Amadio, however, was set for a lengthy conversation, so I picked out a couple of the blankets the children had dropped and the biggest of the cushions and tried to make myself comfortable on the bench right under the window. I folded one blanket to pad the hard surface underneath me and covered myself with the other, a thin, tawny-colored length of wool. It had a pleasantly smooth texture and a faint scent of rosemary.

The fresh night air felt good. The morning sun would wake me early there, but early waking was inevitable when one slept in the most public part of a large household. Amadio continued to pray aloud while I drifted toward sleep.

I couldn't quite arrive at sleep, though, with his epic devotions proceeding in the background. I lay there, feeling the night breeze on my face, listening to the drone of his voice and thinking, against my will, of what was to come.

I didn't see anything I could do that would stop it. Even if I somehow made my escape from this palace and got my information to the Donati or the Buondelmonti, it might not make any difference. Maybe Buondelmonte was prudent enough to stay home on Sunday, but I doubted it. If he hadn't intended to come into Florence from time to time, why did he hire Dino and Vanni?

Thinking of those two hulking brawlers wouldn't have brought me comfort under normal circumstances, but I did feel better knowing they were in his employ. Those two, plus Buondelmonte's own knightly skills and training, might serve to keep him safe, or at least to protect the women, which was my main concern. I welcomed Selvaggia's word that only Buondelmonte was a target, and I believed her, but I knew any Donati women with him when he was attacked would be in danger, if only because of the confusion that holds sway whenever there's a violent clash on crowded city streets.

My mind went over these same points again and again, until finally Amadio yawned, stretched, got up, and selected his blanket. He stretched out on another section of the bench and was snoring raucously within minutes. I was irritated. If I couldn't sleep for his praying, what hope did I have of rest with that racket going on?

Still, I was exhausted, and I was just falling asleep when I heard a thin, high-pitched, despairing sound of animal pain, coming from outside. It jolted me awake, alarmed, until I remembered the owl. I had heard only the bird of the night, taking his prey. And yet that small, helpless scream wove through my troubled dreams, when I did finally sleep.

*

The next day began early, as I had expected. Eager children were all over me before I had a chance to fold my blankets and put them back into the chest. Amadio came to my rescue, telling the young ones to give me a chance to wake up and break my fast first, but he promised them all manner of tricks and songs and fun very soon.

I had my orders, so off I went to the kitchen. The still-silent cook pointed to a trestle table where food was set out. It was Thursday now, so cheese was provided, as well as a dish of fresh ricotta with honey-soaked raisins to accompany it. She had set out fresh bread as well, and a pitcher of watered wine, so I breakfasted.

When I returned to the hall, Amadio and the children were waiting expectantly. Still too stiff for tumbling, I warmed up with a bit of mime and then a few jokes and stories, bringing the livelier children into the act and letting the shyer ones hang back and watch.

178

A question to Amadio revealed that this house had no juggling balls available, nor musical instruments other than Selvaggia's citole, an instrument on which I had no skill. I was left to my own devices, but jesters are used to that. Ingenuity is pretty much a requirement in my profession, and the children were not critical, but eager to be pleased. So I spent a lively hour or so with Amadio and the children before anyone else in the household arrived in the hall.

I was clownishly begging the children for a rest while they laughed and teased me by shouting "No! More jests!" when Lambertuccio came down the stairs. This time he greeted the children, and they him. To me he said only, "Good morrow, Fool," and before I could answer he had gone through the door to the tower.

I got my break with a little help from Amadio, but soon I was back on duty. By then I was ready for a little tumbling. My cartwheels especially delighted the youngest girl, who squealed with glee. The two boys were determined to try it for themselves, so Amadio and I hastily switched over to singing, lest one of them manage to break a bone while in our care.

I was leading them in a silly children's song about animals and the sounds they make, sitting with my back to the stairs down to the street, when I heard someone coming up those stairs. My scalp itched furiously, and I wanted to scratch. Even more, I wanted to turn around and see who it was, but this was not my home, not my business. I did manage to shift positions enough to see the man making his way across the hall toward the door to the tower, and I didn't miss a note or a howl or a meow even when I realized that it was none other than messer Schiatta degli Uberti. He ignored all of us completely, and the children paid no attention to him. He vanished through the door to the tower and it closed behind him.

A planning meeting, I supposed, even as I continued to sing with the children, who bellowed lustily along with me. When a voice joined in from the upper staircase, I looked up, and to my surprise Selvaggia stood there, singing along in a pleasant alto. She was smiling as she came down the stairs.

After watching the other women react to her on Monday, not to mention Amadio's caution around her, I half expected the children to take off screaming, but instead they broke off the song to run to her and welcome her with hugs and wet kisses. I was astonished, and I brought the song to an abrupt close and watched them. Adults might find her terrifying, but she was clearly a favorite aunt, or sister, or cousin, or whatever her relationship was to these children. She smiled and tickled and teased, and they responded with giggles and every sign of warm affection. Perhaps Selvaggia had a twin sister, I thought, and this was not the same woman at all.

I was disabused of that idea when she greeted me. "I see you earn your keep, Fool," she said drily. "Do you know 'The Lady and the Faithful Knight'?"

At that, Lucia's eyes shone, but the boys groaned loudly. The ballad Selvaggia had asked for was romantic to the point of sentimentality, having to do with a kidnapped lady and her betrothed, who would ride through fire to rescue her, if necessary. Naturally, it became necessary. The song was popular among women. I knew it, but it was not a regular part of my repertoire.

"My lady, I do not know it," I lied.

She feigned disappointment. "Then go on with whatever it is you do know," she said, and settled back on the bench to listen. The youngest girl climbed into her lap and nestled there.

A little rattled, I announced that singing time was over, and we would now have more stories. This went over well, and I launched into some tales from Aesop that I could have told in my sleep. The children drank in my tales of clever mice and foolish cats, of foxes, hares, and crows. That gave me a chance to watch and think, even while I worked.

Selvaggia stroked the little girl's hair gently, but her eyes kept traveling to the staircase down to the ground level. My back was still to it, but even as I was telling the story of the Fox and the Billy Goat, I heard the downstairs door open, the guard's voice, and then masculine footsteps coming up. I didn't turn to see who was there, but Selvaggia's face lit up with a now-familiar expression of malice, so I wasn't surprised when the visitor who finally came into my line of sight turned out to be Mosca dei Lamberti. He stared expressionless at Selvaggia for a moment, then inclined his head briefly and moved on, toward the door to the tower. Another member of the planning council, no doubt. Selvaggia watched him, smiling a little, not pleasantly.

Would more be coming? Who else, I wondered? I continued to run through my repertoire and sure enough, I heard the door again, the guard, and more footsteps. More than one man this time. Heavy footfalls, the clatter of metal. Armor or weaponry, more likely both. I began to tell the entranced children the tale of the Donkey, the Fox, and the Lion, and as I spoke I waited for these next visitors to come within sight on their way to the door. I was completely unprepared for who I saw.

Dino and Vanni were the men tramping through Lambertuccio's hall. Buondelmonte's bodyguards. The fable died on my lips, the children started to clamor for me to finish, and Selvaggia watched those brutish hirelings go through the tower door, her expression one of pure triumph and glee.

I could call forth no more words for the children. I took the surge of energy I was feeling and channeled it into a sudden, violent display of tumbling, to the delight of the children and to Selvaggia's amusement. I somersaulted and flipped and leaped my way to a breathless conclusion and the applause of the children, all the while thinking only one thing: Buondelmonte was betrayed.

24. DELIVERY

Amadio's eyes were shining as my bravura explosion of tumbling came to a breathless halt. The children scrambled to their feet, ready to try to copy my antics, but Selvaggia clapped her hands and told them to sit. "Our fool hasn't finished his story," she reminded them, and they settled back down reluctantly.

"Please finish the tale," a small voice begged, and others joined in. Shaken by what I had seen, I couldn't even remember what story I had been telling them. I faked an attack of coughing, to justify taking another break. Amadio sent Lucia to the kitchen to fetch me a drink of water and told the other children to play for a while until I had a chance to recover. Selvaggia just watched us, smiling a little, and I leaned back against the wall and sat, trying to calm myself.

The children fished a leather ball out of the chest and began to play a game, rolling it to one another in turn across the floor. They chanted a nonsense rhyme, a new verse each time a child rolled the ball. I couldn't tell whether the game had any point to it or not. But then, why should children have a purpose to their behavior when the adults did not? At least the children of this family didn't have to plot and scheme and kill to be happy. Not until they were older, at any rate.

And Selvaggia was happy. Her face fairly glowed with it. It disturbed me to see this murderous joy making her oddly beautiful, her eyes sparkling and alive, her face animated, her movements quick and graceful. She was still no Isabella, but at that moment any man's attention would have been drawn to her, even if he could not afterward have explained exactly why.

I took the water from a dignified Lucia, thanked her gravely, and sipped it while the children played. I need some way to get a message to the Donati women, I thought. If they know Buondelmonte and Isabella are riding into a trap, they can stop this madness. Or if I could only get out of this palace and go talk to Lippo, this betrayal need not cause Buondelmonte's death. He would at least have a fair chance to escape, and if he chose not to take that chance, then that would be no fault of mine. But with his own men turned against him, unknown to him, what hope did he have?

Amadio sat down next to me, still flushed with pleasure. "That was wonderful tumbling," he said, blushing a little. The lad was shy. "I loved the way you walked on your hands. I wish I could do that."

"Did you play at such games when you were a child?" I asked.

"Oh, yes. But now that I'm sworn to the church, I must conduct myself with dignity," he said seriously. "I can't do somersaults and handstands and cartwheels any more."

Poor lad. Distracted as I was by Buondelmonte's plight, I liked this kind, hapless young man, and I thought it sad that at his tender years he felt a need to be a model of proper behavior. "I can see why you can't have your robes flying all over," I said, "but I don't know why you couldn't learn to make music, for example, or to jest, or to juggle."

"I have no music in me," he said, "and jesting isn't appropriate for a man of the church." He brightened. "But I don't see any reason why I couldn't juggle. Is it hard to learn?"

I looked him over, appraising him. "I don't see why you couldn't juggle, either. I didn't find it hard to learn, though it does take time and practice." A thought was beginning to form in the back of my mind. I needed to hold Amadio's interest while I figured out how to accomplish what I wanted to do.

"It's a pity you don't have juggling balls here," I told him. "The children would love it if you juggled for them. It would keep them amused, and that would be a help to your parents. If you only had a set of juggling balls, I could teach you." I offered a brief, silent prayer that he wouldn't remember the set at the nearby Fifanti palace.

Amadio jumped up. "But you must have some, don't you? I saw you juggle once, in the street. You were wonderful!"

This was going to work. "Yes," I said innocently. "I have a fine set of weighted leather balls, but they're back at my house, and your father won't allow me to leave here to fetch them so I can teach you."

Momentarily stymied, Amadio stroked his chin as he thought. "If Father says no, then you mustn't leave," he said, drooping a little. Then he straightened and his eyes opened wide as an idea occurred to him. "But could we send someone for them?"

"I do share my house with a musician called Neri," I told him, as if his idea was new to me. "If you sent a message to him and he brought the balls here, I could see if you have a talent for juggling."

"Yes! I'll send a message right away! Do you want to write it?" Amadio was fairly bouncing up and down by now, and the children watched him with curiosity.

"No, Neri can't read," I said. "If you just send a man to tell him I'm here and not at the Fifanti palace any more, and I have need of my juggling equipment, maybe he'll even bring along the clubs."

Amadio quivered with excitement. "What shall I start with, balls or clubs?" he demanded.

I considered this. "Let's try you out on both, and see if you like one better than another. You can always start with one and then learn the other later."

I told him where my house was, and he dashed to the stairs, eager to give the message to a runner. He skidded to a stop at the top of the steps and turned back to me. "I'll just be gone a minute. You won't go anywhere, will you?"

I started to give my word, but Selvaggia, who had witnessed our exchange, answered for me. "He isn't going anywhere, Amadio. Send your message." He bounded down the stairs, and she turned to me.

"Fool, I'll be watching you. Don't think you're going to be able to send any private messages. Your juggling balls is what you'll get out of this, that and an eager pupil, and nothing more."

"My lady. You heard our speech; I have no secrets," I said, trying to look forthright and honest, and she laughed. She sounded genuinely amused.

"You're right, Fool. You have none. Some of us do, however, and we're going to keep them," she said. "And even if you did manage to tell your friend, we'd just keep him here, too."

Fair enough. I didn't know how I was going to manage to talk to Neri without being overheard by Selvaggia, but I would solve that problem when I came to it. Or it came to me. But causing Neri to be imprisoned with me here wasn't something I could risk. His behavior was so unpredictable these days that I didn't trust him not to do something stupid.

I resumed my storytelling duties, and as I was beginning a new tale, Amadio rejoined us. He gave me a nod and a grin and sat on the floor behind the children to listen.

We passed the time with stories and songs and more tumbling until Tana took the protesting children away for lessons and prayers.

I kept watching for Neri. This made no sense, for if he came, I would hear the door, and the guard, and the footsteps on the stairs, long before I saw him, but still I looked for him. Selvaggia didn't fail to notice.

Once he had me all to himself, Amadio wanted me to tell him all about how to juggle. It was impossible to show him empty-handed, so he ran up to the kitchen and returned with three wizened apples, which he offered me. I can tell you, limp and leathery little apples are not the easiest things to juggle, but I managed to give him a demonstration of the basics, and then a chance to try for himself. To my surprise, he took to it.

Still I waited for Neri and hoped he would come, but as the sky grew dark, I knew it wouldn't be that day. Surely, surely he would come on Friday, I told myself, as the rest of the household readied for bed and Amadio lined up his apples on the bench and prepared for his lengthy evening prayers. I knew all was not well with Neri, but I didn't think he would ignore my request. For one thing, Ghisola wouldn't let him.

I stretched out in my place under the window, wondering if sleep would come. Perhaps it would have, if I hadn't allowed myself to look again at that stenciled painting across from me. Seeing it was only a step away from seeing, again, my father's unfinished work as it stared mutely down at its maker's crumpled body, lying on the stone floor at the foot of the stairs, far, far below the broken scaffolding. The scaffolding he had told his employer was too rickety to be safe. The scaffolding he had been ordered to climb anyway.

When my mother and I arrived, out of breath, it was Neri's father we saw kneeling next to mine and weeping, and it was Neri who came to me and took my hands in his. The owner of the half-decorated palace was in heated conversation with the guild steward about who was responsible, and he had no time to spare for a new widow and her bewildered son.

The owner was fined, which did us no good, and eventually he sent us a grudging gift of something like alms, which my mother refused. In fact, she threw the purse on the street and slammed the door on the servant who brought it. I became a member of Neri's family in every way that mattered. When a fever took Neri's father, both of us, his two apprentices, mourned him together. Life got more difficult then, but we helped each other through, and in time made ourselves over into performers, for neither of us wanted to follow in our fathers' steps and paint rich men's walls.

I knew that Neri would come. He was always there when I needed him.

*

Although I expected to wake again to children clamoring for my talents, this time it was Amadio's voice droning his morning prayers that brought me up from sleep. In this household Friday was respected as a day of fasting, Amadio told me, and entertainment was strictly limited. He sounded regretful. The children cast longing looks in my direction whenever they trooped through, but I was left largely to my own devices.

Amadio stayed with me, occasionally talking, but more often reading silently from a book of prayers, his lips moving busily. Selvaggia was not in the room all the time, but she was in evidence often enough for me to feel sure she would make it a challenge to pass a message to Neri, if he came. When he came.

Dinner was over, and I was beginning to despair of seeing him, when finally I heard a rap at the door. The last two times had been disappointments, household business that had nothing to do with me, so I didn't want to get my hopes up too much. Still I listened, and this time I heard Neri's familiar voice. My heart jumped. He had come! And Selvaggia was there, seated by the window, sewing.

Amadio saw me react, and smiled. "Is that your friend?" he asked.

"Yes, that's Neri."

"I'll go bring him up." Amadio was off down the stairs. I heard voices, Neri's and Amadio's and a third, probably the guard's, and then footsteps on the stairs. And there, finally, was Neri.

He looked awful. He was rumpled and unshaven, his hair was greasy, and I'd bet he hadn't slept in days. I smelled wine, as well as the stink of a man who hasn't washed in too long.

Selvaggia looked first at him, then at me, then delicately wrinkled her nose, and that small act of arrogance infuriated me. Impulsively I stepped forward and embraced him, something I normally would have hesitated to do when he was like this. He pulled away from me and held out my leather props bag, at arms' length. I took it from him. A peek inside the bag told me that my motley was there, as well as my juggling balls and clubs.

"I asked him to bring your costume, too," Amadio said anxiously. "Was that all right? I thought the children would like it."

You mean you would like it, I thought, but I only said, "Good idea."

Neri had already started to leave. "Wait!" I said. "I want to talk with you for a moment." He turned and faced me, a blank, listless expression on his haggard face. He still hadn't said anything, and his usual energetic twitchiness had dulled to a sort of lethargy. Selvaggia was watching us, but Amadio rummaged in the bag, pulling out the colored leather balls, exclaiming over each one as it emerged and tossing it from one hand to the other.

Thinking fast, I said to Amadio, "My friend and I need to pray together. We have a companion who lies mortally ill, and we would entreat God to help him in this his final few hours. May we use the chapel, just for a few minutes?"

Selvaggia stood up abruptly and her needlework slid to the floor. She started to speak, but Amadio waved her to silence. "Of course you may," he said. Apparently when it came to matters of religion the priestling's word was law in this house, even if Selvaggia remained in charge of more worldly matters. She glared at me, but she sat back down.

"Amadio, it would be a charitable thing for you to go with them," she said, picking up her embroidery and smiling maliciously at me.

"I'll add my prayers to yours," Amadio said, steepling his fingers and raising his eyes. "Come, I'll lead you to the chapel." That was less than ideal, but I could hardly tell him no.

I tried to catch Neri's eye, but he wouldn't cooperate. He simply stood there, awaiting instructions. Amadio went through the door that led to the rooms in the tower, and I motioned Neri to follow. I fell in step next to him, whispering to him as we walked.

"What's wrong with you?"

"Nothing."

"You look awful. Are you all right? Is Ghisola?"

"We're fine. I want to go."

"Not yet." We passed what I thought must be Lambertuccio's study, a comfortable room with a brazier, a desk, and a shelf with books. The door stood open, but no one was inside.

Amadio led us to a closed room beyond the study. He took out an ornate key and worked it into the lock on the door while I whispered to Neri.

"I need you to carry a message from me."

"No."

"Neri, you have to. It could save a man's life."

"No."

Amadio finally managed to get the lock open, and he ushered us into a tiny room, unadorned except for a crucifix on the wall and a stark image of the Virgin enthroned, surrounded by dour angels holding musical instruments awkwardly, as if they didn't know how to play them. We crossed ourselves and knelt.

"What's your friend's name?" Amadio asked me in a whisper.

"Masetto di Bicci," I told him. As far as I knew, the mangy Masetto suffered from nothing worse than fleas, but I didn't want to tempt God by naming any of our human acquaintances. I thought I saw a tiny spark in Neri's eyes at my choice, but it faded before I could be glad.

Amadio prayed out loud, eyes tightly closed. That gave me the chance to try to talk to Neri by mouthing words at him, but he closed his own eyes and wouldn't look at me. We knelt there for a long time, me frantic with worry and frustration, Amadio dutifully praying for Bicci's mongrel, and Neri, for all I knew, taking a nap. It was enough to drive a man mad.

When Amadio finally got up, we followed him, and I had no further opportunities to whisper to Neri. We came back into the hall, and I was desperate to think of a way to detain him so I could try once more to talk to him.

"Amadio, I'd like to walk my friend to the door," I said. I knew the guard wouldn't let me leave with him, but maybe if I could get downstairs I could pull Neri into the latrine and have a few quick words. It could be enough.

"Of course," Amadio said, his sympathies still aroused by our dying friend. "Go on down. There's a guard, so I'll wait for you up here."

Perfect. We tramped through the hall, where I was careful not to meet Selvaggia's glaring eyes. Amadio wished Neri a good day, thanked him for bringing my equipment, and sent his blessings to our dear friend Masetto. Neri nodded, and the two of us went down to the street level.

The guard reached for the door to open it, but I shook my head, indicating that we were going to make a stop in the latrine first. He probably assumed I was just accompanying my guest out of courtesy. At least, I hope that's what he assumed.

I closed the door behind us. Luckily no one else was in the soldiers' privy. I started to whisper to Neri again, but he cut me off.

"I don't know what it is you're trying to do, but I want no part of it. I'm not running any messages. That's your job, or so everyone seems to think. I'm not getting involved in knights' business. I wouldn't have even brought you this stuff if Ghisola hadn't insisted. I've got nothing further to say to you, so don't even try." His eyes were bloodshot and unfocused, his tone hostile. He looked like a man plumbing the depths of hell itself.

"You didn't take communion, did you?" I said, that thought arriving out of nowhere.

"No. Couldn't."

"But you confessed?"

"I'm going. It stinks in here. Don't call for me again—I won't come." And he was out of the latrine and on his way through the door before I could catch him.

The guard raised an eyebrow as he bolted the door behind Neri. "Your friend needs to clean up a bit, Fool."

"He's going through a bad time," I said.

"Looks it. We paid him for his errand, anyway. Maybe that'll help."

"I hope so," I said, and trudged back up the stairs. When I reached the top, Amadio was reading, with my leather balls strewn around him, but Selvaggia was watching me. Her eyes searched my face and she must have seen what she wanted to see, because she gave a little nod of satisfaction and went back to her sewing.

Amadio was too religious to be persuaded to take his first real juggling lesson on a Friday, though clearly he could hardly wait, but he did thoroughly inspect all of my equipment, including my motley. I think he wanted to try it on himself, but he couldn't quite reconcile that with his churchly dignity, so he just caressed it with his fingers. "Too bad you don't have a hat," he remarked.

The hat. I could have sent somebody for the hat, and given my message directly to Lippo, I thought, my stomach sinking. But no—I couldn't send anyone from this household to a shop housed in a Donati palace. It would have been like asking the Trojans to come out and give the Greeks a hand with their wooden horse. Although in this case I thought that Oddo's people would have been the Greeks, and the Buondelmonti and Donati the Trojans, since they were the ones facing betrayal.

Selvaggia went on up to her chamber. Amadio asked a few sympathetic questions about my ailing friend, but I managed to convince him that it choked me up too much to talk about it, so he respectfully left me alone after that. The day ended again with Amadio praying at great length, and with me staring moodily out the window at Mars, feeling more than ever as if I had failed to do anything to stop this mad rush to murder. I didn't know what was wrong with Neri, but he had been my last hope. I had no more ideas.

25. JUGGLING

The next day, Saturday, was a working day from dawn to dusk for me. I put on my green and yellow garments when I woke, ready to earn my bread, though I wasn't very happy about it.

When I wasn't performing for the children, I was teaching Amadio everything I could about juggling. To his own delight he proved to be an apt pupil, with good coordination and timing and even a fair sense of style. The children clustered around to cheer him on, though they were quick enough to mock him whenever he dropped a ball. Amadio was good-natured about it, for he was having a wonderful time learning, especially when he realized I was genuinely surprised by how well he picked up the skill. Whenever I was occupied in telling stories to the children, Amadio practiced in the background, a leather ball occasionally hitting the floor with a plop.

Selvaggia wasn't much in evidence that day. I did see her around midafternoon, after the children had been called away to prepare for their visit to their Uberti cousins. She and Tana led the file of children down the stairs from their chambers and through the hall, on their way to the great staircase down to the front door. Tana carried a lidded basket, and the two youngest children were clutching favorite toys in their arms, a cloth doll and a carved wooden horse.

"You'll be seeing me later, Fool," Selvaggia said as she passed me. She didn't bother to look at me.

Even with all of the things occupying me that Saturday, I found time to think more than I wanted to about what was coming. I still didn't know where, and I still didn't know exactly what time, but I did know it would be tomorrow, Sunday, and I knew that Selvaggia expected me to be a witness. I assumed that meant I was to be here as the assassins gathered, and to watch them set forth. I prayed it didn't mean they would expect me to go with them. That seemed unlikely, for I was no soldier, and Lambertuccio and Oddo were sufficiently unsure of my loyalty that they were keeping me here against my will.

Running along in the back of my mind as a sort of counterpoint to my dread of the assault on Buondelmonte was a constant thread of worry about Neri. Something was very wrong there. Not long ago, he would have taken my tale of the ailing Masetto and added to it, playing our old game of working a story into impossible twists and turns and then tossing it back to the other one to straighten it out—or tangle it further, more likely. I was impatient to get out of this place where I didn't belong and get home and find out what was going on with him, talk to Ghisola, and start trying to make things right again, even though I knew that getting out of here would only happen once the vendetta against Buondelmonte had been fulfilled—or, better, if this attempt to kill him somehow failed, and the planners had to begin their strategizing all over again. If that happened, next time they would do it without me. What rankled was knowing that we could have made it fail, if Neri had been willing to listen.

No sooner had Selvaggia and the children left with their escort than other people began to arrive. I sat cross-legged on the floor, coaching Amadio this time from a position where I could see all the comings and goings. Amadio put the balls aside and began experimenting with my juggling clubs. I watched Schiatta degli Uberti enter with two of his sons and wondered if one of them was married to the wayward sea nymph. A little later, Mosca dei Lamberti arrived, alone. All of them passed through the hall and into the tower, presumably headed for Lambertuccio's study. A little more time passed, and more juggling—the lad was insatiable— before Oddo arrived. He greeted Amadio and exchanged a few friendly words with the boy before going through the same door the others had used, but he had not a word for me. He must have forgotten about me yet again.

Finally I could stand it no longer. "You need a break," I told Amadio. "Resting from time to time will keep your reactions quicker." Obediently he sat down next to me on the floor, carefully placing my clubs in a line in front of us.

"Are more men coming?" I asked, trying to sound casual.

"I think that's it, at least for those coming through the house. The other men are already in the tower. They came in through the second-level door in the back, up the ladder." I was surprised. I hadn't heard any activity beyond that door, but then, those tower walls were extraordinarily thick.

"They'll stay in the tower tonight," he went on. "I'll have to stay there too, my father says." He didn't sound happy about that.

I looked him in the eye. "Are you taking part in this, then?"

"Probably not, but I'm to be there as a backup. With my father and messers Schiatta and Mosca and Oddo, I can't imagine they'll need me. My father says I have to be there, though, because it's family business."

"Not the business of a churchman, I'll warrant."

"That's what I tried to tell my father, but he just spoke of warrior bishops and family loyalty and all of that."

"So tomorrow everybody troops out and goes off to find Buondelmonte?"

He shook his head vigorously. "No, no. Didn't they tell you? It's to be right outside, on the bridge. Next to Mars. Buondelmonte will come riding past sometime after they finish the chrism ceremony."

Next to Mars. Buondelmonte, sacrificed to the god of war. I should have guessed.

"Do you know when it will be?"

"We don't know exactly when, but we do know the whole baptism party will be taking the babe to the Donati enclave out by San Pier Maggiore, to show it off to the family's women there."

"So not to the houses where monna Gualdrada lives, and Manno and Cione? Messer Cione, I mean?"

"You know them?" He sounded surprised.

"No, I just wondered whether it was those houses," I lied.

"No, not those. The infant was born in one of those houses, so they've all seen it already. They're going to the family's other enclave, all the way out to the east wall. So we're guessing that by the time they leave there, it will be either late morning or soon after dinner, depending on whether they stay for the meal or not. We've got men in his party, and they tell us those are the likely choices."

Dino and Vanni, those doubledealing thugs.

"What about me?" I asked. "If you're sleeping in the tower tonight, who's guarding me?"

He blushed. "I haven't been guarding you, exactly. I've been more like your host, and I've tried to make sure you were comfortable. I hope you didn't think I was just being a—a sort of jailer."

"No, Amadio, don't worry. You've been a gracious host. But I have no stomach for murder, however much Buondelmonte deserves your family's anger. Will I have to be in the tower with you?"

He squirmed a little. "No, you'll be here again tonight, but Selvaggia will be in charge. A guard will be posted at the door and another man will be on duty up here, so there'll be no impropriety, but you do need to do what she says." He smiled a little ruefully. "That's usually the easiest thing to do, anyway."

"What about your lady mother?"

"She has even less stomach for this than you or I do. She'll be praying the whole time. It's right for a woman to dread such violence, even if her family's honor requires it."

"And does your sister dread it?"

He didn't answer.

*

It was early evening when we heard Selvaggia return with her escort. Tana must have stayed with the children, because Selvaggia came up the stairs alone. She saw us both still in the hall, surrounded by my clubs and juggling balls, and she frowned.

"Amadio, aren't you supposed to be in the tower?" she asked.

"We're going up to the kitchen for a bite, and then I'll go," he said, a little defensively.

"I'll come with you," she said, and the three of us went up the stairs to the kitchen. The cook wasn't there, so Selvaggia rummaged around and came up with several things for us to eat. She set them out on a table that was probably used as a cutting board most of the time, judging by the deep grooves and cuts in the heavy wood. Though the hour was late, the meal was substantial: we had bread and cheese, raisins and dried apricots, more of Amadio's wizened apples, olives, some chewy sausage, and a cold dish of grain cooked in almond milk, to which Selvaggia added a hefty dollop of honey. Amadio had told me his sister had a fondness for sweets, and I noticed she took several slices of quince paste.

"What about all the men in the tower?" I asked between bites. "Don't they need to eat?"

"They have their own supplies," Amadio told me. "Father and the other knights will eat with their men tonight. It's military tradition, Father says."

"It also means they can keep an eye on how much wine the men go through," Selvaggia said. "Amadio, you'd better go on over. It's getting late."

"Couldn't I do my evening prayers in the hall first, or at least in the chapel?"

"I think you'd better pray in the tower. The men might need your prayers tonight."

Amadio brightened. "I suppose you're right. All right, then, I'll go. Sister, Fool, God's blessing on you, and good sleep to you both." Not likely, I thought, though perhaps Selvaggia might manage it.

When Amadio had gone, Selvaggia and I sat in silence for a few minutes longer, munching on the leftover food. Finally she put a piece of cheese rind back on the table and stood up. "Sleep where you've been sleeping, Fool," she said. "When you get down to the hall, you'll find one of my father's men bunked down there, and there's a guard at the door, so don't get any ideas about going anywhere. I'll see you in the morning." She turned and walked out of the kitchen into the area where the private chambers of the house were located. The scraps of food and our plates, apparently, were the cook's problem, wherever she was.

I grabbed a handful of apricots and went back downstairs, my thoughts racing. Now I did know where, and I knew as much as anyone did about when, and I was beginning to think it likely that Selvaggia would demand my actual witness to the ambush, a thought which threatened to make me lose all the food I had just eaten. Maybe if I made myself unobtrusive enough she would forget me in the heat of the moment, as her uncle always did.

The man in the hall was lying under a blanket on the floor near the top of the stairs. Apparently his thought was that I wouldn't be able to get past him without waking him, and in fact his belly did form a small blanketed mountain between me and the stairs. He raised his head and grunted at me by way of introduction.

I dug out my own blankets and arranged a bed in the usual place, under the window. After I stripped off my motley I laid out my tunic, ready to pull it on over my shirt as soon as I woke in the morning. I made sure all of my juggling equipment was safely stuffed into the bag, for once I was free to go, no matter what the outcome of Oddo's schemes, I intended to leave this place without delay.

Tonight, even in the absence of Amadio's droning I knelt in prayer, but not on the bricks of the floor. Rather, I knelt on the chest under the window and stared out at the bridge and the statue of Mars, while I tried to find the words to ask God to warn Buondelmonte, to protect the women, to free me from this place, and to deliver Neri from whatever demons tormented him. I could find no peace, nor any sense that God was less indifferent to my woes than Mars himself, and so finally I stretched out and tried to sleep. This night, even exhaustion wasn't enough to help.

*

The next day started well before dawn. I woke from the dozing state I had finally achieved to watch perhaps two dozen soldiers, heavily armed but only lightly armored, tromping through the hall. A few were Lambertuccio's men, but more were Oddo's, and some were Schiatta's. By now I recognized them all. Amadio was with them, looking miserable. He wore a bulky, padded garment under a loose robe, and he carried a short staff, though he handled it as gingerly as if it were a poisonous serpent. His companions were less protected but more dangerous, all with bladed weapons of one sort and another—swords, spears, and long knives that meant business. Amadio didn't look at me as he passed by.

I pulled on my tunic. My minder, the old soldier I had heard called Cenni, was already up and had moved his blankets out of their way, and he watched the armed men with something like envy as they trooped down the stairs. Apparently guarding me and protecting Selvaggia was not the assignment he wanted, but the big-bellied fellow was past his prime as a soldier, and that was how Lambertuccio saw fit to use him.

I heard the men milling and talking downstairs, and I thought I heard the bolt being lifted from the great front door. Cenni called down from the top of the stairs, wishing them good hunting. I shivered. A voice replied, and then the door opened and closed again. I could still hear men in the entry, though—not all had gone.

Cenni turned to me. "Scouting party's off," he said. "They'll relay a signal as soon as the quarry's sighted." Very well, if Cenni was in a talkative mood, I'd see what I could find out.

"Is that all of them?" I asked.

"Don't need many," he said. "The knights'll do the killing. The boys are just there for backup, and to control the crowd afterwards."

"There's a door to the tower, isn't there? Why did they go through here?"

"No door on the street level, and the ladder's been pulled inside. Messer Oddo didn't want them all climbing down. Somebody might've seen. If Buondelmonte knows the tower's being used, even he's not fool enough to ride this way. That's why they won't have used any candles last night, nor any fire. If the men are needed, this way they can go out either the front or the back, depending on where the target is."

"And if the scouting party doesn't spot him, the man in the tower will," said Selvaggia, who had joined us in the hall while Cenni spoke. "You can see everything from up there, as you're about to find out." So much for being forgotten. Her "up there" made me shudder in spite of myself. That tower soared higher than a city boy usually even looked, let alone climbed. And I hated heights.

Selvaggia was dressed in the brilliant red gown she had intended for her wedding. Her dark hair, her one claim to beauty, this time was stuffed haphazardly into a net of gold thread punctuated with pearls, and she wore several rings on her plump hands. She was wide-awake and alert.

"Will you breakfast, Fool? Cenni?" I wasn't hungry, but Cenni accepted with enthusiasm, so all three of us climbed up to the kitchen.

Again, no servants were in evidence. In this household, when business was to be done it was family and only family, plus a military presence. Everyone else simply disappeared. Selvaggia found us simpler fare than the previous night, mostly bread with cheese. Cenni munched contentedly, but Selvaggia didn't eat much, and I couldn't choke any of it down.

She noted my problem. "Carry some with you, then," she said, her tone cool, amused. "We may have a long wait." Obediently I pocketed a piece of bread and a chunk of cheese, though I couldn't imagine eating on this day.

Selvaggia stood up, brushing crumbs from her skirt.

"Time to go up the tower."

26. UP THE TOWER

Selvaggia led us back down to the hall, out through the door at the end and onto the wooden walkway. The wood planks groaned and creaked under our feet, and gusts of cold wind found their way in through the gaps between the unfinished boards of the passage walls. It was a relief to go through the door to the tower and step onto solid rock. We passed Lambertuccio's study and the chapel. Both doors were closed and no sounds came from within.

A door in the corner of the tower opened directly to the stairs, a tight, steep spiral winding up through the very core of the thick stone wall. Even hollowed out to accommodate the stairs, that wall was massive.

Selvaggia led us up and I followed, with Cenni close behind me. The passage was barely wide enough in places for Cenni's ample girth. I had never been inside a tower before and I found the ascent laborious, but Selvaggia climbed like a cat. She clutched her skirt with both hands to raise it out of her way, and I glimpsed sturdy ankles.

The steps were too narrow to rest a foot fully on them, and the walls pressed in on us on both sides. Irregular stair heights and the tight spiral made progress difficult, and footing on the narrow side of each step, at the inside point of the spiral, was treacherous. What uncertain light we had came from far up above, and I feared making a misstep. Would Cenni catch me if I did, or would we both tumble down that long staircase? I kept one hand on the rough stone wall to brace myself, using the other to reach out and grope for the next step before I trusted my foot to it.

I had seen this tower many a time from the outside, but I could not recall how high up its first windows were. Those windows were still above us, but we were slowly moving closer, and the light increased as we ascended.

Some Florentines called this tower La Bigoncia, apparently thinking it resembled a giant wine vat. Others referred to it as the Tower of Two Lions, for the carved lion heads over the doors far below, carvings as old and worn as venerable Mars himself. To me, it was simply a pile of stones that thrust itself impossibly high into the sky. Equally impossibly, I was now inside it.

At last we reached the first landing, where the stairwell opened out into a meager living space with rough wooden flooring. Selvaggia stepped out onto that floor, and Cenni and I followed her. Narrow windows admitted light, but I carefully avoided looking out. The wind whistling through those slits told me I didn't want to see how high up we were.

The soldiers had slept on this level. They had left their straw pallets, as well as a jumble of mugs, lidded chamberpots, forgotten dice and scraps of food. A brazier, large enough to cook on, was cold and unused. This level had one area curtained off from the rest, and I guessed this was where the knights had slept, apart from the common soldiers. No ceiling, but high above us, perhaps two or three times the height of the Amidei great hall, was the underside of another wooden platform like the one we stood on.

We didn't stop, but continued up another stairway, this one wooden and less tortuous. It started in the center of the landing. Daylight came in through occasional slits in the thick walls. These stairs had no railing, only empty space around them, but at least we were no longer tracing a tight spiral. It required my full attention to keep from stepping off an edge. I was tiring with the effort of trudging up so many stairs, and I heard Cenni breathing heavily behind me, but Selvaggia moved briskly upward, and we had no choice but to keep pace with her.

The wooden stairs ended at the second landing, high above the first. The space around the square opening where the stairs came to an end was divided into four open rooms, with rough wooden walls separating them. Above us, much closer this time, was yet another platform. It was close enough to us to give the sense of being under a ceiling, even if it was in truth only the underside of another, higher, floor.

Each room on this level had either a window or a pair of narrow windows, and the one we emerged in, which looked out on the bridge, also had a stout door that led to the outside, where a wooden balcony could be attached or removed from within. I remembered seeing a more or less permanent balcony about halfway up La Bigoncia, facing the bridge. I guessed that we had reached it.

"This is where we'll be," Selvaggia said, not even out of breath. "But first, one more level up, to check on something." More climbing, and this time up a ladder. And what did she want to check on? I caught my breath as best I could and followed her again, Cenni right behind me and puffing hard. I kept a measured distance and tried not to raise my eyes, as I would have found myself looking up Selvaggia's skirt. Following a noblewoman up a ladder is not the sort of social situation my mother prepared me for.

The ladder went steeply up one side of the tower's inside wall. It was secured to the wall, at least, and stable. I avoided peering out the window slits as we passed them, but I had a sense of being much higher up than anyone should be. For an instant I saw in my mind my father's body, lying broken as if he had carelessly discarded it on his way to God. I gripped the ladder hard, and bit back a curse when a sliver came off in my palm.

Selvaggia reached the top of the ladder and hauled herself up in a flurry of red skirt, climbing out onto the sturdy wooden platform that formed a broad walkway all around the walls. I saw plenty more tower above us, but no more stout platforms, only ladders bolted to the walls and a few beams that might once have supported flooring. I halted on the ladder, my head poking out just above the platform, and Cenni panted below me.

This third level had only two windows, and one of them was directly above the room with the balcony. On the side that looked out over the bridge, a burly soldier stood watching our ascent. He was warmly dressed in a heavy knee-length green robe and thick gartered stockings, and on his head he wore a coif that covered his ears. The strings that would have tied it under his chin dangled.

A crossbow leaned against the wall next to him. A low wooden door next to the window was open a crack, and wind whistled through the space. A man would have to stoop to go through that door to the balcony, if balcony there was.

The soldier saluted Selvaggia. From where I had halted on the ladder I could watch the two of them while I worked the sliver out of my palm.

"All right, then, Ruggieri?" she said.

"All right, Lady."

"You keep a good watch, now, and take true aim if need be," she said, and he grinned at her, displaying a blackened front tooth.

"That I will, my lady. Rest you easy," he said, and she smiled back at him. I thought of two dogs about to be released at the hunt, teeth bared, quivering with eagerness. Had one of them barked, I wouldn't have been surprised.

Selvaggia flapped her hands at me impatiently, motioning for me to climb down. Over my shoulder I told Cenni to move, and we started to descend. She stepped back onto the ladder and followed us down to the platform.

We waited for her, and she led us into the room we had been in briefly before, with wooden walls extending up half again the height of a tall man and ending well short of the platform above us. Behind us was the hatch leading to the wooden stairs we had come up. Wind whistled through two narrow shutterless windows on either side of the door in the outside wall, and the floor was slimed with bird droppings, especially under the windows and on their stone shelves. A dead starling lay on the floor, spiky little feet pointing up. Cenni picked it up and tossed it out the window.

The room contained four three-legged stools and a chest, which I guessed held carpets and hangings to display outside on the balcony on feast days. A large chamberpot with a lid was tucked into the corner. On the makeshift wall several cloaks hung from a rail, all in the Amidei red-and-gold broad stripes. They smelled strongly of mildew.

Selvaggia went to the window on the left and stood on her tiptoes to peer out. She motioned me to the other window, and I approached it cautiously. The wind made a restless whining noise around both openings, and I wasn't sure how far up we were. All of the winding around on the stairs had made it impossible for me to gauge distances, and I deliberately hadn't looked out the window slits we passed on the way up.

It was dizzying. I didn't think we had climbed any more than halfway up the tower, but we were higher off the ground than I had ever been before, and I was unprepared for such an expanse of sky, at once terrifying and exhilarating. I stepped back—it was too much to take in.

Selvaggia laughed. "Better get used to it, Fool, for we'll be out on the balcony next," she said, and I groaned involuntarily. To step out that door, into the air, seemed a thing quite beyond me.

She pointed to the door, and Cenni stepped forward to open it. He lifted the bolt and tugged, pulling the door inward, and a rush of brisk air hit us with enough force to make us all take a step back. I pulled back another step from that gusty whoosh of air, flattening my palms against the rough stone wall. My heart was banging in my chest, and I could scarcely breathe. Selvaggia laughed again.

"It's breezy," she said. "I like it that way. Cenni, take the stools out, and grab a cloak for each of us." Cenni handed Selvaggia a cloak and offered one to me, but I wasn't going to wear the colors of these accursed families, so I refused it. He shrugged and pulled one about his own shoulders, as Selvaggia put hers on and tied its laces in the front, and then he took three of the four stools out the door, one at a time. I heard wood knock against wood as he set them down. There is a floor out there, I told myself desperately. There must be.

I yearned to stay inside, but I knew Selvaggia would never allow it, so when she waved me impatiently to the door, I went, though I couldn't imagine walking out into the sky on that wooden platform. I didn't even know yet if this was a covered balcony, or if it had a protective railing. It could have been merely a raft of wooden planks, hanging perilously out over the street and bridge below instead of floating sedately down the Arno, where a raft belonged. I had seen both kinds. Surely if this one was designed for the family's comfort it would have a railing, or walls. Surely I remembered seeing such a structure from the street below—didn't I?

At the door I stopped in spite of myself, one hand gripping each side of the frame. The wind blew in my face, chilling me, and straight ahead all I could see was sky and some buildings far, much too far, in the distance. No human being should be able to see that far—such a view was for birds, or God. I froze and closed my eyes tightly, swaying a little where I stood.

"He's afraid, Cenni," I heard Selvaggia say. "Fool, keep your eyes closed. Cenni, take him to a stool and sit him down."

I felt Cenni's broad hand on my arm as he moved me aside and stood in the doorway. He went through first and then guided me through, my eyes still scrunched shut. My foot crossed the threshold, and I stepped down—and felt nothing under my foot where I expected to encounter wooden floor. My eyes flew open. Panicking, I lost my balance and almost tumbled forward, but Cenni's grip held me firm, and my foot finally found the new floor level a few inches lower than the one inside. My legs buckled under me and I was down on my hands and knees on creaking wood, the wind blowing all around and under me, Cenni's broad hand around my upper arm.

I saw wooden slats ahead of me rather than sky, painted alternately in thick coats of dull red and muddy yellow, suggesting the Amidei stripes. The sense of something there between me and the sky helped me catch my breath. Open sky showed between the slats, but as long as I stayed down on the floor I felt more protected, despite the unnerving sensation of cold wind whistling under my hands and knees.

Selvaggia found all of this hilarious. That would have angered me had I had any energy left to feel anger, but terror will drain a man and not leave much behind. Still holding onto me, Cenni grabbed a stool with his other hand and dragged it as far back to the tower wall as he could without pulling it back inside. He hauled me over to it, hoisted me up, and sat me down on it, saying, "Keep your eyes closed and lean against the wall, Fool, until you get used to it." I did as he said.

I breathed deeply, willing myself to regain control. My hands clutched the edges of the stool. Keeping my eyes tightly closed, I tried to assess what I could feel. Wind, chill and brisk; the platform we rested on creaking and shifting a little but holding our weight; the wall at my back and the hard round seat of the stool under my bum. I could hear

Selvaggia's gown rustling to my left, and I could still feel Cenni's firm grip on my left arm. It was full day by now, but I didn't sense strong light beyond my eyelids, so I guessed we were shaded. Tentatively I reached my right hand out to my side, and it encountered the wooden slats on the right side of our platform. That helped me to calm myself, and cautiously I opened my eyes.

At first I was careful not to look beyond the platform. Selvaggia was wrapped in her striped cloak on my left, and Cenni was between us, crouching beside me. The even row of vertical slats was topped by a rail, about waist-high to a standing man—if any man dared to stand up, out there where only eagles should have been. That flimsy wall was in front and on both sides, the tower's outside wall with its door leading inside making a much more solid fourth wall at our backs. We were indeed shaded, not by an attached awning, as I had expected, but by a second platform directly above us that interrupted our light. Ruggieri's door must open out onto that platform, our ceiling, his floor.

We were facing east, or a little southeast. The market was off to our left, and the near end of the bridge with old battered Mars on our right and close by. I could see the bridge when I hazarded a glance between two of the slats. Were it not for those slats, with spaces only about the width of my thumb in between them, the sun would blind us. It would soon anyway when it got high enough to glare at us over the railing.

I could hear a babble of noises from the people on the street and the bridge below, but with the wind gusting around us, the only words I could make out were those of a cart driver shouting "Arra!" at his donkey, and of a woman screeching at her little boy to stay off the bridge.

Selvaggia sat calmly, close to the rail. She was gazing out between two slats, in the direction of the bridge. All she had to do for an unimpeded view was stand up. Something about her did not look quite right to me, and I puzzled for a moment over what it was, until I realized that the coarseness of her musty cloak was an incongruous contrast to her fine and costly gown. The cloaks with their broad red-and-gold stripes, like the heavy-handed paint job on the slats, were designed to be seen from down below, not from up close.

Cenni relaxed his grip on my arm. "See, it's not so bad once you get used to it," he said, his tone reassuring, as if he were coaxing a child up onto a donkey for the first time.

Yes, it is that bad, I thought. I was trembling, though some of it might have been shivering from the chill wind.

Selvaggia turned to study me. "Fool, I'm glad to see your fear," she

202

said. "There's something I want you to understand. Do you see the bridge over there?" She pointed, and I leaned forward enough to peer between two slats until I saw it again.

"One less-than-noble knight, one Buondelmonte dei Buondelmonti, will come riding toward that bridge. He'll come from our left, out that way," she gestured, "and he'll go directly in front of us, toward Mars and the bridge, and then he will go no farther."

This I knew, but what did it have to do with me, and with my fear? I said nothing.

"He will pass close enough to us that a shouted warning from up here could reach his ears. I merely want to make sure you understand what a big mistake that would be."

Would I be heard from up here? Cenni had the same thought, for he asked, "My lady, can they hear us down below?"

"Depends on the wind. Not when we're speaking normally, as a rule. But just in case, once they're close we will be very quiet. All of us." She fixed me with a meaningful stare, then slid her eyes past me to look at the bridge.

"If you were to attempt any such warning, my only problem would be deciding whether Cenni should gut you with his knife before we throw you over the edge of this balcony, or just go ahead and throw you, living." I felt my bowels loosen.

"That would probably depend on whether Buondelmonte heard you or not, but then again, it might just depend on my mood of the moment. Are we clear on this point, Fool?"

The blood must have drained from my head at the thought of pitching over the side of the balcony and plummeting to the street below, because Cenni grabbed me again, as if he thought I was about to pass out. I think I whimpered a little.

"Cenni, did you get that?" she said.

"Yes, my lady." This man, who was looking after me with efficiency and a certain detached kindness, at a word from her would kill me and throw my body to the ground a hideous distance away. Or just throw me, alive and terrified. I had no doubt of his allegiance. He might have a moment of regret, for he was a decent sort, but it wouldn't slow him down. It was not lost on me that even though Oddo's man Pierino had spoken of Selvaggia with little respect, her own family's men held her in high regard.

"So, Fool," she said, "will you warn messer Buondelmonte and his pretty little bedfellow?"

I swallowed. "No, my lady, I will not," I finally said. She had given me more credit than I deserved. Even without that stomach-churning warning, I didn't think I would have the courage to defy this woman and her soldier.

She nodded, satisfied. "It wouldn't accomplish anything even if you did. If Buondelmonte makes a run for it, Ruggieri—" she pointed upwards, "will bring him down, and if Ruggieri has to shoot, that means more risk to other people down below. He's an excellent marksman, but mistakes can happen. So if you want to limit the killing to the one who deserves to die, as you so nobly suggested when we spoke before, you'll keep silent and enjoy your unobstructed view of the spectacle." Her voice was relaxed, but her hands were gripping the railing tightly, and her eyes scanned the route she had described, from left to right, again and again.

My mind was roiling. The thought of Ruggieri firing a bolt into the street below us was terrifying, but logic reminded me that he was one man, with one weapon and probably only one shot, for it would take him considerable time to reload once he fired. That limited the damage he could do. But what, in any case, would I yell to alert Buondelmonte? I could hardly shout, "Messer Buondelmonte, I think you ought to know that your bodyguards have been bought off and there are soldiers in the crowd trying to kill you." I'd never make it through the four syllables of his name. Defeated, I hung my head. Again, Selvaggia controlled the situation.

With the rules established, we settled down to wait. Shamefaced, I had to request permission to use the chamberpot inside, for my body needed to rid itself of the burning liquid result of my fear. Cenni stood guard next to me, patiently, and afterwards drew me back outside, where I shivered in the chill wind.

Finally I mustered the courage to look around me. Although the height made me shiver, I had to admit the view was magnificent. I had never known it was possible to see so much of the city at once. I could see the river sparkling in the sun. From here I could watch the progress of a cart along a street, and then continue to watch it even after the street curved. Nothing was hidden from me. The world must be so for falcons, I thought. It's a wonder they ever return to the wrist.

I could see other towers belonging to other great families, standing tall and strong and proud, both near and distant. They jutted up into the sky, claiming whole neighborhoods for their mighty owners. I saw churches, palaces, gardens, and streets crowded with buildings of many sizes and shapes, of brick and stone and wood. I could see part of the city walls, with their watchtowers. I watched the business of the city take place before my eyes: the steady traffic of loaded carts, men on horseback, women with baskets balanced on their heads or strapped to their backs, and groups of pilgrims, all making their way into the city across a bridge already crowded with shoppers, and still more people traveling in the opposite direction, going back out of the city.

Gradually the sun warmed me, and I stopped shivering. Selvaggia and Cenni slipped off their mildewed cloaks, and Cenni took them back inside. I watched the little people passing below us. In the utter newness of this experience, I could almost forget, for moments at a time, why we were here.

Then Selvaggia stiffened, and I jumped. I heard creaking and footsteps on the platform above our heads, and Ruggieri's voice saying, "My lady?"

"I see him," she said. "Cenni, Fool, keep down and keep quiet." More creaking told us that Ruggieri had gone back inside.

I peered down to the street from between the slats, to our left, to see what they were responding to. Within my view was no white-clad knightly party on horseback, only the usual crowd of people, laden donkeys, scavenging pigs, children dashing around, and directly in front of us the two beggars who usually sat on either side of the entrance to the bridge, the lame one and the one with a shriveled arm.

Then I noticed the peddler in front of the palace. He wore a pointed straw hat, and the basket that hung over his stomach from a cord around his neck held a colorful assortment of wares. From this distance I couldn't see exactly what he was selling, but he wore a knee-length tunic and particolored hose. One leg was blue, the other white.

He was crying his wares—I heard the word "ribbons," though I couldn't distinguish much else. Selvaggia's attention was riveted by him, as was Cenni's. Deliberately, the peddler pulled a length of red cloth from his belt and waved it in the direction of the palace, once, twice, a third time. No one on the street took note of him as they went about their business.

"How can he see them coming from down there when we can't see them yet?" I asked, surprised to hear myself speaking the thought aloud.

"He's relaying a signal from another man further north, and that one's relaying yet another," Cenni said, his eyes still on the peddler. "We have planned well."

Above us, Ruggieri remained out of sight, but from just inside the door upstairs I heard a ratcheting sound and a series of clanks and clicks, wood and metal. A crossbow being readied.

205

"Stay down," Selvaggia said again. "Here they come."

27. VENDETTA

I peered through the slats, crouching at the front of the platform this time despite my fear, for another fear was overriding it. Unsure at first where to look, I saw no riders coming toward us, but at the far end of our line of vision I did see people moving away from the center of the street and over to the sides, making way.

And then I saw them. Tiny and distant, two gleaming white figures mounted on white horses, their two hulking, treacherous bodyguards close behind them. Following behind Dino and Vanni were four of Buondelmonte's men and a woman in blue. Let her not be Fiammetta, or Bianca, or Gualdrada, or Elisa, I prayed silently. Let them not be part of this. The retainers were too few; they posed no challenge to Oddo's forces. Oh, Buondelmonte, I thought, you are too confident. Was he at least still wearing that heavy quilted perpunto under his festive clothes? I imagined I could see his golden spurs glint in the sun.

We watched them come closer, growing larger in our sight as they approached the bridge. I could now tell that the woman riding behind Isabella was a servant, and not one of the Donati ladies. That, at least, I was thankful for. The peddler was no longer in our view, and we couldn't see what was happening directly below, in front of the house and just outside the door. But the wind had shifted, and I heard voices below. I thought I might have heard a gruff male voice saying, "Ready."

The people on the street and on the bridge were not a feastday crowd, but still there were enough of them to clutter Buondelmonte's path. The riders moved slowly, finding their way down the middle. That didn't leave much space for those who had to step aside for them, flattening themselves against the stone walls of palaces and houses. Many of the people on foot stared after the riders as they passed, no doubt dazzled by all the white and gold and by Isabella's arresting beauty.

Everyone was also well aware of Buondelmonte's act of defiance, and of the vendetta. The riders would soon come within a few steps of the Amidei palace and tower, and Florentines were ever excited by the chance to witness a flagrant insult or a confrontation. But no one, even those who relished the drama of the situation, expected a violent attack in such a public place, and a week after Easter Sunday.

And now the riders were directly in front of us, as close as their route was ever going to bring them. In vain I searched for the telltale bulk of armor under Buondelmonte's sleek garments. Vanity had prevailed. When

I looked down at the fair Isabella, so young and so graceful, something stirred in me, far below the level of thought. I had been certain I wouldn't have the courage to cry out a warning, but whatever was stirring was pushing my fear aside, making its way relentlessly toward the surface.

My mouth opened and I drew a deep breath. Selvaggia heard me, turned to look at me, and scowled. She made an abrupt gesture to Cenni. Before I could let that breath out again, with or without my voice behind it, he lunged at me, clamped his arm hard across my face and yanked me back inside the tower. He held me there in the doorway, and not gently. I struggled, mashed under his broad arm, and I whimpered a little, in pain and terror. Would I now be tossed off that tower in the sky, in punishment for a warning I didn't even manage to deliver? I expelled my breath in a grunt, but I couldn't draw another without choking on his sleeve, and my head was starting to spin.

Selvaggia ignored us. Over Cenni's suffocating sleeve I could just see her as she stared down at Buondelmonte, unblinking, her teeth gritted as her breath hissed through clenched jaws. She turned her head slowly as she watched them pass. "Release him, Cenni," she said in a low voice, her eyes never leaving Buondelmonte. "He'll be quiet now."

Cenni obeyed, glowering at me, and I sank to my knees in the doorway, gasping for breath. He cuffed me hard on my shoulder, and then shoved me aside and strode to the edge of the platform, where he crouched down and peered between the slats.

That could have been my chance to elude them, to slip away and go back down those stairs while their attention was elsewhere. But even if I got away, by the time I reached the street whatever was going to happen would have happened, and I would walk out into a dangerous turmoil.

Instead, I scuttled over to the edge on all fours, still gulping air and coughing. But I had to see. I had to know what was going on below us. Selvaggia was right: I wouldn't call out. That moment had passed. Buondelmonte had moved on, and it was too late. And I was afraid again, afraid at the thought of how close I had come to sacrificing myself without thinking.

I recognized Lambertuccio's men in the crowd. My eyes sought Buondelmonte, and I saw that his horse and Isabella's had just stepped onto the bridge. They were stuck behind a slow-moving donkey cart, and I heard Buondelmonte yelling at the driver to get out of his way, when everything happened at once.

Dino and Vanni peeled away from the party and rode off to either side, just short of the bridge. Selvaggia jumped to her feet, Cenni half a second behind her. Buondelmonte's retainers shouted, and he turned. Whatever he saw made him spur his horse, at the same time reaching over to grab Isabella's reins. But the donkey cart ahead of them abruptly turned sideways, blocking their way. Now we could see that the driver wore the Lamberti blue and gold. The crowd noise got abruptly louder as people realized something was going on.

By now I too was on my feet, although my first sight of sky and city above the railing was enough to make my head spin again. I kept my eyes on Buondelmonte, even as I gripped the railing and kept my feet as far back as I could and still see anything. Selvaggia and Cenni were leaning over the rail, and I heard the tramp of Ruggieri's feet above us as he strode forward into position.

Isabella's horse reared and whinnied, and she struggled to hold on. Buondelmonte reined in his mount and came to an abrupt halt. He turned toward Isabella and reached again for her mare's reins just as Schiatta stepped forward briskly, raising a mace overhead. I held my breath and tried to close my eyes, but they obstinately remained open and staring.

A woman in the crowd screamed. Schiatta swung his weapon hard, and the head of the mace connected with Buondelmonte's side, unprotected as he tried to control Isabella's panicking mare. The blow toppled Buondelmonte from his horse and he slid to the ground and crumpled.

Schiatta's skill was such that Buondelmonte fell to the right and a little behind the horse, rather than between his mount and Isabella's, where he might have found some little protection. But there was none where he fell.

Schiatta stepped back, his contribution at an end, and Oddo moved forward, his knife flashing. Buondelmonte still twitched on the ground when Oddo reached him, but he jerked and lay still as the blade slashed across his throat.

Oddo, in his turn, stepped back, his foot sliding a little in the expanding pool of blood, and Lambertuccio came forward, holding a sword. Selvaggia's father was in no hurry now. He placed his swordpoint on the knight's breast and with both hands shoved it home.

I heard an incongruous little sob, and I turned to Selvaggia. She was as white as Buondelmonte's fine robes, her crimson dress the counterpart to the red blood that soaked those robes, the stain spreading as we watched.

One of Oddo's men grabbed the reins of Isabella's mare and pulled both horse and terrified rider out of the fray, throwing a cloth over the animal's head to calm her. Nothing could calm Isabella, who screamed repeatedly, the clearest sound to us in our aerie of all the chaotic shouts and cries below. Terrified men and women and animals ran, in any direction that sped them away from the armed men. Those who had already been on the bridge were running toward the far end, bumping into each other in their panic. The lame beggar was making particularly good time, shoving others aside as he sprinted. In some distracted corner of my mind I made a note not to drop my coins in his bowl again.

Buondelmonte's retainers and the servingwoman never reached the bridge. One or two of his men tried to get to him, but the soldiers who poured from our palace surrounded them and menaced them with weapons, preventing them from riding on or from dismounting.

In the confusion I couldn't see where Vanni and Dino had gone. Schiatta, Oddo, and Lambertuccio were also nowhere to be seen, and I suspected they had vanished into the palace, their retreat protected by their men. Over to one side I saw Amadio doubled over and vomiting. Then he, too, was gone.

My mind was working with unnatural clarity. From my high perch I could watch everything, yet I felt nothing, only a detached interest in the unfolding scene below. It was as if my physical distance protected me from the horror of what I was seeing, but I feared that wouldn't last. Irrelevantly, I wondered if Buondelmonte had managed to find his way to Isabella's bed before the nozze. No matter; he had had her now for at least a few short weeks.

We watched as a circle opened up around the fallen knight. I heard a shrill whistle, and the soldiers melted away, even those who had been holding Buondelmonte's followers in place, until in a matter of seconds no one from Oddo's party remained on the street. Buondelmonte lay in his own blood, his gold spurs still gleaming in the sun, and no one was within a man's length of him. He lay at the foot of Mars.

When Buondelmonte's men realized they were no longer being held back, they dismounted and rushed to their fallen master, filling in that eerily empty circle as we watched from above. Isabella's lady, with no one to help her dismount gracefully, scrambled down on her own and ran to the screaming young widow, whose agitated mare was now being held with difficulty by a passerby, a man either braver or more curious than most.

Word was spreading rapidly, as it will do in Florence. From the direction of the cathedral we heard the city's great alarm bell sound, and now as many people were running toward the scene as had run away a few moments before. From the north we saw the growing crowd part to let four horses through, moving fast. Three of them were ridden by men. Close behind came a gray horse with two women riders. I felt a sinking feeling in my stomach. I recognized all of those riders, even at this distance. The men were Buondelmonte's brother Gherardo and the Donati lords Cione and Manno, and the women were the white-clad Fiammetta in front, riding hard with her white-gold hair flying behind her, and Gualdrada behind her, head down and arms clasped around her daughter's narrow waist.

All of them stopped at the head of the bridge. They jumped down from their mounts, except for Fiammetta, who remained seated atop the gray. Gualdrada was the first one to the ground, halfway off the horse even before it came to a trembling stop, and she ran over to Isabella, adding her wails to her daughter's. Gherardo's eyes were on his fallen brother. He walked slowly forward until he reached Buondelmonte's side and fell to his knees in the spreading pool of blood.

Cione and Manno followed at a respectful distance, crossing themselves and, I supposed, murmuring a prayer. Gualdrada and the serving-woman succeeded in getting their hysterical lady off her horse, and the three of them clutched each other and wept.

Fiammetta still did not dismount. She looked at Buondelmonte, at the little knot of weeping women, at the palace, at the crowd of people gaping, at the podestà's men who had finally arrived at a run, several paces ahead of their scurrying trumpeter. And then she looked up at us.

No one else had thought to look up. The three of us were leaning over the railing, and above us Ruggieri still stood holding his crossbow. I saw Fiammetta take it all in, and I saw her recognize me. Those blue eyes bored into mine for what seemed like forever, until at last she turned away and nudged her horse into a walk, moving closer to Buondelmonte.

"Better get out of sight, Ruggieri. You don't want the boss to see you," said Cenni to the platform above us, and we heard the tramp of Ruggieri's footsteps, going back inside. That was when I realized belatedly that Ruggieri was Selvaggia's man, not Oddo's or Lambertuccio's. Of course. Honor was not served by killing at a distance, so the knights wouldn't have tolerated it. But Selvaggia had said simply, "I want him dead." And Ruggieri would have obeyed her, had there been need.

"My lady? Will you away?" Cenni extended his hand to Selvaggia, but she didn't take her eyes off the scene below. She shook her head.

"No, Cenni. I'll stay awhile. Go inside and wait for me."

"And the fool?"

"With me." Cenni bowed and backed through the door. He didn't

211

move far away from the door, I noticed. Part of his charge was to protect Selvaggia from me, ridiculous as that may have been.

"My lady," came Cenni's voice from inside, "it's better you not be seen."

She said nothing, but sank to her stool and continued to watch the scene below from between the slats. I sat, too.

Down below Fiammetta had taken charge. First she spoke briefly to her uncles, and messer Cione nodded. I would have given much to know what the girl had said.

She still sat her mount, which must have given her an advantage in making herself seen and heard. She spoke a word here and gave a direction there, and four men walked the short distance to Santa Maria sopra Porta. When they returned minutes later, they were carrying the church's bier.

The Donati men and Gherardo gently picked up Buondelmonte's limp body and laid it on the black-covered platform. A sort of impromptu procession order then formed, with Buondelmonte's men standing ready to lift the bier and carry it through the streets. Fiammetta guided her horse over to her mother and sister, who were leaning on each other and weeping, and spoke to them.

Isabella shook her head vigorously, and Gualdrada appeared to be trying to shield her elder daughter from her younger. Fiammetta spoke again, and Gualdrada stared at her for a moment, then slowly nodded her head. Cione and Manno joined them then, and they guided Isabella, weeping wildly, over to the bier and tried to get her to climb onto it. She pulled away and turned to her mother, who reached out to her. But Fiammetta spoke yet again from atop the gray horse, Gualdrada drew back, and at last Isabella allowed her uncles to seat her on the bier. She shrank from touching her husband's body, even while his head lolled in her lap.

Soon the somber procession was on its way, with two of the podestà's men leading the way. Gherardo, Cione, and Manno followed, then Buondelmonte's four retainers carrying the bier. Fiammetta had dismounted at last, quickly and neatly, and I saw that she and her mother had ridden bareback. She and Isabella's servingwoman supported the anguished Gualdrada as the three women walked close behind the fallen knight and his young wife, now his widow.

A terrible pathos suffused this tableau of the weeping young widow in white, her bloodied husband still wearing his flowery garland. It would conjure sympathy for the slain man and his allies, I realized, while wordlessly blaming those who had caused his death. The image of the fallen, garlanded man with his head in a woman's lap would strike a strong chord among Florentines, who saw such images on the walls of their churches every day. I had not guessed that little Fiammetta was such a gifted strategist.

Selvaggia must have been thinking the same thing, for she murmured, "She's good, that one." I turned to her. She had regained her composure, and a little color had returned to her cheeks, but I thought I saw traces of tears there as well.

I was exhausted and drained, and as usual at such times, I cared too little for what I said. This time what came out of my mouth was "My lady must be well pleased."

She was expressionless. After a moment, she said, "All that was necessary has been done."

"You have ignited a civil war in your city," I said. "Was that part of what was necessary?"

She shrugged. "An insult to the lineage must be answered. We have given our answer. If the townspeople see fit to fight over it, then they'll fight."

"And you don't care."

"Why should I?" Her eyes blazed. "He stole from me my honor, my dignity, and every chance I had for a decent life. There's nothing for me now. Should he not have paid? Would you have him rewarded for his baseness?" Her voice shook a little, but she didn't lower her eyes.

I hated everything this woman had done, and at the same time I felt a grudging admiration for her. Oddo was right: she should have been a man.

"What will happen to you now, my lady?" I asked her. In truth, she had few good prospects.

She slumped a little. "I'll go into a convent," she said, her voice flat. "No one will want rejected goods. I will not marry. I'll live out my life in the service of God, and I will never know a moment of pleasure or lightness again. But I'll live all the years to come with the memory of this day, and it will be enough." Tears sparkled in her eyes, belying her words, but she did not let them fall.

All at once I was finished. The thing was done, as Mosca had said, and there would be no end to it. But for Selvaggia and me the end had come. She had no reason to keep me any longer, and I was going home.

I stood up, not bothering to say goodbye or announce my intention, and started to go inside.

213

Behind me, I heard Selvaggia say, "Go out the back door, Fool. The men will be barricading the front, but you can still get out through the courtyard." I turned to face her. She was still gazing down at the street, and she didn't look at me.

Then I did go. As I brushed past Cenni, I pulled a linty wad of bread and cheese out of my sleeve and held it out to him. He took it automatically, then stood there looking down at it with a puzzled expression as I walked to the hatch, lifted it, and headed down the stairs. I clattered down, first the wooden stairs and then that long spiraling staircase, descending faster than was safe, but not caring. I burst into the empty hall, grabbed my bag of juggling equipment, and ran down the great stairs.

At the bottom, it was as Selvaggia had said. The men were throwing together a set of barricades to protect the palace, and they wouldn't let me pass through the front portal. Instead I went out the back, into the courtyard, where men were building the makeshift walls to serve as protection during the street fighting that would surely come. I was able to wind my way through the workers and find my way out through an alley, and then I was out on the street, and on my way home at last.

28. UNREST

The city was in an uproar. People were running every which way, excited, spreading the news. Already the great families were fortifying their palaces and towers, withdrawing ladders and barricading alleys with stockpiled building debris and scrap lumber. High above the street a tower was being joined to a neighboring tower by a wooden bridge, maneuvered into place and made fast by men standing on balconies like the one I had just left.

With all of this going on, part of my direct route was impassable, so I had to wind my way around smaller streets to make my way back to my own neighborhood, lugging my bag of juggling props with me.

The city's alarm bells rang again, though to what purpose I didn't know. No one heeded them. Certainly no one rushed to the palace of the podestà, and I couldn't believe that city officials would risk bringing armed men together at a moment when passions ran so high. Probably the alarm was meant to call the podestà's own men to receive instructions, but it added an insistent, agitated note to the general hubbub.

I walked fast, for once making no attempt to skirt the filth and refuse in the street. My heart hammered in my chest. The enormity of what I had just witnessed was beginning to catch up with me, and the memory of Fiammetta's blue eyes staring directly up at me was a torment. I wanted to tell her that I tried to shout a warning. But did I try? I didn't know whether I would have shouted or not, had Cenni not stopped me.

But even if I didn't act when it might have helped, I had at least tried to get a message to them earlier, and if Neri had been willing to carry it, all of this might have been prevented. A wave of anger washed over me, displacing my pain at the thought of Fiammetta. I walked a little faster, rehearsing in my mind what I would say to him when I got home, he who had been so quick to condemn my involvement in these knightly follies. Yes, Neri too bore some blame for this, and it was so much easier to think about his role than about my own.

I rounded a corner, by this time furiously scolding at Neri in my head, and ran smack into a man who was standing motionless at the edge of the street. I started to curse, but then I realized he was one of perhaps twenty people lining the street shoulder to shoulder, silently watching something. He ignored me. I elbowed my way into the line of watchers to get a look at what they were seeing.

Buondelmonte's cortege was moving slowly toward us. The podestà's men who headed it scanned the crowd as they rode, and instinctively I moved back a little. The Donati men and Gherardo, grim-faced, walked behind them, striding like the warriors they were. Next came the bier with the bloodied knight, his limp body jostled this way and that with every step, and a disheveled Isabella, no longer screaming but heaving with dry sobs.

Buondelmonte's head lolled in her lap, still encircled by a wreath of leaves and early flowers, and his blood soaked the length of fine white damask that covered his throat, damask ripped from the sleeve of Isabella's festive godmother gown. She rested her hands on his shoulders, resigned at last to touching him, and her fingers plucked agitatedly at his blood-drenched robe. Her thick mantle of honey-colored hair fell like an amber waterfall, veiling both of them, the ends reddened with Buondelmonte's lifeblood.

And then I did duck out of sight, hiding behind the man I had bumped into, for behind the bier walked Gualdrada and Fiammetta.

Gualdrada wailed without ceasing, making an eerie sound somewhere between hysterical weeping and the ancient ritual pianto. Her reddish hair was down in a tangled mass, and for the first time I noticed streaks of gray in it. She had rent her gown so it gapped raggedly open in front, and raked her face with her nails, leaving bloody streaks on both cheeks. She beat her breast with her fist as she walked and wailed.

That vivid picture of the ancient style of mourning caught at people's hearts: a murmur of sorrow and sympathy rose up as she approached, in spite of the earlier talk on the street that blamed her for the great insult that had set the vendetta in motion. She leaned heavily on Fiammetta for support, though the younger woman was smaller and reed-slender.

Fiammetta's pale hair fell loose as well, but she walked in silence. Her face was drained of its delicate color, and she watched the people on both sides of the street as she passed, looking directly at anyone who would meet her eyes. I couldn't have met those eyes again. I retreated around the corner.

From there I could see only that the procession had added many people, men and women who followed behind the Donati women. Many bore lighted candles. Among the women, several made a spine-tingling pianto, their voices high and wavering, interspersed with occasional yelps and theatrical sobs. Bringing up the rear was Buondelmonte's snow-white horse, riderless. A powerful and impressive spectacle, and the crowd was enthralled. People crossed themselves and murmured prayers; some fell to their knees.

The Donati wanted to move the crowds, and they had hit on the perfect piece of theatre to do it. They must be taking this spectacle through as much of the city as they could, for there was no other reason for them to be here on this little street, not close to either the Buondelmonti or Donati homes or to the cathedral. It was probably significant that the podestà's men were with them, although it might only have been intended to forestall any further violence.

Buondelmonte's cortege passed. I was able to continue on my way, but I walked more slowly. I was beginning to understand that this whole conflict was much too big for me to stop. The most I could have done, even if I had taken every opportunity—and I knew I had not—was to delay it a little while.

And yet, had I not been the one to begin it? I shook my head, hard, to dislodge that thought, and picked up my pace again until I reached our house.

Ghisola met me at the door.

"Have you seen him? He hasn't been back since yesterday evening," she said. Her eyes were red-rimmed and swollen. Neri had no business putting her through this, I thought, my anger starting to resurface.

"He's probably at the tavern," I said. "I'll go find him."

"Tavern's closed. It's Sunday." Right. I'd managed to forget that. But then, I wasn't the only man who had kept the sabbath in an unusual way this day.

"Well, then, I'll go find him. I need to talk to him. Maybe he's at the church."

Ghisola shook her head. "I looked there," she said. "There's no sign of him."

I realized I was pacing up and down, the meager size of the room requiring me to reverse direction every few steps. Might as well go out and search for him, I thought, and I started for the door.

"Don't." Ghisola's tone was pleading, and it stopped me. I turned around, really seeing her this time. She had circles dark as bruises under her eyes.

"What's the matter, Ghisi?"

"I just don't want you to go. Please. I'm afraid, and the whole city is going mad, and I've been here by myself all night and most of today, except for when I went out to look for him, and I'm too scared to go out again, and I know there's trouble between you two, and I'm afraid if you find him, you'll fight. He's been drinking, and you know how he gets." This all tumbled out in a rush, and she sat down abruptly on the stool, as

217

if the loss of so many words at once had exhausted her. She clenched her hands tightly together, but she couldn't keep them from shaking.

"Ghisola," I said, trying to sound calm and reassuring, "I don't want to fight Neri. I just want to talk to him, and I want to make sure he's all right. That's all." I sat down, to show her I wasn't rushing out and leaving her alone.

She sniffed, and I saw a tear trickle down her face. "If you go out there, you won't find him, and everybody's gone completely crazy, and then I'll just be worried about you, too." She wiped her nose with her sleeve, something she was normally far too fastidious to do.

I sat quietly for a few minutes, thinking. Neri and I had never fought, but if we did, it would be an interesting contest. He was bigger than me and well muscled, but years of tumbling and juggling had made me quicker and more agile. A juggler's sense of timing versus a musician's, then? I'd not want to bet on such a pairing. I was not intentionally seeking a fight, and yet when she spoke of it, I realized that not long ago fighting would have been a real possibility, so angry had I been. But when I forced myself to think rationally about Neri's crime, I had to admit he didn't know the stakes when he refused to take my message. In our quick furtive conversation, I hadn't been able to make it clear to him, not that he had been particularly willing to listen. If I ever got around to making confession again, I was going to have to confess to anger against a friend. And Neri, in his turn, could confess to being a stubborn idiot.

The remaining rage drained out of me like air out of an inflated pig's bladder. Ghisola's presence was calming to me, even when, as now, she was not calm herself.

And so I agreed to stay with her and wait for Neri to come home. She brightened a little at that, and puttered about preparing a late dinner of pottage and some bread fried in oil, enough for three, in case he returned hungry.

While she worked, I sipped a cup of wine and listened. I no longer heard the city's alarm bells, but I could hear other bells sound sporadically. I heard death knells from more than one parish church close enough for the peals to reach our ears, but not from our own parish. I heard a fire bell, but it was far in the distance. It did not ring for our neighborhood. From time to time I heard men shouting, and once I was fairly sure I heard a clash of arms, too close for comfort. And once we clearly heard one of the podestà's criers in our neighborhood square, announcing an early curfew, telling people to stay indoors and informing us that the podestà's men were patrolling the entire city to keep the peace.

Well, good luck finding any peace to keep, I thought. Peace was not a thing Florence had an abundance of, that spring.

We ate in near-silence, still anxious and worried, listening to the noises outside. Ghisola was about to clean our wooden bowls when we heard a tap at the door. She dropped the dishes with a clatter and dashed over to open it, though of course Neri wouldn't have knocked, but in her anxiety she wasn't thinking clearly.

It was Bicci. We asked him in, and he came and sat with us in front of the hearth. Our fire still crackled from Ghisola's cooking and hadn't yet settled into embers and ash.

Bicci's brow furrowed when we said we didn't know where Neri was. It seemed everyone was worried about Neri these days. It occurred to me to wonder how I could have expected him to be able to carry a message, when it sounded like he'd been so troubled of late that the whole neighborhood feared he would do something foolish or dangerous. What had I failed to see? In my defense, I had been imprisoned in great houses for the past several days, so I had managed to miss his most recent peculiarities.

Bicci brought us news from the streets. Full-fledged civil war had not erupted, though preventing it was taking every man the podestà commanded. Bicci had heard, however, of a number of small skirmishes, and the great houses were arming and preparing for the worst. I had seen the beginnings of that on my way home, so I wasn't surprised to hear that the Uberti had turned their compound into a fortress. Schiatta had been instrumental in creating this situation, and now he intended to profit from it if he could. It was a bitter thought, when so many had been harmed.

"And did you hear about Vanni and Dino?" Bicci asked.

I spat, and Ghisola glared at me. "Those traitors, who betrayed their master? I suppose they're off drinking up their blood money, or selling themselves to somebody new," I said, my anger rising again at the thought.

Bicci shook his head vigorously. "No, no. They're dead! You didn't hear?"

"Yours is the first news we've had. What do you mean, they're dead?" I demanded.

"I mean they're dead. As in not breathing anymore. As in stabbed and slashed and skewered, and off to hell, heigh-ho. Oddo sent his men for them right after the attack on Buondelmonte. Said traitors like that couldn't be trusted. If they'd sell out one master, they'd sell out another, and it wasn't going to be him."

That sounded like Oddo: smart, violent, and practical. "Good riddance to them, then," I said.

Ghisola crossed herself; I didn't. "So they got their money for nothing."

"Yes. Oddo's men killed them, quick and efficient-like, but they were under orders to leave the money. Oddo says he paid them for work done, all fair and honorable, and then he paid them for being disloyal. And they could keep both payments."

"So what happened to the money? Were they carrying it?"

"Oddo's men left them on the street, so people came swarming and took everything. Money, clothes, weapons, all of it. Nobody liked those two." With reason, I thought. Cutthroats and thugs tended to be unpopular, even in this city where much of the ruling class could be described in the same terms. Bicci reported that boys had dragged the stripped bodies off; he didn't know where. Usually I disapproved of the Florentine urchins' unpleasant habit of exacting society's revenge on dead bodies, but in this case they were welcome to them.

Bicci waited with us until we heard the podestà's patrol pass, and then he took his chance to scurry back to his house and Tedora without being taken in for breaking the curfew. As he left he promised to get word to us if he learned anything of Neri, curfew or no.

It was evening now, the sky a darkening blue through our high, small window, and the room was growing dim as the fire died back. The sky was clouded over, no starlight showing through, no moon to light the night. The darkness would give ample opportunities for mischief before the night was done, and the dark lanterns troublemakers carried at night would be everywhere. Such lanterns were illegal for good reason—men of malicious intent used them to light their way and recognize others while they kept their own faces in shadow, so they couldn't be identified.

I thought the podestà had shown good sense in declaring the curfew, though enforcing it was another matter. The city government lacked the power to bring things under firm control, but it could be effective in certain situations, besides being the only protection we insignificant people had when the great families went mad. We would just have to hope it was enough.

We sat in the gathering gloom for quite a while longer, until well past full dark. Finally I managed to persuade Ghisola to go lie down. I promised her I would stay up, and if Neri came I swore to wake her immediately, before I even spoke to him. She was so exhausted that she agreed. In a matter of minutes I heard her soft snoring from the bed alcove.

I'm not sure how much longer I sat, thinking, sorting things out, and sipping wine, before I heard running footsteps and a loud pounding on the door. I jumped up. The noise woke Ghisola, who emerged from her alcove sleepy-eyed and rumpled just as I got to the door. I was about to lift the latch until I thought better of it. These were troubled times, I reminded myself, holding Ghisola back with one arm as she reached for the latch.

"Who's there?" I called out.

"Tomasso. Open up. Neri's hurt. You've got to come." I threw the bolt open, and Ghisola moaned.

29. NERI

Tomasso, flushed and agitated, motioned us outside. He held a lantern, an ordinary one. "Come on," he said, gesturing toward the tavern square. "Hurry up—Neri's been in a fight, and it looks bad."

That was all we had to hear. We took off at a run toward the tavern. Ghisola hadn't even taken time to pull on her shoes, and her bare feet slapped the ground as we ran.

It wasn't far. A few steps and around the corner, and we were on the square where the communal well stood covered, waiting for the morning's traffic. Simone was standing in front of his door. At his feet lay Neri, unmoving.

Neighbors were rushing from their homes and converging on the spot, some still in their shirts, and most carried lanterns or candles or lamps. The night was still; only a few of the lights blew out, and those that did were relighted from the others, so the square was as light as dusk.

Simone stared down at Neri. I thought irrelevantly that it may have been the first time I had seen Simone without his apron. Next to him, Bicci's dog whined.

Ghisola gave a tiny cry and put her hand to her mouth, her steps faltering. I caught her arm, just as Bicci looked at Neri and then at us and grimly shook his head. Ghisola pulled free of my grip and ran to Neri, falling onto her knees and draping herself over him, babbling and weeping. The neighbors stood back a little, respectfully, and crossed themselves and mumbled prayers.

Simone bent down and put his hand on Ghisola's shoulder, but she didn't notice. I began to walk forward, slowly and numbly, and Bicci came to meet me.

He shook his head again. "He's gone," was all that he said, and then he turned and walked with me over to Neri.

My friend lay on his back. A gaping hole in the front of his tunic had oozed bright blood, and he lay in a red lake. He was dirty and disheveled, and a stubbly growth of beard surrounded his mouth, which was open in a snarl. His eyes stared at nothing. His hands were filthy and I smelled wine, as well as blood and the contents of his guts. My stomach turned, and I doubled over and vomited up my dinner. To see this twice in one day was too much, and this time was worse, much worse, for this time it was Neri.

More neighbors came. Clergymen from the parish church arrived and tried to take charge, but they couldn't get Ghisola to move away from Neri. They stood around with the rest of us, unsure what to do, while she held his body and wept and spoke unceasingly to him, too softly for anyone to hear. Tedora, heavily pregnant, knelt behind Ghisola and prayed, tears streaming down her face.

We remained thus until the podestà's patrol arrived at the square. The officer in charge hopped down from his horse and came over to see what was amiss. He stopped in front of Neri's body, and as he gazed down, his expression hardened, and he muttered, "Another one."

He looked up. "Anyone witness this?"

Simone stepped forward, and the podestà's man held up a torch to illuminate him.

"Identify yourself."

Simone blinked in the light. "Simone di Vieri. I run this tavern here." He gestured to the building.

"Who's the dead man?"

"Neri di Paolo. Musician. Lives in the neighborhood."

"Fight?"

"Yes. Two groups of men—"

"Which men?" the soldier interrupted, scanning the crowd of neighbors as if looking for the culprits.

"They're gone now. They were arguing, and somebody said something, and Neri attacked him, and one of the man's friends pulled his knife, too, and—well, you can see what happened." Simone's eyes indicated Neri's body.

"The dead man was the aggressor?"

Simone nodded. "Neri pulled a knife. He was drunk, and he got angry at whatever the man said, and he rushed at him, and then another man stabbed him."

"Anybody else get hurt?"

"No."

"What was it made him so angry?"

"Didn't hear it," Simone said. He wasn't telling the truth, though I wasn't sure how I knew that.

"But you're sure the dead man was the first to pull a weapon?"

"Yes."

"Would you recognize the men?" the soldier asked. "Were they wearing any family colors? Carrying lights?"

"No colors. Dark clothes, pretty ordinary. They were masked, and it was dark. One of them had a dark lantern. He was careful, and I didn't see any faces. I don't think I could recognize them, unless it was exactly the same group in exactly the same clothes."

"That isn't going to happen, I can tell you. Well, it sounds like there's nothing much for us to do here, if the aggressor is the one who died. We've got lots more of these situations to deal with tonight, so if nobody's going to press any charges, we'll be on our way. Anyone?" He looked again at the crowd that had gathered. Nobody spoke.

"All right, I guess that's it. You people have churchmen here? Good. They can make a report later. We've got our hands full right now. There's gangs of young toughs all over the city, looking for trouble. We'll leave you to it, then." He remounted, and the patrol rode on its way. Still nobody spoke.

Someone had closed Neri's eyes. It must have been Ghisola, for she hadn't moved away or let anyone else touch him.

A young priest came over to us, pale, a nervous tic in his left eye. "We'll have to make a report," he said. "Will you tell us what happened?"

"I'll tell both of you," Simone said, including me in his gesture, "but first we need to arrange to get his body home and find a woman to stay with Ghisola."

The priest, who was even newer to the parish than Father Pietro, looked a little abashed that he hadn't thought of that himself. As if relieved to have a task, he issued orders to his assistants: they were to bring the bier and the pall from the church, and with them some candles, and accompany Neri's body back to our house. Two churchmen would stay all night to conduct the vigil. Tomorrow Father Pietro would tell us the time for the funeral, and we would work out the expenses then. I agreed to all of this, as it seemed to have become my responsibility.

While we waited for the churchmen to bring the bier, Bicci and Tedora left to fetch Ghisola's sister Lapa, and also Anselmo and Rufino, assuming they could manage to get to them while the city's patrols were out everywhere enforcing curfew. The priest drew Simone and me aside to talk.

I began it. "So, Simone, what happened?" I asked him. I was numb, and I craved his story to hold on to. A day like this one belonged to the end of the world.

Simone told us, and for once he took no joy in being the bearer of news. He described waking to a loud banging on his door, and Neri below, demanding wine, though it was plain he'd already had plenty. Simone had come downstairs to talk to him, hoping to convince him to go home quietly. It was working, until a party of noisy young nobles arrived in the square. They had been drinking, and they too demanded that Simone open up and serve them. He refused politely, reminding them of the sabbath.

The five young men, all dressed in good-quality but everyday clothing, were in a raucous mood. They demanded to know whether Simone and Neri supported Oddo's party or the Buondelmonti. Simone told them he was a humble tavernkeeper who didn't side with anyone, but only wanted peace in the city.

"What did Neri tell them?" I asked.

"Well, he pretty much managed to insult everyone," Simone said. I could well imagine. Neri, drunk, was the most creatively offensive man I had ever known. I was going to miss that, I realized with a pang.

Neri had called Buondelmonte an idiot, and Oddo a thug. He told them Mosca was an oily bastard who could trick a lot of men who were too stupid to think for themselves and get them to do something ridiculous.

That did indeed pretty much cover everyone, and I heard an echo of my own comments in Neri's rant. Had those words caused his death?

Out of the corner of my eye I saw Tedora and Lapa running toward us, Lapa far ahead, Tedora struggling to keep up, one hand clutching her belly as she half ran, half waddled toward Ghisola. Lapa was carrying a pair of shoes. Good, I thought absently—Ghisola's feet must be freezing by now, for the night had turned cooler. I was glad to see them, but I turned my attention back to Simone's tale, for there was more.

The young nobles became demanding and arrogant, insisting again that Simone open the tavern and serve them. Simone pleaded that he didn't have the key with him, choosing not to tell them he lived upstairs. Fearing Neri would wade in and begin a fight, Simone tried to calm the situation. He was giving the young men directions to a tavern that might be more available, since it was also an inn and had to feed its lodgers, when a second party arrived.

These men were also dressed in unidentifiable dark clothing, and they hid their faces behind black masks with slashes for their eyes. They were four, one older and three younger. The old man was the one carrying the dark lantern. Simone guessed it might have been a father and three sons, and the father did most of the talking.

Simone thought that the father recognized the men in the first group, because he spoke to them rudely, asking whether the men supported the murderers of the good knight Buondelmonte. The first group must have been of Oddo's party, for they began to quarrel, calling Buondelmonte a base knight whose word was meaningless. They said he was dishonorable, and loudly proclaimed that Buondelmonte had given such offense to the Amidei and the Fifanti that death was the only possible compensation.

The masked older man replied that the proper response for a discarded marriage contract was a monetary fine, not a treacherous, foul murder.

This provoked one of the young men in the first party to claim that the strife began when Buondelmonte stabbed Oddo at Mazzingo's knighting, which he called a brutish action unworthy of a knight.

The masked old man took exception to that, saying that Oddo had first insulted Buondelmonte, whose response was only an honorable answer to provocation, and in any case a wound to the arm was no excuse for a vile murder, especially one in which it took a small army to bring down one valiant knight.

Simone and Neri stood to one side and listened to this exchange. Simone had been relieved at first to have the issue of opening the tavern forgotten, but he didn't want to be witness to a lethal encounter between the two opposing parties.

No one knows what might have happened had the argument continued in this vein, but it chanced that one of the young masked men thought to trace the cause of the fracas back even further. Perhaps he wanted to calm the angry speakers by mentioning a cause that didn't accuse either side. What he claimed as the origin of it all was, as he put it, "some idiot jester who stole a plate of food at a banquet and started everything."

At that, Neri growled, and suddenly his knife was out and he lunged forward at the young speaker. He was drunk and moving slower than usual, and that gave another young man—the brother of the first, if Simone was right—time to pull his own blade and slash at Neri's belly. He connected, the knife went in and raked downward. Blood spurted, Neri fell, and both parties, masked and unmasked, thought it prudent to leave immediately. All the rest, we knew.

I stood there, stunned. Always, it came back to me. Neri had attacked a man for my sake, and died. Both Neri and Buondelmonte died because of my jest.

This was the thought that stayed with me, the only thought I was able to form, as we prepared to carry Neri's body back to the house for the vigil. Bicci hadn't yet returned with Anselmo and Rufino, but they would find us at the house, whenever they managed to get back. The clerics reported that Father Pietro said the bier would not be brought round until morning, and Lapa had finally managed to persuade Ghisola to get up and let us take him, so Simone and I hefted Neri gently onto the old cloak Tomasso used to cover his customers when he shaved them. The church in its infinite wisdom had also decided to wait until tomorrow to send the candles, but our own people had the lanterns, lamps, and candles they had brought with them to the square, with even a dark lantern or two of our own among them. We made a sad, tired little procession as we carried Neri home.

30. VIGIL

Neri's body lay in the house all night. We pulled his pallet out of his alcove and put it in front of the hearth, and Simone and I laid him gently on it. The churchmen arrived and formed a knot around him, peering at him by the smoking light of our own tallow candles.

Tedora and Lapa hovered so closely around Ghisola that I only caught an occasional glimpse of her. I heard her sniffs and sobs, but with all of our neighbors outside demanding to hear what happened, I had no chance to see to her. The nervous young priest, who was in charge, told me to keep everyone out except for the three women, who would prepare Neri's body for the vigil and for burial, so I stepped outside to answer everyone's questions and ask their patience.

Tomasso had gone back home to get his razors. When he returned to shave Neri I admitted him, and he performed this last, sad task, working for once without a word. All others, though, remained outside.

Anselmo came, and Rufino. Both were ashen. It took them over an hour to get to us, dodging through dark streets to avoid the curfew patrols. I saw traces of tears on Rufino's cheeks, and Anselmo was angry and belligerent, determined to go inside and see Neri. I asked him to wait for Ghisola's sake, and for her sake he grudgingly agreed. It was the middle of the night by then, but a crowd was gathering. Someone brought a lamp and set it down next to the door, and others held candles.

Neither of our fellow performers lived in our parish, so they hadn't thought anything of it when they heard the death bells ringing, sounding the traditional three peals for a layman. The cathedral had rung those same three hollow notes for Buondelmonte, and indeed, all over the city this night there were many—too many—reasons for the death knells to sound.

When Bicci left the square to get Rufino and Anselmo, Tedora had gone with him as far as Lapa's house. He told the women to wait for his return, for the streets were particularly dangerous that night, but Lapa wouldn't wait, and the two women rushed to Ghisola as soon as Lapa threw on her clothing. They wouldn't leave her side, though Tedora's pregnancy made her pale and tired and Bicci fretted about her. I was glad they were there, for I was too numb to know how to help Ghisola now.

Simone stood with me, answering everyone's questions about what had happened. His public story—the argument, Neri's drunken threats, his wild lunge with his knife, and the other man's thrust in defense of his companion—mercifully didn't include the details of the argument. No one was surprised by this turn of events, however distressed they were by the outcome. I had to conclude that my involvement in the knights' business in recent weeks had blinded me to the magnitude of what was going on with my best and oldest friend.

All around us people wept and prayed as we waited for the churchmen to finish their task. As new people arrived, they brought news of fighting in other parts of the city. The crowd would never fit in our tiny house, and I knew in the morning still more would come, people who lived too far away to risk encountering the podestà's patrols during the hours of curfew. Neri had many friends, and not only in our neighborhood.

When the priest finally emerged to tell us we could see Neri, the mourners formed an orderly file. They went in a few at a time to pray, to weep, and to speak a word to Ghisola. I stood outside and watched them enter our house and then, soon, come back out again, looking shaken. Most of them wandered off toward their homes to finish out the night, but I knew they would be back in the morning, to do Neri honor and to help us get through his funeral.

When at last most of the crowd had dispersed, I went back inside. Bicci and Anselmo stayed with me, but Rufino's worries for his wife and child on this ugly night pulled him away, even though he wanted to stay as well. Tedora and Lapa wouldn't leave Ghisola, who was still wearing Lapa's shoes. Three churchmen stood around Neri's body, now incongruously clad in a coarse robe of penitential sackcloth. Lighted candles, good wax ones this time, had been placed at his head. The church may not have provided, but our neighbors had. Neri's hands were folded across his chest, his face was neatly shaved, and his clothing lay in a tidy heap, the clerics' pay for their work. I wouldn't say he looked peaceful—only empty. Empty and still.

We joined the vigil, praying quietly along with the churchmen. Bicci eventually nodded off, but still he knelt beside me, and the women wept and prayed in the far corner.

I listened to Bicci's regular breathing. Had Neri seen San Cristoforo this day? Had the saint failed him? Where was my friend's soul now, and how did it fare? No answers came to me.

I may have nodded off myself, because I became aware of dawn's light in the window and the first sounds of the pianto at the same time. I hadn't thought to seek out professional mourners, but it sounded as if the women of the neighborhood were taking care of it themselves, as more and more female voices joined in the eerie wailing and keening.

Ghisola and the other two women were alert and listening. A soft tap at the door, and three neighbor women came in, quietly. They crossed themselves and mumbled a short prayer in Neri's direction before turning to Ghisola with hugs and words of sympathy. One of them came over to me to whisper that a crier of the dead was outside, and did I want to hire him to announce Neri's death? I thanked her and stepped outside.

Several neighbors were already gathered, among them the women who were making the pianto. I knew some of the keening women, but others must have been hired. I hadn't arranged for them, so I assumed someone else had made that contribution. The crier told me he would cry Neri's death for half what he usually charged, because he had two others from nearby parishes to announce at the same time. I handed him his coin, and then he was off to inform the city, neighborhood by neighborhood.

Father Pietro was coming toward us. I went to meet him, identifying myself to him under the polite guise of "reminding" him, and thanked him for coming. He mumbled a couple of godly platitudes, to which I said "amen," and then we got down to business. By the time we had negotiated use of the church's large funeral candles, the purchase of smaller candles, use of the pall and bier, and arranged for masses for Neri's soul at intervals of a day, a week, and a month from his death, I was considerably poorer. But at least I knew the extent of the damage, and the use of the church's equipment kept my expenses contained. It didn't occur to either of us that Neri's funeral expenses might not be my responsibility.

I named for Father Pietro the men who had volunteered to serve as pallbearers, including myself, and pointed out to him the only two he didn't know, Anselmo and Rufino. He squinted toward the crowd and nodded vaguely. I fetched the coins from my alcove and paid him what we had agreed, hinting that I might pay for additional masses later. Under the circumstances, I thought Neri might be needing them. We agreed on a schedule for the different stages of the funeral. He said we could begin the procession to the church as soon as he arrived, shortly after we heard the bells for Terce. I asked if he wanted to come and pray over Neri. He was about to demur, leaving the task to his underlings, but then he thought to ask me, "Is there a widow?"

Ah. I had forgotten he didn't know. He had surely seen Neri and Ghisola together many times. If he thought her the widow, she would have the place of honor in the procession that I believed was rightfully hers. If he knew they were not married, she wouldn't even be permitted a place at the graveside.

"Yes," I said. "She's in the house. Would you speak with her?"

"It is my duty," he said, and we walked back to the house together. The group clustered outside parted for us, and the pianto grew quieter, though it didn't cease entirely. The church discouraged mourning in the old ways, and the priest glanced at the wailing women with irritation, but he said nothing and followed me inside.

I strode over to the corner where Ghisola sat with the other women, while Father Pietro bowed his head and spoke a prayer over Neri. "Father Pietro wanted to speak with Neri's widow," I told her, speaking distinctly and just loud enough for all present to hear.

Everyone in that room other than the priests knew the situation, but I was sure no one would contradict me. All the eyes that met mine showed an understanding of what I was doing and why. Ghisola herself simply mouthed "Thank you," got up, and walked over to the priest to await his attention.

With Father Pietro's prayer finished and his underlings praying more fervently than ever under his eye, he turned to Ghisola and said the appropriate things, kindly enough. She expressed her humble gratitude in a shaky voice, and he squeezed her hand sympathetically, then turned to go.

He stopped at the threshold, as if something had just occurred to him, and turned around. "You do know that the funeral must be outside?" he asked me.

I was confused. Outside? Was he trying to tell me Neri was excommunicate? Ghisola made a little sound of protest.

Father Pietro hastily added, "Don't be afraid. He'll have all the holy sacraments and nothing will be omitted, for we have the care of his immortal soul as our charge. Only, he is dead by violence, and we may not profane the church with blood. All else will be as usual, I assure you." He smiled reassuringly, adding, "No matter. The same holds true for great and small. It will be thus for the murdered knight Buondelmonte, for he, too, died by violence. May God grant us a fair day for their funerals." This, apparently, was supposed to console us, and Father Pietro was off.

I did remember this restriction now, though I thought it a stupid rule, since the victims of violence generally didn't choose the method of their deaths. But as long as nothing interfered with Neri's interment in holy ground, I supposed it didn't matter. A glance at Ghisola confirmed that it didn't matter to her, either; she shrugged, and went back to gazing at Neri while tears ran slowly down her cheeks.

The priest's words had reminded me of that other death. Less than a day ago Buondelmonte's fate had been the most important event in the world, and I wouldn't have believed I could have forgotten it so completely in the face of my own loss and grief. I wondered if the two slain men's souls were together, somewhere. Yet Neri had attacked a man and died with a knife in his hand, and Buondelmonte was only riding along in the sunshine. Even so, it was Buondelmonte's actions that had set so much evil in motion.

It didn't feel right to think of Buondelmonte while in Neri's still presence, so I stepped outside. The house and the street outside were full of an ever-shifting crowd of people, and once again they brought news of events elsewhere in the city. In fact, we were hearing a steady stream of alarming reports from those who came to pay their respects: towers and palaces barricaded, skirmishes in the streets, vendettas begetting more vendettas. Boys throwing stones. Fires, the scourge of crowded cities crammed with wooden buildings, set deliberately, sometimes randomly. Only the lack of wind, together with many a weary bucket brigade, kept them from spreading and saved the city from disaster.

The podestà's men patrolled the streets even now, as the day advanced, but they were too few to prevent every eruption. The city government was not yet strong enough to stand up to the great families. They were hard pressed even to police individual incidents, and we would see few if any repercussions for the knightly class, though the rest of us could not brawl with such impunity.

I thought of the soldiers I had joked with, eaten with, bunked with at the Fifanti palace, and those at the Amidei, and wondered how they fared. What was Mosca doing, and Oddo? We heard that Schiatta was using the city's restlessness as an excuse to arm his people, and his palace enclave was taking on the air of a military encampment. For anyone who had been alive during the Uberti's previous takeover attempt, which had occurred not long before my birth, this would be a cause for great alarm.

My thoughts strayed to the women. I couldn't forget Fiammetta's face as she stared up at me. Her name suited her then, for she had been a slender, white-hot flame in the midst of all the confusion. And Gualdrada, wailing as she draped herself protectively over Isabella, and that poor, fair, terrified young widow herself, recoiling in horror from her husband's blood.

And what of monna Ermellina, and monna Lauretta? What had the old woman, monna Ortolana, made of it all? Did Mosca's sea nymph have any idea of the part she had played? What did Lambertuccio and

Amadio tell little Lucia?

And Selvaggia. But before I could wrap my mind around the idea of that woman, I saw another one coming down the street, one I had hoped never to see again. Coming toward us, wearing a widow's dark brown and accompanied by her beetle-browed father, was Duccia.

31. WIDOW

Duccia and her slow-witted father were the last two people I wanted to see just now. Without thinking, I moved swiftly forward to intercept them. They must not confront Ghisola. Not now, not like this.

They were hurrying toward the house, but she stopped short when she saw me, and her father halted just behind her.

"You!"

"Duccia. What are you doing here?" I demanded. Not the proper way to greet a new widow, I suppose, but no love was left between this woman and Neri, only bitterness and shrieking recriminations. I didn't want her to go near his body, and I didn't want her to see Ghisola at all.

"I'm his widow," she said defiantly. I choked on the cloud of cheap perfume that enveloped her. "I'm entitled to be here, and I'm entitled to whatever he left. He hasn't got any other family for it to go to, as you very well know."

"He left everything to the church," I said. A mistake, I realized right away—she'd never believe that.

She didn't. She practically snorted at me, and her father, taking his cue from her, laughed in his coarse, menacing way, displaying rotting gums and a few broken teeth.

All right then, try something different.

"He doesn't have anything left. He drank it all, near the end." That was probably closer to the truth, though I had no real idea.

"He left everything to his whore, didn't he?" she said. At that, I looked down at her, at that pretty face distorted into an ugly expression, at her painted cheeks and pointed chin, and it was all I could do not to strike her.

"You're the whore, Duccia," I said, softly because this wasn't the time to give full vent to what I was feeling. "Remember why he left."

"He owes me my dowry," she snapped. "He gave me part of it, but he didn't have it all. He'd invested the rest of it in some stupid scheme, and I want it back. Now."

"He doesn't have any money," I said, stalling. She probably couldn't make a legal case for inheriting anything he had left, given the circumstances of their separation. But her dowry was hers, no doubt about it. The court could have taken it from her at the time if Neri had brought charges against her for infidelity, but he was not a man to do such a thing to a woman he once cared about. So we needed to find that much money to buy her off, somehow, else she could make a world of trouble for Ghisola.

"You watch what you say to my daughter," growled Duccia's father, who had finally managed to catch up with the conversation. Both of us ignored him, and she plunged on.

"He owes me, and I'm his widow, and I'm going to walk in that funeral procession and his whore isn't. And there's nothing you can do to stop me." She started to walk past me, but she found herself nose-to-nose with Anselmo, who had seen what was happening and appeared at my side with a musician's timing.

Anselmo didn't like Duccia any better than I did. His wiry little body was taut and his hands clenched into fists as he and Duccia feinted, first one way and then the other. She couldn't get past him. Her father, meanwhile, was still trying to figure out what was going on, a puzzled frown on his face and his mouth half open.

"Duccia, if you go away, I swear I'll sell whatever Neri has left and give you the rest of your dowry," I said, putting my hand on her shoulder.

She jerked away. "Don't touch me!" she said, her voice harsh. The dung-colored gown, probably borrowed, strained across her breasts, but even so it was modest by Duccia's usual standards.

"I'm going to join that funeral, and I'm going to tell the priest I want my dowry, and I'm going to tell him about Neri's whore, and you can't stop me." Anselmo and I exchanged a glance. We needed to find a way to end this, here and now.

"Duccia," I said, thinking fast, "if you do that, it will take you weeks, maybe even months to get anything, and that's if Neri has any money, which he probably doesn't. But I'll make you a deal: if you agree to go away and leave us alone, I'll give you the rest of your dowry in cash, right now."

She glared at me. "You don't have that kind of money."

"I do. Or would you rather take it to court? I'll gladly be a witness to why you and Neri parted. Is that what you want everyone to hear? Or do you just want to take the money and go?"

She barely hesitated. "Show me the money," she said. Good; I was right that greed was her reason for being here. If money would make her leave Ghisola alone, I'd give her money.

"It's in the house. I'll go get it."

"Oh, no, you don't," she said. "If you go back there, I'm coming with you." Her father, still standing behind her, nodded his head emphatically.

"Then Anselmo will go fetch it," I said. "And I'll stay here. But you only get the money if you swear to leave us alone from now on."

She exchanged a sly look with her father, then turned back to me. "All I want is what I'm due," she said, suddenly prim and self-righteous. And completely unconvincing.

"And you won't make any trouble for Ghisola?" I persisted.

"Pay me my dowry and enough more to make it worth my coming here, and I'll leave his frowsy blonde whore alone."

No, she wouldn't. I knew Duccia; if we didn't get a binding agreement she'd be back, in a day or a week or a month, demanding more, making threats. We had to settle this now. And we didn't have much time, because soon the bells would sound Terce, and Anselmo and I would have to join the other pallbearers for Neri's funeral.

"Shall I go get your money?" Anselmo asked me. I shook my head, thinking hard. We needed something final, something legal, and we needed it now, before those bells rang. I didn't have a notary on call, but—

I had it. "Anselmo," I said, "bring me the purse. It's in the bag with my juggling balls. And fetch ser Bicci." I met his eyes, willing him to catch on.

"Ser Bicci?" he said blankly. Then he got it. Thank the saints for clever friends. "Ah, of course—ser Bicci, to notarize the agreement. I'll be right back." And he was off.

An uncomfortable silence settled over the three of us as we waited. Finally Duccia said, "I heard he died in a fight." I said nothing.

"He was my husband," she said, her voice rising. "I have a right to know." As she spoke, I heard distant bells chime Terce.

"Yes, he died in a fight," I said shortly.

Anselmo and Bicci were coming toward us. That meant three of the six pallbearers were involved in this negotiation, so no danger of the procession starting without us, but if we dallied too long, Father Pietro would arrive and send a churchman to see what the delay was. That would give Duccia an opportunity I didn't want her to have.

Anselmo had brought me the purse containing my remaining coins. He raised one eyebrow and gave the blue and white silk an appraising look as he handed it over, but he said nothing.

Bicci, who was a man of many talents but no notary, had managed to find a wax writing tablet and stylus. He inclined his head gravely to all of us and stood poised, stylus ready.

"Our friend, ser Bicci," I said by way of introduction. "He will ensure the legality and finality of what we decide." Duccia's eyes were on the purse. Its colors meant nothing to her, only its contents. It was much lightened in recent days, but it still held enough jingling coins to make her mean little eyes glitter.

I named a sum, less than the amount I believed Neri had owed for her dowry, but not by much. She doubled it, naming a figure that was more than I had. I didn't tell her that. We went back and forth in rapid-fire haggling until we reached a number we could agree on. It wiped out pretty much everything I had left except for small change, but she didn't have to know that. If there had been time, I would have tried to argue the figure lower, but Father Pietro had arrived, and the people in front of the house were watching us, waiting to begin the funeral. I had no time to spare. We agreed on the sum, Bicci scratched solemnly on his tablet, and then I started adding a few conditions of my own.

"You will consider yourself paid in full. You acknowledge that Neri owes you nothing. You swear that you will never come to his house nor bother anyone living there. You acknowledge that you and Neri separated due to your mutual agreement. You admit that Neri lived a virtuous life, and you will not at any time in the future say otherwise, because if you do, you will prove that you have lied to a notary, and you will be subject to the full penalties of the law." Bicci kept scratching, and I tried to look stern.

Our "notary" nodded soberly.

"I would advise you not to take that chance, young woman," he said to her. "The courts take such things very seriously indeed." Anselmo's mouth twitched, but he managed not to laugh.

If Duccia felt intimidated, it wasn't in her nature to admit it. "Just give me the money," she said, thrusting her chin forward and holding out her hand. I counted out the coins and placed them, one by one, in her palm, trying not to touch her skin. When I finished, she closed her hand tightly over the coins and she and her father exchanged a triumphant grin.

"Ser Bicci will draw up the document and place it on file. You have sworn to it, and there will be no further negotiations," I told her. This was risky: could she be ignorant enough not to realize that any final document required her mark or signature? "Anselmo serves as witness."

"All right, I'm going," she said. "And you and the blonde whore can rot in hell, for all I care. I suppose she'll be spreading her legs for you next, if she isn't already."

They hurried away, Duccia clutching her coins. Anselmo raised his right hand in the fig as he watched them go. It was an obscene gesture no matter who did it, but Anselmo managed to make it more obscene than anyone else I knew, even Neri. The trick was all in that vicious little twist of the wrist. I moved in front of him, to hide him from the mourners back at the house, for I saw no point in outraging Father Pietro now.

Duccia's little excursion had made her a fine profit, I thought bitterly, but at least she was gone, and I didn't think she'd be back. Between the funeral and Duccia's dowry, I was down to almost nothing.

"Neri would have loved that," Anselmo said a little wistfully, as we watched them go. It was true; our neighbor's sudden promotion to notary would have given Neri boundless amusement.

"Thanks, Bicci," I said.

"That's ser Bicci to you," he said haughtily, and Anselmo and I grinned in spite of ourselves.

"I didn't know you could write," I said.

"I can't." He showed us a crude sketch of Duccia, pointed chin, fierce little smile, and all. The likeness was not flattering.

We had no more time to enjoy the success of our little game or rue the loss of my wealth, because the hour of Neri's funeral was upon us. Four churchmen emerged from our house bearing the bier with Neri's body atop it. Ghisola, Lapa and Tedora followed them out.

Father Pietro waited for us impatiently. He made sure to remind me, under his breath and out of Ghisola's hearing, that if he had chosen to call Neri's fatal fight a duel, he could have declared my friend in a state of mortal sin and withheld not only all burial rites, but even a grave in consecrated soil. I was contrite. I explained that I had been dealing with a potential troublemaker to ensure that Neri's funeral rites would not be interrupted, and that mollified him.

Anselmo, Bicci, Rufino, Tomasso, Simone, and I took our places around Neri's bier. His body had been covered with the church's black pall, but his face remained uncovered. This was the moment for the church's bell to sound its metallic three-note call once more. At the priest's signal, we lifted our burden to our shoulders and slowly, clumsily began the grim walk through our neighborhood, to give those few friends who hadn't joined the procession their chance to say goodbye.

Perhaps it was the sleepless night that preceded the funeral, but I have few memories of that procession. I know that the churchmen walked in front with Father Pietro bearing the cross. The men from the neighborhood preceded the bier, and the women followed it, Ghisola immediately behind and supported by Tedora and Lapa. Many of the men carried lighted candles, including the three enormous ones the church

238

had lent us. The clergymen chanted, but the women continued with their *pianto*, their high voices wavering in a mournful complaint that echoed through the streets and bounced off buildings, coming back to us and blending anew with the women's voices.

I knew that elsewhere in the city Buondelmonte's funeral was proceeding in the same way, but on a much more magnificent scale. The knight would have a forest of candles, a *pianto* that reached to heaven itself, and hundreds of people attending him, including all of the Buondelmonti's allies making their political statement. The exquisite Isabella would be dressed in a simple dark gown, supported by Fiammetta and Gualdrada as she laid her husband to rest.

People crossed themselves and said a prayer as we passed by. I put one foot in front of the other and walked, listening to the chanting, the *pianto*, and most of all to Ghisola's soft weeping behind us.

We approached the church. The clergymen were chanting "Subvenite" as we neared the building, and I saw the two trestles set up in front of the door. I had forgotten we wouldn't be allowed to bring him inside the church. Carefully, my fellow pallbearers and I set the bier down on the trestles, adjusting it a little to make it secure. Neri's feet were pointing toward the church door; thus we would have carried him in, had the priests allowed it. One of the priests stepped forward and drew the pall up over Neri's face, and Ghisola sobbed. Absurdly, I seemed to hear his voice again, telling me to take care of her. I looked down on his still form and touched my temple in acknowledgement.

The service that followed felt interminable, with droning chants and prayers, antiphons and parts of the hours. People edged closer to the bier to touch Neri one last time, to look, to pray. Ghisola stayed back, crying quietly. Father Pietro blessed Neri's body. I caught a whiff of incense as he walked around the bier, moving the opposite of sunwise, but holding the funeral outdoors meant that the powerful scent dissipated in seconds.

When the churchmen began to chant "Libera," it was our cue to pick up the bier again. The women also resumed their *pianto*, but more quietly than before. We had only a short walk to the cemetery behind the church, and the rest of the proceedings took little time compared to what had gone before.

Neri's grave was dug and waiting. With little fanfare we laid him in it, feet to the east. This was the signal for all but close family to leave, and so people circled the grave while the churchmen prayed, saying their last goodbyes, and then filed out of the churchyard.

On her way out of the churchyard, Tedora whispered to me, "I'll take care of the meal." Only then did I remember that we were supposed to provide a funeral meal for the mourners and I had done nothing about it. Food vendors would come to the house, though, tipped off by the criers of the dead, and we could purchase a meal from them. I thanked her and handed her my last remaining coins, for Bicci and Tedora could never afford to make us a gift of a funeral meal for so many. Tedora's ankles were swollen and she needed to get off her feet, but I knew she wouldn't let herself rest until she had the meal set up and ready.

The women picked up the pianto once again, wailing louder as they moved farther away from us, as if to give us their support in our mourning for as long as possible. At this funeral no one had rent their clothes or scratched their faces or torn their hair, though there had been a little ritual breast-beating among the few hired mourners. All of the anguish had been contained in those mournful voices, as if we had known violence enough already. Would Isabella have torn her magnificent hair, I wondered, and did Gualdrada rend her exquisite clothing? I felt a smoldering undercurrent of anger as I thought about it. The knights' stupid feud had taken something from me that could never be replaced, something worth more to me than the lot of them all together.

Ghisola and Lapa remained at the graveside, as did Anselmo and Rufino and I. We were close enough to family and the priests saw I was in no mood to argue about it, so they did not challenge us. Father Pietro sprinkled Neri's body with holy water, and followed with the cinders from his thurible. He intoned the final prayers, one of his assistants deftly retrieved the church's pall from Neri's body with a pole, and the gravediggers began to fill in the grave. The five of us stayed long enough to pray a last prayer, but we were all exhausted, and we still had that funeral dinner to see to.

Our smaller procession back to the house consisted of Anselmo in front, carrying one of the church's huge candles, lighted, and then Ghisola with me on one side and Lapa on the other, and Rufino bringing up the rear. None of us spoke, or sang, or prayed. We simply walked.

My memories of that meal are even more blurred than those of the funeral. The vendors had provided Tedora with bread and wine and other necessary things, nothing elaborate, but still more than adequate, for no one was hungry. The full weight of what had happened, both to us and to the rest of the city, was just beginning to press down on all of us, and it was enough to destroy appetite.

People began to drift away as the afternoon wore on. I was numb with exhaustion. It would have been a relief when the last person finally left, except that the last person was Ghisola. She went home with Lapa, and I was left in our little house with the remains of the funeral dinner. For almost the first time I could remember, I was completely alone.

32. GHISOLA

The weather turned sharply colder that night, one of those wintry spells that sometimes interrupt a balmy spring. I let the fire go out. The cold I was feeling came from inside, and not even a roaring fire on the hearth could have touched it.

For the next three days I remained in the freezing house. I ate, when I remembered, whatever I found that needed no cooking, and when I ran out of those things, I ate nothing. I drank until the wine ran out. I alternated between keeping to my bed while I yearned for sleep, and pacing the length of the room. I ignored knocks at the door, and after the first day no more came. I exercised a constant vigilance, chasing away memories as they tried to surface, but all of my efforts were wasted, for the memories would come, whether I would have them or no.

Once in a fit of helpless rage I swept my arm across the table, knocking everything off onto the floor. The sensation was oddly satisfying, so I continued by pulling down everything that was hanging on the wall—pots, spoons, towels, a net full of onions, and half a cheese in a sack. Let the mice have it all; I didn't care. I knocked over the stools and the small table and kicked the reed mats into a corner. At least now the house was a closer match for the way I was feeling.

Late afternoon on the fourth day I heard the tap on the door. At first I ignored it, then, when the tapping continued, I yelled, "Go away!"

Silence followed, and I thought whoever it was had obeyed me, but then I heard the rasp of the key in the lock. That could only be Ghisola. Even with the key she couldn't get in until I unbarred the door, but I couldn't keep Ghisola out, so when she rattled the door and called to me, I reluctantly got up to lift the bar and let her in.

I wasn't ready to see her, though, so I turned my back on her and went to the bench and sat down, staring into the cold hearth. I heard her make a little sound of impatience or surprise as she saw the wreckage of her tidy house, but she said nothing. She moved quietly around, righting the stools, spreading the mats, picking up the scattered items on the floor. I didn't look at her. I knew I was failing Neri, and it tore at me—how could I keep my promise and care for her when I couldn't even face her?

After she had brought some small measure of order back to the room, I heard her walk to the door. She said, "I'm going to get fire. Don't bar the door. I'll be right back." The door closed behind her.

I sat, feeling nothing. This was Ghisola's house, too, and I had no right to keep her out, but I had no wish to be around another person. Especially the one person who made it impossible to avoid thinking of Neri. I thought about leaving, but I didn't have anywhere I wanted to go, so instead I went to my sleeping alcove and stretched out on my pallet. The curtain was open, and I noticed she had taken my brimming chamberpot and piss bottle with her. I felt ashamed. It wasn't the first time she had performed that service for me, but now it didn't seem right for her to be doing it.

I think that was why, when I heard her come back, I got up and came back out into the main room. I steeled myself to speak to her, but she ignored me as she returned the emptied and rinsed vessels to my sleeping area and brought the firepot over to the hearth. She was also carrying a sack, which she placed on the table. She took kindling from the basket, arranged it in the middle of the stone slab and pulled a smoldering rag out of the pot, touching it to the wood chips and straw until they caught light. She busied herself tending the new fire until it was burning well, and then went over to the bag of onions she had replaced on its hook and took out four of the largest ones. By then she was able to rake some coals over to the side and let them die down without interfering with the rest of the fire. Once they had dulled to embers, she tossed the onions onto them to bake, heaping more glowing ash on top.

I stared into the fire as it crackled cheerfully. Against my will, a tendril of warmth worked its way up my spine, though my hands remained icy. Ghisola sat back on the bench with a soft sigh. She had left space, enough for another person, between us.

Both of us watched the flames as the little room started to lose its chill. We sat like that, not looking at each other, for a long time. The onions began to blacken.

Finally she broke the silence. "It wasn't your fault."

I didn't reply.

"It was his demons, and the wine. Did you know that wasn't his first fight? Or even his first that week?"

I hadn't known. How could I, imprisoned first at the Fifanti palace and then at the Amidei? Performing for them, singing, wishing I had Neri's fine strong voice. That voice I would never hear again. Still I stared into the fire, saying nothing.

"He fought a man because he thought I had been insulted. He fought another one who wouldn't shut up about the vendetta. He almost got himself killed fighting a third man and four of his friends, until Simone stepped in. We never did figure out what that one was about."

I was confused. This wasn't the Neri I knew. But then, neither was the Neri who brought my things to the Amidei palace and refused to deliver my message. Despite myself I asked, "When did this start?" My voice cracked; I hadn't used it in days.

When she answered, Ghisola's voice was muffled, and I knew she was struggling against tears. Still I couldn't look at her, and I wondered what was wrong with me. She loved him too—her pain had to be as bad as mine.

"It started soon after the drinking got worse. He was worried about all the things you were involved in, and about Duccia, and money, but mostly I think he was worried about me. He felt guilty, and he was afraid he wouldn't be able to protect me. So if it's anybody's fault, it's mine." This last part came out in a rush as she lost her struggle and began to weep, in great, shuddering sobs. Awkwardly, I scooted closer to her and put an arm around her shaking shoulders.

"It wasn't your fault either, Ghisola. Neri made his own choices," I heard myself say, and then realized I was beginning to believe it. "But I don't know how I could not have known about the fights, at least before the Fifanti took me into custody. I understand how I managed not to know about the last week, but I don't know how I missed any that happened before that."

She sniffed and wiped her nose with her sleeve. "He didn't want you to know," she said, swallowing. "He said you'd call him an idiot for looking for trouble." I almost smiled at that. He was right, I probably would have.

"So he told me not to tell you," she said. "I did start to tell you a couple of times, but I'd promised, so I couldn't." I should have realized she was keeping something back. How could I have become so absorbed in the lives of the people with surnames that I missed all the signs?

She got up and prodded the smoldering onions out of the coals with the poker. With a towel, she picked them up and put them on a wooden platter. She placed the platter on the bench between us and then fetched a little pitcher of vinegar and a jar of salt, and she added a loaf of fresh bread from the sack she had brought, and a knife to cut it.

"Eat," she said gently. "You need food in your stomach. It's hard enough to go on, even if you take care of yourself, but it's impossible if you don't."

I shook my head, trying to ignore the smell of the hot onions and the saliva gathering in my mouth. "Don't want to go on," I mumbled. She made a little sound of disgust.

"Well, you have to," she said. "You're still alive. Buondelmonte's dead, and Neri's dead, and who knows how many others by now, but you and I are alive, so we have to keep going. Sometimes I think the ones who are dead have it easier, because they don't have to figure out how to keep going any more. But we do, so you've got to take care of yourself better than this." She gestured at the shambles I had made of the room, still only partly put to rights. "This isn't good enough. You've made this place a pigpen."

"I can't. He's dead, it was my fault, and I feel like I'm being disloyal to him if I take care of myself when I'm the one who caused his death."

Ghisola hissed. The unexpected sound made me jump. In one rapid motion, she grabbed one of the steaming onions and flung it, hard, against the wall. It clung there, a thick drizzle of hot onion pulp oozing down the wall. The smell was overpowering.

"Men are such fools!" she said, wiping her hand on her skirt. "You say it's your fault, Father Pietro whines that it's God's will, but the truth is, Neri did it to himself. The man who killed him was only defending his brother, and it was Neri and his demons who killed Neri, and nobody else." She expelled a long breath, and slumped on the bench, staring again into the fire.

As usual, I said the first thing that came into my mind. "You know, Ghisi, if you think the house is a pigpen, you have to admit the onion didn't help."

She stared at me in disbelief, then turned her eyes to the scorched onion plastered to the wall. It was still dripping. The corner of her mouth twitched a little, and then she was laughing, helplessly clutching her belly, laughing and crying all at once, with great gulps of air and noisy sobs, and I was holding her, tears running down my own cheeks. We sat that way until her sobs and laughter dwindled to sniffs and hiccups, and finally we moved apart, she to wipe her tears away and me to sit back and look at her.

She was thinner, even in those few days. For all her insistence that I eat, I didn't think she had been doing much of that herself. She was clean and neat, but her face was drawn. Her eyes were reservoirs of pain, even after the release of tears and laughter. I put my hand on hers.

"Where is his soul, do you think?" I hadn't known I was going to say that.

She hiccuped again, then forced herself to swallow several times in a row, trying to make the little convulsions stop. Finally they did.

"His soul?" I prodded.

245

"With God." No hesitation.

"He didn't make confession. He died with a knife in his hand. Do you think those things don't matter?" My voice was rough, shaky. I needed her certainty, for I had none of my own.

"He didn't choose his demons. If he had lived, maybe he could have freed himself from them. God won't condemn him for what he couldn't help." She sounded so sure of this that I felt a weight lift from my heart, if only a little.

"Ghisi," I said, "how do you manage to go on?"

"You remember when I lost the baby?" I did. Only a couple of months after she had moved in, she miscarried, a tiny little thing barely formed, washed out in a lake of blood. It had not quickened. Neri had been beside himself with fear for her.

"There was another child before that," she said, her voice flat. "I was married, before, did you know?"

"No. Are you widowed, then?" Ouch. With Neri four days dead, that wasn't a good thing to say.

She nodded. "Lost my little boy, three years old, and his father right after, of a fever. My little Taddeo was my treasure. I thought the world ended when we buried him. For a while, I think it did. I don't remember much from that time. By the time I started to pay attention to the world again, my husband was gone, and I had to find some way to go on, by myself."

I hadn't known. She had never spoken of all this before. "It must have been hard, going on without your husband."

"He wasn't the one I missed. He wasn't an evil man, but he wasn't a good husband, either. I wished him no ill, but it made no difference to me if he lived or died. It only mattered that Taddeo was gone. But my point is that even then I went on, if only because I had no choice. I was alone, I had to make a living, and I had no idea what was to come. But I kept going, one day after another, and then there was Neri, and finally the world started to look like a place where I might want to stay for a while, after all." She looked up at me, her expression bleak.

"And now he's gone," I said, taking her hand.

"And now he's gone," she echoed softly.

We sat together then, both of us miserable and not saying much, but we found comfort in just being together, the two of us who had loved Neri best. I still didn't see exactly how I was going to manage to go on, but when I thought about all that Ghisola had been through, it seemed to me that if she could find a way, then so could I.

Afternoon had faded to evening, and the fire burned down to embers. I wondered if Ghisola intended to return to Lapa's house, but I didn't want to ask. Although I had spent the previous three days trying to shut out the world, I found I wanted her to stay. We ate the remaining onions and the bread and agreed that we wished we had wine to go with them, but neither of us wanted to go to the tavern, and I had no coin left in any case.

We talked then of practicalities. Ghisola said her sister didn't have enough room to accommodate her for long, and I made it clear she was welcome to stay here at the house, but I also had to tell her I had no money left, and so was unsure how long I would be able to keep renting the house. She had never known how much money I had, so I didn't have to tell her that Duccia had been around, or what I had done to get rid of her. Ghisola simply assumed I had spent my last coins on the candles and masses for Neri, and I let her think so. She was quick to assure me she would contribute everything she made from her wool carding, and that we would get by somehow. Both of us knew it would take me a while to start working again, without Neri's music and after all that had happened. With the city threatening to explode into a full-blown civil war, jester jobs could be scarce, and anyone who believed I had begun the conflict was not likely to want to employ me.

After a while we were even able to talk of selling Neri's things, to help us manage. She told me Anselmo wanted to buy Neri's organetto. He couldn't afford it all at once, but he offered to pay half our rent when it came due, and then make another payment or two later. It would probably get us through until midsummer or thereabouts, we figured, and maybe by then we would have a steady income again. Also, I was glad to think of Neri's beloved instrument going to a friend instead of a stranger. It was hard enough to talk of selling his clothing and other personal things, though we saw little choice.

Finally it was fully night. Both of us were exhausted, but we made no move to go to our respective sleeping alcoves. We were both staring moodily into what remained of the fire when we heard a little skittering sound and saw a mouse zigzag across the floor in front of us. It was lamed, moving erratically. I wondered if it had escaped from a cat somewhere. It stopped to nibble on a crumb of bread, unaware of being watched. Without thinking, I raised my foot to crush it, but Ghisola touched my arm and shook her head "no," so I set my foot down gently instead, which was enough to startle the mouse. It lurched away in a panic and disappeared into a crack in the wall. Ghisola was right; we needed no more deaths, however insignificant.

I drowsed, wondering why we were still awake, and then finally I realized what was wrong. "Ghisola, if you don't want to sleep in Neri's—in that bed, you can have mine. I don't mind sleeping out here," I told her.

She looked relieved, and grateful. "You are kind," she said. "I want to be here, at the house, but right now I just can't sleep in his bed." I understood. I wouldn't have been able to go into his alcove at all, at least not yet.

"Go on in, then. I'll roll up in my cloak and sleep on the bench."

She smiled wanly, got up from the bench, and went into my sleeping space, pulling the curtain closed behind her. Then she opened it again.

"I need a candle," she said. "I don't know where anything is in there." So we found one, and a holder, and lit it for her from the embers. She vanished into my bed alcove again, candle in hand, and as she pulled the curtain shut, I heard her mutter, "Ugh."

It made me smile, for the first time in days. "Ghisi," I called to her, "just put up with it for tonight. Tomorrow, when it's light, we'll get things cleaned up and sorted out."

"All right. Good night," she said from behind the curtain.

I arranged myself on the bench. I thought I might at last be able to sleep, though I was aware of Ghisola crying softly in my bed. Still, when it was light, we would begin together to put things right, or as right as we could. And we would go on, because that's what people do.

33. WEDDING

Anselmo has learned to play many a lively tune on Neri's organetto, and he was playing one of his favorites as the young people danced and laughed together in the Donati hall. I accompanied him on a small hand drum. We played, watching contentedly as black-haired Margherita and her new husband stamped and twirled in the middle of the floor. Her mother Bianca sat with us, smiling at her daughter and beating time with her slender hand. All three of us were moving a little more slowly than we had fifteen years ago, when Margherita was a baby and the world was in an uproar. We were more likely now to sit on the sidelines than to join in the dancing, but we still took our share of pleasure in the music, the festive clothes, and the pulse of the dance.

Ghisola sat across the hall with Gualdrada. She wore the exquisite dark blue gamurra Gualdrada had worn years ago, that day she married her daughter to Buondelmonte, for the older woman was much too thin for it now. I thought Ghisi looked quite charming, partly because she took such obvious delight in wearing the fine garment.

Gualdrada was in her usual window seat, and in her lap nestled the boldest of this year's crop of gray kittens, the only one brave enough to make its way downstairs when so many people were about. Ghisola gently coaxed Gualdrada to watch the dancing, but the widow's attention frequently wandered, and she drifted back into gazing out the window until Ghisola managed to call her back to the present.

Manno and messer Cione stood talking with the family of Margherita's young husband Arrigo. All of them smiled on the lively young people, the giddy couple and their friends. Arrigo beamed at his bride as if he could scarcely believe his luck, and she smiled back at him with such an engaging combination of shyness and merriment that it was impossible not to join in their celebration.

The dancers signaled us to stop, for they were ready for a rest. They moved toward the food table to refresh themselves, and a young jester did a startling handspring into the space they had just vacated. Everyone turned to watch. The lad performed a rapid-fire series of somersaults and finally sprang to his feet and launched into a flamboyant cartwheel.

He's landed over too far to the left, I thought, watching him critically. We'll have to work on that.

But his youthful audience found no flaw, and they applauded him enthusiastically. When a young man tossed him a juggling ball, he caught it, and the next, and the third, and set them spinning. Not bad, not bad at all, I thought. The boy is a natural. Well trained, too, if I do say so myself. He was wearing my yellow-and-green jester's cap, and it suited his fresh young face and bright blue eyes.

One of the dancers watching him was a yellow-haired girl, not quite grown to womanhood, and her pretty face dimpled whenever she smiled. She was smiling now, beaming at the lad, and it seemed to me that he put forth extra effort whenever her eyes were on him. I couldn't help grinning at the two of them, who doubtless had no idea how obvious they were.

So much has changed in the last fifteen years. These young people have inherited a city more dangerous and more divided than the city their elders grew up in. The divisions are entrenched now, and we cannot return to the days when all Florentines shared their city in peace, if such days ever really existed.

But at least the city they inherited is not, quite, the nightmare we all expected it to be, in those dark days after Buondelmonte's murder. Broken, yes, but not shattered. Much innocence has been lost, but these boys and girls have a chance at a decent life, and in those early days I would not have believed that possible. It looked much worse, that spring.

Despite our fears, the violence stopped just short of full civil war. The podestà and his men worked tirelessly to bring the situation under control, cleverly playing one side against the other to maintain a precarious balance, until at last they achieved a measure of success. And yet even then there was no peace. The great families carried on their feuds, street to street and tower to tower. Life has become harder and more dangerous for all of us, but from time to time there are periods, often brief but sometimes lasting weeks or even months, when things are fairly calm, at least until the next flareup of hostilities. Margherita's wedding had been blessed by such a lull.

The city government grew in power, as much because people wanted the lawlessness brought under control as because it had earned that power, and in time Florence flexed her muscles enough to exercise authority over the families. Of course the government was formed by members of those same families, so the authority has never been absolute. No great house in Florence was spared loss, whether of life or property, and some lost everything. The most violent offenders were exiled, some briefly, some forever. It wasn't possible to outlaw the tradition of vendetta, but over time men have become more constrained to follow its rules.

Always there are bitter contests and too many people take sides, but these days we little people mostly manage to keep our heads down and stay out of the worst of it. Life is harder for the people who live in their palaces and fight from their towers—the people with surnames.

Those who followed the Buondelmonti and the Donati came to be known as the Guelf party, and those who followed the Uberti, Lamberti, Amidei, and the Fifanti were called Ghibellines. Both of those outlandish, clumsy names are borrowed from beyond the Alps. They imply that the Guelf faction favors the pope and the Ghibellines the emperor in those mighty men's perpetual squabbles, though we Florentines see it as a more local conflict than that. Perhaps there is a kernel of truth in those larger loyalties, but what we see in the streets is just the usual struggle for power and supremacy among neighbors, intensified and made more deadly by the Buondelmonte conflict.

Not a day has passed since that fateful Easter octave that I haven't regretted my part in dividing our city, all the more once I became a father. It's painful to know I had a role, however small and unwilling, in making my daughter's world harsher and more dangerous. And yet this flawed world still has room for joy, as she and her mother have shown me so abundantly.

As for what we're doing here, in this palace again—well, right after Buondelmonte and Neri died, I would have scoffed if anyone had predicted I would one day renew my connections to the Donati. I didn't think to ever see any of those people again.

That all changed one day about a year after Neri died. I opened the door to a knock and was astonished to see Lippo and Elisa standing there before me. Lippo leaned on a stick, and he carried a leather bag. We greeted each other awkwardly. I invited them in, introduced them to Ghisola, and offered them wine, which they accepted.

An uncertain silence followed. Finally I asked after the Donati women, and Elisa started to speak, but Lippo shushed her.

"Before we speak of that, I must ask you something," he said, frowning a little. He stared down into his wine cup.

"Then ask," I said, spreading my hands wide to show my willingness to speak honestly. I knew what he would say next.

"Were you complicit in messer Buondelmonte's death?"

"I was not. I didn't will it, and I didn't help to cause it." I still wasn't sure that last was entirely true, but that I did not will it was the truest thing I knew.

"And yet the lady Fiammetta saw you up in the tower."

251

"Yes." I had a bitter taste in my mouth as I said it. "I was there against my will, and I had been held by Oddo and by Lambertuccio for that whole week. I tried to get a message to you, but I failed." I glanced at Ghisola. She knew that tale, and a look of pain crossed her face.

"Ah." Lippo leaned back, and his face relaxed. "She was right, then."

"Who was right?" Gualdrada? The old woman?

"Lady Fiammetta. She said she didn't believe you were our enemy, but I should ask you directly and see what you said. She guessed that you were there unwillingly."

Bless that fair young woman. I was surprised at the wave of relief that swept over me. I still had nightmares about those blue eyes looking up at me in the tower, and I had grown used to believing that she hated me.

"That being the case," Lippo went on, smiling, "we have a proposition for you. I'll let Elisa explain."

Elisa told us how things were in the Donati household. Gualdrada, reviled by the people of Florence as the cause of the great divide, could no longer even go outdoors without being pelted with refuse and cruel words, for the people's sympathy hadn't lasted beyond Buondelmonte's funeral. She fell into a deep despair, which over time had gentled into a sort of vague, unfocused state. She spent her days sitting at a window gazing out, a little to one side so she couldn't be seen from below. On days when the weather required closing the shutters, she sat by the fire and stared into it, often for hours at a time. She grew childlike, unable to do anything for herself. Isabella had taken refuge in a convent soon after her husband's murder, and with her went Gualdrada's last link with the world.

Elisa and Fiammetta had cared tenderly for Gualdrada, but now Fiammetta was to be married, and Elisa was to go with her to her new home. They needed to find a woman to help care and cook for Gualdrada, as well as for Bianca and her child, and also a man to take care of other duties and to protect their honor, or else Manno and Cione wouldn't permit Gualdrada to continue living in her palace. They had come to me at Fiammetta's suggestion to ask if I would be willing to be the manservant, but now, seeing Ghisola there with me, they wondered if perhaps she would be interested as well.

"You could still take your performing jobs," Lippo added, "just so you were available when the ladies needed something. And you wouldn't have to live there, just come in every day and do what's needful. I'd keep doing it myself, but with this gout, I can't be much help to them any more. My apprentice helps out sometimes, but I need him in the shop, these days."

Ghisola's eyes met mine. I read interest in her expression but also wariness, so I told Elisa and Lippo that we would have to talk it over, and I would come and tell them our answer in a day or two. They agreed, and rose to leave.

Elisa smiled shyly at Ghisola and said, "I hope you'll decide to come. My lady needs a gentle, patient woman to help her, and you'll find the Donati ladies are kind and generous. And monna Bianca's little girl is a joy."

Ghisola was polite but noncommittal, and Lippo and Elisa were on their way out when Lippo remembered something. He reached into the leather bag he carried, and to my amazement he pulled out my long-forgotten jester's hat, and with it, the little green and yellow domino mask.

I hadn't thought ever to see those treasures, let alone own them. I remembered with a pang the brash confidence with which I had placed the order, all those months ago. "I can't take them," I said, shaking my head regretfully. "I had the money when I ordered them, but too much has happened since, and I have nothing to spare any more. I'm sorry, Lippo. They're magnificent." And they were. The craftsmanship was remarkable, they would have been perfect, and I looked at them with longing.

Lippo grinned. "It's all right. They're paid for, a present from Fiammetta." Then, guessing what I was about to ask, he added, "Even if you don't take the job."

I wanted to speak my thanks, but my throat was constricted and I could say nothing. I felt the pinpricks of tears. Ghisola beamed and took the gifts from him, since I couldn't make myself reach for them. "I think we'll probably take your job," she said, "but we'll come to you tomorrow and tell you our decision. If we do say yes, then the Donati ladies must meet me and decide whether they want me."

They took their leave, and we heard Lippo's awful singing start up and then slowly recede as they moved farther away. Ghisola placed the flamboyant cap on my head, adjusting it a little. It was perfect.

We went to them the next day. Gualdrada trusted Ghisola from the first moment they met, and Ghisola's warm heart opened wide for the fragile older woman who had been through so much. Ghisola was so enchanted with little black-haired Margherita that I think she would have stayed to cook and clean and care for them even without pay, but as it happened, Manno and Cione were prepared to pay generously to keep that household functioning.

Since I was last there the house had acquired a middle-aged Donati woman who was a penitent, as well as an elderly widow. In the next few years they added a young girl who was simple, and another who had been blinded by illness. Others came and went, young Donati widows who soon remarried, a Donati woman estranged from her husband and later reconciled, and a high-spirited young girl whose family thought her a troublemaker, in residence until she was married off. That last one found loyal friends in the Donati house, and when her father finally produced a suitor she would accept, she married with a trousseau containing more fine embroidery than Florence had ever seen before.

The house became the repository for all the Donati family's unwanted women, and as such it is useful to Manno and Cione. It has taken on a lively, eccentric character of its own, and Margherita, who charmed everyone, gave all those different women something in common, for all of them love her. Bianca manages the household with grace and efficiency, especially since Ghisola arrived to help her. The two of them are an effective team, more like sisters than lady and servant. We settled into this new routine with surprising ease, and as Lippo promised, I still find plenty of time for my other work in between moving the occasional load of firewood or accompanying ladies to the market.

Our new association with the Donati naturally brought us closer to the conflict, but the house of women has never been directly involved in the feuds. Not that we always feel safe there, and not that we don't sometimes find ourselves buffeted about by the struggles of the warring parties, but for the most part the house remains a sort of haven, or refuge.

Next door, Cione and Manno carry out their military exploits and their intrigues, and we watch their swaggerings and strivings from our windows with alarm or amusement, as the times require. Once in a while we find ourselves confined to the palace for a few days, behind barricades, carefully measuring the water we take from the storage barrels until the Donati men send someone to tell us it's safe to go out to the well again. Now and again a woman in the house expresses concern or sorrow for a kinsman or husband or son, but for the most part, it doesn't touch us directly.

While we have lived thus, others involved in Buondelmonte's story, or in ours, variously lived and died, prospered and suffered. I'll tell you what I know of them.

Schiatta degli Uberti died a couple of years ago, and Lambertuccio just last month. Neither died from the vendetta they began, but both lost close kinsmen to it, and lived long enough to mourn them. Schiatta never succeeded in becoming lord of the city, and to this day I believe he failed only because of Fiammetta's quick thinking and flair for theatre.

Oddo is still a major power in Florence's governing elite. He has changed little over the years except to grow grayer and more grizzled. He is still hotheaded and ruthless, yet he mourned long when his lady wife died of a fever.

Mosca has become a condottiere, a leader of soldiers, and by all reports a good one. Now he leads Florentine troops against Siena. It gains him honor and distinction, and keeps him busy, which to my mind is a great advantage. Sometimes when I hear tales of his valor in battle, a picture comes unbidden before me of a younger Mosca, gleefully lobbing wads of bread into a roomful of scuffling men.

Lambertuccio's boy Amadio was so horrified by what he had seen on the day Buondelmonte died that he withdrew from the world, joining with six of his highborn friends to form a religious confraternity in honor of Our Lady. It's said that all seven young men will be saints one day. They have chosen to live apart, outside the city, and I've heard that the seven of them have pledged their eternal salvation, all to one, one to all. If one falls, they all fall. That must have taken courage. I don't think there are six people in the world I would trust with the fate of my soul, though I can think of two, and I'm quite certain that no sensible person would choose to link their soul's fate to mine. I doubt the lad still juggles. It's a loss; he had talent.

Poor eager Guido was one of the casualties of those first weeks of furious fighting. He died as he had lived, trying to please Oddo. Oddo no doubt promptly forgot about him. Pierino, who had learned to be tight-lipped, eventually took on the captaincy Guido had held. I see him sometimes, on horseback, leading Oddo's soldiers off somewhere or another. He is always scanning the streets for signs of danger. He doesn't acknowledge me, but only rides on by, unsmiling. The first few times I saw him, he was riding Windbag.

Bicci—or "ser" Bicci, as we all came to call him—died four years ago, but not before apprenticing his son Foresino to me to learn the fools' arts. The boy is promising. He has his father's skill at conjuring, as well as what I can teach him. The gift for mimicry, however, died with Bicci. Ghisola and I lend a hand to Bicci's widow Tedora as needed, and the two women remain close friends.

Lippo grew increasingly troubled by his gout, until finally he was unable to work. The Donati took care of him, seeing that all his needs were met, and they were generous to his family when he died. The leather shop is now rented to a mercer who swears he does half his business with the ladies upstairs.

And speaking of those women, what of them? The old woman is no longer among us. I didn't learn it until later, but that terrible day, when Gualdrada took off riding after her girl, Ortolana in her turn ran after hers. She was old, and fragile, and she fell hard on the street. She broke her hip, and they carried her to the Ospedale of San Giovanni, still calling for her Drada. Had she lived, the Donati women would have brought her home and cared for her, but she only lasted two days. Gualdrada never came to see her, too lost in her own downward spiral. Fiammetta saw to the burial, as she saw to everything in those days.

Isabella never emerged from her convent. I heard she was content to stay there, for she wanted no more excitement in her life and she no longer trusted the world outside. In time she took her vows and became the bride of another man brought down for no good reason. Selvaggia, as she had predicted, also was bundled off to a convent. There, thanks to her family name, she became abbess in fairly short order. Either God's wisdom or man's made sure it wasn't the same house that took Isabella, so the two wouldn't spend their lives tormenting one another. Beauty and intelligence were never meant to become enemies. Either might win a battle, but neither one alone would ever win the war.

Fiammetta, who partook generously of both, did marry. Her husband was a much older man, wealthy but not a knight, and faultlessly loyal to her uncles' party. I was not invited to perform at her wedding. She returned now and then to visit at the Donati palace, but always when she was coming she sent word for me to absent myself. She forgave me and held me guiltless, but she, too, couldn't forget that moment, and she didn't want to see me again. Fiammetta bore two babes in quick succession. I trust she had joy in them while she could, for the third died inside her and took her with it. Her funeral, too, had to be held outside the church, for her body held an unbaptized infant, and the church must not be defiled. Ghisola, who had gotten along well with Fiammetta, was among the mourners, as was Bianca.

As for Ghisola and me, we kept our little house, struggling with grief and practical matters alike. Anselmo's payments for Neri's organetto got us through that first spring and summer, and by fall I was working regularly again, trying without much success to avoid becoming known as the jester of one of the factions. Florence was running out of uncommitted families to work for.

For several months Ghisola and I lived as brother and sister, but the day came when we sought a deeper comfort in each other. From that time on, Neri's bed alcove was used only for storage.

We had been working for the Donati for close to a year when Ghisola conceived a child, but it slid from her womb unformed, as the earlier one had. It was another loss, another sorrow, and she took it hard. Still, we had each other, and Ghisola had little Margherita to dote on, and so we kept going.

And finally she conceived again, and this time the child thrived. Because we wanted to make our peace with God in hopes that He would spare this one, we held another wedding in the Donati palace, where our friends and all the members of that unusual household gathered to wish us well. Their wishes must have worked, for even though we hardly dared to hope for Ghisola to bring the child safely to the light, God smiled on her at last, and she did. That beautiful child is our daughter Costanza, the bright-eyed, dimpled twelve-year-old who dances before us this night, now a boisterous child, now a shy young woman, celebrating her adored Margherita's wedding.

But Costanza's birth, however welcome, was hard on Ghisola, and the midwife took me aside and impressed upon me that for the sake of Ghisola's life we must not risk another. No matter. There are many ways to love, and I feel sure that by the time Ghisola and I are laid to rest in the parish churchyard where Neri's bones lie, we will have discovered them all.

The dancers are ready to dance again. They clamor for music, and pull this rambling old man back to the present, which he finds not such a bad place to be. Mosca was wrong, I think. A thing done has no end, only more beginnings. I suspect it won't be many years before we gather again to see my fair little daughter joined in marriage to my limber apprentice, and I'll wish them well with all my heart. Mosca was wrong, I think. A thing done has no end, only more beginnings.

Finis

Thank you for reading *A Thing Done!* If you enjoyed it and would like to help others find it, please consider writing a review, either on a retail site, a review site, or wherever you are in the habit of looking for books. It needn't be lengthy - even a line or two with your honest reaction to the book would be enormously helpful in improving this tale's visibility and findability in a world where many new books are published every day.

You might also enjoy Heath's second novel, Lady of the Seven Suns: A Novel of the Woman Saint Francis Called Brother. This book, published in September 2019, is available from online retailers or can be ordered through any bookstore. Like *A Thing Done*, it is based on fact and is set in early 13th century Italy.

About the Author. Tinney Sue Heath has a journalism degree, but somewhere along the line she realized that for her, the classic journalistic questions of Who? What? When? Where? and Why? were getting shunted aside by "What if. . . ?" And thus a fiction writer was born. She lives in Madison, Wisconsin with her husband. The two of them enjoy playing medieval and early Renaissance music on a variety of period instruments. They travel to Italy as often as possible; while research may be the excuse, they also take pleasure in that country's natural beauty, art, music, food, wine, language, and history, as well as the wonderful people they meet there.

For more about her work and about the history of medieval Italy, consider signing up for her monthly **newsletter** on her **website:** http://www. tinneyheath.com. New subscribers will be able to download her *Cantilena for Seven Voices: Dante's Women Speak*, a novella-length collection that channels the voices of seven women we know from Dante's life and works. These reminiscences, character sketches, and vignettes will give you a picture of life in Florence around the turn of the 14th century, and it is not available elsewhere. She is also on **Facebook**. Search for "Tinney Sue Heath" or go to https://www.facebook.com/tinneyheathauthor/.

Author Notes

Florence in 1215. In that year Florence was in a period of intense growth, expanding from 15,000 to 90,000 residents between 1150 and 1250. Already an important city, she had not yet achieved the preeminence in Tuscany and in Italy that she was later to enjoy. Most of the familiar medieval landmarks (the Palazzo Vecchio, the Bargello, the mendicant churches of Santa Croce and Santa Maria Novella, the Badia as it is today) were not yet built. The cathedral was not the well-known Santa Maria dei Fiori of today, crowned with Brunelleschi's famous dome, but a smaller, much earlier church on the same spot, dedicated to Santa Reparata. The Baptistery was already venerable, but the area between it and Santa Reparata was filled at that time with the tombs of prominent Florentines, many of whom rested in recycled Roman sarcophagi. Only one bridge spanned the Arno, in the spot where the Ponte Vecchio is now. The bridge present in 1215 had been reconstructed in stone after a flood in 1117 washed away the previous wooden structure. This bridge, in its turn, would be destroyed by another flood in 1333 and rebuilt yet again.

Houses, many of wood or a combination of wood and brick, were crowded together, with overhanging additions jutting out over the narrow and winding streets below. The city bristled with tall defensive towers, used in urban warfare. Yet even then, orchards and gardens existed within the city's walls.

The Roman walls that enclosed the early city had been replaced by a new circle of walls, finished in 1177, which more than doubled the protected space. The walled area was to more than double again in the 14th century, when new walls would be built.

Florence was ruled by a *podestà*, a fairly short-term position which, since 1207, was always filled from outside the city to try to ensure impartiality, and by councils made up of her prominent citizens. Powerful families retained a great deal of control and influence, both as part of the governing elite and unofficially because of the money and military strength they commanded.

In the year 1215, Europe was in between the Fourth and the Fifth Crusades. The man who was to become known as Saint Francis of Assisi had gained papal approval for his religious activities, but his order was not yet officially recognized. Frederick II, the Holy Roman Emperor, who would be known as "Stupor Mundi" or the antichrist, depending on who was describing him, was a young man in the fourth year of his reign. The future Saint Dominic founded the Dominican Order. The Fourth Lateran

Council had just established the doctrine of transubstantiation, and had forbidden the clergy to conduct trials by ordeal or by combat; elsewhere, Genghis Khan had captured Peking. In England in the year 1215, King John reluctantly signed the Magna Carta. Dante would not be born for another 50 years, and The Black Death was more than a century in the future.

Dates and Times. Chronicles of the events in this story split about evenly between assigning them to the year 1215 or to the following year. One reason for the confusion may be that medieval Florence began her year with the Feast of the Incarnation, March 25.

Time was relative. Daytime hours in winter were shorter than their summer equivalents. Bells marked the liturgical hours: Terce, the third hour, would have rung at about 9:00 a.m., and Sext, the sixth hour, around midday. None was not noon, as one might expect, but rather midafternoon, and Vespers rang at dusk. Florentines ate their main meal early, probably between Terce and Sext, and then took a light supper later in the day after work was over.

Homes and Towers of the Elite Families. Stone buildings were the ideal, but brick with stone facing was not uncommon. Walls might be hollow and filled with rubble, and upper stories were often built of less durable materials than lower—brick above stone, or wood additions built onto brick. Overhanging jetties (*sporti*) jutted out from upper floors and gave people some much-needed additional living space. These were of necessity made of lighter-weight materials; still they constituted a danger to people in the streets below as well as anyone unfortunate enough to be in them at the wrong time, as it was not uncommon for them to collapse. Buildings might be joined to other buildings over the street level with balconies or passageways, blocking still more light from the street below.

Wall fireplaces and chimneys were rare at this time, if they existed at all. (Historians disagree on precisely when this improvement occurred.) Colder parts of Europe embraced this innovation sooner than the relatively mild Mediterranean countries, and a central hearth, with ceiling ventilation and with additional heating provided by portable braziers, was more usual. Kitchens were often in separate buildings, perhaps behind the house in a courtyard, or else on the top story, to minimize the risk of fire. Windows might be covered with treated cloth, but would not yet contain glass.

The towers so characteristic of medieval Italy were military in their original purpose. In their soaring height they demonstrated graphically a family's might and wealth. Typically these towers reached a height of as much as 120 braccia (70 meters, or 230 feet). To put these dimensions in perspective, a building in New York, one of the skyscrapers of its day before it was demolished in 1955, was 82 meters (269 feet) in height and had 17 floors. Later, in 1250, the city government—briefly under the control of the popolo and not the elite families—decreed that private towers be reduced to no more than 50 braccia (29 meters or 96 feet).

These strong structures had massive walls, especially at their base. Towers as short as 39 meters (128 feet) have been found to have walls 2 meters (or over 6 1/2 feet) thick, narrowing to a thickness of 0.8 meters (over 2 1/2 feet) at the top. When a family found itself on the losing side politically, confiscation of its goods often included destruction of its towers, a symbolic as well as a practical gesture. In World War II, the German army destroyed much of Florence's remaining medieval center with bombs, but not even twentieth-century explosives could destroy all of the towers. Damaged, truncated, but stubbornly still there, several of the mighty towers stand even today. The Amidei tower in this story is one that remains.

Towers were usually owned by a consortium, often made up predominantly of members of a single extended family but possibly also including their political allies. Shares might be as small as a seventeenth part or a twentieth, but membership in a consortium meant that one had the right to use the tower defensively. While it did not automatically mean that all other members of the consortium would actively come to a member's aid in case of need, it did suggest that members would refrain from siding militarily against other members. Shares in a tower were inherited, but only by males, for a woman could marry someone who would one day turn against the consortium, and the risk of such a person obtaining the right to a share of the tower was considered unacceptable.

Names, Titles, and Heraldry. As the Jester's comments about the "people with surnames" suggest, most Florentines at this time did not have a family name. Men were known by their first name and that of their father, possibly going back another generation if necessary for clarity (Neri di Giovanni di Ugo), and women were known by a first name and the name of a father or husband (Selvaggia di Lambertuccio degli Amidei).

All of the family names cited in this book did exist, and their affiliations were as shown. Oddo Arrigo dei Fifanti is sometimes elided to "Oderigo." Berto degli Infangati is more traditionally called Uberto; I changed his name to avoid confusion with the Uberti family. Gualdrada was sometimes referred to as Aldruda; Isabella is called Beatrice in some histories; no one cites a name for Selvaggia, so I have provided her with one.

"Messer" designates a knight, "ser" a notary, and a married woman is called "monna".

Heraldic colors and devices were as I have shown them. The Buondel-monti did have a device which I have not described in the book, because I cannot find evidence that it was in use as early as 1215. It consisted of a stylized mountain ("monte"), which resembles three gumdrops, one stacked atop the other two, the whole surmounted by a cross (the "buon" or "good" in their name). It was in their traditional colors: white and blue.

Amadio. As the Fool suggests in the final chapter, young Amadio did indeed achieve sainthood, along with the six companions with whom he founded the Servants of Mary (Servites), of which order he was the third General. He was probably about twelve years old in 1215; for fictional purposes I have made him a little older, so he could take part in the events of this story. He is sometimes referred to as Saint Bartolomeo degli Amidei. He was beatified in 1717 and canonized in 1887. He did, as stated, make a pact with his companions that either all of them would be saved, or none of them. It is said that when he died, on 12 February 1266, the others saw a flame shooting up into the sky.

Danteisms. Two items in this story may be considered the author's homage to Dante:

1. The Fool dreams his uneasy dream of a man whose hands have been cut off, holding up his bloody stumps. This is how Dante depicts the shade of Mosca, in the Inferno, where he is placed in the Eighth Circle among the Sowers of Discord.

2. One of the small children the Fool entertained at the Amidei house was the young Manente degli Uberti, later to be known as Farinata, the great Ghibelline leader memorably described by Dante, who places him in the Sixth Circle of Hell among the Heretics.

Marriage Rituals. Marriages in Florence during this time period con-sisted of three separate stages, stages which could occur very close together in time, or which might be separated by years. Betrothals of children, for example, might occur years before the ring-giving and the bride's transfer to the husband's home, and even once the ring was given, considerable time could elapse before the bride changed her residence—for example, if her father found himself unable to pay the dowry in full.

None of these ceremonies required the church in any way (though a nuptial mass could certainly be part of the later stages), but they did require witnesses, consent on the part of both spouses, and usually a notary to record the contract. A marriage, whatever else it might be or become, was first and foremost a business transaction.

Preliminary to everything else was the *impalmamento*, or handclasp, which sealed the agreement between families, an agreement which may well have been facilitated by a marriage broker or a family friend. It was not necessary for either bride or groom to be present for this agreement; it was strictly between the families, and the only essential ingredient was the presence of the man who had authority over the bride-to-be, her father or guardian.

Stage One of a Florentine marriage was the *giure* (general term) or *sponsalitum* (notarial or legal term): a binding betrothal ceremony with only males present. As many male friends and family members as possible gathered to witness this agreement, which included the specifics of monetary exchange, such as dowry, trousseau, and morning gift. The *giure* often took place quite soon after the *impalmamento*.

Stage Two took place at the bride's home. Kin and allies of both sexes and both families gathered to witness; the notary obtained the spoken consent of both parties, and the husband gave the wife a ring (the *anellamento*). He also presented gifts to the members of the bride's family at this time, and they in turn played host at the feast that followed. After this ceremony, the couple was considered man and wife.

Stage Three completed the transfer of goods (dowry, trousseau, gifts, woman), and saw the bride transferred to the husband's home via a public procession, to be followed by another feast at her new home. This stage was called the *nozze*.

At this time in Florentine history, consummation typically followed the *nozze*, but this was by no means an absolute. Customs could vary with time and place and level of society, so Buondelmonte's wish to consummate his marriage with Isabella before the *nozze* was not necessarily inappropriate.

What the Chronicles Say. The earliest extant record of these events appears in the Chronica of Pseudo Brunetto Latino (so called because for a long time scholars thought it was authored by Dante's contemporary Brunetto Latini, but then they decided it wasn't), written at the beginning of the 14th century—that is, less than a century after these events took place. The banquet, the jester's prank, the insult offered by Oddo, the injury inflicted by Buondelmonte, the ensuing councils and agreements, Gualdrada's persuasion, Buondelmonte's betrayal of his betrothal to the Amidei girl, and finally the vendetta against Buondelmonte and its outcome appear in this book very much as they are set forth in this and other early chronicles of Florentine history.

Later chronicles (Dino Compagni, writing in 1311; Giovanni Villani, writing in the 1330s; Marchionne di Coppo Stefani, writing in the mid-1380s) and histories (Machiavelli, in the 1520s) tended to begin the story with the broken engagement and say little or nothing of what preceded it. Taken together, the accounts demonstrate some uncertainty as to details: Did Gualdrada summon Buondelmonte, or did she hail him as he passed in the street? Did they already have an understanding, or did she present her lovely daughter to him then for the first time? Did the ambush take place on Easter Sunday or another day? Was it Buondelmonte and Isabella's wedding day or after their wedding?

They agree that there was a daughter of Lambertuccio degli Amidei, and that she was jilted by Buondelmonte, but we don't know her name, or how she felt about the things that happened to her, or what, if anything, she may have tried to do about it. Thus, the character of Selvaggia is my own invention, as is Mosca's motive for influencing the council as he did—though the chroniclers unanimously give him credit, if credit is the right word, for his famous declaration: "Cosa fatta capo ha." (A thing done has an end to it; or, Once it's done, it can't be undone.)

Later chronicles put greater or lesser emphasis on Buondelmonte's guilt, according to their own political leanings, for the Guelf-Ghibelline split divided Italians for centuries after this incident. Villani, for example, says that Buondelmonte was influenced by the devil, thereby providing him with an excuse, and he places the greater blame on Buondelmonte's enemies.

And for anyone wondering how things played out for the redoubtable Oddo: The vendetta reached its tentacles far into the future. In 1239 the Buondelmonti and Uberti made a brief peace with the marriage of a daughter of messer Rinieri Zingari dei Buondelmonti to messer Neri Piccolino, brother to messer Farinata degli Uberti. Shortly afterward, the Buondelmonti faction lured the Uberti into a trap, and Oddo and a son of Schiatta's were killed—by a Donati.

Acknowledgements

First and foremost, I want to thank my husband Tim for his consistent encouragement and for his insightful observations and comments (not to mention all the trips to Florence). Not the least of his contributions was his gentle suggestion that perhaps this tale would not quite fit into a short story. Or a novella. Or a novelette. Okay, Tim, you were right.

Three readers gave me useful comments. My thanks to Barbara Oelke, Dorothy Pugh, and Linda Wendt for their input as fellow fiction writer, journalist, and astute reader, respectively.

And special thanks to Beverly and Holly Stuart, writers and mentors extraordinaire, who provided me with the kind of detailed critique every author needs and wants, and at the same time managed to shore up my confidence and keep me going through the rough spots. For their steadfast support, I will always be grateful.

This book could not have been written without the work of generations of historians who focused on Florence and its fascinating past. For their meticulous scholarship and their determination to present this city's story to the modern reader, I owe them a great debt.

And finally, back to Tim, who managed to come up with the best description of the headstrong knight Buondelmonte I have ever found anywhere when he proclaimed Buondelmonte to be "a goofball of a major order." That pretty much says it all.

Tinney Sue Heath

Made in the USA
Middletown, DE
12 March 2020